RUN, RUN, RUN AWAY

The Ivy Chronicles – 1

C. R. Cummings

This is a work of fiction. Any references to historical events, real people, or real locales are used fictitiously. Other names, characters, places, and incidents are the product of the author's imagination and any resemblance to actual events or locales or persons, living or dead is entirely coincidental.

Editorial advice provided in part by Practical Proofing; practicalproofing.com.

Cover Design by Nichole Cummings
Book Cover Photography by EmoCookiez

ISBN-13: 978-0-9966050-0-7

For Linda – You will never be forgotten

ACKNOWLEDGMENTS

I would like to thank my husband, Glen, for being patient, supportive and putting up with me disappearing into my own little world for days on end.

Nichole and Vale…you both are awesome, thank you for taking the time to review, give suggestions and for all your snarky teenage comments. (Many of which somehow found their way into the story.)

Special thanks to Jena at Practical Proofing for her wonderful editing and insights, and a huge hug to Maggie Shayne for her guidance and support.

And a big sloppy kiss to all my family and friends who suffered through countless re-reads and who still like me even though I'm horrible at returning phone calls.

RUN, RUN, RUN AWAY

THE IVY CHRONICLES - I

CHAPTER 1 - Ivy

I woke with a start when a bright beam of light hit my eyes. I was about to jump up and run, but the light veered to the left. A truck passing by, my mind finally processed. We were at yet another stop along the bus route. Sitting up, I could see that night had fallen while I'd slept. Street lights glowed dimly against the brighter lights of a bus terminal. The bus had pulled into a parking spot and almost everyone was standing up, getting ready to disembark.

My head felt clear and I stretched leisurely. It was the best sleep I had gotten in I didn't know how long. No screaming in the middle of the night; no sounds of things being thrown or torn apart. No pounding on the walls by my insane mom, shrieking that the demons were after her again. I felt refreshed for the first time in months.

"Excuse me," I said as I touched the shoulder of a man about to stand up in the seat in front of me. "Where are we now?"

"In Medford...Oregon. If you're going on to Eugene, this is the last pit stop. If you need to go, you know..." he said, clearly uneasy talking to a kid about bathroom stuff. "Now's the time," he finished lamely and stood up, moving into the aisle to wait his turn to get off.

I hurried to pull out my map and check it. Medford wasn't hard to find. It looked like the first real town inside the state. I had already checked the bus routes and this one actually did have a route to Coos Bay. I shoved everything back inside my pack and pulled out a black slouchy beanie. Pulling it down over my forehead I checked my reflection in the window. The hat didn't hide the ugly bruise, but it was late so maybe nobody would notice. I stood and shoved my arms in my coat, then followed the others off the bus.

A few went into the terminal and straight to the restrooms. Others were greeted by people who had come to pick them up, or walked over to cars. I pushed open the doors and took a step inside. The few people that were in the waiting area were picking up their luggage and moving outside. I watched them through the plate glass window as they talked to the bus driver, then board the bus. After a few minutes the people who had hit the restrooms came hurrying back, and headed out to the bus. I waited quietly as I watched the bus driver greet the last of the passengers and close the door. With a swooshy air sound, the bus started up and pulled out.

I was alone in the waiting room now. A clinking noise drew my attention up to a large, metal grated clock, which informed me it was just after 10:00pm. I could see a brighter light coming from the ticket booth and movement inside. Walking over to it, I stood and looked in. One person was in the cubicle, safely tucked away behind the glass.

I had to knock on it to get the guy's attention. There was a little round metal plate thing like at the movie theater. He pushed a button and leaned close to it.

"Yes, can I help you?" he asked as he stifled a yawn.

"When does the next bus leave for Coos Bay?" I asked him with a tired smile.

"At 3:30am miss. In a little over five hours," he replied checking his schedule.

"Can I purchase a ticket please?" I tried not to look him in the eyes.

"$75 one way, or..."

Interrupting him, I quickly answered, "One way is fine. Thanks."

I put four twenties in the weird little slot thingy.

Without even looking at me he pulled a lever, efficiently moving the cash to his side of the glass. My change and the ticket were pushed back to me within seconds and for the first time he looked closely at me.

"Thanks," I said as I retrieved the ticket and my change.

"That's a nasty bruise you got there missy."

My hand went instantly to my right eye to cover it. "Tripped over something," I mumbled and turned my head away from him.

"Uh huh," he said, giving me an appraising look before he turned around on his stool until his back was to the window. He had already dismissed me from his world.

Suddenly weary, I slowly walked to the first line of chairs that faced out the large windows of the terminal. Moving to the far end of the row, I dropped my backpack on the last chair of the row then removed my coat, laying it down on top of the backpack. I sat down next to them and stared out into the night.

I had made it this far with no hiccups; maybe I really could get away with this. Since yesterday morning I had been bus hopping north from San Diego. At first it was scary and I was worried that Mom would find a way to come after me and drag me back. I constantly watched the faces in the cars passing by the bus and scanned the people at each of the bus terminals, terrified I'd see her.

I had been preparing for this day for months, but yesterday it had come to a head. I just couldn't take any more of it. Knowing I didn't have a choice if I wanted to stay safe I had quickly dressed in my best pair of old jeans, thrown on a long sleeved t-shirt and finished off my outfit with an old vest that Marmaw and I had found at a garage sale. It had beads and sequins sewn all over the front and sparkled delightfully. The best thing about the vest was the multitude of zippered pockets on the inside which now held the bulk of my stash of money.

After grabbing up my coat and a backpack loaded with

my spare clothes, a travel bag, Marmaw's books and my sketchpad, I had unlocked the padlock on my door and ventured out into the hallway. I found Mom lying on the floor of the front room in the same sweats and tank top she had worn for close to a week. A bottle of something was in her hand; a joint was in the other and there were a couple of lines of white on Marmaw's antique hand mirror on the coffee table next to her. Her head was lobbed sideways away from me, giving me the full view of the vivid white puckers on her neck. Another one of her suicide attempts gone bad. I had stared at her with repulsion…and fear. Some scrum bag was out cold on the couch, just another in the long line of losers she had hooked up with.

I lived with Mom; I used to live with Mom, Marmaw, and Granddad. But my mother's parents had decided to die on me last year, leaving me with a space cadet mom that even they couldn't seem to handle. Mom had gone and gotten herself pregnant at 17…consequently me. She never grew up, got in all types of trouble, ended up in jail a few times, rehab even more times and tried to commit suicide twice. She was always leaving for long periods with new boyfriends, only to return, broke, beaten and sick. Then she'd be off to rehab or a hospital again. Marmaw and Granddad dealt with her, and took care of me.

They said we just had to try to understand her; that she had a hard time dealing with her reality. Good one Mom, mess up everyone else's 'reality' while you're at it. I didn't hate Mom, I just didn't like her. I think you're supposed to love your mom, but I have a hard time doing it. Besides that woman I lived with now was anything but mom-like. Nope, didn't like her one bit.

It had been good when Marmaw and Granddad were alive. Marmaw cooked and cleaned and loved me. She wrote children's books…cute little ones about fairies… and even did the illustrations. Beautiful water colors of bright painted fairies in tutus, sporting butterfly wings. She was a wonderful grandma.

I loved my Granddad and Marmaw. I missed them both, so much. I never even got to say goodbye; not when they were alive and not at a funeral. Mom didn't want to have one, said it was dumb since their bodies were never found. Mom had been the last to see them. She had gone with Marmaw on a short trip and then Granddad had left to get them, but it was only Mom who ended up coming home. She announced that my days were numbered now that they were gone. She said she was going to kick me out…nice mom, right?

That was until Uncle Geraint showed up the next morning. He really wasn't my uncle, just this old guy that Granddad liked to hang around with. We always knew when he came 'cause he drove this old restored car from the 1930's that made funny noises as it went down the road.

He said he was the executor of Granddad's estate and tried to explain it to me. I didn't know where Mom had gone…she hid when anyone came around…so it wasn't surprising that she had disappeared. I had to listen to all this stuff about Granddad having to leave along with Marmaw, and how sorry he was, and how I shouldn't worry, because I'd be taken care of. I remember being numb from shock and really didn't understand anything he had said after the part about Marmaw being lost and Granddad going with her.

Mom had understood though. She might have been hiding, but she was sure listening. After he left, she came out and threw a fit. She lost it big time...she recognized what she saw as the most horrendous thing; that everything had been left in a trust to me and nothing to her. Not one dime. I listened as she let out a barrage of foul language, stomped down the hall and slammed her door. While the house echoed with her screams and the sounds of glass shattering, I quietly went into my bedroom and cried myself to sleep.

After that Mom said I could stay as long as I signed my checks over to her. Thanks Mom.

Life had turned to hell after that. The checks came, I cashed them and Mom took the money. She spent it mostly on her drugs and loser boyfriends and I went hungry a lot. After a couple of months of her having all the money she wanted for her *pain* medication, the beatings started. From her mostly, but when one of her boyfriends decided I looked like a good punching bag she never lifted a hand to protect me.

Granddad and Marmaw had always kept to themselves in our little town so we had no friends in the community. And with all the trouble that Mom got into, I don't think anyone wanted to know us. So there was no one left in my life to ask me why my arm was in a sling, or comment on another black eye. I had made up so many stories to explain them at school that my classmates either thought I was the clumsiest girl in the world or the worst bad-ass. I was growing weary of the charade and I had somehow lost every friend at school I once had. There was no choice in the matter, I had to get away and started to formulate a plan.

Mom had declined so far into hell that she could barely speak, let alone read. I told her that Uncle Geraint had written that the money had to be reduced a few hundred a week so it would last me longer. She was livid and threw another wild temper tantrum, but other than that didn't question it. I pocketed the difference and after five months had just under $4000.00 saved up.

Yesterday morning had been bad and had made the decision to finally leave easy. Mom had surprised me when I came out of the bathroom with only a towel wrapped around my small frame. She'd grabbed me from behind and chomped down on my shoulder, leaving behind a raw, red, bite mark. I had screamed and pushed at her, trying to get away, which only seemed to agitate her more. I had taken a number of blows to the head before I managed to escape to the safety of my bedroom.

The time had come. There could be no more putting it off, hoping I could wait until school was out. No one would miss me anyway.

Mom would really miss the money though, and I have to admit that I felt enormously satisfied when I mailed the letter to Uncle Geraint before boarding the first bus. I told him I was going away for a while, and if he needed to get ahold of me he could send a letter to 'general delivery' at the Coos Bay post office. I couldn't tell him about Mom, probably didn't need to, but I sure didn't want her to continue to spend my trust fund the way she had been. I asked him to hold my money and if I had a need, I would contact him. I guess telling him that Mom was staying at home and wouldn't need anything did seem a bit mean, but I wrote it anyway.

My trek down memory lane was interrupted suddenly as the outside doors of the bus terminal were thrown open and a group of backpack toting college kids noisily entered the terminal. Quickly gathering up my coat and pack, I hurried around the edge of seats towards the restrooms. Something stopped me though, a faint aroma along with a puzzling sensation. Both struck me as somehow familiar.

Nervously I looked over at the crowd of kids trying to figure out what it was and where it had come from. I relaxed somewhat when I was sure Mom wasn't there and I recognized the odor...weed. Our house reeked of it, however I knew Mom wasn't the only one who smoked the crap and even though the smell was slightly different, these *were* college kids after all.

As I turned to continue walking, my eyes locked with those of a boy with the group. He had long, wild dreadlocks and he was staring right at me with an odd look on his face. It felt like he knew everything there was to know about me and could see inside my thoughts. I couldn't pull my eyes away from his and it wasn't until another of his friends distracted him that I realized I had been standing there like a dork just staring at him. Somewhat embarrassed and horribly bothered, I hurried on to the safety of the restroom.

Pushing open the door I dashed to the oversized stall and locked myself inside until my pulse calmed itself. I didn't know why seeing that guy was so disconcerting; he'd probably noticed the horrible bruise like others had today and that's why he was staring at me. Pulling myself together, I left the safely of the stall and moved over to the counter to look at myself in the mirror.

The bruise *was* ugly and I hadn't taken the time to put makeup on or even brush my hair this morning. I dug in my pack for my travel bag, pulled off the dumb beanie and went about freshening up. I busied myself washing my face and brushing my teeth before taking a hard look at the bruise. There really was no way to hide it, but maybe I could diffuse it a bit with some makeup.

I didn't have much makeup and never used foundation or anything like that. What I had were a few odd things I'd found in the girl's restroom at school: a half-used mascara, a couple of small cases of eyeshadow that were almost used up, a strange collection of lipsticks and a couple of pencil eyeliners. My favorite was the dark green one and when I had found it laying discarded on the bathroom counter at school, I wasn't surprised that someone had left it. Not too many girls wore green eyeliner.

But I was anything but the typical teenager, I actually liked wearing it. I set about putting some soft green eye shadow on, feathering it out from my eyes a bit more than normal, then began adding the liner. I used it generously around my eyes, playing with it, making cool little swirls down and up from the corners of my eyes. By the time I was done the bruise wasn't noticeable at all and the lines looked sort of like a henna painting. I added some black liner around my eyes to emphasize the green before adding loads of blue/black mascara, making my eyes seem to glow. Reddish purple lipstick completed my look.

I didn't need to do anything with my hair except brush it. I loved my hair. Last year, right before Marmaw and Granddad had left, I decided I needed a *new me*. My little white-haired grandmother had driven me right down to the salon, and said whatever I fancied was fine with her. I knew exactly what I wanted. I had them cut the dark red mop off to a short little bob and cut the bangs in a cool curved 'v' to the center of my forehead. The hairdresser called it an updated Pixie cut...which Marmaw loved. My hair is perfectly straight, and the lady who cut it understood just what I wanted.

Then, when I asked for purple highlights, looking sheepishly at Marmaw for the okay, she had clapped her hands together and encouraged it. So the purple highlights went in. When we got home, Granddad loved it, Mom hated it and I was thrilled.

The strange thing was it had been almost a year and my hair was exactly like it had been then. It hadn't grown at all, nor had the purple highlights faded. I really hadn't thought about it much since so many other things had happened in the last year, but it was rather peculiar. Not that I was complaining, I really did love my hair this way and didn't want it to change.

I took an old sweatshirt from my pack and pulled it over my head. It had grown chilly in the room and I had started to shiver. No way was I going to chance catching a cold now. I took another look at myself in the mirror. My eyes looked amazing...they seemed to shine out through the makeup. They were deep nut brown with little rays of blue in the right one. Granddad said it meant we were family, and he'd wink with his matching one at me. I smiled at the memory and winked at myself in the mirror before I gathered up my things and steeled myself to go out to the waiting room.

The group of college kids was still there, loud and annoyingly rowdy. They took up a good part of the seating area with their camping gear and packs. Most looked like a new generation of hippy wannabes; Granddad would have loved them. The guy with dreadlocks to his butt was standing on the other side of the room. His hair fascinated me and I wondered if people really used pee to make them. I had read that somewhere and thought it was rather disgusting. The hair probably smelled like urine. Yuck. I moved as far away from him as I could and sat down by some girls who looked like they had been partying all night.

No one seemed to notice me. I pulled a sandwich from my pack and ate quickly, washing it down with bottled water. When I was finished, I pulled out one of Marmaw's books and my MP3 Player and put my earbuds in. Another of my *finds*. Someone had thrown it in the trash at school, its front cover cracked. I wasn't above pulling things from the garbage and the thing worked fine. It was a rather nice one too. After I had deleted all the music stored on it, popular crud that everyone my age seemed to like, I had loaded it up with the right tunes for me. I loved the vintage music from the 50's and 60's.

It was what Granddad had listened to. He always had his little paint splattered radio tuned to the oldies station and would sing every song loud and off-key while he worked in his shop. Buddy Holly, Roy Orbison, The Monkees, Creedence Clearwater, Del Shannon, Ricky Nelson; all names I shouldn't know from the 50's and 60's, but I did. Mom always grumbled. I wasn't sure if it was Granddad's singing or *what* he was singing, but it would piss her off and she would go into her room, slam the door and hide. Maybe that's *why* he sang so loud, I thought to myself as I pushed the 'on' button and Simon & Garfunkel started to sing *The Sound of Silence* to me.

I closed my eyes and tried to picture Granddad. My memories of him were so clear and the mellow music allowed me to almost feel his presence.

Granddad had been retired. I never understood what he had done before, but his entire life was wrapped around Marmaw, me and woodworking...oh and sometimes going off and hunting down Mom. Granddad was an old fart. That's what he called himself. An old fart. Built like a barrel, he could do anything. He made furniture, and frames, and fancy doors, and jewelry. I loved his jewelry. We all wore one of the necklaces…except for Mom. He made the teeniest, tiniest hearts and fashioned necklaces out of vines. He called them our fairy talismans. I loved that I had grandparents who believed in fairies. Pretty cool.

The old fart only had one real quirk. He refused to buy his lumber for anything he made. It had to come from his 'special' wood, the wood he cut and harvested himself. He would take trips four or five times a year, hiking deep into the forest to get his supply. As I got older, he let me come. We would drive for hours up the coast and spend the night in the camper on the back of the pickup. Then before the sun even gave a thought as to whether it wanted to rise or not, we would start out.

There was this river that emptied out into the ocean and Granddad knew where the path was that lead up, into the forest, to his special grove of trees. The first time I remember going alone with him, I had been in the third grade. I was excited that I was allowed to take a trip just with him, leaving Marmaw alone to deal with Mom. Seven wonderful days alone with my Granddad in the forest, with no one but the birds and weird bugs to keep us company.

I had laughed at 'the old fart' as we moved along the path that lead into the forest…he would tell me that the path was special and only certain people could find it and use it. He would point out the mark carved into the wood of a large tree and say we were stepping into the 'world between'. It was just two straight lines with a circle in the center joining them together. I knew Granddad had put it there; it was high up, but within his reach. I'd giggle and hug him; it was his trip, his spot, his right to make stories up if he wanted to.

The path itself was a magical journey. Granddad had names for all the special areas, where the boulders hung above us on a ridge or where the trees grew close in and made an arch over the path. He loved to make up names and was always calling out to a tree or rock, "Hello, Pavali" or "Good morning to you, Tavish!"

At the end of the path was paradise. A grove of trees grew in a wide circle, creating the most amazing clearing almost two full acres deep and wide. It glistened with sunrays. It was green and lush, bursting with life. Flowers of all kinds grew in masses: hollyhocks, roses, jasmine, lily-of-the-valley and so many more I couldn't name them all. They sparkled with dew and filled the air with intense fragrances. Some were lovely, while others were too heavy. Marmaw always said that the aroma was like the ups and downs of life, all the smells combined, the enchanting mingled with the unpleasant and you had to sort them out to decide what your focus in life should be…the good…or the bad. I couldn't disagree with her on that one.

At the far end of the clearing sat a small cabin. Granddad said the fairies had created it just for us. I loved that old guy.

I understood why he would make that story up. The forest had almost reclaimed the cabin with trumpet vines. The cabin sat in a nest of gargantuan ferns and multicolored foxglove; it *did* look like a fairytale house, all green and spouting flowers.

I loved it there. I loved the trips.

When I had started to make plans to run away, the cabin was the only place I could think to go to. Mom hated the cabin and detested the forest even more. If Granddad or

Marmaw even mentioned the possibility of going there, she'd get hysterical and it would take days to calm her down. She would never think of looking for me there, nor would anyone else. I only needed to stay hidden for a couple of years and then I wouldn't have to worry about being sent to a foster home...or even worse, being sent back home to Mom. This was the best way, the only thing I could think of. I would just disappear until I was 18 or until I needed money.

I flipped open the book I held and buried myself in the pictures of Marmaw's fantasy world and re-read for the hundredth time her story called *The Forest Fairy.* I hid away in my own world of music and fairy books.

The time seemed to drag by though, the college kids were annoying and loud, and the things they were talking about bored me. The guys seemed to know a lot about beer and the girls seemed to be all about saving things: frogs, trees, dirt...I found them rather mind numbing. Every now and then I'd feel eyes on me, but when I looked up I couldn't see anyone looking my way. It gave me the heebie-jeebies.

Just as I thought I couldn't take the wait any longer, the bus pulled up and the route was called out. I stood, along with the college kids, and together we boarded the bus. I planned on falling back asleep as soon as possible. The seats were uncomfortable, the other passengers were disorderly and even asleep they were noisy. The guys' snoring was beyond belief. I turned up the music on my player and tried to drown them out. I stared out the window of the bus trying to ignore it. The countryside was blanketed in darkness, the only light came from the stars, until finally the sun started to rise. Then it was more interesting, the road was windy and on one side there was an unnamed river or stream and on the other side, there was a forest. I really missed the forest.

The other people started to wake up around me about

9:00am or so. We didn't make any stops; there was a restroom in the back of the bus and, stupid me, I had sat as far back as possible. Now I was stuck sitting next to the door to it. The college kids came and went, came and went. Sometimes smells would come to me when they opened the door and I had to hide my nose in my shirt to keep it out. I decided I hated buses with restrooms.

I started to get really hungry around 10:00 and took some power bars from my bag. It wasn't the best food, but it stopped my stomach from growling. I pulled out my sketch pad and rummaged around until I found one of the pencils. Bored, I picked the first thing that caught my eye; a blonde girl who had fallen asleep, her mouth wide open. A dumb thing to draw, but I was enjoying making sure she looked like a real hag in the drawing.

"Not bad." A cool voice came from behind me, making me jump. I looked up and into deep green eyes. The dreadlock guy was standing just behind me, leaning on the back of my seat. Quickly I closed the pad and glared up at him. His hair was unusual; I'd never been so close to someone with hair like that. Around his neck hung several long pendants, some were pretty cool looking. However it wasn't nice to look over people's shoulders. I gave him a snarky look and narrowed my eyes at him.

"Oh sorry...I didn't mean...it's good." He stammered before he gave up and went back to his seat. As he passed, I noticed that both hands were covered with heavy silver rings and his wrists bore wide leather wristbands set with stones. He had so many friendship bracelets on that you could barely see the leather bands on his wrists. He wore normal jeans along with a purple vest that looked like something a prince should be wearing. He was interesting, a walking new age jewelry advertisement. Every now and then, I would feel his eyes on me and would look up. He was watching me, studying me...I didn't like it.

Zack marched back to his seat annoyed with himself. It made no sense. Up until this morning all he could think of was this camping trip. That was until he had walked into the bus terminal and saw her. She had been walking towards the restrooms and had stopped midstride to nervously scan the room…their eyes had locked and for a moment time seemed to stand still.

She was small, with interesting hair and a heart shaped face marred by a revolting bruise around her right eye. His protective instincts had kicked in; he felt the need to find who had done this to her and beat them to a pulp.

He broke eye contact when one of the guys asked him a question about water purification, and when he looked back the girl was moving away towards the restrooms. He followed her with his eyes until the door closed behind her.

He had tried to push her from his mind as he waited with his group for the bus, but couldn't stop himself from glancing at her now and then when she came back out and took a seat across the room. He decided if she was taking the same bus he would find a way to talk to her during the trip. Trying not to think about her, he fell asleep soon after the bus pulled out.

When he finally woke, he got up and walked to the bathroom at the far end of the bus. The girl was sitting by herself and didn't notice him as he went by. When he came out he paused behind her, trying to decide if he should say something.

But then he smelled *it*; a heady, fresh fragrance.

He was *compelled* to lean down and sniff her hair, then felt exceedingly stupid. She didn't realize he was standing there, as she was concentrating on drawing a picture of a girl in the seat in front of her. It was pretty good.

"Not bad," he said, expecting her to say something back.

The look she gave him was ice cold. There was no

doubt that she didn't want to be bothered. It shocked him back to reality and he stammered something and then hurried back to his seat feeling like a complete ass. But still he couldn't stop himself from looking back at her.

CHAPTER 2 - Ivy

I knew we were getting close by the sound of seagulls and the smell of wet sand and seaweed. The breeze brought it in through the window I had finally figured out how to open. The smells from the restroom were about to gag me if I didn't do something. Now I had the wonderful wet smell of the ocean to mask it, and the promise that we were not too far from the end of this ride.

The bus turned off of the highway and made its connection with Highway 101. *Yeah!* I thought as the ocean came into sight. It was bright and sunny and people were all over the beach. I wanted to be out there too. I got up on my knees and sat staring out the window, watching the birds and the tourists and everything. I was the first one up and out of my seat when the bus finally pulled into the station, stopped and opened the door. I didn't give anyone a chance to get into the aisle before me. I didn't care what they thought of me. I just wanted to get outside, into the sun and feel the breeze. I wanted the memories to come back of Granddad and me walking hand in hand down the little streets, peeking into the shops, exclaiming over the elaborate kites and creations with seashells.

I felt really stupid after I got off the bus. My eyes had started to tear up and I couldn't see where I was going. I bumped into the dreadlock guy, mumbled an apology and hurried away. Oh man, I had missed this place.

Once out of the terminal I hurried to the main street, still full of shops. Food first, I thought as my mouth started to water at the aromas coming from a little family restaurant just ahead of me. It sat between two shops, one advertising books and the other filled with tourist-type junk. I stayed focused on the food. The door opened just as I got to it and a family with noisy kids came out. I held the door open for them as they exited, then hurried inside. The sounds of waitresses taking orders, glasses clinking and tourists talking in soft muted tones floated through the air to me. Cool, I thought. Normal people, doing normal things. A smile erupted on my face as the plump waitress came up and asked the number in my party. She seemed unfazed that it was just me and lead me to a small booth for two.

I dropped the pack on one side and slid into the other, taking the menu from her outstretched hand. Opening it greedily, I scanned the items. Shrimp, hamburgers, salads, fish sandwiches, fries, milk shakes... My hands were shaking I was so excited. I couldn't remember the last time I had been so keyed up about food. Since Granddad and Marmaw died, food was just something I made sure I had so I could go on living.

This was different. This was real food, not something that I grabbed at school, or shared with my friends, when I still had some, at the mall. Real food, like Granddad and I used to get. I noticed the waitress was coming my way and hurried to pick something out. I was right; she stopped next to me, her little pad all ready. Trying to stay calm I ordered the biggest fish burger they had, curly fries, a side salad, and for good measure a bowl of chowder and a Pepsi. I was a little perturbed when she reached for the menu, I wanted to keep reading it, but I gave it up with a silent sigh.

While I waited, I dug into my pack and pulled out a notebook and a pen and sat back down to write my list. I had planned this over and over again in my mind, but couldn't risk writing it down. Someone might have seen it and known what I had been planning. Now I needed to make sure I remembered everything. I didn't want to have to come back to town, unless I wanted to, for a few months.

1. Fishing pole and gear
2. Plates, silverware, tongs and long spoons
3. Sleeping bag
4. Matches, lighters
5. Flashlights, lantern and batteries
6. Tarp
7. Lightweight food; dried and some canned
8. Bucket
9. Kerosene
10. Hatchet

I sat there looking at my list. It was long. How in the world was I going to carry all of this? I thought about what was already at the cabin, or at least what had been there last time I visited. There were the cast iron cooking things, some blankets stored in the ancient trunk, the old propane lantern that I had always been scared of, some buckets, a broom and a bunch of stuff that Granddad had collected over the years and stored there. I thought there was an axe, but it was a huge thing that I didn't think I could even pick up, let alone use to chop wood. I needed my own little hand hatchet.

I crossed off the fishing gear, since that should still be there, and then added it back on just in case. By the time I was done, the only thing I had taken off was the bucket. Then added books, sketch pads and more pencils. I needed a way to carry everything, but the most challenging part was where was I going to put all this stuff as I collected it? I sat there pondering the question and watching people walk on the side walk outside the window. People came and went. Couples, kids, families...one was going by the window right now on the way to the beach. The dad was pulling a large plastic wagon piled high with a cooler, towels and a little kid riding on the back. I watched them as they stopped at the crosswalk and then made their way across the street.

My brain must be on slow motion due to lack of food,

because it took a minute for it to sink in. That's what I needed, a large wagon like theirs. I could get all my stuff in it and pull it along the path to the cabin. It would be hard, but easier than carrying everything. I was smiling at the thought when a hand and a plate appeared in front of me. I looked up to the fake smile of the waitress. I didn't care what mood she was in, mine was awesome!

"Thank you," I said and meant it.

"Anything else you need?"

I looked around and saw the ketchup and tartar sauce was already on the table, so I shook my head no and started to pick up the burger, and then I had a thought as she started to turn away.

"I mean yes. Do you know where I could find a beach wagon?"

"There's a hardware store just down the road…they might still have some," she said as she moved away, back to the kitchen.

I stored the information and dug in. It was wonderful. I had to keep telling myself to slow down. I had finished my meal before she came back to check on me, and was fine with her just giving me the bill.

Soon I was making my way down the road, heading in the direction of the river inlet. I needed to see it, see the path, *know* it was real before I continued with my plan. The line of shops disappeared behind me as I walked down the road. I saw the hardware store across the street, in an outdoor shopping center between a radio shack and a grocery store. I knew where to go now, once I'd made sure...

The sidewalk ended and I found myself trudging down a dirt path. A small run-down motel sat back from the road and as I passed it I heard a familiar voice. The college crowd had ended up there. I stood and watched them milling around outside the little building that looked like a shed, near a sign that said "Office". A thought was forming, but it didn't take shape until I had started to walk some more. When it finally hit me, I stopped and looked back, then turned and went to join them.

No one paid me any attention. Dreadlock guy was handing out keys to the group and the rest were picking up their packs and luggage, and started to walk towards the line of rooms. I waited until they weren't looking, then walked into the office and set my pack down. There was an extremely large woman sitting in a chair, I thought she was sitting on a chair anyway, I couldn't see any sign of one under her. She smiled a rather horrifying smile of brown crooked teeth at me. The place looked like she lived in it; there were pictures of people on the beach: a sea shell collection covered in cob webs, old maps littered the counters and hung from the walls, and the whole room was painted in faded flat aqua green paint.

"What ya need, sweetie?" Her voice surprised me. It was higher pitched than I'd expected and younger sounding.

"Another room, if there are any left." I leaned closer over the counter and whispered. "I just can't spend another night with my dorm mates, it would just kill me." I said with a grimace. She shook her head in understanding and turned to look at her computer screen.

"I have one left. It has a queen bed, no smoking and the TV doesn't work."

"That's fine with me," I said with a grin.

"I can give it to you for $55 since the TV's broken." I got the impression that she thought I wouldn't take it, but she was wrong. It would solve my dilemma of staging for the hike. I pulled some cash out of my jeans and handed it to her. She took her time writing a receipt for me, then handed me an old tarnished key with a tag that said "Room 15". I noticed that the receipt was filled out with a name I didn't know. It looked like she had just copied from the college kids' registration. Cool.

"Thanks!" I said, flashing her a polite smile before heading out into the warm sun shine. All the college kids had made their way to their rooms except for a couple of guys smoking by the ice maker. The room next to them was 10, so I started walking towards the other end. The parking lot was dirty gravel and little dust clouds followed me as I walked.

I put the key in and turned the lock. The room was bare minimum: a bed, a dresser with the dead TV sitting on it, a table and two old chairs. The art work on the wall looked like it was from a garage sale and the curtains looked worse than ours did at home. It was perfect.

I locked the door, dropped my pack and stripped on my way to the bathroom. Oh, the shower was wonderful. It was clean, cleaner by far than the one I was used to. I used a couple of the little bottles of shampoo and scrubbed myself until I was red all over. Grabbing a scratchy towel, I went back into the main room and dug out clean clothes and got dressed before I was even dry. I brushed my wet hair, glad I never had to bother with styling it, and put my makeup back on. I really liked my green liner with the swirls. A faint stain showed me where to put it again and I smiled at my refreshed *new me*. I looked all wonderland woodsy like and the dumb bruise was started to fade a bit. I winked in the mirror, my *I love you Granddad* and put my makeup back in its little pouch.

Making sure the curtains were closed, I picked up the vest with all my money in it and started to empty the pockets out. I had just crammed the money into the vest pockets, so it was all mixed up and scrunched. I laid the bills out, sorting them into piles of twenties, tens, fives and ones. There were loads more of the twenties than anything else. I figured I needed a lot today, and didn't want to have to pull it out of hiding if I ran out. I counted out a thousand, folded them neatly into three piles and put one wad in each of my shorts pockets and in the small one inside my pack. It was supposed to be for a cell phone, like I'd ever had one of those. It worked perfect for my stash.

It was hot outside and I had already put on a tank top and my jean shorts, and the little vest would complete my outfit. I returned the rest of the money to the zippered pockets inside the vest and was pleased that the bulges were barely noticeable. The vest had one button that pulled it tight around my waist and since it was dark and heavy with the beads it hid the little lumps.

I was set. It was a nice day and I decided I needed to see the path before I made any more detours. I walked the highway on the dirt path until I came to the bridge that spanned the river. A main hiking trail was advertised with signs posted on my side of the river. I barely glanced at it as I stood at the rail and looked across the expanse. I could see the path Granddad and I had taken from here. It snaked up the small hill on the other side and disappeared into the trees.

I couldn't wait...well, really, I could, and I had to. I had things to do first. I turned quickly around and came face to face with the guy from the bus. The green-eyed jewelry store guy. I stopped and stared at him.

"Hi," he said almost too cheerfully. Was he following me?

"Uh hi?" I said, squinting at him.

"Are you scoping out the trail for tomorrow? I didn't know you were with our group. I haven't seen you at SOU," he said, his voice still friendly. He was checking me out, I could tell. I didn't like it, not that I didn't like boys. I just didn't like boys who checked me out when I didn't want to be checked out. I thought about what he'd said. He thought I was going on the hike with his group, he must mean the trail beside me.

"Uh sure, I wanted to see where we would be starting," I replied, still cautious.

"Didn't realize what you signed on for, huh?" he said

with a laugh, moving his dreads out of his face with a swipe of his hand. Okay, he was a hunk, a college kid and all, and even the dreadlocks were kind of cool. Besides I couldn't think of a time an *older* boy had paid me any attention. But this guy was getting on my nerves, hunk or not. I had things to do.

"Of course I do, do you?" I replied as I started walking right past him back up the road.

"Hey hold on. I'm Zack, and you are?" He hurried to catch up with me.

"Busy," I said, looking at him with a side smirk.

"Sure, okay," he said with a confused look on his face. I wondered how many girls walked away from him. "What's your name?"

"Why?" I asked as I walked faster.

"Uh, because it would be easier than saying hey you," he said with a crooked little grin.

"'Hey you' works for me. I gotta run." And I took off running.

CHAPTER 3 - Elsie

June 21, 1861 –

Dear Diary,

Milton came home early to surprise me. He knew what a rough time I am having with Clara. I would never say it aloud, but Clara is not a nice child. She bites and hits and is prone to have the most horrible of tantrums. None of the other mothers will let her play with their children and I feel alone with my troubles. I strive daily to love this child Milton and I created, but she does make it hard.

Only in the forest does she seem at peace. Bless my man for coming for us today, we be going to walk the paths up to the deeper woods, it may be the child will give me rest from her frustrations.

June 25, 1861 –

Life is unkind to me and I know not what I have done to bring this. Milton took Clara and me up into the forest as he had promised. We had been having a wonderful time, just a simple walk. Milton done brung his axe, looking for a good burl to make a new chair out of. Clara was happy, skipping and laughing and picking the flowers. She went ahead of us on the path to the huge roots of a hemlock tree. We gave it no mind until the odd mist rose from the roots and a small male child appeared out of nowhere holding a large stone. He was startled to see us and dropped the stone at Clara's feet. A mighty thunder and bright lightning shot out from the stone.

The boy rose up into the air and before my shocked eyes, he became a small pretty bug. Then as the stone threw out another bolt of lightning, it struck him and he transformed into a large draping willow tree. I could see his face that had become part of the trunk and no greater panic have I ever had. The stone continued to send out angry lines of lightning, hitting Clara and then reaching out to strike trees and animals. Birds fell at our feet and to my astonishment strange creatures started screaming around me. Beautiful wispy beings, male and female were standing near me and sitting on tree branches, where they came from I do not know. The lightning seeming to seek them out and I did not move quickly enough and felt the line of fire hit my arm as it shot by. My mind was too full of the horrors I was seeing to care about my arm. Creatures were shrieking all around me as they were hit. Some seemed to melt and then form into something altogether different, terrifying creatures that I never heard tell of. They were the fortunate ones as others had their bodies shattered into bloody pieces. Many died as I watched and I do not have words for all the terrors I saw.

The stone shot lightning out again and again and I could not reach my Clara. But the child hadn't moved and didn't seem hurt by the tongue of lightning. Milton pushed forward to snatch her away from the evil stone and a ribbon of lightning burst forth straight at him. He held his axe out as if to hit it and the lightning struck the axe instead. Bright lights shot out around us and I was so feared that my Milton and Clara were gone. Then, as suddenly as it all had started, it ended... the forest was quiet once more...save for the wails of a babe.

Fire had spun up around us and except for the hemlock trees every other thing in the forest around us was either destroyed or on the verge of being consumed by the fire. I followed the sound of crying and found the babe nestled in a vine. As I came close I could see one of the strange creatures was holding the babe. Flames were shooting up all around it and the mother wilted like a plant and I knew she was close to death. When she saw me, she held the babe out and I didn't even hesitate, but ran into the flames and took the little child from her.

My Milton grabbed me then and rushed us from that place, me, Clara and the babe, and had us hide a good distance away. Against my protests, he left us and went back into that firestorm. When he returned he was unhurt but would not say a word about why he had left us or what he had been doing. We hurried out of the forest and back to our home. We have not spoken of what happened, but my dreams are troubled. Clara has crawled into her mind and will not come back out. The little one is no nuisance at all and I find I love having such a babe to cradle.

November 14, 1861 –

We are being forced to move out of our home. Our neighbors call witch at us and there is none to make it stop. It is Clara. I did not think she could get any worse than she was, but now my girl draws stares and words from those in this town. She is at most times a beauty, golden wavy locks and a smile so bright that a person would wish to embrace this delightful child of mine, nay it is in a mere second that she becomes the demon-spawn. She screams most awful, speaks in a language that only she understands while shaking uncontrollably. It is her eyes that give a person fright. When a fit strikes, her eyes roll back into her head as she spins and spits foam from her mouth. I wake in the morn not knowing which Clara I will see, the beautiful one or the other. Milton has taken to tying her down in her bed at night, he says it is to keep her safe, but I'm thinking it is to keep us and the little one I named Ruth protected from her. We have another worry on us. The babe Ruth is not growing as a babe should.

It has been five months and the babe is no bigger than when we found her. It does not matter now. The town folk have told us to leave and we fear for our lives. Milton said the forest will welcome us and that is where we will go. I dare not fight with my man as I see things I should not be seeing and know things I should not be knowing and need to stay close to him. We will leave when the sun has set tonight.

CHAPTER 4 - Ivy

I ran till I got to the crosswalk to the shopping center that sat on the other side of the highway. I looked back, but the guy, Zack, was nowhere to be seen. Good, I thought as I slowed and waited for the light to change for me to cross.

The hardware store was my first stop. It was cool, not just hardware, but camping and outdoor stuff. I found everything I needed, plus a nice heavy duty beach wagon. They even had a ton of dried food meals. They were really compact, so I got four cases of the things, explaining to the salesman that I was buying for a large group of hikers. My little wagon was full when I left and I had only spent about $400. Not bad. I made a few impulse buys, like a fish knife and some mini fire-starting logs. I wasn't too sure of my fire making skills.

I pulled the wagon back to my room and unloaded it before heading back out. My next stop was the grocery store. I had my earbuds in and was oblivious to everything around me as I did my shopping. I was having so much fun. I decided I loved spending money. The store was interesting. I couldn't buy *normal* food, and now that I had the meal things, I wanted only things to add to it. Peanut Butter, jam, a ton of canned meats, flour, sugar, instant cocoa and teas and some coffee…I really didn't like regular coffee, mochas were more my thing, but thought it might grow on me…and bags of pasta and oatmeal. They had these really cool bulk bins were I found deals on a ton of things I could use, some munchies like nuts and crackers and processed cheeses in packs. If I was actually able to fish, I'd be able to live pretty good this way. I stood looking at the bread for a while, then went and looked at the flour again.

Marmaw used to make bread. I needed a cook book I thought, adding it to my list. I read the recipe on the back of one of the bags, and got the yeast and other stuff it said I needed. That reminded me of things like salt and pepper. I grabbed big containers of those. My wagon was pretty full by the time I finished there. I knew I'd have to repack to get it to fit…but told myself that I could make a couple of trips to the cabin…if I had to.

After I unloaded for the second time, my motel room was looking like an ad for disaster preparedness. I was going to have fun, I told myself as I looked at it all. I glanced at my watch and decided I had plenty of time to get the books and other items I wanted to look for in the little tourist shops. I almost skipped out my door and down the highway, back to the busy part of town, with my handy dandy wagon along for the ride.

I peeked in a lot of shop windows once I hit the sidewalks again. The bookstore smelled like mold, but I found a cool palm sized camper's cooking guide. It even showed how to gut fish and make hush puppies and Indian bread. Crud! I needed corn flour and honey. I'd have to pick them up later, if I could remember.

I found a couple paperbacks. *My Side of the Mountain* just screamed at me, as did a book of poems by Shel Silverstein. Good time to read the classics I figured, since I had only brought Marmaw's books with me, and I had already read those.

One of the stores had art supplies and I got the sketch pads, along with some water color paints, brushes, and more pencils that came with a sharpener. Except for getting something to eat again I was pretty much set. I smiled at everyone, the little kids, the old people, the ones who worked in the stores. I felt alive for the first time since Granddad and Marmaw had left. I was heading towards a little café with a sandwich board out front that said "Fresh Fish," when I passed the antique store. I had the oddest feeling that someone had called my name from inside the store. My first thought was to run…but the voice I had heard, *if* I had heard it, pulled at me. I stood and looked at the window display of old pictures and glossy fancy furniture, with doilies like Marmaw had used; there was something about this place and I had to go in.

A little bell chimed as I opened the door painted with the words *Winnie's Whimsies*. I felt instantly at ease and a feeling of safety settled over me. A girl about my age looked up from a book she was reading and grinned widely.

"Hi," I said, liking her immediately. She had pig tails high up on her head, with curly blonde hair that was barely long enough to fit into the rubber bands. They looked like little blonde teddy bear ears. She was wearing the most bizarre assortment of mismatched clothes. Combined with white lip gloss, they looked perfect on her. I noticed right off that she was void of any piercings or tats, and my opinion of her rose. I hated seeing girls with metal in their noses and eyebrows. Mouth piercings of any kind really creeped me out...I wouldn't even talk to anyone who had those.

"Hi, can I help you find something?" she asked me, hopping off her stool.

"I just kinda want to look around. Can I park this thing somewhere?" Pointing at my wagon.

"Sure, let's pull in into the back room. I'm the only one here until 6:00 so no one will touch it." She skipped away from me, down one of the aisles towards a closed door. I giggled as I followed, wondering if she was always this childlike. As I caught up with her, she opened a door, displaying a stock room. "Will this work okay?"

"Sure, thanks," I said as I pulled it in.

"Are you staying at one of the beach houses?" she asked, looking hopefully at me.

"Kind of, I'm staying with some family at a cabin up in the mountains. We just came down for the day," I said, feeling bad about my half lie.

"Oh." She pursed her lips disappointedly. "I was hoping you were a new local or something." Her face brightened and she said, "I like your hair and makeup. Wish I could wear more makeup, but my grandma won't let me. She's got some strange ideas about what things 'fit' with my aura."

My first thought was she had a grandma who cared enough to have a say, then I wondered what her aura had to do with anything. But I understood what she meant about her grandma and grinned back at her. "And I wish I had pretty blonde hair that curled so I could wear it like yours." And we both laughed.

"Hi, I'm Margo," she said, sticking out her hand. I took it, as she whispered "It's short for Margaret, but I hate that name."

"I'm..." and I stopped. Did I give her my real name? What if someone started to look for me? What the heck, my first name wouldn't hurt. "I'm Ivy," I answered, feeling comfortable with her. I started to look around the store; it was really cool. It was like junk store meets antique store meets new age hippy head shop. I looked at everything, not that I needed any of it, but it was a fun way to spend my time.

We ended up in the back corner of the store where there were racks of used clothes. I found some tie-dyed tank tops. Margo would pick something out and hold it up; mostly I shook my head no. But when she held up the little dark blue beach cover-up dress, I had to have it. After that, she knew what I liked and before I knew it, I had a couple more summer shirts, leggings, and the dress thing. There were some discounted bags of underwear and socks, so I grabbed some of those also.

The two of us spent almost an hour trying on an

assortment of outfits in the little dressing room, each combination getting wackier and we passed most of the time laughing. It was so much fun...something I hadn't had in a long time. But at the end of the hour, my arms were getting kind of full of clothes and I really didn't need anything else. Margo was still looking through the clothes racks, but I stopped her.

"Margo, that's all really. This has been so much fun, but I need to pay you for these and get going." She looked crestfallen as she walked me over to the cash register and started to ring the clothes up, folding them neatly and placing them on the counter.

As she was doing her thing, I was looking around. There were jars of stick incense and candles and really cool crystals on chains. A pile of fist-sized rocks sat on the corner of the counter, each unique and amazing. Beside the counter there was a tall glass case filled with oils, perfumes, incense and little trays of polished rocks.

"That's my grandma's stuff. It's that aura thing she believes in…she says this stuff all has them too," Margo said. She rolled her eyes and finished putting my clothes in a cute little bag for me.

I raised my eyebrows and grinned. "Really? Like what you said about certain makeup and hair styles fitting your aura?" I was trying not to laugh. It was cute.

"Yeah, she's kooky, but I love her. She's into this like Wiccan thing," she said as she went over to the case and brought some polished rocks out on a tray. "Grandma Winnie picks these up on the beach and polishes them. She says they 'call' to her."

I looked at them. They were really something. As she put the tray back on the shelf, I noticed that just above the case, mounted on the wall was a framed box displaying a necklace. The necklace itself was made from vines, braided into a tight cord. Hanging from the cord was a tiny heart shaped bit of wood. It looked very old and the wooden heart was faded like beach wood. I had only seen a few other pieces of jewelry like it before and pulled out my own necklace and looked down at it, then back up at the framed one. Mine looked almost new compared to that one. The vines that made up my cord were still green and my little wooden heart was highly polished, bringing out all the grain variations in the wood. The one in the box was similar…really similar. I couldn't stop looking at it.

"Something wrong?" she asked as she followed my glaze.

"I don't know," I replied a little disorientated. "That necklace up there, it looks like mine. Where did you get it?"

"This is going to sound really bizarre. Grandma said she found it and it is supposed to be calling out to someone or something."

She laughed a bit nervously as she looked at it. "Grandma says it's very unique, but she won't let me touch it."

"Calling out?" I responded in disbelief.

"I know. It's really embarrassing at times. Grandma is always going on to anyone that will listen about places in-between and the balance of the worlds. She thinks there are like other places, and we can move between them if we have the right *aura* about us," she rolled her eyes at this point. "Anyway, she said this is from *the other side* and she thinks she is keeping it for someone special."

"Special? Like the right colored aura?" This was interesting. Margo had a family as outlandish as mine had been, there was a bond here.

"I guess. I wish she'd stop talking about it. It's stupid," she glanced up and saw the look on my face. "Oh please, don't get me wrong. I love my grandma, she is really sweet and everything. But the people here in town make fun of her and it kind of falls over onto me. I don't have many friends." Her voice was so sad. Boy did I understand. My mom had done a job on me when it came to having friends. I didn't even think about bringing anyone home, not ever. Even when Granddad and Marmaw were around, I couldn't do it. Mom would have ruined everything with her bizarre behavior. I felt tears coming on and reached out and hugged her. After a minute she pulled back and wiped her own tears away.

"It's okay, really." She looked up at the necklace. "I wish grandma would just get rid of that thing, but she says she has to keep it since she is the caretaker of this town."

"Can I buy it? I think maybe my Granddad made it," I said as I held out my necklace for her to see. "Doesn't it look like mine?"

"It does. Wow that's amazing. But I'm sorry, I don't dare even take it down. Grandma would have a conniption fit if I even touched it," Margo replied shaking her head.

"Well okay," I said disappointed. It really did look like my necklace and I would have loved to have something else that Granddad had made…if he had made that one.

"Maybe you could come back tomorrow when Grandma is here," she said hopefully.

"I wish I could, but it will be a few days before I get back into town." She made a pouting face, but didn't push the subject and I was glad.

We talked some more, but finally I had to pay her and take the bag she handed over to me. She collected my wagon, pulling it up to the door. Smiling, I took it from her and started to leave, stopping only after I had opened the door and the little chime had gone off.

"Margo, it was really nice to meet you. I hope we see each other again. Next time I'm in town, I'll stop by."

Her face brightened. "That would be great. Do you have a phone number so I can call you?"

I shook my head no and answered, "It's kind of remote where I live. How about I come back in a couple of weeks?" She nodded okay glumly and I left, pulling my wagon behind. I made a friend and I thought she was probably the one person that someday, maybe, I could really talk to about my mom. It was something to look forward to.

I wasn't in the mood to eat inside. I walked almost aimlessly. I stopped at an outside stand and got a bag of fish and chips and a soda. Finding a bench no one was on, I sat down to eat. The fish and chips were hot and greasy, and pretty good.

The wind was starting to blow off the ocean, and a fog was rolling in with it. The sun was still out, but it had turned chilly. I watched as people packed up and found their way off the beach. I put my earbuds back in and started listening to Elvis belt out "All Shook Up". Throwing my trash in the can next to the bench, I got up and started walking back to the motel, pulling my wagon behind me. I found myself singing along with Elvis, getting odd looks from people as I passed them. Better me than Margo, I thought.

I didn't care about the stares; I really got into the "all shook up" part and it carried me all the way back to my little motel room. I was feeling good that maybe I gave the locals something to gossip about instead of my new friend.

CHAPTER 5 - Ivy

I spent the next couple of hours sorting everything. My food went into one pile, it was the largest. The camping equipment didn't look like much once I got everything out of the boxes. I put things inside other things, put the cases of food in the wagon first, then the odd shaped camping items, but it wouldn't stay put. I ended up using a couple of the larger boxes that other things had come in to re-pack some of the stuff. The lanterns were the only things I was worried about breaking, but the little glass parts came out and I was able to pack them in one of the new, cheap towels I had brought. I got everything in; it was piled high, but it fit. I covered it with the tarp and used a lightweight rope to tie it all down. It was heavy, but once I got it rolling, I would be fine.

I changed into jeans and pulled on a sweatshirt and went back to the store to get the few items I now knew I needed after reading the camping recipes. I could put the last few things in my backpack.

Once I was back from the store, I cleaned up the room, taking the trash out so no one would question all the purchases I had made. I was anxious to leave, but knew I couldn't until after midnight. The little town seemed to stay up late and I didn't want to be pulling my wagon down the highway with a bunch of cars going by.

I went out again, just down to the McDonald's in the shopping center, to grab some burgers and fries. It wasn't until I was in line that I noticed that the college kids were in there also. I could hear them talking about their big hike tomorrow up to a remote camping site. The girls were complaining because there weren't any showers and the toilets were outhouses. I laughed to myself, trying not to smirk, when I thought of my bars of soap and shampoo, and rolls of toilet paper that had to last me for a couple of months. I'd be bathing in the sink or the cold stream and surviving with only my outhouse. They had no idea what roughing it was.

When it was my turn, I ordered double what I really wanted. McD hamburgers are good hot or cold, and it would be a nice snack along my hike tonight. I got a large coffee also. When my order came, I moved over to the condiment table to put as much sugar as possible in the coffee. I was standing there, opening 3-4 packs at a time and dumping them into my cup, when I felt movement behind me.

"Hey you." There was that annoyingly nice voice again. Crud. I really didn't want to talk with him. I thought about ignoring him, but that was just plain rude, if my running away today wasn't rude enough. Turning my head, I looked up at him. Green eyes smiled down at me.

"Hi Zack," I said, trying to sound as bored as possible, and then turned back to putting the sugar in the large cup.

"That stuff will stunt your growth, you know," he said leaning on the counter to look at me, pushing his dreads back over his head. I 'hmmmed' at him as I started to open creamer packages.

"So 'Hey You', are you coming with our group or with another one?" I just looked up at him, trying not to be annoyed at his questions. He wasn't put off by me it seemed, since he answered his own question. "Okay, another. No one in my group seems to know the purple-haired girl."

I grabbed some napkins, and then reached for the packages of ketchup, making him move out of my way as I did so. As I took a handful of the ketchup packets, I realized I had forgotten mayonnaise completely. My tuna would be icky without it. Another 'Crud!' I did not want to go back to the store. He was watching me, studying what I was doing, and then looked at the bin with the condiments. With a little chuckle, he grabbed a handful, looked around and motioned for me to open my bag. I did, narrowing my eyes at him. He dumped the handful of mayonnaise packets in and grabbed another large handful and put those in too. The he leaned close and whispered. "Do you want some of the other ones too?"

I held back a giggle and whispered back, "No, my bag is full." I couldn't help grinning at him. Okay, he was growing on me. He opened his eyes wide in fake shock, then leaped away back to his table, quickly shook out the bag his food had been in and was back standing next to me with a charming smirk plastered on his lips. He made sure his back was to the workers as he filled the bag with more of the mayonnaise, then ketchup and mustard. Boy, I was set, I thought as he handed them to me with a cute little smirk.

I really tried not to smile as I turned and started to walk out with my two bags and coffee. He followed and opened the door for me as I mouthed a thank you to him.

"You're welcome," he whispered back. "Hope to see you on the trail tomorrow Hey You." He gave me a playful wink then went back in to join his friends.

"In another life," I whispered as I walked away. "See ya Zack, been nice knowing you." I walked back to my room feeling rather depressed. At one time I had friends at home, but I never missed them that much. Now I was thinking I just might miss Zack and Margo, which was pathetic since I had just met them and there was no way they could be considered my friends.

I sat on the bed in the room and ate my late dinner, while I shoved all the little packets into one bag. If I only used one a day I'd have enough for a couple of months, I reasoned as I finished the burger and laid back on the bed.

I looked over at the alarm clock. 11:00pm. I set the alarm to go off at 1:30 and closed my eyes and tried to let sleep come. No such luck. After about fifteen minutes of trying to sleep, I reached into my pocket and got out my MP3 player. Without opening my eyes, I put the earbuds in and turned it up. The Everly Brothers were up next on the play list, then I listened to Neil Sedaka sing "Little Devil," then The Doors sang "Light my Fire"...I fell asleep singing along with Del Shannon. His song "My Little Runaway" spoke to me in so many ways and I felt the tears building as the pain and misery I'd been living with for the last year took hold of me. The recording must have been an original taping, since it had that tinny sound to it. Del's voice was haunting as his words empathized with my situation. My last waking memory was murmuring, *run, run, run, runaway* over and over again.

The loud annoying ringing woke me. The lights were still on and the dumb alarm clock had actually worked. I hit it hard, then again for good measure. "Sorry," I said to it as I sat up. It had done its job after all, and I shouldn't be mad at it. I could hear faint music and realized my earbuds had come out, the MP3 was still on.

"Good one Ivy, run down the batteries before you even leave," I mumbled to myself. I grabbed my pack and hunted around until I found my power cord for it. If I plugged it in now, there was a chance it would charge before I left. I found a wall plug and connected it, then dropped it on the little table as I yawned and staggered to the bathroom.

I took a quick, hot shower, then as I was drying off, I gathered up the little bathroom things that were included in the room; some soaps and lotions, one shampoo and a couple of conditioners. I brushed my teeth, cleaned the residue of makeup from under my eyes and then packed all my stuff. I was fine wearing the same clothes, so I pulled them back on, along with the sweatshirt. I used the toilet one last time, took the extra roll of toilet paper, shoving it in my pack, along with anything else that was still lying around. I put the remaining hamburger in last, clipped my MP3 on, straightened the bed, and turned off all the lights. The little clock showed that it was 2:00 am.

I moved the curtains about an inch and peered out. A heavy fog had settled, and only the faint glow of the motel sign could be seen. Ideal. I left the key on the dresser and made sure my flashlight was in the front pocket of the sweatshirt before I opened the door. I peeked out gingerly. No one was out and there was not a sound of human life. I could hear surf crashing against the rocks in the distance. It seemed to echo in the fog.

Trying to be quiet, I pulled the wagon out the door. It was really heavy, and once I got it moving, it was hard to make it stop. As soon as I achieved stoppage, I closed the door, grabbed the wagon's handle again and started to pull it through the gravel to the dirt path next to the highway. The fog swirled around me, hiding me completely as I laboriously dragged the wagon across the gravel. It was a bit easier once I was next to the highway, but still not fun. I trudged along slowly, making my way to the bridge. I was hating life at that moment; the darn wagon did not want to move. When I finally got it up on the road, it rolled a lot easier. Half-way across the bridge, an owl startled me, hooting directly overhead.

I jerked to a stop and looked up. The fog was thick overhead and whatever had hooted was completely hidden from sight. Crap…I had lost momentum and had to really yank on the wagon to get it rolling again. No cars came as I crossed, but faint headlights started to glow in the distance just as I pulled the wagon from the pavement and onto the dirt on the other side of the bridge. I had to hurry to get under cover before the driver saw me. I used every bit of strength I had to get that stupid wagon started up the little hill and around the first tall spruce tree. I could see

Granddad's mark carved into its trunk and relaxed, knowing without a doubt that I had found the right path.

CHAPTER 6 - Elsie

August 1862 –

I know not where to begin. We found our way back into the forest and were met by the oddest of creatures. I was feared of them and kept the babe hid. Clara was no worry as she fell asleep and stayed that way for many a day. Milton has been meeting with the others that he calls fey and he thinks that we be safe here. I do not understand all that he speaks of, and do not want to know.

I do know that it was the hemlock trees that saved us. I hear them, which sounds odd to write. Milton seems to understand and told me it was the hemlock trees that protected the forest from that horrible stone. He told me that he had put the stone into a hemlock stump that first day and covered it with hemlock wood before he had come back to us. What a sacred magical tree the hemlocks are to be able to lock up the stone and shield its power to destroy. These fey that have come do not know the stone is there and I'm thinking they cannot see past the magic of the hemlocks.

I have taken to drawing pictures of the forest and the creatures that I see. Some are so beautiful it does hurt to look on them, but I do not trust them and told Milton to be watchful of the things. He learned to give heed to my words when the fey grew infuriated with him when he would not hand Ruth over to them. They said we had stolen her and she belonged to them. Of course Milton said no. I had heard their words and ran with Ruth to where Clara was sleeping, thinking to hide, but they found me.

One pulled hair from poor sleeping Clara's head and I knew not why it would do such a thing. The others tried to take Ruth from me, but Milton was able to get to us and stop them.

Milton knows I will not give up my Ruth to anyone. This child was put into our care on purpose, my dreams tell me this and even if Milton does not believe in my dreams he does loves me and will stand with me. Besides he loves this tiny child as much as I do.

He was full of anger and did something awful to the fey to stop them from taking her. I think he is wonderful. He turned all those creatures into a type of butterfly and demanded that they leave the forest...and they instantly did. No one, mortal or fey is going to take Ruth away from us.

May 1863 –

It has been a long year in the forest. I grow tired of making a home in a tent and cooking over an open fire. The forest is unhappy without the fey...how I know this I do not fathom. I have convinced Milton to try to make peace with the fey and allow them back into our forest.

He has opened the doorway and the fey have come back. They seem humble and willing to work with him this time. Milton and them have come to an understanding. They have accepted that Milton has a magic about him that they cannot overcome.

I do not comprehend fully the magic my man now holds, but he has control over this forest and the fey that come here. They have taken to calling him the Woodsman and his axe, the very axe that shielded us from the magic of that awful stone, is now the key that opens the doorway the fey use to come and go. Milton has decided which fey are safe to be in the forest with us and has locked the rest out. He knows how I feel about the creatures, so they are not allowed to be around me or the girls unless they are Wisps, as my man calls them. I must say they are very becoming as little harmless bugs.

Milton and the fey have finished the cabin that is to be our home. It has a fine roof of hemlock slates and is sturdy and built from hemlock wood. He didn't tell them why he wanted the cabin built with the wood, but when they finished the building and were gone he went and retrieved the stone from where he had hidden it.

The fey are not to be trusted and more and more they are asking about it, wanting it back. Milton and I both know that can never be allowed to happen. Our new hemlock cabin will keep the stone's wicked magic locked and insure the fey cannot get to it.

Milton used the river stones to lace the fire hearth and has set it amongst them. I do not like the thing he calls the Sumair stone, but it seems quiet now, and I know this cabin has swathed its power. I like the thought that the stone is a prisoner within the hemlock wood, as well as that the creature that brought the evil stone to the forest in the first place is also a prisoner. It will be a long while before I find any forgiveness to give to the Willow. I know it is not *all* his fault nor did he bring all evil things to us. Clara was already not a good child and I do love Ruth, she is a blessing...but Willow changed my family's life path without so much as a by-your-leave and it can never be the same again. I guess if I were to be honest with myself it is just that I need to be mad at someone and he is it.

After all Milton had done I still did not feel we were safe, so he fashioned necklaces out of vines and little hemlock wood hearts for each of us that gives us protection from the fey. He says the hearts are talismans and have a magic within them that no fey can overcome.

At my bidding, he also put a 'lock' on this forest, so no other will ever be able to innocently stumble upon this place and possibly meet the same fate as us. I would not wish this life on anyone. He left us for a time and went into town to gather a stove and other items for our home. It must have been mighty hard to cart the heavy load up the path but I am thrilled to have a nice little stove to cook on.

CHAPTER 7 - Zack

Zack couldn't sleep; he had come back with the rest of the hiking group from McDonald's and hung out with the guys. They had wanted to play some cards, but the game didn't go anywhere. He had gone back to his room around 1:00am and undressed down to his boxers. And lay there. He was thinking about the girl. What was it about her?

Yeah, she was cute, with that purple hair and strange makeup. And she was so petite she looked like an imp, but that wasn't it. She didn't act like any college girl he had ever met. Even the ones on this trip either flirted all the time or were so involved in the save-something thing that they drove him nuts. This girl acted like she just wanted him to go away. That made him even more curious about her.

He knew his behavior since he had first seen her had been odd. But he couldn't get the smell of her out of his mind. She smelled like clean, fresh-cut grass and it was hard to explain, but he just *knew* that she needed his help. On the bus he'd ended up just feeling like a dope and really hoped no one had seen him sniffing her hair. Then again today out by the bridge she hadn't been responsive to him, but he had gotten close to her long enough now to know the smell wasn't from her hair, but from all of her.

He couldn't believe she had actually run away from him. He didn't know if that meant she was scared of him or really didn't want anything to do with him. Still he had followed her to the shopping center. She had purchased a large amount of camping equipment, food and that large wagon. No one went camping with a wagon or that much stuff. Then it was like she was just a tourist, walking around town, buying this and that. He had loitered outside the antique shop when she went in. He watched her through the window and saw she was enjoying her time with the blonde, and then he had to hurry and hide when she came out.

He had hoped she'd talk to him when he saw her come into McDonalds tonight, however again she really didn't want anything to do with him. It was a bit odd about the condiments, but even he had taken them before and they were handy on camping trips. Strange and interesting...a real mystery.

The crunching sound of something on the gravel outside pulled him from his thoughts and he got up to investigate. He looked out the window, but it was foggy and hard to make out anything in the dark. A faint outline of something moving in the fog got his attention. He strained to see what, or who, it was. A clearing in the haze gave him a glimpse of the back of something bulky, and then the fog closed in again. Curious, he pulled on his jeans, slipped his feet into his tennis shoes and went out.

He couldn't see anything now, not even the office. But he could still hear the sound of something moving on the gravel. He walked out into the parking lot, trying to follow the sounds. Again the fog cleared a little…an owl shrieked overhead and on the bridge he saw someone. The figure had stopped and had turned to gaze up at the owl, when he finally got a look at who it was.

"Damn, it's her!" he hissed under his breath and started running. What was she doing out at this time? And pulling that stupid little wagon he had seen her with? He ran after her, not caring if she heard him or not. She had moved off the pavement on the other side by the time he reached the bridge and he was distracted by the headlights in the distance. When he turned back she was gone. He ran down the road, but she wasn't there. He hurried back to the bridge and tried to see where she could have taken that wagon. He found wheel tracks in the dirt by the bridge, but they disappeared up a small hill. He started to climb and had to hold on to small trees to make it up.

He gave up after a few minutes. There was no way she could have come this way, with or without that wagon. After standing there for ten minutes he started to feel foolish. Maybe it was just a weird dream, or the fog... He gave up and went back to the motel. He'd find out who she was hiking with tomorrow, and maybe he would switch groups.

CHAPTER 8 - Ivy

It was easier than I thought it was going to be. Once I cleared the road and the little hill, the path leveled out and the wagon rolled along behind me almost merrily. I had moved out of the fog and now the stars and the moon provided me with light. I didn't even need my flashlight to see. I stopped to put my earbuds in and hummed along with the familiar melodies. Granddad would have liked hiking at night. It was the perfect time for one of the stories he always made up for me on the walks.

I thought of that last night with him. Marmaw had taken Mom somewhere a few days earlier, and Granddad said he was going to meet them. I had already been missing Marmaw but not Mom, and I sort of wished she would stay wherever they had gone when Marmaw finally came back. Granddad and I had spent those few days together working around the house, and that last night we had reminisced about our trips here.

He told me that any time I needed to be somewhere safe, this was the place to be. Granddad had been really insistent on that point; he wanted me to repeat to him that the cabin was a safe place. I still think he was talking about later in my life, using the phrase 'somewhere safe' to mean a place to get away, to relax, or reconnect with nature. He was strange sometimes like that, saying things that made no sense. I'd just agree to whatever it was he was talking about, hug him and go on with my life. I did the same thing that night, not giving what he was talking about much weight.

I wondered now if he knew it was his last night and he

was telling me that I might *need* to go somewhere to be safe.

No matter what he meant, Marmaw hadn't come back, Granddad had left and Mom had returned instead of them. It was my worst nightmare come true, and as things went from bad to worse with Mom, I had three choices. 1. Live with it, 2. End up in a foster care, or 3. Run. I had kept coming back to the third choice, *run*, asking myself, run where? I had gone out to Granddad's shop before Mom had sold everything to catch the scent of him again. The aroma of sawdust and the grease he used on the saws, the raw smell of the wood; it was all Granddad to me. I had stood in the shop and closed my eyes; thinking about Granddad had led me to thinking about the cabin. A place to run *to*. After that the plan occupied my every waking moment and probably my dreams too.

I thought of Granddad and me walking this path and wondered for the hundredth time why we had never seen anyone else on it. It was easy to find, right by the bridge. I could see it just standing there yesterday. But not once had I seen anyone on the path or in the forest or at the cabin. I hoped that it would remain that way. I wanted to be alone, I needed to be alone. But still I wondered why no one else used the path.

It should have been eerie to be in the forest alone, but it wasn't at all. The moon-light filtered through the tall fir and hemlock trees, casting a glow down onto the path. It was edged with all sorts of ferns; mostly huge sword ferns, almost taller than me, but there were little lace ferns and deer ferns and maidenhair and so many I couldn't remember all their names. The trees started to get larger, the forest denser...wilder. Vines grew up the trees' trunks, mixed in with mosses and night blooming irises and strange mushroom growths on the trees' sides, like little shelves. The forest seemed to emit acceptance; I felt embraced by it. The weird little bugs appeared, surrounding me, keeping me company.

Eventually I came to the place 'of the rocks' as Granddad had named it. It was where the path lead up the side of a mountain, one side was stacks of boulders, held together with a multitude of moss and ferns. The other side started to angle down and soon I'd be able to look at the tree tops below. It wasn't a dangerous walk…the path was wide and I knew it well. My wagon gave me no problems at all. I could easily pull it with one hand as I walked. I knew that was a little peculiar, but I wasn't going to start complaining about it.

The climb lasted for over an hour until I entered the 'hollow', another of Granddad's names. The forest was so thick here that even sun light couldn't get through. The trees had grown together forming an arch over the path. Granddad had made up a story about the fairies putting the trees there as guardians of the forest where our cabin sat. It was dark inside the hollow and I had to pull out my flashlight to see.

Neil Diamond started singing in my ears. I knew the music, but it wasn't his earlier work. It was the more classical one from the early 70's, about the Seagull. I always liked this album, even if it wasn't really classified as an oldie. The song seemed to fit the mood on this part of the path.

The path twisted and turned many times before I finally came out from under the arches and was once again in the normal forest. The moon light greeted me and shone down on the path as I continued on.

I reached the clearing just before sunrise, passing under the arch of twisted branches Granddad had used to form the entry. The glade and the cabin looked just as I remembered. The cabin sat off to one side, backed by tightly packed trees. Granddad had woven woody vines between the trunks, until it was like a fence behind it, with blackberries and other thorny bushes making an additional barrier. He had continued the 'fence' around the entire glade, making the arches over all the little paths that led off into the forest or down to the stream. The cabin looked like a large bramble itself, covered almost completely with trumpet vines. Marmaw had used this setting for almost all of her books…no offence to her, but it looked better in person.

"I'm here Granddad," I said out loud. Damn I missed him. The sound of wind chimes came to me from behind. I whirled around and looked at the trees close by. I didn't remember us ever having put a wind chime up. The bugs were there though, staying back from me, hovering in a tight little group. They were really weird and I only remember seeing them here, in the hemlock forest. They reminded me of hummingbirds that had combined with dragonflies. I had to really work at not swatting them away, which would have brought a sharp word from Granddad if I had done so. He was always telling me we couldn't hurt anything in the forest...then he'd contradict himself and go fishing. It never made any sense to me.

I pulled the wagon up to the door and lifted the rock that was hidden under the vines. The tiny pill bottle was there with the key. Popping the lid, I dropped the key out into my hand. Eagerly, I put the key in the lock, turned it easily and opened the door to my new home.

CHAPTER 9 - Elsie

April 1871-

My dreams have been powerful of late and Milton understands my need to leave this place for a time. Ruth been growing nicely, looking a great deal more like a normal little being. Clara is in a good way, awake again and cheerful. We leave on the morrow.

June 1871 –

When we left the forest this time we were concerned that we would need to move farther away so that we would not come across ones that knew of us. We found our concerns were ground-less as we are not remembered by any. Many years seem to have passed while we lived in the forest and we thought it had been only couple.

Ruth looks like a child of 5 or 6 now, still growing only when in the forest. For us, it is different. Neither Milton, myself nor Clara age a bit while in the forest and though we do in the normal world, it is slower than common people. Dark creatures are still drawn to us, my head hurts from hearing them. Clara is terrified of them, more than people seem to be of her. It is a strange life we have.

August 1871 –

We move yet again. Five towns we have set up home in and in none can we find peace. Clara causes us problems wherever we go; she is but a pale shadow of who she once was. She may not have been a sweet thing, but this switching of herself from normal to a creature of nightmares is disturbing. It is a hard task to keep her oddities hidden from people.

September 1876 –

We find we never seem to feel at home outside the forest now and must frequently come back for short periods, before leaving yet again to find a new place outside to live. But always we have to move on after just a few short weeks. We are plagued by the things of the night that continue to hound us. Milton and I seem to be able to disregard them as they do us no harm and little Ruth gives them no mind at all. It is Clara who they torment and it is for her that we return to the forest so often so she can sleep and have control of herself again.

September 1883 –

Milton has met others of our kind out here in the real world and we are learning that we are not alone. There are good folk, fey, that have decided to live in our world and call themselves Alltha, wild ones. There are others like us that have been touched by the fey's magic and been changed, shifted. We are told that fey magic will attach itself in ways that enhance what a person already is; if the person is good then the magic will be in some form good, but if the person has an evil soul the magic will form around that aspect of them instead. Oh my poor Clara, I once had hopes that she would outgrow her meanness. Maybe it was my fault since we did spoil her so as a babe...but in my soul I know that is not true. She was born this way and the magic took hold of that part of her...she will never be better.

July 1932 –

I have not written for a long while. We come back and forth; Milton has found a trade that supports us well. I have taken to writing stories and drawing pictures of fairies that are posted in weekly papers in a number of cities in California. I do not like moving so much, but it is necessary. I have made some wonderful friends, other shifted mortals like us and a few women of the Allthas. Now no matter where we end up, I have help with Clara.

Milton has used his magic to protect Clara and Ruth, blocking their memories of the past. We do not want them to get lost in them and live confused. Clara is confused enough so this is a good thing he has done for her. I wasn't sure it was the right thing to do to Ruth as she is a delight and seems to have no problems in either realm. But whether I like it or not, it is done.

CHAPTER 10 - Ivy

It looked just like we left it last time. A small homey rectangle. The door opened to the hall, which was really just an add-on to the original door. On both sides were the familiar bench seats that lifted up for storage underneath, and rows on each side of wooden pegs for hanging up coats and things.

The inner door was open and I pulled the wagon all the way in, then went back and closed the outside door. Coming back into the room, I just had to stand and look around. It smelled like home, like Granddad. The aromas from the trumpet flowers permeated the cabin, giving it a deep heavy scent.

The far side of the cabin was almost taken up with floor to ceiling shelves, mostly used for things other than books. Baskets held craft stuff and miscellaneous items, most just clutter gathered over the years. There were still some books lying amid the disorder, worn and well read. Two oversized, handmade chairs sat in front of it. Granddad had purchased them in town years before he brought me here. He'd had to take them apart, carry them through the forest and up the mountain and then put them back together. They were lumpy and old and I loved them.

The stove sat in the back left corner, with a mixed selection of stones set in mortar running beneath it and up the wall behind it. Granddad hadn't been picky when he'd chosen the stones; some were flat, some kind of round, there were tan ones, white ones, dark brown ones and one really cool stone that was black with crazy lines of blue running through it. Granddad always joked that it was our 'family stone' since mine and his eye matched the blue in it.

There were hooks and little ledges all over the stones with large metal spoons and tongs. A well-worn set of heavy fireplace tools leaned against the stones. The stove was big and black with a little door for the wood, and an inside shelf for baking. There were four round burners on the top with a cast iron pot and frying pan, and an old coffee pot sat off to the side.

To the left of it was our sink. Granddad had built a set of low cabinets, placing an old metal trough on top. Somehow he had drilled a hole in the bottom of the trough and connected a piece of garden hose that allowed water to drain outside. There was a hand pump to bring water into the sink. It was old and rusty and I hoped it still worked.

Above it was a line of open shelves that still held some mugs and cracked plates. A couple of misshaped baskets held some silverware and other kitchen things. Next to it was another floor to ceiling set of shelves. My food could go there.

The table sat in front of the shelves, across from the stove. Granddad had made it from one slab of a tree. It was thick and about 2 feet wide and only 5 feet long. We had used it to eat on, draw on, cut up fish and meat on…and play cribbage on. It was dented from knife marks and years of use. A bench seat sat under the window, with more storage under it and two red square boat safety floats to sit on. We had brought those the second time I came with him, so I could reach the table better. There were a couple of handmade stools in front of it. I used to use one to sit on when I washed dishes at night.

There was a ladder made out of branches that went up to the open loft, where I would curl up with my blankets and quilts and watch the fire burn out in the stove through the slates in the rail. Under it and to my right was another bed made from pieces of wood and woven with vines. It was like lying on a large hammock. Granddad's and Marmaw's bed. A couple of Marmaw's handmade bright colored scrap quilts were folded up neatly at one end.

Home.

I had to close my eyes for a moment after I took it all in. Home. I felt like I had come home. When I opened them, they were moist and I was barely able to hold the tears back. Dropping my bag on the bed, I started to unpack my wagon. For the next hour, I put things away, organized the shelves, found places to put all my food, then grabbing my new sleeping bag, I climbed the ladder.

It hadn't changed from the last time I was here. My old blankets were in the trunk that Granddad had somehow gotten up the ladder. I made a nice nest of them on the floor, then climbed into my sleeping bag, clothes and all, and fell instantly asleep.

I'm not sure what woke me; it could have been the light of the sun coming through the bottle window next to my head, or my dream...laughter...joyful laughter. Sitting up, I was disoriented for a moment, the window Granddad had put in for me was casting a light display around me. He had collected a bunch of different colored glass bottles and cut off the bottoms. Somehow he had fitted them together to form a thick multi-colored window. Rays of pinks, greens and blues were illumining my loft, with bits of dust motes visible in the rays.

I disentangled myself from the sleeping bag, then crawled to the ladder and went down. The sun was beginning to set, the air was feeling chilly and I hadn't chopped any wood yet. Taking a bottle of water and gulping it down, I stood there trying to figure out what to do first. I decided that nature was calling. Now I really was missing the old fart. He had always made sure the outhouse was clean and ready before I had to use it.

There was no avoiding it. I grabbed some cleaning stuff, a couple of rolls of toilet paper and went out. I'd missed most of the day by sleeping in and now couldn't put off this chore any longer. I walked behind the cabin to the little funny house at the edge of the trees and opened the door. It didn't smell; that was good. I swept, then wiped everything down, used the bleach spray that we had left on our last visit, making sure the toilet seat was spotless and clean. I did my business, trying not to think about what was beneath me and missing a real toilet.

When I came out, I could have sworn I heard something in the brambles behind the outhouse, but the thicket was too dense to see into. Chills ran up my spine and for the first time it dawned on me that I really was all alone in the forest. Memories of horror films came back to me and I almost ran back to the safety of my cabin. I picked up my new hatchet and instantly felt better.

Taking it and my wagon I went back outside. My wagon now had a new function. Wood hauler. Pulling it into the closest thicket, I gathered up small, dry branches, and a few slightly larger ones. I'd have to chop them down to size and wasn't sure I was looking forward to that part. What if I chopped off a finger? I chastised myself for being such a weenie and forced myself to continue with what needed to be done.

It wasn't long before I had a nice pile of kindling in the wagon and another pile next to the stump Granddad had used for chopping wood. I didn't think about it until now, but his old large axe wasn't there. Maybe it was in one of the benches inside the door. I couldn't remember if Granddad stored it there or someplace else. It had never really entered my mind before.

But my hatchet worked fine. I spent time just creating kindling and breaking down medium sized branches into bits that would fit inside the stove. Before I knew it, I had amassed quite a few neat piles of bits of wood to start fires with. It was only the larger pieces of wood that gave me more trouble, but I put aside the ones I couldn't handle. The axe would work better for those. I needed to find it and try swinging it...tomorrow.

My evening was spent getting the wood into the wood box and starting a fire. I did it on the first try, without the little fire starter things. Granddad would have been proud. Soon I had water heating in the large pot and the coffee kettle. I found Marmaw's little checked tablecloth stored in one of the bench seats and put it on the table. I turned the MP3 up as loud as possible and sat it on a shelf. The Foundations were singing "Build me up Buttercup", one of my favorites, and I sang along as I cleaned and straightened, and made myself some food. It was happy and upbeat, and I always wondered why anyone would name someone Buttercup. It sounded like the name of an old farm horse to me.

The music followed me through the night, until I found myself having trouble keeping my eyes open. I collected one of Marmaw's tattered quilts off their bed, curled up in one of the lumpy chairs and drifted off.

CHAPTER 11 - Ivy

For the next few days, I puttered around the cabin. I wrote down my stock of food, and then did up a menu. If I held to it, I was good for about one, maybe two, months. I tried recipes from my camping book starting with pancakes. The first couple of times they came out horrible, but by the third day, they tasted close to how Marmaw had made them. I gathered wood and then gathered more wood.

I looked everywhere for Granddad's axe but couldn't find it. I thought I finally had when I discovered a long thin wooden box shoved way in the back under Granddad's bed. But when I opened it, instead of the axe, I found items that could have only been Marmaw's. It was packed full. On the top there was a tray with art supplies: oil paints and brushes and a couple of used up watercolor trays. In between two pieces of old cardboard were a bunch of watercolors Marmaw had painted. The rest of the trunk was filled with notebooks.

At first glance they looked like those composition books that my English teacher always made us use. But those were black and white. Most of these were older, light brown with thread stitching on the binding and an odd size. Smaller than the 8 by 10 notebooks you could buy anywhere, but bigger than the composition books at school. I flipped though some, and the paper was yellowed and brittle. There were a whole bunch of the things, but some looked newer…metal spiral bound notebooks in blues and greens. There was one big fat volume on top with some watercolor pictures between the back pages. This must be her stash of writing she had never finished. I made myself comfortable and started digging through them.

I decided to read the fat notebook first. When I opened the first page, I discovered it was different than the other stories that Marmaw had written. Those books had been picture books; all cute and fun, with a simple little story to go along with the illustrations. This one was more like a real book, not quite a novel, but if she had finished, it could have been close.

On the first page she had written "The Tale of Willow of the Wisps by Elsie Glenwood". That was Marmaw's real name and I couldn't wait to read this new discovery. But after a few pages I flipped back to the first page again and made sure again her name was really on the page. The writing wasn't the same as her other books. It was written in a different tone and was kind of scary. It *was* interesting though and it did start the same way all of her books had. I started over from the beginning and tried this time to really *hear* the story she was attempting to weave:

"Once upon a time, in an age of wonder, the fairy folk of Firinn discovered a curious new doorway inside their land. The more adventurous of them went through the doorway and to their delight found a new Meadhan. A Meadhan is an enchanting place, a little bubble of energy and life that sits between the different worlds. The fairy folk then ventured out from the Meadhan into Alainn, the Realm of the Mortals in a land mortals called Scotland, and they found they enjoyed the Mortal Realm very much, so much so that a number of the fairies made it their new home.

These first fairies that took the journey from Firinn into the Meadhan and then out into Alainn were called the Seelies. Over eons of time, these folk divided into two parts, the Blessed of the Seelies and the Fateful of the Seelies.

The folk of the Blessed were woodland fairies; Brownies, flower fairies, Elves, Pixies, Druids, the Friths who were shape shifters, or Wisps as most knew them, and more. All are good, wonderful, playful, helpful, charming, and a total delight to come across in one's travels. They lived in the air, woods, ponds, flowers, trees and anywhere the sunshine could reach.

The Fatefuls, on the other hand, were dark fairies. However that doesn't always mean that they were bad fairies, but they did like the dark. If they lived above ground you would only see them at night or on a dark stormy day. They loved the netherworld the best and tended to find caves and tunnels and holes in the ground to live in. The Boggarts were one of these types of folk.

Boggarts are interesting creatures; they can be good or bad, but they are always mischievous. Some in the fairy realm knew them when they were completely fair and good, and they called them brownies. Some of the brownies found they liked the dark better. Over time, the cute little brownies who were normally helpful, fun and a tad mischievous became a bit more malicious in nature. From living deep inside the earth where the varied combinations of magic soaked into the ground and penetrated the very soil in which they dwelled, they were changed, their appearance and their magic distorted. Thus was born the Boggarts.

Everyone, both in the fairy realm and the mortal realm, stayed as far away from the devious little creatures as they could. If one heard their horrible cries ring out, it was always best to turn and go the other way. The Boggarts liked to steal and wreak havoc wherever they went. If a person or fairy was found to cherish an item, whatever it may be, a shoe, a horse, a child...the Boggarts would find a way to hurt the thing, or steal it away never to be seen again. The few Boggarts that retained some goodness were known to give things back, but they were not good at giving items back to the rightful owners. The owner of a missing green shoe might have found a cow in their kitchen, and so it went.

It got so bad that the Boggarts decided to use what remained of their good magic to form a magnet to capture as much of the dark magic that soaked into the ground as possible. In this manner, using the magnet they created, the Boggarts were able to stop their descent into revolting foulness, keep some of their good magic, and remain a friend of sorts to the fair folk. They named their magnet the Sumair stone and never told any others of its creation. It started out as a very powerful inanimate object that's only purpose was to emit its unique Siren Song to seduced dark magic and imprison it within its sphere. Unfortunately over time the Sumair stone developed into something more...something even the Boggarts hadn't planned on. Once the stone had soaked up all the dark magic it could find, it wanted more. At first it was content with taking what good magic it could find, along with the dark. But when that proved still not enough to satisfy its thirst, it began to release some of the dark magic it had collected, planting seeds of evil that grew and created even more dark magic. The Sumair stone then soaked that magic hungrily back up, making it stronger and stronger. Finally the remaining good Boggarts took action. They took the stone and went as deep as they could into their tunnels and imprisoned the stone where it could not release any of more of the dark magic and cease taking their good magic.

After time the stone was forgotten and life went on. Many years passed and there came to be a young Boggart named Nosen. He had traveled deep into the woods searching for a spoon one of his brothers had stolen away and instead found a group of lively Wisps.

The Wisps were fair and good and a delight to be around. They were playful and loved to dance while in their folk form. They would flitter about playing or sit on flowers in their Wisp form. They were thoughtful creatures, quiet and full of sunshine. If one happened upon a Wisp it was always best to tell the little creature how beautiful they were and in their happiness they would bestow good fortune.

Nosen, being young for a Boggart, had never encountered the Wisps before and he found himself enchanted as he watched them dance and frolic in the woods. Soon he was pulled into the merriment by a young Wisp named Willow. The two played together throughout the night and from then on, the two were inseparable.

Both loved to play mischievous and charming games to the amusement of any that happened upon them. It might be a game of tag with Nosen chasing after Willow in his Wisp form, or lost treasure where one would seek what the other had hid or the very best game, hide and seek. Many a time other fairies joined in with their play, and all about them would be sounds of merriment when the game was afoot.

One fine day the two were playing a game of hide and seek in the Boggart's tunnels. It was Willow's turn to hide and he had almost run out of places where Nosen couldn't find him. Willow went deeper than he had ever ventured before into the tunnels and ended up at a sealed door. Undaunted, he changed into a Wisp and entered through a small crack at the base of the door, thinking surely Nosen wouldn't find him there.

In the center of the sealed room sat a marble pedestal with a round stone perched on top. The stone was black and riddled with purples and blue streaks that seemed to pulsate within the stone. Willow changed back to his fey form to get a closer look at this magnificent thing just as bolt of purple fire shot out from the stone and zapped him.

As he fell back he felt a surge of darkness he had never experienced before; a yearning for something that did not belong to him. He looked at the stone and had *to have it. As the stone continued to zap about the room one bolt hit the sealed door and shattered it. Willow plucked the stone from its resting place and ran from the room. Up the tunnels he scampered, through the passageways and past any Boggart he happened to encounter.*

The Boggarts knew what the small fey had taken; all the Boggarts had felt the disruption in magic when the stone had been activated and knew what it meant. They gave chase, trying to catch Willow so as to retrieve the Sumair stone. But Willow was enthralled by the wicked magic of the stone. He ran and ran until he was out of the Boggart's burrow home. The stone continued to shoot bolts of blue and purple, zapping trees and shrubs and birds and anything that happened to be in the way.

The stone had no care what it zapped and many good Frìth fairies were hit. The evil magic changed some of the fairies into something quite different...a flower or a bug...while others it sucked the magic from completely, until the fairy was no more. Some were transformed into Gnomes or one eyed Fachans or strange feathered creatures.

But Willow didn't see the chaos the stone was creating. The need to possess this thing was too great and he ran deep into the woods leaving havoc in his wake. Boggarts by the hundreds chased after him, screaming for him to give it back.

Willow ran though the Meadhan until he came to the silvery doorway into Firinn. Luckily, the stone fell silent once in the world of Firinn, nullified by the heavy magic in the Realm of the Fairies, but not so lucky for the Boggarts as they couldn't find the Willow in the vastness of Firinn.

All would have been fine if Willow had stayed within the fairy realm, since the Sumair stone was just a pretty stone there in the realm of goodness. But Willow didn't stop; he ran and ran and ran until he reached the other side of the realm to a small hamlet called Rootmire and another Meadhan doorway, and out into the Hemlock forest.

Willow passed through the doorway without hindrance

and bumped right into a cute little mortal girl with a bounding blonde ponytail, a huge smile and a handful of flowers. With the little girl were her parents...a kind woman carrying a picnic basket and a huge man wearing a backpack and carrying an axe.

Startled at seeing mortals, Willow changed into a Wisp without thought, dropping the stone as he did. It fell at the little girl's feet and started to zap. It zapped the little girl with bright blue and purple lines of magic. It zapped the trees, and the fairies in the trees...fairies that had been invisible to the mortal family until the moment they were zapped by the stone. One fairy, horribly disfigured, fell dead in front of the little girl, who had opened her mouth to scream, but no sound came from her.

The stone continued to send out bolts of fire, zapping around itself over and over again. It sought out anything of magic that was in the area, killing, changing, maiming, and revealing all the magically things to the horrified family. It lapped up the magic as it went and then dispelled it back out again.

It zapped Willow too, extracting his magic and then zapping him again. The little fairy was changed into a large tangled willow tree, his grief-stricken face etched into the bark. The stone pulsed and zapped and sucked the magic from the forest, then it shot it back out in changed forms, shifting all the remaining fairies into Wisps. Then it zapped the man.

Now as anyone knows, fairies' magic can only do so much to a mortal. If the mortal is good, the magic has to be good in some form. Of course it will still hurt the mortal, but there will always be goodness somewhere. But if the mortal is bad, evil beyond belief can be inflicted upon them. As luck would have it, the man was good and the magic the stone threw at him tried its best to hurt him, tried to change him, tried to inflict evil into his soul. But the man was strong and his only thought was to protect his family.

He held up his axe as if to smash the stone and the magic hit the axe the hardest. Only the fairest, lightest bits of magic rolled around the axe to hit the man. It opened his eyes and mind to the fairies. It gave him knowledge that no mortal should have about the fair folk; it touched his very being and shifted him.

However the main force of the enchantment bounced back and hit the Sumair stone and then ricocheted at the silvery doorway into Firinn and lastly splintered out, dissipating its magic into the hemlock trees. Everything went silent as the stone lay stunned by the reverberating magic.

The family was frozen in shock. The quiet in the forest was broken only by a baby's wail. The man gathered up his little girl who was staring blankly and hung limp in his arms, while the woman searched for the baby. She found it nestled in a large vine. The vine had wilted and now looked more like a woman than a plant. The Frìth fairy was near death, her new born babe held tightly in her arms. As the mortal woman came close, the fairy held out the baby to her. Hesitating only a moment, the kind woman took the little new-born fairy and watched tearfully as the fairy mother turned to dust before the mortal woman's scared eyes.

The man hurried his family from the area and they didn't stop until he felt in his bones that they were safe.

Alone, he went back to where the Sumair stone lay. He knew that this thing needed to be put somewhere quickly so if it awoke once more it could not continue to wreck its havoc.

Nearby was an old hemlock stump, its center hollow. Instinctively the man knew that's where the stone needed to be put. Gingerly he picked it up and dropped it into the cavity of the stump. Using his axe, he chopped at the rim of the stump until it had fallen in, and whispered a prayer that the stump would hold the evil tight. All around him, fairies who hadn't been touched by the magic of the stone came out of hiding and tried to go through the doorway, but the doorway was sealed.

The man walked close as he heard their dismay and his axe started to vibrate in his hand. He held the axe up and touched the doorway with it. To his shock, the doorway opened. The fairies fled the forest, back into their private realm of Firinn, without even a thank you to the mortal with the axe.

The man and his wife, along with their now changed daughter and the baby, left the forest…for a time. It wasn't long before they discovered how much they had been shifted, how much their lives had been affected forever by what had happened to them in the Hemlock forest. The man and his wife in their goodness decided it was just another adventure in their lives and dealt with all the changes with diligence and great courage.

The baby…"

Marmaw ended the story right there, just as it was really getting good. I turned the page and found a bit more she had written, but I didn't find it very interesting. Just some notes about Scotland and how bad it got there for the fey after Willow left. There was something about creatures called Eilibear, demons, Druids and a war they were all involved in, but it read like a history lesson so I barely glanced at it. There wasn't anything else written after that.

I was a bit miffed that Marmaw hadn't finished the story. I wanted to know what had happened to the baby and to their little girl. It wasn't really one of Marmaw's best writings, though. It was rather dark and depressing overall, but I was captivated by it.

I looked through the pictures Marmaw had painted and found that they were nothing like her others. The ones of the woods with all the fairies playing were fantastic and the picture of Nosen the Boggart was really good. I had never even heard of a Boggart before and the little guy didn't look very friendly to me. He was exceedingly skinny, with a really long peculiar nose, and a mouth so wide it looked distorted. His ears were large and droopy, with wild hairs sticking out from the pointy tips of them.

Willow, on the other hand, was splendid. He had a boyish look to him, with wild curly short tan hair, high cheekbones and almost pouty looking lips. His frame was sturdy; shirtless his chest was riddled with muscles, like a young body builder. Marmaw had made faint shadows of him, blurred as if he were moving quickly.

The painting of inside the cave chamber was really detailed, with treasures of all sorts lying about and the pedestal in the center with the stone. There was something about the stone that looked familiar to me, but I couldn't place it.

There were a couple of pictures of Willow running with the stone; one in the tunnels and another in the Scottish woods. A very light silvery scene could only be what Marmaw thought the fairy realm of Firinn looked like. It was another of those Thomas Kinkade type paintings, all shiny with glitter and bright cheery flowers and cute little houses. It was the only one that reminded me of her published storybooks.

The really scary ones were of the hemlock forest. They were very dark pictures, with flashes of lights and deformed creatures in the throes of agony as they fell from trees. I hated the one of Willow changing into a tree. The look Marmaw had put on his face was one of pure terror. Then there was one of a half-plant, half-fairy, holding a small baby. Marmaw had given the fairy a look of such gentleness that my heart went out to her. I found myself starting to cry and didn't know why. I wiped the tears from my face and turned the picture over, not wanting to look at it any more.

The last picture in the stack was of the man chopping at

the stump with determination and power. The man glowed as little fireflies darted all around him.

Almost everything about this story and the pictures was peculiar and maybe I could see why Marmaw had never finished the story or published it as a children's book. It wasn't really a child's story, but I would have enjoyed it if she had finished it. This must have been her first attempt at a novel, but was still in draft form, with little handwritten notes and crossed out words. The writing itself was neat, but the words seemed too simple for the type of tale she was trying to tell. I started to feel rather bad…here I was picking apart her story and she wasn't here to defend it. It was more than I could do. I would never have been able to make up a story like that. I felt ashamed of myself.

I thumbed through the other notebooks, but they looked more like random thoughts, maybe ideas for this and other stories done in a sort of diary form. There were a couple of folded up sketches in the back of one. The first one brought a smile to my face. Marmaw had done a pencil drawing of Granddad wielding his axe against the remains of a huge hemlock tree. The other picture was a bit shocking. It was a drawing of Mom, I guess on one of her better days. Mom was lying in a hollow of moss and ferns. She was curled up, sleeping, her hair fanned out around her, a dream like work of art. Marmaw had captured everything that should have been and could have been, beautiful about Mom. It gave me the chills looking at it.

Quickly I folded them back up and went to stuff them back between the pages of the notebook when I saw the writing on the back. "Clara 1915" and "The Woodsman 1892". Surely those couldn't be dates. That would be a bit bizarre since that would make Granddad something like 120 years old. It was unnerving that Marmaw had drawn a picture that looked like Mom but was someone else. Maybe Clara was my great-grandma and my mom, Skyler, looked just like her. I shook it off, besides it just looked like Marmaw was using Granddad as her model for the story, the same with Mom. I gathered the notebooks and paintings, and put them back in the box. I slid it as far under the bed as I could and tried not to think about it. But it haunted me; those pictures...and the story of Willow and the family.

CHAPTER 12 - Elsie

July 1955 –

I teach the children from home, wherever that may be from year to year. The outside world has continued to change in wonderful ways. To my eyes it seems to overshadow the wonders of the folk even. Clara has come to be a young teenager and our hands are full. She declared she hated her name and has changed it, demanding that we call her Skyler instead. For me, it seems to be yet another step away from being the child I gave life to.

Little Ruth liked the idea of having a different name and informed me that her name is Ivy. I do not know if she made it up or if she has some memory of her mother naming her. She dances around, making up silly little songs about her new name and I have to admit with the bit of magic she displays, the name suits her well.

Clara...Skyler, is getting better at having control over changing from one type of image to another...blurring she calls it. She can look like a beauty one moment and something loathsome and grotesque another. I do not know for sure now which is really her, or if either are. But no matter how in control of that aspect of herself she is the other natural parts of her being get her into trouble almost daily. She is a mean and cruel person, spiteful and wicked to everyone she comes in contact with. But it is the fey child who she hates more than anything or anyone else.

Milton has to continuously refresh the veil he put on Skyler's memories as it fades quickly from her and she remembers how much she loathes Ivy. She has taken to telling people that Ivy is an evil fairy and that the child cohorts with demons. Many people in the cities have tried to get her locked away, thinking her to be insane. We protect her from the authorities in this world as best we can. I do love my child and pray for her to find balance and happiness in both realities.

September 1969 –

We have lost Skyler again. She's grown into a bright pretty teenager with a mind of her own, when she can use it. For the first time in her troubled life, she was seeming to fit in with a group of young ones. We were living in the Bay area when she took off with a bus load of kids that called themselves flower children.

I truly hate to admit it, even to myself, but I was glad that she was gone. Ivy keeps me happy and it was nice to have my life feel just a little bit normal for once.

November 2, 1969 –

Milton worries about Skyler as she has yet to come home or contact us. He has gone to look for her. Ivy and I have been listening to all the news about Apollo 12 being launched into space. Such wonders.

December 11, 1969 –

Milton tracked Skyler to the Greenwich Village. With help from the wild fey, the Alltha, he finally found her. She had been with a crowd who were following a musical group named the Mugwumps. How she kept herself from blurring and terrifying those around her, we don't know.

She was a mess, strung out on every sort of drug, and Milton had a time getting her to come with him.

CHAPTER 13 - Ivy

I spent the next few days either sitting by a window in the cool of the mornings or out and about during the day. Summer in the forest, and my glade, was magnificent. The wild roses and morning glories twisted up the brambles, birch trees and the fencing that surrounded the glade, to create a hedge of color that even the early morning haze couldn't hide. Foxglove, fairy bells, lilies and lupine sprouted out from the lacelike ferns. Creepers with bright blossoms intertwined in the old growth azaleas and rhododendrons, creating an explosion of color. To top it off, butterflies fluttered about, mingling with hummingbirds and dragon flies, and, of course, the weird bugs.

I sought the comfort of the trees, paths and meadows. On the walk to the stream, the blackberries and huckleberries were flowering also, which meant by late July or August, I'd have berries to pick. Everywhere I went, the weird little bugs followed me, as if they were so interested in what I was doing they'd put me on their priority watch list. They never tried to come into the cabin, which I was grateful for. Now and then there would be rustling in the leaves near me and I'd catch sight of a squirrel or chipmunk. They were cute and I started leaving bits of crackers out for them. A family of foxes was living by a boulder, and I saw rabbits sitting on logs, watching me with their little noses twitching. There were even deer. I'd seen their tracks in the mud of the pond. I got up real early one morning and saw them as they drank from the edge. It was a Disney fairytale.

It was peaceful and quiet, and I took to making myself a small lunch and walking deep into the forest every day. The trees towered over me, sheltering me. It was green and fertile; where the ferns ended, moss and creeping vines took over, enveloping the entire forest in hues of emerald and jade. It was like the forest was barring any un-green thing from entering. It was fresh and alive, and all mine.

My granddad had always left me in the glade near the cabin when he went into the forest to chop his wood, but I knew which path he took or thought I did. I hunted for days to find the right one, thinking that maybe he had left his axe behind. It was as if the forest was hiding it from me, the path, not the axe. I'd think I'd found it only to wind up at a dead end, the path stopping at a pile of huge fallen trees, or a wall of blackberry bushes.

I finally gave up at one such barrier and sat down on the mossy forest floor, mindlessly picking the few newly-ripened blackberries. They were small and tart, but a welcome change from my normal diet. As I sat there, the weird bugs started buzzing around my head, more annoying than normal. I tried to move away from them, resisting the urge to swat them, and ended up falling sideways into the blackberry bushes. The darn things hurt as the thorns snagged my clothes. I had to struggle to get loose, ignoring the stupid bugs in my fight with the barbs.

When I had finally pulled myself free and inched back from the bushes, the dumb bugs flew at me again, but this time zoomed right by my head and went straight into the undergrowth. I followed them with my eyes and saw that my struggles had opened up the outside foliage to reveal the dead older growth underneath...and the rest of the path. There was a tunnel of sorts along the path that snaked its way into the snarl of thorny vines. Without giving it much thought, I crawled into the passageway.

Thorns scratched at me, grabbing my clothes and hair,

but they didn't stop me. Crawling forward, I made my way through the mess, and before I knew it, I had come out on the other side. I found myself in a dense, dark hollow of tall hemlock trees. Off to the left was a gigantic tree stump; nearby was what remained of the toppled tree that had drilled a path through the other vegetation. Ferns and moss had taken over, saplings and shrubs had spouted from its sides, creating a long line of tiny Christmas-like trees.

It was eerie in the small clearing, if I would even call it that. It was so dark I could barely see and a heavy mist seemed to have settled over the area. It was too quiet. There were no sounds at all: no birds, no tree frogs, or rustling of leaves by the wind. Not even an insect dared to chirp or buzz in the gloom. But the weird bugs were there. They would zoom to one place as a gang, hover for a second, then zoom to another place. Stupid bugs.

I disregarded them as I looked around. All the hemlock trees were gigantic, but these were monsters; their roots bulged out of the ground, and some were even lifted completely off the ground by the over-zealous roots. A carpet of moss and leaves covered the forest floor where the smaller forest of ferns didn't conceal the ground. Trees beyond time had fallen in tangled masses, only to be covered by more ferns, vines and moss. The word *lush* came to my mind as I took it all in.

Off to the right was one of the largest hemlock trees I had ever seen, looming up into the sky. It was so ancient that the roots that had pushed it up were as large as the trees themselves. It was raised so high that a grown man could easily walk underneath it. The whole place shimmered with tiny sparkles. Marmaw had used glitter on her paintings to get this effect, but here it was natural.

It was really cool.

I had never been here before, but I recognized it at once. Marmaw had painted this setting. Not once, but many times. This was the setting Marmaw had used for the story paintings. There was the hemlock with the roots where Willow had come out of the *doorway* into the forest and bumped into the little girl. The huge stump looked like it had been hacked on by an axe, and had to be the one she used for where the man had hidden the Sumair stone.

I could picture the fire bolts shooting out from the stone into the trees, and the poor fairies that were hurt by it. I didn't dare look around for a bush that might have held a baby. It would have been unnerving to find it.

This just had to be the place; Marmaw had to have been here, had to have painted it. It was a sight that begged to be painted. A photo couldn't capture this...this enchanted sensation. The whole area seemed to radiate with anticipation, as if waiting for something.

Just standing there, I felt spellbound...overcome with a need there was no name for. The dumb bugs brought me out of my trance by whooshing past my head, ending at a fallen tree. They lingered there, then as a group darted back to me, flitting around my head and near my ears. Before I could even reach up to whack them, they shot back to the fallen tree.

A silly thought entered my head, I watched way too many re-runs, and I murmured out loud at them. "What is it Lassie...is Timmy in trouble?" My voice sounded out of place here, and whatever humor I was feeling evaporated as the weird bugs drove back towards me, halted halfway and went back to the tree.

Weird. Did they watch re-runs of dumb dog sitcoms?

I was intrigued by the bugs. Narrowing my eyes, I bit my lip in consideration as I watched them do their weird little flight path thing, back and forth a couple more times before I finally decided that I was going nuts. "I really need to get back to town and be around people," I murmured, since I was starting to think the bugs *were* trying to tell me something.

Yep, I was losing it. But I still walked over there, trying

hard not to smash ferns along the way. Around the stump, some of the ferns were almost shoulder high. It felt strange pushing my way through them. The ground seemed to rise a bit on the far side of the stump, making the ferns seem even taller. I pushed a huge blade aside and found myself looking again at the fallen tree lined with cute little Christmas tree growths. There, stuck in the wood, as if Granddad had just swung it hard, was his axe, shining bright silver in the browns and greens of its surroundings.

The bugs whirred around me as I reached out to grab the handle. As my hand closed on its smooth polished surface, a tingle started in my fingers and traveled up my arm, ending as it vibrated my teeth. My whole body felt as if I had poked my finger into an electrical outlet, which I had done once when I was five…I wasn't the brightest bulb in the pack back then. I was thinking the same thing about myself now, as I reached out with the other hand to get a good grip on it. That didn't seem to be too smart as my feet suddenly felt on fire and a line of heat instantly traveled from them up to my throat, causing me to yelp.

"Enough of this shit," I yelled as I yanked hard on the handle…too hard it turned out, as the axe easily came loose from the wood and I stumbled backwards and ended up flat on my back with the axe on top of me. The darn thing was heavy. I was looking straight up, and overhead I could just make out the graceful branches of a willow tree. It was completely out of place mingled with the hemlocks and other evergreens. The shock of seeing it there overshadowed the weight of the axe on my chest. Scrambling awkwardly up, I heaved the axe into my arms, and like I'd seen Granddad do hundreds of times, rested it on my shoulder. It was easier to carry this way. I turned to leave the ferns and was met with a swarm of the weird bugs. Not just the few that always seemed to be around me, but at least five times the normal number. Their bright bizarre colors glowing in the shade like fireflies.

My mind tried to process two things at once; how really mystical the place looked with all their hues of sparkling colors and how much I wished Marmaw could paint *this* scene. At the same time, I was thinking that seeing the willow tree here was beyond spooky.

None of the bugs touched me. They seemed to move out of my way as I hurried back to the path...yes path. If I thought the new multitude of glowing bugs was bizarre, or the misplaced willow tree, or even the spine-chilling feeling when I touched the axe, the fact that the brambles had parted and now there was a clear path before me paralyzed me with terror. The bugs seemed attracted to me and I felt closed in by them. I started to run, not caring that I was damaging a multitude of plant life along the way.

All the times I had been told not to run while carrying something sharp left my brain altogether. I ran through the neatly parted blackberry bushes, past my basket that held the remains of my lunch and down the path. The bugs followed me. I could see them in front of me, to the sides of me, and knew the rest were close behind me. I ran, holding tight to the axe as if my life depended on it, and didn't stop until I was at the cabin door.

I had to pause to open the door and it registered that the bugs had left me. I looked back and saw them. They were holding back, hovering, lingering, and dancing in the trees and flowers and bushes. They glowed brightly in the sun-light. The sight reminded me of my bright sequined vest, as if the sequins had come to life and were playing cheerfully in the garden. If I wasn't so creeped out, I would have stood and watched the amazing sight, but I *was* creeped out by it.

"I wish I had someone to talk to," I mumbled as my normal little group of bugs flew close by me. It was odd that I could recognize them from all of the other weird bugs that had taken over my garden. I glanced at the smaller group that was now flittering just off my right shoulder.

Looking at them, I shrugged and said to the cluster, "I liked it better when it was just us. Wish you guys could talk. Bet you'd agree with me." As if in answer, they bunched together, closer to me.

I opened the door and went inside, closing it tight and leaning against it, still holding firmly to Granddad's axe. I felt faint; whether from the dash through the woods or my fear, I didn't know. I stood there for some time with my eyes closed until my breathing calmed. It seemed rather silly now. It was only a forest, only bugs, only a tree, and only an axe...Granddad's axe.

Being inside was a quiet relief. I laid the axe down on the bench inside the door and went to get something to drink. I stayed inside for the rest of the morning and early afternoon, cleaning and puttering around my little home. I pushed what had happened out of my mind. I refused to think about it; it was too different, too strange. Somehow I convinced myself that it had only been a combination of hunger, loneliness and the workings of my vivid imagination brought on by Marmaw's story.

I tried to make a different recipe with what food I had, but it was a disaster. I ate it, or at least I tried to. How was I to know that after only a few weeks I'd get tired of the same thing every day? I didn't want to be finicky, but I wanted a cheese burger so bad I could taste it. But there was no way I was going to go back into town. I needed to suck it up and deal with it.

Frustrated with the mess I had made of my little kitchen, I just stood there looking around the room until my eyes fell on the fishing gear in the corner. That's what I needed; fish or crawdads or even frogs. I could eat any of those.

I had visited the pond only a couple of times since I'd been here, finding the quiet of the forest more interesting. Besides I had been looking for the axe. I had it now. I wasn't sure I wanted to try to chop wood with it; it was heavy and a bit ominous to me at the present. A nice late afternoon by the pond was just what I needed.

I took my fishing pole and one of the cheese packs to use as bait. With a bit of trepidation, I left the cabin. The weird bugs were nowhere to be seen, which thoroughly convinced me that it had been my imagination. I walked out of the cabin glade to the path that led down to the pond. A few bugs joined me, my normal little crowd of purple and green dragonfly things.

I had to walk down a short hill to the bank of the stream, then rock hopped upstream until I came to the pond. There was a path, but for some reason I liked this method of getting there better. The pond was like a hidden treasure. The forest enclosed it on both sides, with only a small clearing with a bit of sand on one side. A couple of big boulders made a small waterfall that flowed into it. It wasn't very deep, maybe 6-7 feet, but it was wide, with one section taken over by mammoth water lilies. I called it the water garden. Granddad used to pull root things up from the pads and they tasted like potatoes. I planned on trying that soon, but today I was going to fish.

Climbing up the rocks, I found a place to sit and put some cheese on the hook. I tried to cast and got tangled in the tree branches behind me.

I tried again and forgot to let my finger off the line, so nothing happened except a snarled mess of fishing line by my hand.

I tried again and tangled in the weeds on the shore.

And I tried again, only to catch the hook up on the rocks next to me. A soft sound of laughter came to me and I quickly looked around. Other than the weird bugs, I was alone.

I gave up casting. It wasn't my *thing*. I just dropped the line in the water in front of me. I was shocked when almost immediately the pole jerked in my hand and I hurried to reel in the line. It was tangled in the reel and wouldn't move. Dropping the pole, I tried to bring the fish in by just pulling up the line. A fish came out of the water at the end of it. A nice big rainbow trout. It wriggled and flopped, then jerked loose from the hook and fell back into the water with a loud splash. The woods seemed to sigh along with me.

I was working hard at untangling the mess on the reel when a twig snapped nearby on the bank. I looked up, expecting to see a deer, but instead I met the eyes of a boy. Startled, I lost my balance and fell sideways into the pond with my poor fishing pole going along for the ride.

I came up sputtering and swam a couple of strokes until my feet hit the bottom, then looked around. No one was there. I hurried out and stood dripping on the bank, my pole better off than I was.

"Hello," a soft voice said from behind me. I just about jumped out of my skin and turned around. No one was there.

"Sorry, I did not mean to startle you." The voice came from my right and I turned quickly. He was standing there, the one I had seen before I fell. I hadn't imagined him. He was tall and slightly thin, but with strong looking shoulders and arms. His face was perfect, like a movie star or a deity. He had deep-set, misty, violet-gray eyes, and his hair was brownish blond, wavy around his face and rested on his shoulders. He stood there, picturesque, waiting for me to speak.

I couldn't. I could only stare.

"I am sorry to disturb you, but we were wondering when you were going to open the door," his voice was velvety, and his words had a stilted, ancient sound. I just stood and gaped at him. Laugher sounded around me, sweet and faint. He turned to look over his shoulder and said, "Hush now," to nothing. Turning back to me, he cocked his head to the side and studied me. I was starting to shiver…I *was* wet.

"You are Ey-vey are you not?" he asked, seemingly puzzled. He pronounced my name strangely and looked at me with those deep, misty eyes.

"Ivy," I finally said, as my teeth started to chatter. I was standing in the shade and was soaked and this strange guy had scared the shit out of me. I started to get mad...this was my place.

"Who are you?" I asked, and then realized he *had* known my name. "How do you know me?" I asked, a deep fright settling in on me.

I was alone in the forest with this guy. I finally pulled my eyes away from his face. He was wearing...I couldn't describe it even to myself. It was like leaves were glued to his body, forming pants. He had on a vest thing that looked like flattened moss. My eyes met his again, and he smiled...what a head rush. I almost fell backwards.

With a mellow tone, almost a whisper, he said his name as he came closer, "Laven." His name seemed to echo back into the thicket. "I am Laven and I've always known you, though you have grown since the Woodsman brought you last."

"I don't know any woodsman; I used to come here with Granddad," I stammered confused.

Voices rang around me. "The Woodsman"

"The Guardian."

"Forsair."

"The Gatekeeper."

"Forest Keeper." Soft as the wind, the words came to me as the weird little bugs appeared and flew past me and settled on the ground behind the boy.

Six persons appeared. I jumped back in shock and fell flat on my butt, my eyes so wide I was sure they were going to pop out of my head. Three girls, and three more boys, all older than me, maybe college-age. They were fair skinned and flawlessly beautiful. The girls had a mystical wispy look. The boys had the same feel about them as Laven. Deep set eyes, longer hair and a softness that was unusual to see. One of them had raven black hair and eyes dark as night. He started to move forward to say something to me, his face stern, as if upset. Laven held out his arm and stopped the boy from coming closer.

"May I introduce our brothers and sisters of the folk," Laven said, his voice silky. "Sisters Aireen, Myste and Whisper." As he said the names, the girls would nod their head at me and smile gently. Two had pale red hair that simmered in the sunlight and the other's hair was a warm honey color. They were wearing clothes that looked almost translucent, in misty colors of flower petals. "Our brothers, Bryear, Rayni and Aishal." The boys did not smile, though they did not frown. Their expressions were more curious, inspecting me, and somehow I felt like I had failed a test.

"Ask the Alltha child," the dark haired boy, Aishal, hissed at Laven. "When?" Laven gave him a long look, glanced sideways at me, then back at the dark boy.

Laven nodded agreement to him, and slowly, gracefully, walked over to where I still sat on my butt, leaning back on my hands. He held out his hand to me. I wasn't sure what to do. These kids seemed harmless enough... but they were acting like they wanted something. I took the boy's hand and he easily helped me up, then just stood and looked into my eyes expectantly. I was getting nervous and started moving back, but stopped as he reached up and touched the faint outline of the swirls on my face. I was frozen in place. His breath was sweet and his touch was soft, his skin felt like velvet.

This is absurd, I thought as he continued to trace the design, then he stopped and looked down at me and smiled the most radiant smile I had ever seen. He looked over his shoulder at the ones he called brothers and sisters, and smiled at them. All but the dark one smiled back.

Then he fixed his eyes on mine again and spoke softly to me. "May I ask when you will open the door?"

"What door?" I asked transfixed by his eyes.

"The hemlock door to our home," he replied with

mellow sweetness. I felt like I was in a trance. I couldn't look away from his eyes. "You came...you have the key. You unwove the magic. It would please us for you to open the door. We have waited for the Woodsman and he has not come. You have come in his place; the magic has blossomed."

"What? Who is *he*? What do you mean, the *magic has blossomed*?"

"The guardian," he responded with a move of his shoulders and slight tilt of his head studying me. "The Woodsman."

A frustrated snort from one of the others broke my trance. I looked away to the others behind him. He turned around angrily and said in a low stern voice, "Be gone." And they were. Gone… Poof... Not there anymore. I fainted.

CHAPTER 14 - Zack

Zack was torn. He hunted for the petite girl the next morning before everyone else was up. He went back to where he saw her last on the far side of the bridge. But the morning light did little to show him anything new. The wagon tracks were there, in the dirt just off the road...then they weren't. Halfway up a small incline, maybe 10 steps at most near a large tree, they just disappeared. He was baffled. Now he couldn't decide if he should continue on his hike or blow it off and go to that antique shop and see what the blonde girl knew.

Still at odds with his decision, he opted for continuing with the hike. He had paid for it and had looked forward to it for months. He wasn't sure if he'd enjoy it as much now that he was distracted thinking about the girl. Maybe the girl *was* up the trail with one of the other groups and he would find her again.

It was possible that she had forgotten where the trail had started and felt dumb when she ended up on the wrong side of the river and hid from him. It was a longshot. Then there was that stupid wagon she had piled high with camping equipment…what was she thinking? Everything about her was a mystery; he didn't know who she was, where she was going, what the wagon was for or why she had departed at 2:00am. She intrigued him and he had an uneasiness he couldn't explain.

He had left with the others of his group around nine that morning and he kept his eyes glued to the trail looking for signs of her wagon, but never found any. The group arrived at the remote camping spot in the late afternoon. By then everyone had given up trying to get him to interact with them. His focus was on the girl with the purple hair.

Once at camp, he dropped his gear and started questioning other campers in the area, asking if they had seen the girl or the wagon. No one had, and after wasting the rest of the daylight away, he'd come back to find his friends upset with him for not helping set up camp.

Shaking the ominous feeling off, he decided to push the girl out of his mind and attempt to be part of this group and enjoy this adventure as best he could. On the eighth day he gave up trying…there wasn't anything he could do about it. He had to find that purple-haired girl.

CHAPTER 15 - Ivy

I came to lying on the upper part of the path that led into the glade of the cabin. I was alone with my pole and my little basket of fishing items, along with a beautiful trout lying across its top. My butt hurt, I was wet and when I stood, I felt dizzy. I must have fallen in the pond and hit my head. I thought I had lost the fish. How bizarre was all that? Trying not to tumble over, I slowly made my way back to the cabin, locking both doors behind me.

Filling the coffee pot with water and building up what was left of my fire, I stripped off my wet clothes, dried myself and pulled on leggings and a tee. My head hurt something awful and I dug around in the first aid kit until I found some aspirin. I gulped two down dry and prepped a mug with cocoa mix for when the water was hot. I was hungry, and yet I wasn't. My head throbbed too much to even think about making food, but there was the fish. While the water heated I cleaned it quickly and sprinkled it with salt like I'd seen Granddad do. It would keep in the cast iron pot until I was ready to cook it. As soon as the water started to boil, I poured it into the mug, drank it quickly, then went up to my loft and buried myself in my nest of blankets.

It was dark when I opened my eyes. I lay there thinking about what I had seen and heard. I must have hit my head and somehow got Marmaw's fairy stories mixed up in some form of a hallucination.

I went over everything in my mind trying to remember all the stories Granddad had told and the ones Marmaw had written, so that I could make sense of the weird dream I'd had. Some of it made sense, but most of it didn't, and I decided I needed to take another aspirin...and go pee. Crud, there was no way I was going to go out in the dark to the outhouse. I was still more than a little creeped out about what had happened today. I decided instead to go in the bucket…yucky I know, but sometimes you just gotta do yucky things. I put the bucket in the little entry hall and put a towel over it. I'd empty it when the sun was up.

But now I was up and awake. I turned on my music and found the list of Roy Orbison songs and let them play quietly while I stoked up the fire and filled both the coffee pot and the larger pot with water. My hair felt all dirty from the pond water. While the water heated, I put the plug in the sink and pumped it halfway full with water, then poured the water from the coffee pot into it. Using a generous amount of shampoo, I started washing my hair.

By the time I was done, I had given myself a pretty decent bath. The floor was wet, but I didn't complain. I felt clean and now hungry. The Everly Brothers kept me company singing "Bye Bye Love" while I cooked the fish and made some coffee. The fish was delicious, the best I'd ever had. Of course I had been craving fresh food for days now. I sat at the table until the sun started to rise, staring at nothing for quite some time, thinking about Granddad, our trips, my life up to this point as a whole. It had been relatively normal until they went away. Even Mom's behavior was normal…for her, up until then.

After that it was like she couldn't handle anything and wanted to escape into whatever she could find to do so with; drugs, alcohol or men. That got me wondering if she even realized I was gone...maybe she would when the money ran out. I was the one who tried to clean the house and get her to eat. She normally didn't notice me at all, even before Granddad and Marmaw had left us.

Dark thoughts were getting me nowhere, but thinking of

Mom made me think of the pictures of her Marmaw had painted, which made me think of the stories, which lead me down the path of wondering. Okay, I wasn't wondering. Some deep part of me knew. I just didn't want to believe it. If I believed it, then the story I'd read was true. It couldn't be...it wasn't the way things worked. Maybe somewhere else people won the lotteries, got the perfect boyfriend, or never had a zit pop out on their nose on picture day...but not in my world. Wonderful things didn't happen to me.

I wondered what else Marmaw had written and knew I needed to read the other notebooks. I had to know more and maybe Marmaw had finished the story in one of the others. I pulled out the box and stared at it for a time.

"Stop being such a chicken," I mumbled to myself as I knelt to open the box and took out the notebooks. The one on top was the one I had already read. I took it out and put it aside, then took out the next one.

This one was older, kind of faded, the cover tattered as if used a lot. On the cover Marmaw had drawn the same little symbol that Granddad had put on the tree. I flipped it open and there was a date on the top of the first page. I did the same with all the other notebooks, noting the date in each and putting them in order. Then I started to read the one I thought must be the first.

I couldn't make any sense of the words for a while, but I kept at it. Marmaw had written it, that I could tell, but the language she had used was strange. It was old fashioned, like the notebook. The first entry was June 21st, 1861, the story the diary entries told was sad and after the first few I knew that these were somehow connected to the story of Willow.

I found it a little disturbing that she had used Granddad's name and her own for this strange story, but I did find it interesting and continued to read. When I got to the end of the first notebook, I re-read the last few entries.

Since it seemed to follow along with the story she had written I wondered if these were her notes when she had started to write it. It wasn't bad, just hard to read, and kind of boring at times. I was really impressed though. I always knew that Marmaw was an awesome storyteller, but this was beyond that. Maybe the writing wasn't that good, but the conception of the story-line sure was, and I couldn't put it down. This is what I had craved after reading Willow's story. I wanted to know *what had* happened to the family and the baby they had found.

I just found it creepy that she had used my name also, but maybe this was meant to be a surprise book dedicated to us or something. A memory exploded in my mind. I was really little and Marmaw had made me a green tutu. I had it on over my clothes and was dancing and singing in the living room. I remembered the dumb song I sang.

"*My name is Ivy, I am teeny tiny, Look at me, I can dance, oh my there's ants in my pants*," I whispered the words and gave myself the chills. I tried to tell myself that Marmaw must have used things I had really done as ideas for her story.

I knew I was trying to make up a reason...something to believe other than what was right in front of my face.

I attempted to keep reading, but had to stop after the entry for December 11, 1969. I was shaking and couldn't stop. There was so much that rang true in my life. I forced myself to re-read some of the passages and consider everything as level-headed as I could. Here I sat in a cabin, that Granddad had told me countless stories about with fairies always as the center piece. We moved...a lot. I had no memories of the years, but after the first few pages, the way Marmaw had written the words reminded me of how she spoke…and I *had* made up dumb songs about my name.

Also, the word *Alltha* sounded familiar and when I placed where I had heard it before, I realized that the dark haired boy had spoken it. I had never heard it prior to that and wondered how I could dream a word before I'd seen it.

I needed to do something. I took a couple of deep breaths trying to calm myself before I quietly got up and collected my MP3 player. I needed to hear it. I knew about the group that had called itself the Mugwumps and what they had changed their name to after Mamma Cass had left the band. I rolled through the list of songs and of course it was there. I wondered if it had anything to do with Mom. I pushed play and sat heavily as I listened to the Lovin' Spoonful sing about magic. I sang along with it.

I remembered singing this song with Granddad...in this cabin. There hadn't been any music, but he had taken me in his arms and swirled me around in a fanciful dance. I felt the tears starting to fall. Why hadn't he told me? Did Granddad really put some kind of spell on me to make me forget all this? Or was it just a tale she had made up, or was there a balance of realms that had to be kept and like my mom, I was now fighting with my *reality*.

When the song ended, I pushed the stop button and whispered the words again;

"Do you believe in magic?"

"Maybe," I answered myself. "Maybe I do."

CHAPTER 16 - Ivy

I exhaled and pulled myself together. I wasn't like my mom, I wouldn't go wacky just because something didn't make sense or if I didn't like it. Then I wondered again if Skyler *was* my mom. There was more to read and although I wanted to just stay there and read it all, I felt I had enough to work through as it was. Besides, magic, or even this new *reality*, wasn't going to tidy up my messy home...or take the pee bucket out to be dumped.

I busied myself with cleaning up, threw a knot of wood in to burn slowly and went up to my loft to fold my blankets and get some clean clothes to wear. The day was already warming up, so I pulled on my only other pair of jean cutoffs and a tie-dyed tank top. As I went down the stairs, I noticed the pile of wet clothes by the door and remembered the bucket again. Yuck.

Somehow dumping a bucket of pee had brought me back down to earth. Whether a fairy or not, still just a girl, a run-away, alone in the forest, doing unpleasant stuff. Going out into the entry, I moved the towel and tried not to look as I opened the door and went to the outhouse to dump it. When I came back inside, I retrieved the wet clothes. I took them and the bucket down to the stream to wash them out. I stopped before I reached the pond, feeling odd about going back there right now. The day was just too normal. Birds were chirping, critters were buzzing around, and a lone frog made a splash in the stream as I came close.

I washed everything and started back up the path, noticing the start of berries on the brambles where just days before had been only flowers, when the weird bugs made their first appearance of the day. They flew past me, up the path and then hovered in the air a few feet in front of me. I had to stop and really look at them. Were they just bugs, or fairies hexed by Granddad? I had never been apprehensive about them before, but I sure was now.

After a few moments of hovering, they started to fly back towards me and I ducked as they went past. All sounds ceased around me. The chirping of the birds was replaced by the sound of footsteps behind me. Frightened, I started to run up the path, peeking over my shoulder as I went.

The boy was there, following me. His face was full of anguish as he looked at me. I turned and ran for all I was worth. I didn't stop until I was at the cabin and only then risked another glance back. The boy was still there, standing just outside the arched fences that lead down to the stream and pond.

"Ey-vey?" he called to me, his forehead wrinkled with worry, his eyes sad.

"Don't come any closer! Go away!" I screamed at him and started to open the door to the cabin when his words came to me.

"I can't Ey-vey. Not in this form. We need to speak, you and I." His voice was just so sad. It stopped me and I looked back at him. He was wearing the same clothes as yesterday, his face glowing in the semi-shade of the trees...and he wasn't moving. He was perfectly still, just standing there, pleading with his eyes.

"Why can't you?" I asked narrowing my eyes with distrust.

"The Woodsman sealed us out," he stated and pointed to the arch in front of him. I looked at it and then at him again. Granddad had put that fence and the arches up years before I came with him; they seemed to have always been there. But I knew he would spend time each visit adding to it, repairing it where the vines had pulled it down.

"Why did the *Woodsman seal you out*?" I asked, curious whether his answer would match the story. He took a moment to consider before he finally replied.

"Some of the folk broke his trust. They tried to take what the Woodsman did not want them to take. Until you unwove the magic, we could only be in our other form, but still we may not enter into the private glade. It is protected...you are protected."

His voice was so gloomy, yet rich with sincerity. I sat down on the doorstep and looked at him, then at the glade with its wonderful garden of plants and flowers. The sun was almost all the way up over the mountains, yet the glade was shaded by the trees that circled it. I watched a couple of yellow butterflies dance around each other as they flew from flower to flower. Many of the new weird bugs were fluttering around too. As I studied them, I thought hard about what he had said.

Laven. That was his name. It sounded so mystical to me. The name of a make-believe prince in a fairytale...or a fairy. I'm losing it, I thought, as I looked at him again...or maybe I'm just coming awake.

He was just standing there on the path, motionless... waiting.

"Why are you here?" I asked him.

"Because of the..." he started to answer me, when a deep harsh voice cut him off.

"No!"

I looked to the other path, and there stood Aishal. I surprised myself that I could remember his name. His face was twisted in anger, glaring at Laven from across the glade. "Don't forsake us for the uncivilized, my brother." His words were spoken with heavy feeling. I watched the two as they made silent communications across the expanse of my glade. Laven sighed deeply and then looked at me once more.

"We are here because we love the forest," he said, his voice for the first time ringing untrue to me. Whatever he had been about to say, he had definitely changed his mind, or Aishal had changed it for him. I decided to switch directions...I did have a ton of questions; I could come back to this one later.

"What is your other form?" I asked already knowing the answer. If this was my imagination, then I was really messed up...*or* Marmaw's stories were true. A large part of me wanted to believe. What was it that Granddad used to say? *When you have ruled out all the possible explanations and you are left with only the impossible ones, you should consider them.* Wise words, and rather absurd, I had thought at the time he had said them. Now they didn't seem so nonsensical.

"A Wisp," he replied with a sly grin as he suddenly vanished and in his place was one of the weird little bugs. It flew over to me, lingered in the air in front of me. It was a bug. Smaller than a hummingbird, but its wings were just as fast and colored like a dragon fly's, shimmering as they fluttered. It was a nice looking bug, a bright glittering lavender colored bug, unique...but still a bug. It hovered for a moment more, then flew under the other arch leading into the hemlock forest.

Laven reappeared outside the arch with a wide grin and a slight crook of his head. Aishal had backed up the path and now stood with the others I had seen yesterday. I knew they were there, but only looked at Laven with incredulity...*he* really was the bug? Then corrected myself...Wisp, he called himself. I shook my head no, trying to deny what I had seen with my own eyes. The impossible...remember Marmaw's story. I had to keep telling myself that.

"Ey-vey?" He called my name quietly...a plea.

"What?" I snapped at him. I had no reason, really, to be mad at him, but I was.

"If you unlock the door, our kinfolk can go home. It's been a long measure of time."

"Where is home?"

"Firinn, the realm of the folk." He spoke in such sweet sounds, it was so mellow.

"How long have you been here?" I asked, feeling strange. I was dizzy, I think from shock.

"For this occasion or...?" He asked softly.

"How long?" I asked again, not wanting to clarify since I had no idea how to.

"For this time; since the Woodsman came last. He would always set us free when he left and open the door back up when he returned."

Okay...that was like Marmaw's story. I pinched myself and yelped. I was awake...or dreaming I was awake. I know, maybe I had hit my head really hard when I fell into the pond and was unconscious and in a coma. That made no sense either though. Do you have to go to the bathroom in dreams, or get hungry, or still sing off key?

I thought about it...as bizarre as all this was, there had to be *some* sense to it. I made a list of what did have logic... weird logic... but logic. They were bugs, Wisps... whatever. If Marmaw's stories were true, then Granddad was the Woodsman. The Willow kid had brought a stone here that hurt everything and changed my family...and if my brain pushed further, then it killed my real mother. Granddad had to keep coming back here to keep us alive, but some of the fairies didn't like us. He had to protect us from them, turning them into Wisp things.

I tried to remember everything I could about my visits here and the weird bugs...but my memories came back in bits and pieces. I remembered the bugs... I remembered the cabin, the glade full of flowers. I remembered sleeping, cooking, fishing, walking in the forest...but no matter how hard I tried, I couldn't put all the pieces together. Had Granddad been chopping wood when we were here? Of course he had, he would go off every morning and I would hear the echoes of his axe chopping, and he could come back with slabs of wood for us to take home.

But I had never gone with him...into the forest when he chopped. What *had* I done? Had I come here over and over again as a child, and just didn't remember? I looked back at the boy who was waiting patiently as he studied me from the path. Did I know him? He seemed nice enough...if he was here and Marmaw's stories were factual, didn't that mean that it would also be true that Granddad only let the good fairies in? Hmmm…I thought.

"How long have *you* been coming here? Before this *time*?" I asked. He looked young, just barely older than me.

"Just a few years."

"What are you?" I asked, again thinking I already knew the answer and for the first time in my life beginning to get mad at Granddad. He should have told me.

"I am fey," he answered with a smile, and then it faded as I frowned at him.

Right...I thought skeptically to myself, still not fully wanting to believe. Fairies were cute little butterfly-girl things with acorn hats and ballerina skirts. They had wings. This was a boy, maybe 18-19 years old. Sure, he could become a bug, but my mind would deal with that later.

"You can't be a fairy, you don't have wings," I announced smugly at him and crossed my arms. I didn't have wings either, how could I be a fairy?

He sighed, looked back over his shoulder at the others, shaking his head and glowered at something that I couldn't hear, before he looked back towards me.

"We do not like that name. *I* do not like that name. I am fey. I...we do not have wings." He said with gentle force. "Others may use that name, but *fairy*," he spat the word as if it was foul and disgusting, "...is a thing of human legend, something made up in Alainn to explain what *they* perceive as the unexplainable. I am fey...of the Frìth fey. The Woodsman must have told you this," he said with self-righteous indignation.

"What is Alainn?" I asked getting frustrated with all these new words that I didn't understand, then shook my head as I remembered the writing once more. Marmaw had called the world that...Alainn.

"Alainn is the name of the world they took you to, where all the mortals live. Did he teach you nothing?" he asked with amazement.

He was pissing me off. How the heck was I to know what to call him or what those words meant? I'd only just learned about all this, and then to slam Granddad! I rose dramatically to my feet and stomped over to him, my eyes flaring. No one criticized my Granddad.

"Listen here you... you *Fey*. I'm not sure if my Granddad was this Woodsman you keep talking about, but he never used the word fey. He talked about fairies. *Fairies*. And, if it's such a bad term, then maybe you did something to deserve it." I all but screamed at him, while the others popped out of sight.

He seemed shocked, then humbled as he lowered his head and stood there listening to my rant. When I had got it all out, we stood there... silent... till the birds started to chirp again in the trees. I saw the others appear on the path deep in the thicket beyond him. The boy, Aishal, looked infuriated, glaring at me with apprehension or hatred, I couldn't tell which. The others spoke in soft anguished tones to each other and kept giving me fleeting looks.

When Laven finally raised his head and looked at me, his face was tormented. In the most sorrowful voice I had ever heard, he whispered, "Please open the doorway. This is all we ask. We will leave you to your peace Ey-vey-Frìth."

I was still upset; I wanted them gone, and I wanted my

tranquil safe feeling back. I snarled at him. "How?"

"You need the iuchair, the Woodsman's axe," he stated as if distressed.

I turned and stomped back to the cabin, threw open the door and grabbed Granddad's axe that I had laid on the bench. Then clomped back to him and held it up.

"Okay, got the axe," I stated, still infuriated at him. "And what the hell is an iuchair?"

He didn't move, but his eyes followed the axe in my hand. The others had grown quiet, looking at the axe, then at me, hope in their eyes. The multitude of other bugs started to gather on the path, almost blocking my view of the boys and girls...fey. "An iuchair is something that unlocks...a key," he answered.

"Really?" I asked, calming a bit. "Granddad's axe is a key?" I thought again of the story.

Laven nodded at me and licked his lips, before he bit down on the bottom edge of one. He had sucked in his cheeks as if in fear or astonishment or reverence; I didn't know which.

"Tell me what to do," I said, deciding that if this was what they wanted and if it would make them leave me alone, I would do it.

"Where you retrieved the axe. The ancient hemlock towers over the doorway." And he was gone, along with the others. I heard, rather than saw, the sound of little fluttering wings as they hurried down the path. I hesitated only a moment before I followed. The path turned and snaked its way through the thicket until the trees grew bigger and I entered the main part of the hemlock forest.

I followed the horde of bugs on the same path I had run down just yesterday, tramping after them, carrying Granddad's heavy axe. I followed them through the strangely parted blackberry bushes into the enchanted sparkling hollow. If anything, it seemed lusher than when I had left. The ferns seemed taller and healthier, shade flowers had blossomed in hues of blue and purple. The mist was ever present, a soft refreshing reprieve from the summer's heat. The birds were chattering excitedly high in the foliage and cute chipmunks scurried around on the fallen logs. It was peaceful and surreal.

I saw the tree they meant even before they had all gathered around it. It was the large one standing off to the side of the stump. It was so ancient that the roots had pushed it up, four roots bigger than the other normal hemlock trees. It was raised so high that a grown man could easily walk into it. Smaller trees and giant ferns grew on three sides, creating a perfect natural cave. And like the rest of this hidden glade, a dense growth of vegetation created a barrier from the rest of the forest behind the hemlock.

The Wisps had stopped at the tree and were flittering around in excitement. Then Laven appeared, standing off to the side by the stump. I was still so agitated that I didn't even think of whether I wanted to be near him or not. I huffed up at him, the axe held in both hands and asked, "What do I do now?"

"Move towards the doorway and ask it to open....and it will," he replied, his voice silky soft.

You've got to be kidding me, I thought, as I stared at him and then the tree. Whatever. I walked forward, whispering for it to open and let these guys leave. I started into the cave of the tree roots and the strangest feeling came over me, as if I were walking through a heavy fog. I sucked in my breath as I felt resistance. My feet did not want to move and I had to force myself forward. I pushed, and tried not to see the shimmers of lights that erupted in the space. Suddenly I was pushed backwards, stumbling against Laven who took my arm to stop me from falling with the heavy axe.

I shook his hand off and glared at him.

"What? What pushed me?" I asked him in a state of

confusion.

Aishal appeared next to him and angrily whispered something to him. Then the girls and the other boys appeared and joined in with the heated debate. I couldn't tell what they were saying; I didn't seem to understand the words. It sounded like gibberish.

All of them were troubled by me *not* going through the doorway…that I understood. I started towards them to find out what the deal was, when I noticed the flight of the other Wisps. They were flying straight at the tree roots and to my surprise were disappearing from sight as they entered a weird shimmering film that glowed faintly in the root's opening. It dawned on me that that must be the doorway.

I had opened it.

Turning back to the group, I saw that Laven had a look of pure determination on his face. He was being stubborn, I knew that look. I had practiced it many times on Granddad and Marmaw. The girls had calmed down and each in turn gave Laven a sweet airy kiss on both of his cheeks before they smiled at me, then walked into the film and disappeared from sight.

Shockingly, to me anyway, the boys Bryear and Rayni also kissed Laven on both of his cheeks, and then came to stand in front of me. Bryear reached out and touched the side of my head where the drawings of swirls had been, smiled brightly at me, then left with his brother through the tree roots.

Aishal, however, did not budge. He was arguing with Laven, their words seemed all jumbled up. I concentrated hard on what they were saying, as if my mind was hiccupping, trying to decipher the sounds.

"Crap!" I muttered to myself. "I want to know what they are saying," I stamped my foot in frustration. Slowly, like a clearing in a haze, the words started to have meaning. They were both completely ignoring me, as I stood there with my mouth agape listening to them quarrel.

"You cannot tell her anything. What if she brings Willow back and he tells her where it is? What then? Have you thought about that? She might claim it for her own." Aishal all but yelled at him.

"If she does, then she does, and we will deal with it if need be," Laven countered, unmoved by Aishal's passion.

"How? It's not right that the Meadhan was taken away from the fey and given to a human. Now this Alltha is in control, and we almost had her and the iuchair."

"You saw the same thing I did, she was forced back. What we do not know is if it was her or the iuchair.

"No, we do not, and now we may never know."

"We will. The light will shine on the rightful owners of this Meadhan yet. This will be simpler. I was not comfortable dealing with the Woodsman, but Ey-vey is now the one."

"She is Alltha! She is not real fey. She has been raised outside, corrupted by the mortal realm. She, like all the Alltha, shouldn't even be allowed to live. It is not right!" He sounded like a bratty kid to me, and I expected him to start throwing a temper tantrum.

"I would like to be there when you tell that to a Druid, my brother," Laven replied smirking at the dark-haired fey.

"They are different, and you, my brother, know that. The warriors cannot live in Firinn. They, at least, have no choice. The others do…they are schemers who have turned against their own kind."

"Ah brother, but are we not the same?" Laven asked silkily, looking with contempt at the other.

"It is not the same and you well know it. Besides, she still wears the talisman to protect her against us, her own kind! The glade is still protected. We cannot even leave from this Meadhan to Alainn from here. I am tired of being without a home, without a doorway of my own. Isn't that why we are here? Aren't we all tired of being doorless? Isn't it the reason we made the bargain, to open the area for the fey and give Shivf what he wants...how can we do that if we cannot bring the stone back or at least the iuchair?" He screamed at Laven, his face twisted with childlike rage. The darkness of his eyes and hair made him seem sinister. I got chills from just watching his facial expressions.

Aishal had started to pace in his frustration, his back was now to me and Laven had moved so that he was within my sight. As Aishal made mention of the talisman, I couldn't stop my hand going instinctively to it at my neck. Laven caught the movement; his eyes widened in surprise. He blinked quickly and looked back at Aishal trying to control a grin that almost escaped the corners of his mouth.

"That was the goal...it still is the goal. Understand this, Aishal, the fey cannot force their will on another fey, and it remains to be seen what sort of fey Ey-vey will be." He reached out and took his brother by the shoulder. "Speak no more of this now. Go. Spend time with our folk, speak with Shivf and see what he makes of this. I will stay and try to understand what we are dealing with. Maybe she knows more than we think she does." At this, a small smile played on his lips as he peered at me over Aishal's shoulder. "If she locks the door, I will make sure it is opened in no more than a fortnight. May the dew follow you, my brother."

Laven had started to walk towards the tree grumbling about me and how everything was going wrong. Laven bade Aishal goodbye again and I mumbled *You're an ass Aishal, get out of my forest.* A look of surprise and anger erupted on Aishal's face as he was instantly sucked into the film, his eyes locked on me.

Once he had disappeared Laven called out to me. "Quickly Ey-vey, touch the doorway with the iuchair." The urgency in his voice made me do it as fast as I could. I held the axe up to the shimmering film stuff, and as it made contact, the film evaporated before my eyes.

He stood near the tree framed by gigantic ferns, smiled a

sweet radiant smile at me and bowed.

CHAPTER 17 - Elsie

December 20, 1969 –

Skyler isn't well, even for her. The distance east was too great from the forest and it wreaked havoc with her balance in the realms. She has completely lost control of her personas and switches back and forth constantly.

We've come back to the forest now, dragging Skyler with us, and will stay until she wakes...it will be a long while.

Ivy is happy to be back and spends her days with her friends, the Wisps. There is no doubt that this is where she is meant to be. Keeping a balance of our lives with this realm and the other is tiresome and it makes me wonder at times if it would be best just to stay here. Ivy is better off and as for Skyler...she sleeps. I can't help but think that the real world would be better off without her chaos in it.

February 1971 –

Skyler woke up today and is almost normal. We go back to our home in San Francisco. I am glad as the dreams that come to me in the forest are dark and I wish not to hear them. We made the decision this time out in the world to tell people a different account of who Ivy is. It was an easy thing to change Ivy's memories to fit the lie.

March 1971 –

She has gone and done it again. Skyler got herself in trouble with the law, drugs this time and they have locked her up. The Uncles had to get involved to get her released. I did not wish her to come home right away so they put her in a nice safe home with Allthas to look after her.

April 4, 1971 –

There will be no end of trouble from Skyler. She tried to kill herself again. How many times will she try? We have to keep the veil on her memories, so she doesn't remember that it's almost impossible to do what tries to do, and only ends up making herself more miserable. If she does remember, then she would also remember all her hatred for Ivy...and now us. We do not know what to do to help her.

I told Milton it was time for us to go back to the forest so she can sleep. God forgive me, but I can't handle her.

CHAPTER 18 - Aishal

Aishal entered the fey realm in less than a good mood. Laven had out-maneuvered him... again... and he didn't like it one bit. The two were brothers by clan only, but the sibling rivalry was as intense as if they were true brothers. He was humiliated that Laven had somehow gotten to be the one who spoke first to the Alltha. He wished now he had pushed harder to be the one. Then, Laven would have been the one forced to come back and deal with Shivf. Even the others of their small clan had taken off, probably not wanting to meet up with the old fey with this news. They, no doubt, had blinked off to do Laven's bidding. Besides, who would want to linger in Rootmire?

He walked the silvery path between the gently waving beech trees, towards the center of the township. He and Shivf had been living in one of the original dwellings. It had been where the elders of the old Hemlock clan had lived once upon a time. Now, all that was left was the ruins of Rootmire, piles of rubble taken over by vines and brambles. It was not the best that Firinn had to offer.

If it hadn't been for the legend, none of them would have even thought to come to such a place. They had formed their clan only a few years before, coming together as castoffs from other larger clans…seven doorless young fey who loved adventure and a good challenge and couldn't seem to keep out of trouble. And the tale had drawn them in; how the Hemlock clan had lost their doorway to a mortal because of a stone called Sumair from the Meadhan in Scotland, and the young fey, Willow, who had the gall to steal it away from the Boggarts.

Everything about this tale stroked their imaginations. How a mortal had been given power above and beyond the elder fey, and how he had even outwitted them. The Hemlock clan had stayed in Rootmire, after the Sumair stone had done its damage to their doorway. The clan requested help from the fey Elders, when all attempts to deal with the Woodsman on their own had failed. They discovered they were no match for the shifted mortal. When the Woodsman had finally opened the doorway again, the fey Elders were there waiting.

The fey Elders had been rather full of themselves, telling themselves how charitable they were, meeting with a non-fey. How generous and sympathetic they were towards the mortal, whose family was damaged by the Sumair stone. Most had already decided what the outcome was going to be. They didn't care that he had saved the Hemlock clan; only that he had taken one of their own, and horded magic he shouldn't have. They would listen to the mortal's pleas; then they would take their magic back, as well as the fey child, and reopen the doorway for the feys' use.

They entered the forest and inspected the mortal with their eyes, and their sensitivities, and found nothing that was remarkable in this one man. The Elders started asking questions of the mortal, and he, in turn, asked his own questions. All of the fey indulged him for a time, but a mortal asking questions about magic and other realms and gaining information about the folk was too much for them. They demanded the mortal bring forth the fey child he had stolen and threatened him if he did not.

To their shock, he had ended up turning them into Wisps and then banishing them from the forest. They learned much later that the mortal had sealed the Meadhan from the outside and created talismans for his family, giving them the only access to it. He wielded the iuchair to open the doorway only when it pleased him, and used the spell of

Wisp more times than not. Eventually the Elder fey gave up and declared the doorway spoiled. They made the decision to make a new doorway, a new Meadhan to another hemlock forest, located in a place called Revelstock. It was a larger forest, different in the types of mortals and magic, but a good place all the same. The displaced fey joyfully took their new doorway and left to form their new homes.

A Meadhan, by fey decree laid down when the silvery doorways had first been discovered, had to have a fey owner. So the Elders declared the Frìth babe the owner, with the Woodsman as the keeper until the babe came of age. After that, the Elders wiped their hands clean of the problem and gave it no more thought.

From then on, only the brave, adventurous or curious came to Rootmire to beg the Woodsman for entry into the mystical hemlock forest. Aishal wasn't sure which category their clan fit into…right now he figured there should be a fourth just for them…the very stupid. The Woodsman let their clan in, all but him. For some reason the Woodsman didn't like him, so he was left behind in Rootmire, while his clan went through the doorway time and time again, trying to figure out a way to take it for themselves.

It was only a little over five years ago that the strange old fey had shown up out of nowhere. He whispered that he could gain the Meadhan for their clan if they would do something for him in return. This fey knew things, dark things, and he understood Meadhans and mortals, and shifted beings, and most importantly, the Sumair stone. He knew what its power had been and did not doubt that it was still there, locked away, still giving the Woodsman its power.

He brought with him hope for their clan. They overlooked the shadow that hovered over them as they deliberated and planned and schemed. Laven, Bryear,

Rayni and the girls accepted Shivf's offer to help and agreed to what he asked for in return. They found themselves sitting with him for days on end, pouring over the information about how best to gain access to the Meadhan and take the power away from the Woodsman. Shivf was always more interested in how the Sumair stone might be recovered, and what he and his kin planned on doing to Willow when they could get their hands on him. After many days discussing and arguing, they came to their agreement, formed a plan…and waited for the right time to implement it.

Laven and the others had continued to go through the doorway and spend time with the Woodsman and his small family. Aishal, on the other hand, had been stuck with Shivf in this run-down hamlet and it had not been the most pleasant of experiences. The old fey knew some very dark magic. He reeked of it. It seemed to seep out of him and into very air around them, changing the little neglected village into a toad infested, rank wood. Shadows and creepers seemed to corrupt the area, and over time, less and less outside fey came to visit.

Aishal had been torn at first. He really wanted his own doorway, but he did not wish to tarnish his life thread with darkness. Shivf finally won him over though when the old fey had discovered how to disguise Aishel's fey glow enough for the Woodsman to be fooled to let him through the doorway. Twice he had been allowed to come and go, until this last time when the Woodsman had not returned to open the door for them.

He had almost gotten to the point where he did not want the forest. Being locked inside, the Meadhan had begun to feel like a prison, and his only thought had been to get out, get back to Rootmire and Shivf. But now, here he had returned, and all he could think of was that Laven had deceived him somehow. He didn't know by what means, but somehow Laven had come out on top this time, again.

And that Alltha child had actually used magic against him, pushing him into the doorway against his will. It was just like what the Woodsman would do, when he tired of having the fey around.

The boy slowed his pace. He was livid at this turn of events, but Shivf was going to be even more so. They had prepared for so long; it was all set. They only needed the Woodsman to return and it would be done. Laven had turned against him, or at least it seemed so. Maybe he wished to get the Meadhan and Sumair stone for himself. But it was more likely he just wanted to be the one that everyone could praise for taking the Meadhan back from the mortal.

He was worried about what the old fey would do. Over the years Shivf had shown himself to be cold hearted and rather ruthless at times. Fey that came to Rootmire hoping to gain entry through the doorway tended to disappear. Shivf was not someone Aishal wanted to cross.

"Mayhap he'll not have waited," he grumbled to himself. It had been so long. "No, he must have waited, he'd better be here."

No one was about on the paths, normal now for Rootmire. Very few of the buildings were full structures. A pillar rising out of the vines or a tumble of cut stones that he passed, were the only indications that once more fey had lived here. He made his way through the overgrown path to a small rusted gate that bordered a once-grand building that had fallen into a state of disrepair. One side had toppled down, crumbling away as the vegetation and vines overtook it.

The courtyard was overgrown, uncared for and all but ruined. Luckily for it, residue magic worked even here and it was beautiful in its confusion of plant life. Off to the side was a water fountain. Frogs and toads seemed drawn to the garden. Their mingled croaks and chirps made a curious chorus of sounds. A huge frog statue spat a stream of clear water into its round basin, where bits of leaves floated, along with various frogs. He flicked his fingers at the creature as he passed and watched as its beady stone eyes winked and followed him as he went up to the door.

He opened it and stood in the dimly lit vestibule. The frogs were in abundance, even inside, he had to side-step so as not to tread on several of them. At one time, this dwelling had been grandly decorated with furniture, statues and fine art. Now it was a representation of all that was decaying in his life. It was a depressing sight but a familiar one.

"Shivf are you about?" he called out, almost hoping for no answer. The only response was the croaking of the frogs. A door to his right stood open and he could see the chamber where he had begun this whole affair. Aishal entered and closed the door behind him. It was cold in the room, and Aishal's ill-temper was growing as he shivered.

The chamber was meant to be the grand dining room, but a wall had fallen and the remains of the kitchen could be seen through the gaping hole. He could see that some shelves were still hanging on the walls, holding unnamed ingredients, herbs and strange bits of something unrecognizable that Shivf had brought with him. A couple of old benches and a table sat in the middle of the floor. It was piled high with dusty scrolls, misshapen books and scraps of paper intermingled with mold covered plates. Toads sat in the middle of all of it.

The door to the cellar yawned open and a flash of deep blood red light exploded from it. Aishal knew what that meant and stayed where he was, waiting for the old fey to step out before he moved over the pile of fallen stones into the room.

The creature did not look like it was fey or human. Twisted and burnt, it walked out of the doorway and stood before Aishal. With a flick of its hand the fire receded, though the air grew heavy with the thing's breathing.

Another moment and the thing started to change shape, molding itself into an ancient person of the folk. His hair was non-existent; his bald head glowed from the light that had started at the newly formed fingers. The fey snapped them and lights turned on in the room, giving Aishal the full spectacle of Shivf's transformation back to the form he knew him by.

He was meaty for a fey, a bouncing round belly started to grow out of the thin frame, as white hair erupted on his head and face. When Shivf was done, he stood barely taller than the boy, twice as wide, with a full pudgy face, thick white eyebrows and shoulder length white hair. To complete the alteration, the beard kept growing until it rested on his fat belly in a tight ringlet of hair.

"Aishal ye have finally decided tae return tae ole Shivf." His voice was gravelly with a thick Scottish brogue, betraying where the professor had originated.

Aishal was not put off by the display of magic. Shivf liked to show off, but he couldn't stop the queasy sensation that started in the pit of his stomach as the professor pushed in at the side of his neck. Part of a hand with two twisted fingers had thrust out from Shivf's skin and started to wiggle. Shivf didn't seem concerned as he forcefully pushed at the hand, shoving it back down into the skin of his neck.

The younger fey looked away, not wishing to think about what that could have been. Maybe it was good that his brothers and sisters had not come with him this time. The darkness that surrounded Shivf was visible, and the fair folk would not have been pleased.

"The Woodsman went and disappeared it seems," he answered with as much brashness as he could muster.

"That be sad…then the magic he be using, has it disappeared also? We'll have tae find another way tae seal the Meadhan fer a wee time while we look for the stone." The old one crackled as a line of snot dripped out of his nose and hung sloppily till it dropped off into his beard.

Aishal turned away and found something else to focus on as he countered, "You get ahead of yourself Shivf. It wasn't his disappearance that allowed me back through the doorway, but what *kept* us sealed inside the Meadhan. The magic has passed to the Alltha one." He all but spat the words; his nerve returning as he spoke. He turned back and faced the old fey. "And to make matters worse, Laven has decided to go against me."

"Has he now? That be what ye be thinking?" Shivf asked as he took a seat at the table and motioned to another chair for Aishal to sit on. "Take ye self back to the Meadhan and kill the thing, kill the Alltha. Not a body in the realm wilt know what ye did," he spat with a mischievous smirk. "We will just git rid of the pest, find the Sumair stone and be done with it." He clapped with glee at his plan.

Aishal looked with disdain at the old one. He was really beginning to unravel at his life thread.

"Shivf, the Alltha *is* a problem and maybe so is Laven. I don't know what he is planning and we cannot 'just get rid of the pest', as you say. She is no longer a babe, but grown now. And I cannot just kill another fey." Not that he wasn't opposed to the idea of getting rid of Ivy...in some manner. However, that would mean stepping over the line of light if he took the life of another fey. He had done some horrible things, bent the rules of the fey many time, however he had never broken the steadfast laws of the folk; letting a mortal know he was fey, giving away magic to a mortal or killing a member of the folk. That was stepping over the line of light into the darkness and if any knew he had done so, the Elders of the folk would ban him forever and he would have to become an Alltha and live in the Mortal Realm.

Shivf's gruff voice bellowed at him.

"It does nat matter that the babe be grown, still a babe

tae us. But what about Laven? Ye be a thinking he'll honor our bargain? Maybe he be thinking to git the doorway all fer himself?"

His voice dripping with scorn, the dark boy took his time answering.

"Yes...No...I don't know for sure. I think that the Alltha interests him. He said he wanted to learn more."

"Well, Laven be right smart…I nat be a bit surprised. Don't ye be worrying, Laven will do as he be told," Shivf announced firmly, aggressively cleaning his ear with his finger. Aishal tried hard not to watch what the old fey was doing. Shivf could find multiple means to sicken him, but at least he was on his side.

It felt like it was all rushing away from him. No one else seemed to care as much as he did that a Meadhan forest was in the hands of a mortal, or now an Alltha. No one else seemed to care about the Sumair stone, that it was still out there, somewhere, still full of power. Power he could use. He wanted the clan to look up to him, to have others point and say, there's Aishal, the owner of a Meadhan and his own doorway.

The old fey was not the most enjoyable fey to be around, but at least he cared. Shivf wanted get the Meadhan as much as he did; he wanted to find the Sumair stone and take it back to Scotland to bury it once more in the deep caves. The ancient fey wanted to reverse what had happened to his homeland, and didn't care who he had to hurt, or what he had to do, to obtain that goal. He wanted Willow as well…another prize.

Aishal remembered what had happened at the doorway, and his blood began to boil anew, as he forced himself to look at Shivf who had finished cleaning his ear.

"The Alltha, Ivy, had magic and a strange gift. She was able to unweave the Woodsman's spell and she opened the door and pushed me out. It was just like what the Woodsman would do when he wanted us to leave," he spat as he clenched his fists.

Shivf had leaned forward and studied the scowling boy.

"Whit gift?" he asked in a whisper, his apprehension showing in his voice.

"On her face. Vines were starting to grow and bud around her eyes and the sides of her face. Laven was sure it meant something important," Aishal hissed.

"Och my!" The fey said as he jumped up and stood towering over Aishal. "Ah believe we have a wee problem," he spluttered. "That be new magic. It means that the stone gave her làidir power." The strange looking fey started to shake. "We fey be one thing or another, but never both. Did ye see any other of her powers?" His words ran together in his panic.

Aishal just stared at the old fey. Shivf's words were so heavy with accent that what Aishal heard was only sounds.

"Speak clearer Shivf, what did you say?" he exclaimed leaning closer, but he got a whiff of the old one and had to pull back.

"Open ye ears! I said the stone gave her làidir power, strong power. Shape shifters can only be fey or something else, not both. The babe was born from a Frìth fey, so a plant would be her other shape. So a plant showing itself as part of her fey form tis a bad thing. It means she be special. Did you understand *that*, you sniffing little worm?" Shivf spoke slowly, forcing his words and Aishal knew he had offended and angered the old fey.

"What do you mean? How could she be special? Her mother was just a Frìth that was allowed in live in the hemlock forest. The stone couldn't have given her any more than it gave the mortal, and there is no way a Frìth is better than any other fey," Aishal responded in exasperation.

"Shape shifters have a magic stronger than the Wisps or other types of shifters, they almost have magic as strong as a Druid. But they can only be a body or the other self, it takes a great force of magic tae be both, that is what I be trying to make you understand. She cannot find out what power she has, she cannot become stronger!" he screamed at the boy.

Aishal finally understood and shuddered. He had left Laven with her. Laven might know, and might tell her. Maybe he should have stopped Laven from talking to her. He should have been the one to speak with her. He hated to admit it, but he had been afraid of her, so he had let Laven be the one. There were not many fey who could un-weave another's magic...which she had done when she released them from Wisp form. Which also meant that she might be able to undo the stone's magic. He should have been stronger, braver. Enraged, he let loose a bone-chilling scream of anger and frustration.

His face, red with fury, he roared at Shivf, "You really think she is stronger than any fey?" He was trembling and could hardly get the words out. "I bet Laven knew and that's why he wants to make friends with her," Aishal rambled on. Shivf ignored him.

Instead the old fey had started to pace, his body seeming to melt and slide in places as he muttered to himself frantically. Aishal waited for the old fey to speak, working hard to keep his panic at bay.

"Ye ask tae many questions, Aishal and ye not be thinking straight. Listen closely, ye must go back. Ye must kill her afore she comes into her full power, or the forest and the stone wilt be lost tae us forever. If ye cannot kill her, take something of hers and force her tae give the forest and the stone tae us." Aishal's face had gone pale with fear as Shivf spoke, his voice trembled as he replied.

"But I can't kill her; my life weave would be blackened!"

"Then take something of hers!" Shivf bellowed at him.

"What could I take? I know nothing about her."

"Think Aishal, she must have mates. She must have

feelings fer someone."

Aishal thought about it. Who would this Alltha have feeling for? Maybe the mortal family…though he wondered if that was even possible. But it might be worth a try.

"How about the family? The Woodsman didn't come, so maybe he's gone to the worms, but there is the lady and their girl.

"Ahh, the fair-haired lass might still work," he said as he played with his beard. "Go git that one, even if the Alltha ends up not caring, there be other uses fer her. Laven would know how to use the shifted lass."

"But how? I don't even know where to look in Alainn. If I find the Woodsman he could kill me, and if I try to harm the old woman or his child, he'd do the same," he whimpered woefully…his panic at the thought of what Shivf asked of him overtaking whatever bravery he pretended to have.

"You won't be finding the Woodsman or his woman. They've been taken care of, me pals have seen tae it, and the lass should be easy, they've been working on that one."

That stopped Aishal cold. He stared at Shivf with dread, wondering if he should ask, then decided he needed to know no matter what Shivf had done.

"How Shivf? How could that have been taken care of? And just who are your pals?"

"I have me ways. Don't ye mind. We wanted to get our hands on one of the talismans the shifted mortal had created, but his woman didn't have one. The lass doesn't either it turned out, but she may be aknowing where tae look. Find a talisman if nothing else."

Aishal felt as if his fair life thread was sinking, his mind saw it spinning down into a deep chasm filled with shadows. He knew there was no going back now. Shivf must have known all along why he and Laven and the others couldn't come back. Whatever dark magic he had spun had sealed them on the other side and he had just left them there. Aishal tried to feel hatred for this old disgusting fey, but he couldn't. He was still his only hope of getting this doorway. Doing so had consumed his entire life, and he resigned himself to his fate. "How?"

The old fey went to one of the shelves and took down a small wooden box. He froze for a moment then snatched a large toad from the counter with his other hand.

"Gezz me room," he said looking at Aishal, then at the table. Aishal had no idea what the fey had just said, his accent seem to get deeper by the minute. Shivf saw that the boy didn't understand him, and his anger flared again.

"The table…clear the table ye fool!" he shouted at the boy.

Aishal looked down at the table in dismay. It would take forever to clean up this mess. Shivf glared at him until he finally just wiped the table clear by pushing everything onto the floor with a loud crash. Shivf gave no heed to the commotion as he sat the box on the table and took a nasty looking knife from the folds of his robe. With one swift motion he cut the head off the toad and squeezed its life juices onto the table in a sickening mess.

Aishal watched in fascinated horror as the old fey threw the squished toad absently across the room and opened the box. He couldn't resist and leaned forwards to see what Shivf had inside. A screech escaped from him as he realized what it was.

"Where did you get that?" he called out, his eyes wide with shock. "Is that what I think it is, the shifted one's hair? I'd heard about it, how one of the Elders had grabbed some of the mortal's hair, thinking they would be able to take the magic back from her. The Woodsman caught them and banished them from the Meadhan. That's her hair isn't it? It smells like shifted magic. How did you get it?"

"Not ter worry yourself about this, just be grateful we have it," Shivf snarled at him.

Aishal watched as the old fey took a couple of strands of blonde hair and dropped them in the goo from the frog.

"I be needing some magic," Shivf said looking up at him. Hesitantly Aishal held his hand out, which Shivf grabbed and held tight.

Time froze, as did Aishal, while the old fey siphoned magic out of him. Aishal could feel the magic being taken. He started to feel lightheaded and knew the old fey could care less if he drained him of all of his magic and left him dry. When finally Shivf stopped siphoning, Aishal could barely keep his eyes open and started to shudder and then screamed as Shivf sliced his palm with the same knife he had cut the frog's head off with. A spray of Aishal's blood splattered the table, mixing with the rest of the mess.

"Why did you do that?" Aishal cried, holding his hand close to his chest, tears of pain welling up in his eyes. "I let you take my magic."

Shivf didn't respond, instead he leaned gleefully over the table, and began to speak in the old tongue. He spoke in a low reverent voice and Aishal could only catch a couple of the words. He understood the word 'blood' and 'we give our life to you'…which scared him to no end.

He couldn't move. Trapped somewhere between horrorstruck and mesmerized, he watched as the liquid begun to swirl, mixing the blood of the toad with his own. The bit of hair pulled together in a tight wad, as a hazy view of a thin shallow woman standing by the side of a road developed. She was shaking and talking to herself. Her body was bent over, her face and arms peppered with oozing sores.

"Ah, the Eilibear still be with her now," Shivf called out gleefully. "We be in luck."

The old fey moved over to a sideboard and rummaged through the clutter till he found what he was looking for. He moved awkwardly over to Aishal and held out a bit of wood.

Aishal didn't know what it was or what he was to do with it, but took the piece and looked questioning at Shivf.

"It 'tiz a bit of redwood, a marker for you to pass. The lass is near the Sequoia fey doorway. She is still moving and if she has any magic left in her, she'll be close to the hemlock forest by the time the sun sets in the mortal realm today. You must hurry. Go naw!" he yelled pointing to the door.

Aishal had never been near the Sequoia fey, but he knew where they were. He was irritated that Shivf had cut him, but satisfied with this turn of events. He moved with renewed purpose towards the door, then stopped to look back at the old fey. Shivf had dismissed him and was passing through the doorway to the cellar. He didn't even want to know what was down there. Shivf was strange enough in the light of day.

He started to wonder anew just what Shivf really was, what type of fey...then pushed the thought from his mind. He really didn't want to know, and turned…hurrying, as he had been told to do, out into the fresh air. He tried to blink out and discovered that he didn't have magic to use. Blinking was something every fey could do, they only had to think of where they wanted to be, blink, and were instantly there. But that took magic and he had let Shivf siphon his from him; there wasn't any left in him now. He needed to refill his body with some or he would have to walk. Pulling what magic there was from the nature around him he was able to gain enough to blink and transported himself to the place in the fey realm where the Sequoia fey had their doorway.

CHAPTER 19 - Shivf

Shivf waited until he felt the absence of the youth before he used a locking spell on the old house. His body was aching as he forced himself down the cellar stairs. Pulling together was a strain on his magic. When he reached the cool, darkened room below, he lit three tallow candles on a small side table. As the smoke started to rise, he spoke the words of release. His body seemed to melt into a wide pool of mush, separating before gathering in three separate puddles. It took longer than it ever had before for the elements to congregate together. One final gasp and the three Boggarts emerged into beings.

They were ugly, small things with crinkled blotchy skin loosely covering boney limbs and fat bloated bellies. All of their eyes were too large for their faces and bulged out like a toad's. Their long hooked noses jutted out from between their eyes and then twisted downward to their thin, wide mouths. The three lay on the ground gasping for air until one let out a shrill piercing scream as it curled into a ball and rocked itself.

Only one had any strength to stand and hobble over to a low shelf to retrieve a handful of dried, shriveled mushrooms. He greedily popped one in his mouth and, with loud smacking noises, ate it quickly. He let out a grateful sigh as the fungus softened in his mouth and released the life giving spores into his emaciated form. Feeling restored, he moved to his siblings and forced one between each of their lips.

Poor Ganee could barely open his mouth enough to take

it in. He always had to be the main body and the toll it took on him was gruesome. Tubaw was faring better and was able to sit up as soon as he had chewed a couple of times. Both brothers knelt by Ganee and rubbed his limbs and stroked his thin hair until he relaxed and opened his eyes.

Tubaw sat back and looked at the other two. "Tis becoming harder to join. We need to travel home for a' wee bit o'time," his voice was thin and raspy as he looked wearily at the head of the little tribe. "We be needing the Sumair stone right soon I'm thinking or we'll be a'failing our kinsmen."

Pengal nodded agreement as he pulled Ganee into his lap and held his brother, whose head lay limply on his shoulder. He couldn't yet speak, and both the others knew they didn't have much longer. Their fair magic was all but gone, and the little bit they got from Aishal was barely enough to work the simplest of spells now. They were going to need to pull on the Eilibear pool of magic again and soon.

Tubaw pulled a blanket from the corner of the room and wrapped it tightly around the three as they dozed, holding each other, dreaming of dancing in the dark caverns and bogs of their homeland.

When Ganee stirred, his older brother, Pengal, was instantly awake. The three had used the Eilibear magic for too many years, their minds connected, even when their bodies weren't. Pushing Ganee and the blanket aside, he rose and made a meal for all of them. By the time it was prepared, the other two were up and had thrown some clothes on before sitting at the table. The food disappeared quickly, but they lingered over their hot tea until Tubaw broke the silence.

"Tis not working, having those fey look for the stone. Ah don't think they'll ever find it, they don't have the need like we do. Those young fey only wants it fer the doorway. They have a' *want*, but not a *need,*" he announced as he slurped his drink.

"We need tae kill them all. Kill them, tear them apart, rip their limbs aff an' dance on their bones," Ganee hissed. "Ah care not fer any of them. It was them that started all this, our kin was happy in our lots before Willow came. We shouldn't have tae play nice with them. Kill them all," the little one spat, as he caught a frog that had made the mistake of hopping too close. He tore off its head with his teeth and spat it out, then proceeded to suck out the insides.

"Naw Ganee, we cannot just kill them all. Ye know that. We be needing them. Tis the balance we be needing, the balance that was broken by the Wisp clan. Willow Wisp was ravaged and still stands there. Jist the fact that all the chaos happened in that forest tells us the stone was at play. It is there, it could not have left. The forest has bin sealed fer too many years. I'm thinking we be needing tae stay till the doorway be opening. Laven will be a doing it fer us, he is a bright lad and he wants that Meadhan for his own. We will stay and wait."

"What do we do now? The Woodsman's woman didn't have the talisman and somehow she got away. Even the Eilibear's can't catch the Woodsman and he's been running around free in their realm for nay onto a year now. He be somewhere in Ifrinn, him and that Druid with white fire. We be no better off naw than we were before, nor any closer tae getting the Sumair stone back, and what if the Druid finds us, what then?" Tubaw asked scornfully.

"No worries. The Eilibear will keep the Woodsman busy, those two wilt be in Ifrinn a long time. And what of his woman? So she got away from us, she's in hiding. She had no powers that would hurt us and I think she wouldn't want to mix up with us or the Eilibear's again. It's their blonde lass that be a help now. The Eilibear have found a home, a wee hole to climb into. I don't think she even be knowing they are inside her. The Eilibear can be good at staying silent when they want tae be," Pengal countered, rubbing his belly where it had joined with Ganee earlier. It still hurt and he thought maybe his brother had left another piece behind this time. "We have no need to worry about those three shifted mortals. It's the fey they raised as their own that may be a problem.

"Then why send Aishal after the lass? What purpose?" Tubaw questioned with a tight jaw. "Tis a waste of time, I be thinking."

"We be needing a talisman and she may know where one is, besides Aishal be needing tae keep busy," Pengal admitted, as his probing of his belly hit pay dirt as he found a small protrusion near his belly button. It rolled under his skin when he touched it. He decided not to tell Ganee, the lad would not be happy that he had lost another piece of himself.

"I jest don't like waiting," Ganee complained snippily, as he drummed his fingers on the table.

"I be trusting the lad Laven. He wilt know how tae turn the Alltha," Pengal informed his brothers, while trying not to notice Ganee's fingers tapping on the table. Another one was newly missing and he could guess where it was now.

"So it all rests on the lad," Ganee scowled.

A muffled sound came from a large box sitting by the wall behind the three. It shook and then a thin cry rang out. "And feed the thing, Ganee, tis your job. The Eilibear will need that body to feed on and incubate in when we finally let the rest through." Pengal said gesturing with his head towards the box.

CHAPTER 20 - Elsie

May 12, 1971 –

We are back, but this may be the last time for me. Skyler got away from us on the way here. She went and cut the talisman off herself, giving herself a bad cut on her neck. We spent a couple of nights at the hospital and Milton had to make up a story about camping on the beach and her falling on the rocks in the dark.

The people at the hospital didn't believe us and had Skyler taken away. That mean woman, with the squinty eyes said Skyler was schizophrenic. She found the medical and police files on Skyler and the woman was almost happy to keep our child from us.

She told us that our daughter was paranoid, with delusions about evil creatures talking to her and touching her. Skyler had told her the forest was after her and that Ivy wasn't her daughter but instead a weird creature and had to be killed. The woman laughed when she relayed that Skyler thought she had powerful magic, but was worried for our safety. This woman decided it was time to take our child away. Skyler was committed to an institution in Salem for treatment.

If that woman only knew the truth.

We could only return to the beach and search for the talisman. We could not find it. Milton thinks it must be buried in the sand, or washed away by the tide. He said he couldn't 'feel' it, so he supposes it is gone for good.

There is nothing we can do except give her one of ours...when we can get her back. Milton says he doesn't have the power to make more of the talismans and I feel he needs his more than I need the one I wear. I told him he will take mine. I won't need it. I am tired with this life. Milton has promised me that I can stay in one place now. He promised that we will find a nice place to live this next time, someplace new and just cope the best we can. I do not wish to deal with Skyler, only madness surrounds her. Am I a bad mother that I've given up on my child? Our friends tell me I'm not, a shifted child is difficult for any person. But it is hard to believe I am not the one at fault as I'm the one who gave birth to her and I am responsible for her actions.

For now we have come back to the forest with Ivy to wait. Milton thinks he can get our daughter back soon and we will go on. He says he will bring Ivy by himself and start to teach her, start to unweave the glamour veil he put on her. It won't happen, he won't do it. We will get Skyler back, have some peace for a time and then Milton will have a reason to delay his promise to me. I believe part of him does not want to tell Ivy and risk losing her.

I wonder sometimes what my life would be like if that one decision we made, that one walk in this forest we took, could be undone? A 'do-over', like in a children's game? That's what I want: a 'do-over'. I know it's not my fault, I had done nothing but try to be a good wife, a good mother and a good person. I feel the need to scream to the world how unfair this all is.

October 13, 1971 –

I waited until Milton was away collecting Skyler and walked the path to the place where Willow stands. If I could hurt that one I would, hate festers in me at this one and will not go away.

It was his fault. I asked Milton years ago to cut it down, kill it, and burn it, anything to get rid of it, but he will not do it. He has the same memories, the same experiences and was changed even more than myself...however he is peaceful with it, has accepted it all. He even went as far as to say he felt sorry for the willow. Not I. Never...not even knowing what I know.

October 20, 1971 –

Milton is back with Skyler. I took off my talisman and while my daughter slept, Milton cut a small opening in her side. He took the small hemlock heart from the necklace and put it in the opening. I sewed her back up and we know that there will be no harm to her now. Without my protection, the forest is not safe for me, nor is the real world. I'll take my chances there though, the demons hold no power that I do not give them and I will give none. Part of me will miss this place, I do love my garden. Now I wait.

CHAPTER 21 - Ivy

"Why are you still here?" I snapped. Okay, I know that was rude, but this really was just too much. Laven, however, did not seem put off by my insolence. He just smiled that smile that I was beginning *not* to like…kind of gentle and tolerant.

"It has become obvious that there is more to you than we were led to believe. I have remained to assist you," he stated, his voice courteous though I thought it was a bit too arrogant.

I didn't know what to say, so I huffed past him back the way I had come. I decided I would go back to my cabin and pretend he wasn't here, that none of this had happened. It was good that he couldn't come into my glade in his fey form. Even if he came as a Wisp, there was only one of him. I could swat him like a bug. Smiling viciously at the thought, I clomped down the path.

My glade looked like it always had, bright and cheerful. The cabin looked the same too. I don't know why, but I had this feeling that everything *had* changed. I stomped right to the cabin door and went in, locking it behind me. I didn't come out for two days, except to use the outhouse, and then I never looked right or left, just straight ahead. I did not want to see him, I did not want to hear him, and I did not want to accept the truth.

It was the next afternoon when I had the memory. I was washing my dishes and dropped a plastic cup. When I bent to pick it up, I remembered. I had been little, really little, 4 or so…and I had gotten myself a cup of Kool-Aid and was drinking it standing by the ice box, as Marmaw had always called it, while she folded the laundry on the kitchen table. Granddad and Mom had pulled up in the driveway and were arguing as they came in the kitchen door.

"No, you can't make me! There's no way I'm going back there!" she had screamed at him, her face contorted in anger.

"We must, I must and you must! It will heal you. Don't you want to be better? It will make the bad things go away for a time. It is who we are now, Skyler, we don't have a choice. We must go back so you and Ivy can live," Granddad had pleaded with her, shouted at her, and then pleaded again.

"It's all a lie. You are a mean, hateful old man. That thing is not mine. You and Mommy did something to me...I know you did. I did not have a baby, I would have remembered. That lady in the parking lot asked about my little girl. I don't know where you got her from, but I won't be part of your lies and I will not go back to that disgusting forest!" she spat with loathing.

"I'm sorry, darling, that we have to tell people that. But it's the best story, the only story we could think of," Granddad said in a low tone, as if uncomfortable.

"It's a lie...all lies. Horrible, repulsive lies. You and Mommy are whacked. You keep trying to tell everyone that I'm the one not right in my head. But why don't you tell them about the fairies and weird things you see. Huh? Why don't you do that? I bet they would lock you up! They would! I'm going to tell them...tell everyone what nut jobs you are. I'm going to tell them about the thing you keep calling a girl. It's not! It does things, it's the one that brings the monsters to attack me, and you don't even care! You love it more than me; you are evil, hateful, freaks! I detest you!"

"Now Skyler, don't you be speaking of Ivy that way. She's a joy, you know that and we only want what's good

for you," Marmaw had said, going over to her and trying to hug her. Mom had pushed her away and glared at them both.

"No! You just want to lock me up again with those things. Or hurt me again with the needles and this thing you did to me..." Mom had screamed as she pulled up her shirt and pointed at a small pucker of skin. "You did this to me! You put something inside me, I know you did. I can feel it and the demons keep telling me to cut it out...and I may. I'll cut it out and you'll see, I'll tell everyone what you did. I hate you!" she had hissed at them.

"Skyler we had to. You kept taking it off. Last time you lost it. You aren't protected from them unless you have it. You gave us no choice. Your mother gave you her talisman to protect you. Don't you realize that? She did it for you!" Granddad had cried, tears running down his face.

Mom had scowled at them, then turned abruptly and ran into me, making me drop the cup. I had reached down to pick it up and she had kneed me in the face. I don't remember crying, only being stunned at the blood that had poured out from my nose. She had laughed and looked back at Granddad and Marmaw with hatred. "Look, the thing doesn't even feel pain, it's not normal."

I had looked up at Marmaw with shock, and she had taken me in her arms and then cleaned me up. Granddad and I had gone to the cabin that night, and it had been all better.

I remembered it…all of it. How Mom had looked deranged and scary. She had called Granddad a freak and had laughed at making me bleed. Granddad had spoken calmly to me and we had come here. I couldn't remember anything else except coming here when I was older. Granddad and I had stayed only a couple of days, then he had taken me home, and left Marmaw and I alone for long periods of time after that. Until I turned nine and he said I could go with him and I did, four or five times a year after that. And he made up stories about fairies.

I grabbed the cup and tossed it into the sink and sat on one of the stools, dazed. I had questions…lots of them. Every time I thought of a new one, ten more would pop up. There was no one to ask; Granddad and Marmaw were gone, Mom was unhinged, that left only one person...fey...crap. It only left Laven.

I debated with myself. I lost a lot of the debates. I tried arguing with myself as I made a lunch of peanut butter and jam cracker sandwiches. I was beginning to miss bread. Tomorrow, I told myself, tomorrow I would try to make some bread. Filling up one of my empty water bottles, I shook some lemonade powder into it and shook it hard while I argued some more with myself. I sat down at the table and ate my lunch, not tasting a bite.

The box. There were more entries, more notebooks I hadn't read. Maybe my answers were in there. I could see just the corner of it under Granddad's bed. I delayed as long as I could, taking small bites and chewing slowly. I must have muttered every foul word I knew as I finished and continued the argument with myself. I had to do it. I had to read all of them. Either I had gone off the deep end and was as loony as my mom...or... It was the 'or' that was giving me pause.

I took my time cleaning up, then slowly made my way over to the bed and pulled the box out and opened it. They were all still there. For some reason I was sure they would be gone, that it was just my imagination. But it wasn't. I scanned the dates and found the newest one. The date was long before I remember coming here with Granddad. '1970's' was written on the front cover in Marmaw's pretty handwriting. I opened it and started to read.

I discovered we had once lived in San Francisco, found the entry were Marmaw told about telling everyone that Skyler was my mom and how they had tried to wipe Skyler and my memories.

I had to stop reading after a couple pages and took great gulps of air. This *was* about us… it *was* real. I wasn't nuts, I couldn't be. Mom wasn't nuts...or maybe she was now…and she wasn't my mom. I had to close my eyes as I grew dizzy. The feeling passed swiftly though and I opened them and forced myself to continue to read.

My stomach started to roll, and I could feel bile rising as I read what Marmaw and Granddad had done to Skyler. It was horrible and my mind was having a hard time deciding if they did right cutting her open like that. March 1972 was the end of the diary entries. The last few pages of that notebook had been ripped out and the rest were blank.

It was enough for me though; I knew I had a choice to make. On the one hand, I could believe that Mom was schizophrenic and a drug user and a low-life. It would be easy to believe that I had lived a rather normal life with Granddad and Marmaw, just like any other kid. And we just liked to go camping...and Granddad liked to do woodwork...and they both liked to make up fairy stories...and my life was just shit now that they were gone. Or...

There it was again, that 'or'. Or...I was a fey, and Skyler and my Grandparents had been *shifted* by the fairy magic and both of them had spent years keeping us safe. Fleetingly I tried to tell myself that I was nuts, then stopped. This made more sense...weird...but it did. I had seen it with my own eyes…Laven and the others. I had seen the doorway and felt the power surging through the axe. I had seen it...I believed it...I had no choice.

Dropping the notebook down on top of the others, I stood and went out the front door. The sun was hot on the doorstep, and the wonderful bright light blinded me for a moment, but I didn't mind. I missed it, I missed the forest. Here I was in the forest and yet I wasn't going into the forest. I was making myself a prisoner in the cabin.

I looked around the beautiful glade, just bursting with

flowers; then I gathered my courage and turned towards the path to the pond. I strolled purposely down it, enjoying the absence of the *bugs*. Only what I perceived as normal sounds surrounded me. The bubbling stream, crickets or frogs, or maybe both; birds and the breeze rustling the leaves in the trees.

I found a spot in the partial shade by the pond and sat down. A chipmunk crept close, but I had nothing for it and it scolded me for forgetting to bring something before it scampered off. Tiny butterflies fluttered in the foliage, and dragonflies zoomed in and out around the pond. The largest frog I had ever seen sat on a lily pad in the water garden of the pond, and croaked at me: *jump up, jump up, jump up*.

I didn't speak frog after all, that's just what it sounded like. And life at the pond was how it had always been. I lay back and looked at the sky, watching a couple of birds that were putting on an air show for me, when I heard something off to my right in the tree branches. I glanced over and I saw Laven was sitting almost delicately amongst the leaves, looking down at me with that look of his, like he didn't know what to make of me. I locked eyes with him and stayed like that for a while until I had to ask. "Who am I?"

That seemed to be a question I kept coming back to. All of the *if's* lead back to this one question. I know I had already asked Laven this, but I just needed to have it answered again.

"You are Ey-vey," he answered as he appeared sitting next to me on the ground.

"Stop that. If you want to move around, at least let me know where you are going to end up!" I cried out as I sat up and inched away. I composed myself and tried again.

"Okay, maybe we should start somewhere else. How about, what I am?"

"You are fey, Frìth fey of my clan," he replied in his

mellow voice.

"How are you so sure of that?"

"You are showing the magic of it," was his calm response.

"What? You mean the axe and opening that doorway thing?" My voice was a little shaky as I said this, it sounded odd.

"Yes, that is part. You also unwove the enchantment on us so that we could show ourselves to you. However I was meaning that you are marked with it, you are Frìth." He answered as he reached out and touched the sides of my face.

I scooted back away from him, unnerved by his touch and then really looked at him. His eyes were so misty violet that they didn't look real. His skin was almost translucent, perfect in every way. He radiated tranquility and calmness; it freaked me out a bit.

"I am sorry my lady, I..." he started, but I put my hand up stopping him.

"Is this a test or a game Ey-vey?" he asked with a wide grin, seeming to be up for either.

"Just answer my questions. What *enchantment* did I unweave?" I snapped.

"The veil on us, the glamour that the Woodsman put on us...or maybe you. I am not sure which held the spell. Did the Woodsman teach you the spell to unweave?" he asked cheerfully in his sing-song silky voice.

"What spell?" I asked confused. I hadn't done any spells. I wasn't a witch... at least I didn't think I was.

"You can see me," he responded.

"Yeah…you are right in front of me," I said sarcastically. I am sixteen; I'm allowed to be a pain now and then...then my thoughts froze. Was I sixteen?

"I could only appear as a Wisp to you, but you broke the spell. You unwove the bindings of the glamour. How?" he asked, studying me with that completely focused look of his.

Geez he had pretty eyes; I wished mine were that violet color. That violet-gray was like a stormy night...or a lavender field.

"How?" he repeated and I sighed. I'd rather think about his eyes.

"I don't know. When did it happen?" I huffed out at him.

"We felt it leave outside of your hovel."

"You mean the cabin? When?"

"The night you retrieved the Woodsman's axe," he said tilting his head with a cute grin.

"Oh...." I started trying to remember what had happened. "I was running. Then I stopped at the door and looked back. All the weird bug things were playing in the glade, it looked really cool. I was feeling lonely. I don't know, I think a little group of the bugs were following me and I told them that I wished I had someone to talk to, that I wished they could talk." I shrugged my shoulders. I really didn't remember what I had said, but I did remember feeling alone.

"You broke the spell with simple words? No clustering of three?" he gasped, seemingly shocked.

"You are speaking in riddles. I don't know anything about a spell, or what a clustering of three is." This was frustrating. I didn't know any more than when I'd started.

"Ey-vey, we have been here for many human years, coming and going, and never could we understand what you were saying to us. We understood happiness or sadness in you, but never your spoken words. Only the Woodsman could allow us to revert to our fey forms if he wished to speak with us. Are you sure all you did was say you wished we could talk to you?" His voice was insistent, but I found that he was annoying me. I didn't like someone even implying that I wasn't telling the truth. Well…I had bent it a lot in the last few weeks at home and to get here, but for the most part, I didn't lie. I didn't know what to say...so I glared at him. That always seemed to work on the boys at school.

"I apologize to you, Ey-vey," he said humbly. Wow, he understood that look well enough, I thought with an inward smirk.

"What is that three thing you said." I decided not to be mad. I had just too many questions, and if I had to get the answers from someone, I was rather happy that it was from a cute, polite boy. I didn't meet too many of them. I suddenly thought of Zack back in town…he had been cute and kind of polite, I guess.

"For any true spell, you need a cluster of three items. Herbs or personal things or other items, but it always takes three." He closed his eyes, and for the first time I could really look at his face. His eyes had always drawn me in. His features were defined, very male, but there was gentleness to them. I couldn't place the features, not American, maybe English...no, it was Irish or maybe Scottish. That was it; he looked like he should be wearing a kilt. I smiled at the thought of him in a dress, it didn't seem anymore odd than the leaf stuff he was wearing. I was wondering how he made them when he suddenly opened his eyes and said.

"Ey-vey. I have magic, all fey do. A normal fey magic is blinking."

"Blinking?" I repeated, narrowing my eyes at him. Was he pulling one over on me? I could blink, anyone could.

"Like this," he said and he was gone. "See, that is what we call blinking." His voice came to me from the branch above my head. "You try it, just close your eyes and tell yourself where you want to be."

I rolled my eyes at him and sneered. Really? He had to be kidding. If I could do this blinking, I would have been doing it for years. Who wanted to walk…or ride in a car for hours? But he was waiting, his eyes pleading with me.

Okay…I guess I thought it was lame, but I did want to try. I closed my eyes and thought of the sand by the edge of the pond. I felt a little woozy and opened my eyes. I was now sitting by the pond on the sand, the water within reach of my fingers. I looked up with amazement at Laven. That was simply pure unadulterated awesome. He clapped joyfully as I looked up at him grinning stupidly.

Then he blinked and was instantly standing in front of me. Grabbing my hands he pulled me up and started doing this bizarre little dance. He was so excited that he was jumping up and down, and swirling us in circles. I could only follow along and watch in wonder at his charming display of the most un-masculine thing I had ever seen.

"Wait...stop," I giggled, as I pulled away and watched as he kept up the hops and bounces around me. Laughing, I finally grabbed his arm, but he swung me around with him again and together we danced another weird little waltz. When he was finally spent, his laughter still ringing in my ears, his face lit with joy, he stopped and stood grinning at me.

"Okay, that was fun," I announced out of breath. I had to hold my sides and take a couple of deep breaths before I could talk again. "So...I can blink. That's normal right? For a fey, that is normal?"

"Yes my Ey-vey, it is normal for a fey, all of the fair folk can." He laughed out loud, his grin so wide I could see his perfect white teeth gleaming at me.

"So I *am* a fey," I said quietly to myself.

"Not just a fey, Ey-vey, a Frìth fey. A very special Frìth fey," he announced proudly.

"I'm filth?" I repeated. What did that mean? That I was dirty or something?

"Not filth, Ey-vey... Frìth, it means forest in Gaelic. The Frìth have their own personal magic, shape shifting. Your mother was a Frìth from my birthplace. She lived here until..."

"Until Willow brought the Sumair stone and he killed her," I finished for him sadly.

"So you know?" he asked surprised. "If you knew, why did you not say?"

"Marmaw wrote stories…in notebooks. I read them. Just now. I never knew before," I said haltingly.

"The plump female mortal who painted the pictures?" he asked, shifting his body to look at me uncertainly.

"Marmaw. Yes, she painted and wrote wonderful stories about fairies," I said, and his face looked pained. "Sorry, *fey*…she wrote about the fair folk. She called them that, but her stories that she published were about little things with cute wings and she called them fairies," I said, correcting myself quickly. His face cleared, but remained thoughtful.

"Yes, I remember the Woodsman saying she wrote stories to go with her pictures. I believe she knew that mortals would not be able to comprehend what the fey really were. They do not have the sight and do not wish to see," he said in a condescending tone, as he moved away and turned his back on me.

"Well, I don't really know what the fey are either. I grew up thinking I was just a mortal, remember?" I snapped, upset at his self-righteousness.

He turned and looked hard at me, studying me, and then bowed his head. "My deepest apologies, my lady," he whispered.

"Stop that!" I shouted at him as my tongue did a weird thing, its tip tingling suddenly. "I'm not *your lady*!"

His eyes went wide, and he held his lips tight, as if in fear or pain at my tone. It took me back that yelling seemed to hurt him. He blinked his eyes a couple of times, but did not disappear. Maybe fey blinked like mortals did too. I found that interesting, and felt bad, though I didn't know why.

"Sorry, I shouldn't have yelled at you," I said, looking

down, feeling uneasy.

"Tis not the volume, my lady. You are throwing a power at me when you do so. It does cause pain," he whispered, his eyes heart-wrenchingly woeful.

"I'm throwing something at you? What?"

"I do not know how to explain it, but magic seems to show itself in your voice. I can feel a difference in the thread of power by how you speak and the force you put behind it," he said a bit louder and moved closer to me again. This time I didn't stop him as he reached up and touched the side of my head. What was the fascination with where I had drawn those lines? They couldn't still be there; it had been days since I'd drawn them on. I waited until he was finished and removed his fingers from my face before I spoke again. He was standing inches away and looking down at me with those melting eyes.

"Why do you keep doing that?" I asked.

"I've never seen a Frìth enchantment like it before," he answered with a weak smile.

"It's just eyeliner I painted on. You know…makeup? Really, it must be gone by now, it was days ago that I drew it on," I stammered at him.

"Tis not this *makeup* Ey-vey. Tis a vine."

"You aren't making any sense to me. What do you mean, a 'vine'?" I snapped at him again. I was doing that a lot, and chastised myself when I saw the look of agony on his face.

"When you entered the hollow of the doorway and retrieved the Woodsman's axe. The vines started to grow," he answered as if that explained everything.

"Well Laven, I don't have a vine on my face. I don't know what the heck you are talking about! Geez, get real!" I shouted in frustration at him. The large frog that had been croaking stopped and jumped into the pond, the birds grew quiet and Laven looked like I had slapped him. I turned and stomped over to the pond and looked down at my reflection. The water was rippling from the frog jumping in and as the water cleared, I turned my head to see the sides by my left eye.

I saw the prettiest little vine, with teeny tiny leaves and little purple flowers, following exactly where I had drawn on the eyeliner. I reached up to touch them and screamed as my hand felt what my eyes were seeing. I fainted again. I was a wimp.

CHAPTER 22 - Ivy

I woke up lying in the deep of the forest. Ferns and moss seemed to be closing in on me. I felt safe. Laven sat next to me, watching me with those beautiful eyes of his. I didn't even ask how I had gotten here…it didn't matter. Sitting up, I tried to smile at him, but it felt weak.

"How are you, my lady?" he asked as he pushed my hair out of my eyes.

"Hungry," I announced, just realizing it. My stomach was gurgling at me. The cracker sandwiches just were not enough. I really wanted a big juicy hamburger with all the fixings. Laven grinned shyly, and held out a hand full of berries. Not what I wanted, but it was something. I took them and tried to eat them without getting my fingers all purple from the juices.

When I was done I hesitated, trying not to look at him as I said, "So, it's all true isn't it? What Marmaw wrote, the notebooks, they were diaries of their life having to raise a fairy, uh sorry, *fey*." Laven didn't say anything, just looked at me. "Mom isn't my mom, and Granddad and Marmaw aren't my grandparents. I'm just some baby they got stuck with."

His eyes sad, he nodded at me.

"Willow Wisp really did steal the Sumair stone which ended up killing my real mom and hurt my fake mom and really screwed up Granddad and Marmaw's lives. Does that about cover it?" I finished sarcastically, and then remembered. "Oh and I've got weird plant things growing out of my head to really polish this picture off," I said as I reached up and touched them again, needing to make sure I hadn't dreamt it. They were still there. Weird.

"I am not sure of all of your words, but I believe you have an understanding, my lady." he answered oh so politely. He was really starting to piss me off with all this *my lady* stuff.

"Why? Why do you keep calling me that? It's creepy," I said as I stood and tried to find my bearings.

"Because you are my sovereign," Laven said standing along with me.

"Right. I'm like what a queen?" I asked as I started pushing my way through the ferns. He followed, a bit quieter and gentler on the foliage than I was being.

"Yes, my lady. The Elders gave the forest and doorway to you if you should want it. You do want it, do you not?" His voice was filled with concern. Maybe, for the first time, it was dawning on him that I might not.

"How would I know what I want?" I snarled back, as I found myself blocked by a huge tangle of blackberry bushes. I had to turn around and found him directly behind me.

"But, all fey wish for their own doorway," he stated, astonished that I wouldn't jump instantly on board with him. "The Frìth has never had their own. We can now grow and flourish and cultivate a new line of Frìth. You have been given a great and wonderful gift, my lady. We have much work to do in order to bring the rest of our clan here and begin," he said, perplexed that I didn't seem to understand what he found to be such a wonderful thing.

I found myself looking at him again...I mean really looking at him. He was beautiful. Not handsome or a hunk…he was beautiful, and a bit naïve, and a whole lot annoying. He was watching me with those simply gorgeous misty eyes from his exquisite perfect face and I found I wasn't sure I liked him. I needed to think…and not with him around me…but there were other questions that were swirling around in my head.

"Laven, doesn't the forest really belong to the fey who used to live here?" I asked, thinking about how I would feel if someone took something that special from me.

"It did, at one time. The Hemlock clan grew the hemlock trees and it was their forest and doorway. However the Elders gave it to the Woodsman...and to you," he answered.

"Wait, where is this Hemlock clan now? Don't they want their forest?"

"The Elders gave them a new doorway, they are content now," he answered sweetly.

"But what about the Sumair stone and Willow? Is anyone concerned about him or that horrible stone?" I could see I was making him uncomfortable. Maybe he didn't think I had a brain or would think to ask questions. Like that was going to happen. He was taking his own sweet time answering me, and I raised my eyebrows at him and crossed my arms, scowling. Laven looked down, as if he couldn't meet my eyes.

"Yes, there are those who are troubled."

"Ha!" I exclaimed, feeling I had won some point.

"But my lady, that is not something to worry yourself with. Once we find the Sumair stone, it will be returned to its home and the forest will be safe for us."

"Wait a minute. You say you want to find the stone and return it? Was all that with Aishal about the stone? He was mad about something," I snapped at him, as I tried to fight my way through the bushes.

"There is no need to worry about Aishal. He wanted to show you Firinn, your true home, but the iuchair did not want you to leave. He only wanted to take it away so that you could come and go as we do. We have a doorway, we have our own forest. I thought you might wish to keep the iuchair for when the Woodsman came again. When might he come again?" he asked, turning away so I couldn't see his face.

"Granddad is dead, he won't be coming back," I said, trying not to cry.

"Oh my lady," he called out, turning to me and acting like he was going to hug me. I pulled back so he couldn't. He stopped and bowed his head. "I am sorry for your loss. It would be good to rid ourselves of the iuchair and the Sumair stone...and Willow."

That stopped me, and I turned to face him. I was sweaty and tired and hungry, and he looked so cool and right, standing there amidst the ferns. "You want Willow back? There's a way to take him? Like what, to change him back into a fey?" I asked in a rush, then paused as what he said sank in. "Wait you want Willow back? Why?"

"To punish him," he stated calmly.

"He's already been punished."

"Not by the fey. Not by the Boggarts or the Frìth or the Wisps or any of the other fey who were damaged by his deed."

"You don't think he's been punished enough?"

"No, my lady. He has been allowed to live as a Frìth would. He gently sways in the air of the between realm, tis not a real punishment," he said as if speaking to a small child. I detected just a bit of superiority in his tone.

Choosing to overlook it this time, I thought about what he'd said. If I understood the nature of the Sumair stone, it sucked up magic, bad and good magic, then spat it back out. If anyone took it back and put it once more in the ground, then those weird little Boggarts might be good again, or at least not bad. On the other hand, they could get worse, even more evil, but maybe the fair folk who lived there would have their lives back. I didn't know if that big war Marmaw wrote about, between the Druids and the Boggarts, was still going on. Would the return of the stone and Willow stop it or make it worse? There were a lot of questions. What about Willow? He had been a kid…an old kid by mortal standards, but still a kid…under the influence of the darn stone. He couldn't be held accountable, it wasn't right to keep this up. And my mind jumped to thinking about the mortals in Scotland.

I took history in school, hated it, but took it, and one of the girls in my class had done a report on Scotland. It sounded like a cool place as it was. If the stone went back, wouldn't Scotland be changed? I wasn't sure I wanted to voice my thoughts to Laven, but I think Granddad was right in that the stone should never be allowed into fey hands again. It was too powerful and too unpredictable. No one could really be sure what the thing would do, or what would happen with it around.

Something about this tale of Laven's was off. I could feel it. There was more that he was not telling me, but I didn't know what. I didn't even know the questions that I needed to ask to find out. I had to grasp at what I could. He said that the Elders had given the doorway to me and the Woodsman...Granddad. They had given the doorway to a mortal?

"Laven," I began, trying to keep my voice nice and level. "Why would the Elders give a doorway to a mortal? You guys seem all hot and heavy about it…why did they do it?"

My question seemed to take him back and he stopped as if shocked. "Because he wasn't a mortal any longer…none of the mortal family was. They had been shifted, given fey magic by the Sumair stone."

"Shifted?" I asked, going over Marmaw's writings in my mind.

"Yes, my lady…shifted…changed…given magic."

"So Granddad and Marmaw and my mom...ah, Skyler, all had...have magic?"

"Of course, my lady. The fey do not like their magic being given to mortals. They wanted it back."

"The Elders didn't seem to mind," I countered.

"I believe that is because the Woodsman was too powerful for even them. They planned on taking it back at the Gather, along with you, my lady," the jerk actually bowed a little at me when he said that. It gave me chills…not good ones. "But the Woodsman turned them all into Wisps. It was very powerful magic, and they all knew it. The Elders decided it was best to wait it out. Even shifted mortals only live for a short time compared to us, at the most maybe five hundred or so years...if the Eilibear don't get them first that is, a fey will eventually find them and be able to reclaim the magic. The council knew they had only to wait long enough and they would have it back anyway," he stated with smug confidence, and I glared at him. I didn't like where this was going.

"Just how do they *reclaim their magic*?" I asked.

"By soaking it away from the mortal."

"What happens to the mortal after it's *soaked away*?"

"They die, of course. Mortals are meant to die. They are born to die."

What a full-blown ass this guy was becoming. I couldn't believe it. This meant him and all the other fey were just waiting for my family to die? Or...wait a minute; he said they had planned on reclaiming it at the Gather, and taking me back. My eyes grew wide as I realized what he had so calmly just told me.

"They wanted to kill Granddad and Marmaw and Skyler? It wasn't their fault!" I shouted at him, and he backed up away from me, his face going white. "Is that what you are telling me? Just kill innocent mortals to get something back that a weird stone had given them by mistake?"

"Mortals are not meant to have fey magic; it opens ways for the Eilibear to crawl in. It is the way, Ey-vey. It is the only way to get the magic back. They are just mortals, my lady. Just like it is wrong for a fey to live in Alainn, a fey becomes an Alltha…a wild thing. But that is not what upset the fey, my lady. We were more upset by the Woodsman creating the talismans...Alltha talismans. That was...is, an affront to us. That you still wear one is an insult to your birthright," he whispered with feeling, as he looked at my necklace.

I was flabbergasted. Words would not come to me. This...this fey didn't care about my family...they were just *mortals* to him. I needed to know more about the talisman I wore. If it was so offensive to him, to the fey, I needed to understand why. I steadied myself...I really wasn't liking Laven at all right now.

"Tell me more about the talisman," I whispered tightly, working at keeping my voice low so my anger didn't show.

"The Woodsman would not agree to let any fey back in unless he and his family were protected. The Woodsman worked the magic into the hemlock wood. He locked not only the doorway, but the forest also with the iuchair. He sealed it off from Alainn *and* Firinn. The talismans allowed any who possessed them to come through the veil into the Hemlock Mendhan," he explained gently to me. "But, my lady, in addition, the talismans made it impossible for any creature or fey to permanently harm the mortals. The Eilibear are still attracted by the magic, could still be seen and heard, but couldn't really harm them. Fey do not need this protection, no Eilibear would dare harm a fey or have the opportunity to do so. Why do you still wear it Ey-vey? Why do you not let the fey in now? You are one of us."

"So the fey are to blame for the forest being locked, not Granddad," I stated, quite amazed that I could overlook all the other horrible things he had just told me and stay focused on that.

"No, the Woodsman is to blame. The fey would never have attacked the mortals if they hadn't taken something that belonged to the fey," Laven countered, quite sure of himself.

"Wait a minute," I snapped. "You all were trying kill the *mortal*, take me away from the only family I knew, while it was your magic that changed everything and you blame *him* for wanting to keep his family safe? You don't care that to get your precious magic back, you would have had to kill my family?" Laven started to speak, and I put my hand up to stop him. I was really on a roll.

"The fey created this Sumair stone, didn't keep it safe, allowed a little fey to play with it...never even thinking that something like this could happen," I waved my arm around the forest. I was agitated at him, mad...this guy was unbelievable.

"You stand there telling me that now I am some sort of queen, and own a doorway and how you are thrilled that now you have your very own little play area. You don't care that the Hemlock fey lost their home. You and your friends want to kill Willow, and that guy, Shivf, actually wants to find the Sumair stone and take it back to Scotland? Really? That's what you want to do? Put the thing back and let it soak up more magic? Or worse, put it back so it can attack innocent people again? Then what, someone else can get their hands on it, and do this all over again? Are you out of your mind?" I was screaming now, I was in a full blown tantrum of anger. My tongue felt like it was on fire and I had to keep swallowing so it would cool down.

"You do not understand, my lady," Laven finally cut in, "It is true that magic does as magic does…but fey magic is not meant to be gifted to mortals. All the shifted ones put us in danger. It does not matter how the mortals gained the power…only that they must *not* have it." He reached out to touch my face again.

"Stop that!" I said, as I swatted his hand away. "What do you mean, *all* the shifted ones? Who else was shifted, and what is this horrible danger that you are so afraid of?" I said glaring at him; he was just too arrogant for my liking.

He was talking down to me as if I was some little kid who didn't understand anything. "Explain what an Eilibear is."

"The Eilibear are demons that live in the realm of Ifrinn. They depleted their realm's magic long ago and now seek ways to obtain more. There are countless shifted ones. Somehow mortals have a knack for stumbling on magic and taking it. The shifted ones are easy prey as are many of the Allthas. The Elders locked all of the Eilibear's doorways; they cannot get into Firinn or a Meadhan..." I put up my hand like I was asking a question at school. It worked…he stopped talking.

"What is Meadhan again?" I asked.

"Ey-vey, there are three realms that create the balance; Firinn, the real realm that the fey live in; Ifrinn, where the Eilibear dwell; and Alainn, where the mortals live. There are pockets between all three realms, fourth realms would be the best way to explain them. It is our way into the other realms; it is called Meadhan, or the middle realm. This..." he said, motioning around us, "is part of the Meadhans, but cut off from the other parts because of the veil the Woodsman put on it."

"Okay, got it. Go on with your story," I said, wondering if I'd remember all this.

He looked at me with a bit of annoyance before he continued. "I was speaking of the Eilibear. A powerful magic was woven so that they couldn't affect any of the other realms; they cannot enter, they cannot be seen or heard, or in any manner affect the realms, except by the shifted ones, or the Alltha if they wish to see them." He looked like a prince from a fairytale, standing there in the ferns, using words from some little kids' twisted story.

He was actually trying to make me believe that there were things called Eilibears that the fairies had locked up. I wanted to slap him…hard. Instead, I took a couple of deep breaths and took care to speak slowly before I responded to him.

"Let me try to understand this. The Eilibear thing is a demon that likes mortals with magic. You call them shifted mortals, and Eilibears can suck magic out of them. An Alltha is a fey that is wild, and you think I am wild…I heard what you and Aishal said. He called me an Alltha. But instead of taking care that the Eilibear things don't get magic, you kill mortals that somehow get it so the Eilibear can't get it from them?" I stated with a hard voice.

"You understand, my lady," he answered with a huge smile.

Geez he was so...so... infuriating! He didn't see it, he really didn't. Between clenched teeth, barely keeping my temper, I replied, "You mean that my grandparents and my mom...I mean Skyler...were plagued by these Eilibear things?"

"Yes, Ey-vey, all shifted ones are. That is why the Woodsman made the talismans, to protect himself and his family from the Eilibears. It would have been far better to just give us the magic back...and you also," he answered with a sweet smile. I really wanted to smash in his gorgeous face now.

Demons, he had called them...that's what Skyler was always yelling about...that the demons were after her, talking to her, watching her. She wasn't insane. She was being attacked by demons… Eilibear... and the fey did this to her.

"The talisman kept my family safe from these Eilibear, let us come to the forest and kept you all from hurting us, and you are somehow affronted that I wear one?" Boy, it was hard keeping my voice level.

"Yes, my lady. You have no need for one. The demons cannot harm you and a fey would never harm another fey," Laven said, still smiling as if he thought that all this was really good and I was on his side. Somehow I doubted his words. There was no way I'd believe that one fey wouldn't harm another fey. I'd seen Aishal's look.

"How about if someone else got a hold of one of these talismans. Could they work for another person?" I asked, thinking about Marmaw saying that Skyler had cut hers off, and Marmaw had given the one she had worn to her in its place. She couldn't leave Skyler without a talisman. What had happened to Skyler's first talisman? I wondered if whoever the Uncles were that Marmaw had written about, had found it...and what about Granddad's? There had never been a funeral, was Granddad buried somewhere still wearing it?

I was thinking all this when I saw the look on Laven's face. It had fallen, his smile dried up and he was avoiding my eyes.

"What?" I snapped at him.

"My lady...I..." he stammered.

"What Laven? What would happen if someone else got one?"

"They could come into the veil and into your glade and hovel. I am not sure, but we believe the doorway could be opened also, even without the iuchair." His voice was so low I could barely hear him.

"And?" I knew he wasn't telling me everything.

There was a long silence. Laven continued to look down at his feet. It dawned on me that he might just blink out and leave me here, avoiding telling me what I wanted to know.

"Laven, if you like me at all, you will tell me. Don't you blink out on me. Spill it," I yelled at him, letting that weird ball of heat out on my tongue.

To my shock he dropped to his knees bowed before me as he started to whimper. "Oh my lady. I did not know," he sobbed.

"Did not know what?"

Laven had covered his ears with his hands and it was very apparent that he did not want to answer me.

"Tell me!" I demanded, letting the little fire out again.

"That you were so special. You are fey, and are the rightful owner. Please forgive me," he pleaded, still on his knees.

"Forgive you for what?"

"Aishal and Shivf...and I, I'm ashamed to say, came up with a plan to bind the Woodsman and take his talisman. We were sure that if we could get our hands on it, we could re-open the door and release Willow from the hex. We have been searching for the Sumair stone for Shivf who only wishes to help the fey where he lives. Once we got the doorway open, we were going to give Willow and the stone to Shivf and he would take them away. The fey only wanted the Meadhan to be owned by the fey and the magic kept safe. You are fey, you are our sovereign."

Wow...okay...wow. I sat on the ground and just looked at him in shock. My body went numb. I had to admit it; that someone might get their hands on one of the talismans and come here scared me the most. I'd always thought in the back of my mind that this was my home and no one could take it from me. Granddad had instilled in me that I was safe at the cabin and now I find out not only was I not safe, but anyone who got their hands on a talisman and knew what it was, was not a friend of mine. I was not safe. There was no way this side of hell I would ever take off my talisman. Granddad and Marmaw had been so brave, all the things they did because of these stupid fey. I was never prouder of them than I was at that moment when everything began to clear in my mind.

I wished Granddad had told me, and I wished I could remember my real life. Marmaw had written that Granddad had put a veil on my memories and part of me was very irritated with Granddad right now.

"Laven, I don't remember any of my life here. I've met you before haven't I?" I asked, wondering if he would be truthful. I thought I would know if he wasn't. It was some time before he answered.

"The Woodsman," was his simple answer, as he rose and stood next to me, his face still pasty looking. "He felt that if you couldn't remember, you would not be a danger to them. He did it to you, Ey-vey. The Woodsman took your magic away from you. He made you Alltha."

I could tell that he thought I would be upset by this, but instead I felt like I was going to cry. Granddad had loved me so much that he had protected me from all of this…maybe I wasn't as irritated with him as I thought. I missed him so much. A tear escaped me and I wiped it away.

"I know, my lady. It was horrible of the mortal to do that to you. We will make it right."

There was nothing I could say. This fey was just too *fey.* He couldn't understand, not if I tried for the rest of my life to explain it to him. I resigned myself to that fact as I looked around us.

"Where the heck are we, and how do we get back to my cabin?" I asked in frustration, completely ignoring his statement.

"Blink." he replied with a shy smile.

Right. I closed my eyes and thought of my glade right by my front door and said I wanted to be there. The woozy feeling came and went, and I opened my eyes to find my pretty little cabin right in front of me.

CHAPTER 23 - Ivy

"Ey-vey! We need to talk." Laven's voice came from the path. I turned to see him standing outside the arch. Good, he still couldn't come in.

"Later Laven. I may be fey, but I still need to eat, pee and sleep." I opened the door, and called out as I entered, "And I need to think about this." I closed the door behind me and only then remembered I really did need to go pee. What a pain. I opened the door and Laven was in his bug form, sitting on a flower right outside the door.

"I'm just using the outhouse. Later Laven, not now," I huffed out as I walked over to the little house, used it and went back, trying not to look around for him. That soft fluttering noise might have been him, but I didn't care. He was really good looking, but not my type. I wanted a friend who was loyal and kind to everyone, not just their own kind. I'd seen it in my other life, at school. Some girl with a nose longer than others, or someone weighing more than the average kid, or someone of a different color…all made fun of, bullied or hurt in some way. Not on my watch and I wouldn't be friends with someone like that. Besides, there was something slimy about him. He seemed just too nice to me.

I made one of the instant meals and ate fast. An idea was forming and I was really good at planning things out. When I was done, I cleaned up and completely cleared the table. I got out a notebook I had salvaged from my school locker, and a pencil, putting them neatly on the table.

The notebooks and stories Marmaw had written were the

last things I needed. I spent some time organizing everything on the table and then sat down. I was ready to do the hardest, most in-depth research paper I had ever done. I loved writing…essays and articles for the school paper, and study papers. It would mean spending hours at the school library or at the public one where I could get on the internet. I wanted a computer so bad it hurt, but Granddad was beyond against it. So I learned my way around the libraries and made friends with the librarians, and I did awesome on my homework.

My teachers loved me; my homework was always done, always perfect and I always got straight 'A's. Now I wondered if that was because I had spent more years in each grade than the average kid. Forcing myself away from that path, I got down to business.

Opening my blank notebook, I wrote down all the variables: Fey, Frìths, hemlock forest, Boggarts, Granddad, Marmaw, Skyler, myself, Wisps, the stone, and on and on. When I was done I was shocked at the number of variables I had. This would be so much easier with a computer, but it was only my notebook, a pencil and my brain. It was a rather daunting task, but that only made me want to do it more. Next I gave 2 pages to each of the variables and wrote the intended topic at the top of that page. I opened the story Marmaw had written and started to read it again, this time looking for any of the variables I had decided on. When I finished with it, I started on Marmaw's diaries, in the order she had written them.

It took quite a while; I had to stop for a couple of potty breaks, and get something to eat and drink a few times. When I was done I had filled my notebook with information, composed a couple of questions at the bottom of each of their pages and really read every word in all of Marmaw's diaries.

"Wow," I said out loud when I had finished it all. Marmaw had given me a wealth of information, whether she had meant to or not. Needing a break I hunted for my MP3 and found it up in my loft. I had left it on and the batteries were beyond dead. That meant more hunting for where I had stashed the spare ones, discovering that I had put them in a basket on the bottom shelf of the bookcase. By the time I got the new ones in, I was agitated and hot and just a bit on edge.

I set the thing on random play, put the earbuds in and clipped it to my shirt, making sure the cord was tucked inside before I sat down again. While I was reading, I had marked pages in each of Marmaw's notebooks. I opened to the first one and took up my large eraser. It was easier than I thought to erase the lines that I knew needed to be gone forever.

I knew what I needed to know, and no one else could ever read these. Luckily for me she had written in pencil most of the time and all the entries that gave a clue to where the stone was hidden, were easily erased. And just to be sure, I filled in other words that made it sound like she was speaking of something else entirely.

When I was done, I gently repacked all the notebooks into the box and returned it to its home under the bed. My next piece of business was worrisome and I wasn't sure if it was even needed, but I wasn't going to take the chance. While I listened to the Everly Brothers and The Hollies and others singing to me, I dug through the baskets on the bookshelves until I found Marmaw's paints and the largest brush I could find, then stood facing the stove hearth. I knew where the Sumair stone was. I couldn't believe I had been so blind or so dense. Granddad had shown me, Marmaw had told me, and today Laven had given me the reason.

I took all the shelves and hanging items off the stones, until it was a blank canvas of rocks. The black stone stood out like a beacon alongside the lighter tan and brown river rocks. I mixed the paints in a cup until I had almost an exact match to the other rocks, dipped the brush in and started to paint. The stone was silent, but I could feel it trying hard to reach out to me. It was really persistent, but I was even more so. I covered it up, playing around with the paint colors until it was a pretty good match to the stones that made up the hearth.

It didn't take long for the paint to dry and soon I was putting the shelves back and rehanging everything exactly the way it had always been. Now the odd stone did not stand out. The Sumair stone was hidden even more completely.

I built a small fire in the stove. While it started to burn I opened my own notebook to the pages about the Sumair stone and ripped them out. Crumbling them into wads, I threw them into the fire and watched them burn. I only had one concern now; that Skyler might know where it was. Somehow I really didn't think Granddad or Marmaw would have trusted her enough to tell her. Add to that the fact that for many years now Marmaw really didn't even seem to like her anymore...which I did find sad. I understood why…Mom *was* a royal pain in the ass. I realized I had thought of her as *mom* again and sighed. I wondered how long it would be before I stopped thinking of her like that.

She was my next concern. I knew that I had to go back. I had left Mom, crap, Skyler, all alone. She couldn't handle the demons by herself. I understood now why she took the drugs and drank so much. I knew it was hard on Granddad and Marmaw, but they were adults and had the will to fight back. Skyler had been a little child; she must have been tormented by those things 24/7. For the first time in my life, I felt sorry for her.

I now knew why Marmaw had gladly given up her talisman for her daughter and what the pucker in Skyler's side was. It was just plain gross that Marmaw had sewn the talisman up inside Skyler, but it made sense. And here I had left her there all alone. I had left her without money, and no one to watch over her. The drugs and boyfriends and all the other shit she pulled couldn't kill her. No wonder Granddad had looked the other way with all the stuff she did. He knew she couldn't be hurt by it, and if that was how she managed to handle her *reality*, then that was what he had to let her do. I was so dumb.

All the research I had just finished told me one important thing about Skyler. Once Granddad got her here to the forest, she slept. Every entry Marmaw had made that spoke of Skyler being in the forest had the same theme…*she sleeps peacefully, Skyler rests, she slumbers on.* I didn't know how or why, but I hoped that I was correct that Skyler would sleep until she was rational, if I could just get her back here. I didn't know if that meant she would like me then. I doubted it, I was just another creature to her, and that kind of hurt. But for Granddad and Marmaw, I would do it. I owed them this.

I busied myself with cleaning up the cabin, putting out the fire and getting ready. I needed a real bath and had a bunch of laundry to do and debated whether I should take the time when I got to town before I caught the bus back home. Then laughed out loud…I could blink right? Just think about my house in San Diego and blink there.

I put on my cleanest clothes, packed some of my favorites that needed to be washed and shoved them and a large amount of cash into my backpack.

When I opened the door, Laven was hovering just outside. He fluttered excitedly around me as I closed and locked the door, then flew over to the path outside and appeared.

"Ey-vey, what are you doing?" he called out to me.

"I need to get something. I'll be back," I said as I walked towards the path leading down out of the forest.

"But Ey-vey, you cannot leave. The doorway is closed and if you do not return, I cannot keep the forest magic alive by myself. At least wait for all the others to come," he begged me as he passed back and forth in agitation.

"What do you mean, until *all* the other fey come?" Startled, I stopped and looked at him.

"Whisper and the others went to get them. We have a doorway now, a real home. Our sisters and brothers went to gather all of our clan. I told them we would open the doorway on the new moon, that's only a few days away my lady. You cannot leave," his voice was irritating me…somewhere between pleading, whining and ordering. He had a lot to learn about teenage girls.

"That's your problem, Laven. I didn't tell them to do that, you did. I didn't say your clan had their own doorway now, you did. Just who do you think you are?" It really bothered me that he would take such a leap of action on my behalf, thinking he knew me, knew what I would want just because I was born a Frìth-fey-thing.

I had made my mind up, at least on some things. There was a lot for me to deal with and I didn't know what I was going to do about some of the things…like Laven and Aishal. But I didn't have time now. I didn't answer him and started to walk towards the path that would take me back to Coos Bay. Laven blinked and was now at the path ahead of me. I wasn't sure what he planned on doing, but it slowed my walk as I considered all the possibilities.

If he had indeed sent the girls out to gather the Frìth clan and others, they might be assembling right now on the other side of the doorway. I felt bad that Laven would be stuck here alone, but he had done it to himself. He made the decision to call other fey to the area on the assumption that I would want him to. Well he was wrong; I didn't know what I wanted except to leave right now. And he was blocking my way. He might not be able to come into my private glade, but he still had the run of the forest and I didn't trust him. I had no idea what he could do; maybe he *could* let a bunch of fey in.

I decided to try something; he wasn't going to like it if it worked. That little bit of fire on my tongue was still playing there and I rolled it around, and then put it in my words. "Laven, go to your safe place in the forest and sleep peacefully until I return and call for you." I yelled out at him, feeling the fire loosen as I spoke. As I finished speaking, he vanished from my sight with an almost comical look of surprise.

"Cool," I exclaimed. It worked…it had really worked. This fey thing was growing on me. Then I had to roll my eyes at myself and reach up and touch the vines. Funny...fey growing on me...I was a hoot. Since that had seemed to work so well, I might as well go for the gusto and try something else.

"Lock this glade and my cabin and the doorway from anyone but me," I yelled, using the little fire. I wasn't going to take any chances. I didn't know enough about the demons to know if they could circumvent Granddad's magic or if they had his talisman, or if something else did. No one was going to get their slimy hands on the Sumair stone or step foot in my glade or home unless I wanted them there.

I was looking forward to going back, for a short trip at least. A big juicy hamburger was screaming at me and I was going to find it as soon as I hit town. Maybe I'd go see Margo before I left and maybe she'd let me take a shower at her place. I had my game plan: food, see Margo, clean up and then blink back to the place and person I had been running from.

I really needed to get ahold of Uncle Geraint also, who handled the trust, but that would have to wait. He had to know more than he'd told me. Then I remembered that I had told him where he could contact me, maybe I should pop into the post office also and see if he had sent me anything.

My feet were almost skipping as I starting walking. I was going back, and I was happy about it. That really blew my mind.

CHAPTER 24 - Skyler

Skyler made her way up the highway. It was a cold walk; her feet were wet, her hair damp and wild in the wind. The last ride had dropped her off just inside the border of Oregon. She'd been walking ever since. Brookings was a memory now, lost in the fog behind her. Her arm ached from holding it with her thumb out. People in California seemed more apt to pick up a hitchhiker; Oregonians just zoomed by without even seeming to notice the lone figure hobbling on the side of the road. She tried to use her *special* trick of blurring herself whenever a car came close, but still she was having no luck. It had always worked before. No matter how horrible she looked or felt, she only had to think of herself as beautiful and that's what people saw.

The sores were back. They hurt and she had begun to remember things. Too many things. And she was missing her daddy. Daddy always made it better. She couldn't remember how...it was there, the memory, just out of her grasp. But he had always somehow achieved it, in spite of her fighting him. She knew she had been difficult, but she had to stop it, had to stop the voices and the strange creatures that were always gathering around her.

Daddy had tried to take her back, she remembered that, and the creatures had taunted her, telling her they would leave her alone if she gave them what they wanted. It was hard pulling herself together, but she did and Daddy thought she was better and left her alone. The rest she remembered as a dream, cutting the talisman out and hiding it in the little wooden box Daddy had made for her. Even with her mind all twisted up, she knew the creatures shouldn't have it, but hoped that if she didn't have it on her person, they would leave her alone. She was so scared that Daddy would find out and be mad at her.

But she didn't need to be scared of him; it was the *things* that scared the shit out of her. It didn't get better though. The things came more often and they were more gruesome each time. So she told them if they would just leave her alone, she would give them something else. They wanted the magic and she didn't know how to give them that. Finally Mommy had convinced her to go shopping though she hadn't wanted to leave the house. She remembered telling Mommy to wait for her in a small store. She had left Mommy there where all the creatures had congregated. Mommy hadn't even tried to get away from them, almost going willingly and they had accepted the old woman with glee, sucking up what little magic she bore and taking her away.

But the demons hadn't kept their promise to leave her alone and Daddy had been mad at her. He had found her, given her to the Uncles, left without a word and the creatures still came to torment her.

They were with her now, laughing, telling her to walk faster, to speed up. She couldn't… her feet hurt and she felt sick to her stomach. The hole that she had dug in her side had opened back up and was oozing pus. She wanted to stop, to give up…but they wouldn't let her.

They spoke of what they had done to her parents and thanked her for the meal. It was depraved and revolting and they told her she was next if she didn't keep moving. As she got closer, she could feel the forest calling to her, a tiny bit of power started to grow outside of the energy the Eilibear were feeding her. She had to get there...it would all be better when she got there. At first she just wanted to find the creature called Ivy. Mommy and Daddy had been passing it off as her child. They said they had no choice; that was the only explanation they could think of to use. It disgusted her, always happy, always right, always small. When it had finally started to grow and look like a child, she had thought her parents would give it back.

The other things wanted it. She would have given Ivy back, she still could and that's what she planned on doing. If she gave the weird girl to the *things*, they would give her Mommy and Daddy in return. They said so. Be rid of that thing forever and have the nightmare end.

She hadn't even noticed Ivy was gone for at least a couple of days. When the haze had cleared from her mind and the pain came back, she started looking for the little creature. The house was beyond dirty; it smelled bad…trash, soiled clothes and clutter covered every inch of the floor, counter tops and furniture. Someone had been sick in the corner of the front room and a fine green slime had begun to grow on the top of it, adding to the rotten smell of the place. She made her way to the bathroom, only to discover someone had been sick in there also, and in addition, had missed the toilet multiple times.

The smell made her gag and she realized that she had made the mess. She started screaming for the creature, first angrily calling out foul names and then switching to yelling out pitifully for Ivy to come help her. In desperation, she moved from room to room, hunting for where the thing had hidden. She was always doing that...hiding. It always seemed to be when she needed her the most.

When it finally dawned on her addled mind that she was alone, the panic set in. She couldn't be alone...without the drugs...that's when the things came. Dark horrible images that entered her mind and she did not want to see them again.

Thinking about the horrible creatures made those images creep into her subconscious. She closed her eyes and tried to focus her mind on Daddy and any happy memories she could dredge up…and that made her think of the forest. It didn't take more than a moment before she could *see* the forest, smell the deep lush aroma of earth and hemlock trees. The image of the large swaying willow came to her mind and the memory turned sinister. She bit her lip so hard that she drew blood and opened her eyes with a renewed hatred for the thing that lived with them. She hurried down the hall to *its* bedroom door, tried to open it only to discover it locked.

No amount of pounding on it or kicking it would open it. Her head and heart were throbbing; she had felt faint and leaned against the door, slowly sinking down by it. That's when the large looming Eilibear had appeared and pulled her up. Told her she had to go to the forest, go now. She tried to fight it, but it hurt so badly.

Everywhere she looked, the demons were jeering and ridiculing her. They came out of the walls and up through the floor. They crawled towards her like slugs or jumped from the backs of chairs, calling her name, telling her what they did to her mommy and daddy.

Her ear-piercing screams must have been heard in the quiet neighborhood. She ran screaming from the house and down the road. Nothing stopped her; she ran until her feet had worn though the slippers she had on. Her feet were bloodied, but she continued to run. Every time she tried to stop, they would come and force something vile into her mouth and whatever it was allowed her to continue.

She had slid on gravel and had fallen and had lain there sobbing uncontrollably until a motorist stopped. The Eilibear gave her power and she was able to blur herself enough to look normal. The large tattooed man had taken her to the nearest truck stop. Frantic to get to the forest and rid herself of these things, she had made herself suck it up and focus.

That was the trick, focusing. She had to tell herself she was okay, tell herself she could do it, be who she wanted to be so that normal people wouldn't shrink away from her. It was hard, but she was able to clear her mind and blur herself enough to beg a ride to Highway 101. She knew where the creature was and she knew how to get there. The forest was their only other real home now that Daddy had sold all the other houses.

He had tried to tell her about it, what he was doing, what Mommy wanted. She didn't want to hear it and had run from it into the dark recesses of her mind. There she remained until the demons had finally been able to break through to her and start telling her what her life would be like if she would just give them the magic.

If only Daddy hadn't followed after the things that had taken Mommy. The voices said it could still be okay, but it was a farce. She had gotten away from the Uncle. She hated the Uncles as much as the little creature she had to share a home with. She knew what they were; they were just like the thing Ivy and it appalled her that Daddy would just give her to them. She had given the Uncle to the demons also and found her way home. She had thought she was finally free of the thing that Mommy and Daddy liked so much, but it turned out to be another piece of the same disgusting reality when another of the Uncles showed up.

She had hid when Ivy had let the Uncle into their home. She heard what he had told the thing; that everything had been left in trust for *it*. All the checks came made out to Ivy and the thing had to sign them or she wouldn't get a cent of it. Nothing she said or did could change what Daddy had forced onto her. She felt betrayed by Daddy. He was supposed to take care of her, not just turn his back on her.

Luckily there were the drugs and someone always willing to provide them if she had the money. All she had to do was keep Ivy around to sign over the checks and she was good to go. It had worked well for her, escaping into the drug induced haze, even if she had to see and hear Ivy every day. That's how the last year had been…without a rationale thought or goal she had just found a way to stay alive and mute out the voices and stop the pain.

And she was going to find Ivy again, this time with a clear mind. She had a well-defined purpose. She would find that creature that had ruined their lives and give *it* back to the others. Then they would give Mommy and Daddy back to her and leave her alone. This was the only thought she had as she lumbered up the foggy highway, getting closer to Coos Bay with every step.

CHAPTER 25 - Zack

The small coastal town was even busier than when Zack had left. People crowded the sidewalks and covered the beach with towels and umbrellas to keep out the hot sun. The sounds of the surf mingled pleasantly with the laughter of kids playing on the beach. Zack felt good about coming back. He liked hiking, but finally felt more relaxed than he had since he'd first met the purple-haired girl.

When he reached the store, he could see it was doing good business and the blonde girl and another older lady were bustling around, trying to take care of all their customers. He picked up a late lunch and found a seat across the road on the beach walk and waited. He didn't mind lounging in the sunshine and watching the people passing by. The sun was starting to set when the store finally started to empty. He watched as the girl and woman brought racks and benches in from the front of the store before he got up and went over.

The bell over the door chimed as he opened it and the girl looked up expectantly as he walked in.

"Hi, can I help you? We're about to close up, but if you know what you are looking for, maybe we can find it for you," she said, a tight, tired smile on her face.

"Well, I'm not sure if you can help or not. I'm not looking for something, but someone," Zack responded, not quite sure how to proceed now that he was here. He didn't want to come off like a stalker. He didn't even know *hey you's* real name.

"If you've lost your friends, there's a police station just

down the road a ways. They have a beach patrol that might be able to help," she said as she gave him an appraising look.

Zack knew he didn't usually make a good impression on adults. His wild dreadlocks and clothing choices always put people off. This girl was looking him up and down like she was trying to figure out everything about him. The odd thing was, it didn't make him apprehensive. In fact, just being with her made him feel rather calm.

"No, I don't think they can help. This is kind of embarrassing, but I met a girl a few days ago and I'd like to find her again. I saw you two talking and thought maybe you might know her." He felt rather foolish, as he said it. It sounded dumb now that he had spoken it out loud.

"Okay, well I've talked to a lot of people today," she countered, "What does she look like?"

"It was over a week ago. I don't think you'd forget her. She was small and had red and purple hair and..."

"Ivy!" She exclaimed with a huge grin. "I've been looking for her, too. She said she was coming back and I've been hoping she would."

Zack wondered why he had been worried that the girl wouldn't remember her…she was hard to forget. "Ivy. Her name is Ivy," he mused out loud to himself. Then looking back at her, he laughed at himself. "Sorry, she wouldn't tell me her name. I've been calling her *hey you* for days now."

"Boy that does kind of sound like something she'd do. I'd only just met her, but there was something rather mysterious about her, you know? I'm Margo, by the way," the cute blonde said as she reached out her hand.

"Zack," he said, shaking her hand. "I felt the same way. It was like she had a secret or was hiding."

"Yeah, I know what you mean. All I found out was that she was staying with friends up in a cabin somewhere and they didn't have a phone," Margo said.

"Did she say where the cabin was by any chance? I'd really like to find her. And this is going to sound really odd...don't take it wrong...but I followed her and then lost her," he admitted sheepishly.

"Really? Followed her from where?" Margo asked and then paused. Footsteps could be heard coming from the back of the shop and Margo turned to look as the old lady Zack had seen earlier came out from behind an antique armoire.

"Hi, can I help you?" she inquired.

Margo didn't give him the chance to reply as she took his arm and pulled him over to the door.

"Uh no Grandma, this is Zack. He's a friend of that girl I told you about, remember? Ivy, the girl staying with friends. Do you mind if I cut out early and have my dinner with him?" She picked up a large multi-colored bag and pushed Zack out the door in front of her. Standing with one foot still inside, she looked hopefully back at her grandma.

Grandma Winnie was looking intently at Zack. She even reached out her arm like she was feeling the air around him, before she answered. "Okay dear. Go have fun; I'm sure you will be safe with this young man." She tilted her head as she continued to inspect him. Margo grinned and waved at her through the front window as she pulled a confused Zack down the sidewalk with her.

Once they had walked past a few of the other closing shops, he finally spoke.

"You just lied to your grandma you know, about Ivy and I being friends. I really just met her," he said clearly uncomfortable.

She waved his worries away. "It wasn't really a lie. I just met her too and I consider her a friend. It's like I've known her a long time…kinda strange for me too."

Stopping at the corner, she pointed at a little coffee shop and looked at him questioning. He nodded and they walked over to it. Once inside, they ordered coffee and he got the largest burger they had on the menu. After the waitress had taken their orders and left, she leaned forwards on the table and whispered, "So you followed her? From where?"

"I came here with a group that was going hiking up to the Hazelin camp, you know, from the trail head by the river." She nodded that she knew the place. "Well our group was staying at that motel near it, and she was staying there too. I watched her go and buy that wagon and fill it with camping stuff, and then food, and then she came to your store. I thought maybe you guys knew each other." Margo shook her head no. "Well I thought she was really interesting, she wouldn't talk to me and she was doing these really strange things. Buying so much stuff all by herself, no car or friends…it was odd. I thought maybe she had signed up late for our group and just didn't know anything about camping or hiking. Then early the next morning…and I mean really early, before the sun was up, I heard something outside the motel."

"What?" she asked captivated by his story so far.

"At first I didn't know. It was foggy, but then I saw her on the bridge. It was Ivy, pulling that wagon filled so high with stuff that she could barely move it. You should have seen her; she was straining and yanking on the thing to pull it across the bridge. I ran and tried to catch up, but this car was coming towards me, and the lights blinded me for a minute. By the time I got to the other side, she was gone."

The waitress came with their order and both Zack and Margo fell silent.

"Gone where?" Margo asked after the waitress was out of ear-shot.

"I don't know. I found prints from the wagon in the dirt going up the hill on the other side. Then they were gone," he responded as he took a bite of his hamburger.

"But there's nothing on the other side. It's just

blackberry bushes and a steep hill."

"I know…but that's where the tracks went. I looked all over, up and down the road and she wasn't anywhere."

"Could someone have been waiting in a car for her? Maybe she left with someone."

He hadn't thought of that. But there had been no sounds of a vehicle, it would have echoed in the fog. He shook his head and he tightened his lips as he thought about it.

"No," he finally decided. "I think I would have heard it. I asked around our group and even called the camp organizers. No one knew anything about this girl. In fact, you know how I said she stayed at our motel?"

"Yeah?"

"Well I found out that she didn't even register. The lady said she acted like she was with us, so she just gave her a private room when she asked for one without taking her name or anything. Wait..." he said looking up at her hopefully. "Do you know her last name? Maybe we could search for her that way."

Margo shook her head no.

"But I did grow up here. I know all the trails and stuff. Why don't you show me where it was, and maybe I can guess where she was headed. My car is parked in the back parking lot."

"You sure?"

"You're kidding right? This has to be the most interesting thing that's happened in years. It's a real mystery, exciting you know? I want to help you figure this out," Margo said, her eyes glistening with excitement.

They sat there discussing all the possibilities, but none seemed reasonable. Zack paid the bill when they had finished eating and the two walked between the stores to the private parking area in the back to retrieve her car. He had to smile when he saw it.

"I know it's not much, but it's mine and it runs," she said as she unlocked the door of the small green jeep. It had a rag top and looked like it could have been used in a war in some remote country. "It belonged to this old guy who lived on the wharf. He moved east last year and sold it to me for almost nothing. I love it, so don't say anything mean about it." She gave him a look that dared him to try.

"No...really, it's great. I have an old beat-up truck my dad gave me and it's not even running right now. I like yours better," he said quickly. He got in and buckled up as she turned the key and the jeep rattled to life.

She pulled out of the parking space and maneuvered through the lot and onto the main street, heading down toward the bridge. He pointed out the motel as they passed, the jeep making too much noise for talking. As they neared the bridge, she pulled off on the side by the trail-head that he had taken with the group and they both got out.

"Is this the one you guys took?" she asked.

"Yeah, it's the only one I know of on this end. Are there others?"

"There's a couple that lead down to the beach, but they are on the other side and down the road quite a ways," she said as she followed him out onto the bridge and they started across. The river was low, making the bridge seem even higher. They stopped halfway and looked down.

It dawned on him what she must be thinking. "No...She couldn't have fallen. The guardrails would make that almost impossible," he said trying not to think about what a drop like that would do to someone.

"You're probably right, but there's no rail in the trees. Could she have started up the hill and fallen?"

"I hope not and I really don't think it's possible," he answered moving away from the side. That was too horrible a thought and he shivered as he turned and started to walk to the other side where he had found the tracks from the wagon. He stood, looking up at the hillside. It was a dense tangle of trees, blackberry bushes and low scrub bushes. There was nothing up that way.

"That's where I found the tracks," he said pointing at the only spot that was dirt. "They ended by that big tree, there."

Margo could see the tree he meant. It was a fairly big hemlock, but there was no way Ivy could have pulled a heavy, loaded wagon up that hill even to that tree. You'd need both hands just to climb up and the tree was surrounded by thick old growth blackberries. It was a fire hazard waiting to happen, not a place for someone to take a hike in the middle of the night.

"There's no way Zack." Turning she looked at the other side of the road. This section of the highway was on the beginnings of a cliff that lead down to the rocks and ocean. They could hear the surf from here. There were no paths down that way either. It was a sheer drop down with tall trees bent by the wind. If she had gone that way, it would have meant a nasty fall that no one could have survived.

The two spent as much time as they could in the fading light walking the edge, looking down. When the sun's light turned to hazy reds and the fog started to roll in around them, they had to give up.

Making plans to meet up the next morning, Margo dropped him off at the motel and then went home.

Margo was up before her grandma, showered and had pulled her hair up into its familiar twin ponytails. She quickly dressed in her favorite capri jeans, her orange tank top that read *A day without sunshine is like night* and finished off the look with purple knee socks and hiking boots. She spent a considerable amount of time making a large lunch and was almost done when Grandma came into the small kitchenette.

"You're up early, honey. Looks like you are going for a hike. The youth group?" Grandma Winnie asked as she gave her a peck on the cheek.

"No…with Zack. Neither of us have heard from Ivy, so we are going to look for her. I know I have the afternoon shift, but do you think you could call Stacy to see if she could take it?" she asked sweetly and batted her eyelashes at her grandma playfully.

"Well, we are pretty busy," her grandma replied trying hard to keep a stern look on her face. When Margo started to pout, Grandma Winnie rolled her eyes and smiled. "Of course, go have fun and if I don't hear from you by 9 or so, I'm calling Harold at the station."

"Love you Granny, see you tonight." Margo gave her a huge, tight hug, grabbed her pack and almost skipped out the door.

The jeep was cold blooded and gave a few coughs before it finally made noises indicating that it might be alive. It backfired a few times down the street before it settled into its lot in life and behaved for its owner. Margo made one quick stop and then headed for the motel.

Zack was waiting for her in the parking lot. He watched as she waved at him before parking the jeep and then getting out, holding onto two very large streaming cups of coffee.

"Good mornin'!" she chirped as she bounced over to where he stood.

"You look just too awake," he quipped at her and thankfully took the offered cup of java. His eyes felt tired and puffy. He hadn't gotten too much sleep, disturbing dreams of Ivy and the possibilities of what could have happened to her plagued him throughout the long night.

"Stay up all night?" she asked as she adjusted her pack.

"Didn't mean to, but I was poring looking over the maps I had and couldn't find anything. The motel office light was still on so I went to see if they had better ones. The gal had a bunch of maps, some really old ones. I looked them over until about 3," Zack replied, not wanting to admit he couldn't sleep.

"Find anything in them?"

"Maybe. She had two old maps from when the town was first settled as Marshfield. She wouldn't let me take those, but allowed me to use the copy machine. Both looked like they were hand drawn and there was a place where someone had penciled in a heavy wooded area named simply 'the hemlock forest'. The next map she had was dated in the 60's, and the forest wasn't noted on it. So either the first guy had just thought the place was special, or maybe all the trees were cut for lumber," he said between sips of coffee.

"Well it might mean there is a trail there somewhere, or there was at one time. You ready?" she asked holding her pack awkwardly.

"Yep, let's get to it." He heaved his own pack up onto his back and helped her get hers on and together they headed towards the bridge. A light misty haze hung low as they started across. The sounds of the ocean and seagulls wafted around them as they walked silently out onto the bridge. Zack shivered in his heavy sweatshirt as a bird he couldn't identify called out a mournful cry. He felt a bit of panic as they came to the other side, but he couldn't figure out why. It was like an old horror movie, all hazy and lonely and for the first time wondered if they really should be going off alone into the woods.

Zack waited for Margo to catch up when he reached the other side of the road. She stood next to him and looked up the hill. They couldn't even see the tree as the haze had thickened, an intense mist soaking them. It was a gloomy gray sight, and again Zack wondered what in the world he was doing.

CHAPTER 26 - Elsie

June 3, 1972 –

Milton has kept his promise and we have purchased a house in San Diego. It is a nice little home for us, in a quiet neighborhood and I do feel comfortable here. Skyler hates it and wants to go back to San Francisco, she says this is a dull town and is too hot. Ivy likes it here, but she is happy anywhere.

October 1972 –

Just like always the demons have found us, thankfully it took them a bit longer this time. I thought I was ready for them, not having any protection now from my talisman, but I was wrong. It was a nightmare and I wasn't sure I would survive it. I need not have been worried. Little Ivy saw my fear of them and shooed them away. I wished I could have taken a picture of this little dear, with her hand on her hip and wagging a finger at them as she scolded them for bothering me. I was glad that she loves me so that she would protect me. But it did make me wonder why she didn't do the same for Skyler. I asked her and she looked puzzled. When she answered, it floored me. "I tried, but she called them back. She doesn't want me to help." I cried myself to sleep.

Milton has let her veil loosen so she can help me, for a time.

February 1973 –

I have settled into a nice routine in my new home. I get to play the part of a normal grandma, keeping house and baking cookies. I've made some friends around town and joined a knitting club. I do not have to worry about the demons bothering me anymore now even though Milton did take her memories again. She has a routine now where she kisses me on the forehead every morning and says a sweet little prayer for me to be safe from all evil.

I know she had no clue that she is casting a protective spell around me every day and i haven't told Milton as I'm sure he would worry about her being able to do this. He worries enough about what she does to plants and I've had to tell her several times not to make the plants in our yard so happy. The neighbors are wondering how my garden is already producing and I made up a story about special fertilizer.

June 8, 1974

Milton is gone again. He is becoming a very active member in the Order. It is very seldom that I get to go. Taking Skyler anywhere can be taxing and I can't just leave if she has disappeared again. She just comes and goes, and I am resigned to the fact that she will always be in trouble one way or another. It is a weekly event to have to clean up some mess she created, pay some fine or go pick her up at the police station.

August 2, 1974–

The dream came again. I haven't told Milton. It will occur and there is nothing he can do about it. It would just worry him. I will fight against what is to happen, but it will still happen. There is no changing that. I just have to figure out how to help.

CHAPTER 27 - Skyler

Skyler had given up walking when it was so dark she couldn't see any longer. She had spent the night curled up in a bed of ferns, her thin coat her only cover. Her body and mind were so tired from fighting off the demons that constantly kept at her that she was asleep before she even relaxed. It was the best sleep she'd had in days, if not months. Whether it was from exhaustion or nearness to the forest, she didn't know and didn't care.

She had woken to an overcast morning, the air laden with dew. The things seemed to have left her in the night, which made for a quiet time to hurry and go to the bathroom without their vile comments. Her side was throbbing, but even it didn't hurt as bad as it had. She must look a sight. It had been a long time since she'd even cared. She felt good...an odd feeling. Being without any sort of drug or drink was hard. She wanted to forget and they made it easier.

But now that she was almost to the forest, she felt restored, healthier. It was easier to breathe and think and function. Now she remembered. This is what Daddy had done when she had gotten sick; he had forced her to come here. Kicking and screaming and fighting him the entire way. Even when she used her special power to blur herself into a picture of perfect health, Daddy hadn't been fooled and would still hold on tight. It was when she wasn't here that she was tormented by the demons. This was the safe place…why did she always forget that? It felt good to be here, to be this close. There was something else...another memory about the creatures…but her goal to find the one she'd had to live with all these horrible years pushed everything else aside. Making her way back to the road, she continued enjoying the peaceful stillness of the fog.

The air around her seemed to pulsate with life; she could feel something soaking into her, giving her strength, power, clearness. She was close; she could feel the pull on her, making her walk faster towards where the path began.

She came to a turnout on the highway, a place for families to pull off, have lunch and maybe take a walk. There was a picnic table and a water faucet. Someone had left the place a mess, the remains of a meal and all the trash that went with it scattered about. She dug through it and found a couple of napkins that weren't used and wet them beneath the faucet, then she washed her face and hands as best she could. Blurring herself so that others would see a nice version of her was great for others, but it didn't change that she hadn't had a shower in weeks.

Something hit her in the back of the head, and then she heard a high insane giggle. They were back. Turning, she saw the things hopping around like misshapen frogs with bug eyes and ten legs. They were laughing and calling her foul names. For some reason she wasn't scared, they looked outlandish and she saw the foolishness of them. She felt so good, felt herself blurring into her other self.

"Get lost," she said, annoyed with them and waved her hand down the road the way she was going. Instantly the things were gone. She raised her eyebrows in consideration. That was different. She tried to remember if she had ever told them to just leave and couldn't think of even one time. Odd, she thought. She felt outside of herself and it was a strange sensation as she started to walk the road again.

She smelled the coffee before she saw or heard them. Two people were up ahead in the fog; their forms, when she came close enough to see them, were like shadows in the dense haze. They were talking, wearing backpacks and holding delicious smelling cups of coffee. She stayed back, uncertain. They were talking about hiking, looking for a trail, looking for a friend.

The fog cleared a bit and she could see them better and her heart jumped with joy. She knew this type of person, dressed differently, but the hippy crowd none the less. The boy had long wildly twisted hair pulled back in a large tail in back. The girl had crazy little bobs of hair on the top of her head. She wished she had some pot; that always opened friendships. She missed those years, those had been the best.

She watched, mesmerized as the girl took another sip from her coffee and she couldn't stand it.

"Good morning," she called as she started forward, hoping her voice was as merry and clear as it sounded to her own ears. The two saw her and the girl moved closer to the boy, as if seeking protection. She tried hard to stay focused, blurring herself so she would look right. It was hard to hold on to it though as the thirst for that coffee was confusing her mind.

Zack and Margo both jumped at the sound of a voice coming out of the fog. It was a woman, about 30 or so. She looked like a bag lady, Zack thought, without the grocery cart of junk. She was dirty and her face looked like someone had used it for a punching bag. Her lip was split, puffy with dried blood. The amazing thing was she was almost glowing in the fog, her eyes so bright they looked like flashlight beams. She didn't look dangerous but disturbing, all alone just walking along, and her voice...it was too chipper for the way she looked…off somehow. Zack moved a step closer to Margo, neither of them finding their voices for a moment.

"Nice day for a walk," the woman announced in a bright sing-song voice.

Zack composed himself, taking in the weird stranger's appearance with caution. "Good morning. Out for a walk yourself?" he asked hesitantly. The woman smiled and her yellow, blackened teeth flashed at him for a moment before turning pearly white. Zack stepped protectively in front of Margo.

"Sure am. I'm looking for someone," she said, eyeing his coffee.

"That so? Maybe we've seen them. Who are you looking for?" he asked, noticing she never took her eyes from the cup in his hand.

"The cret..." she started, and then stopped. "A girl...my...daughter," she stammered. "I've somehow lost her. Do you mind if I have a drink of your coffee?"

Zack didn't know what to say. The woman in front of him was switching back and forth from a beautiful woman to an ugly hag. His body had started to shake and for some reason his arm had grown weak. He looked down at the coffee in his hand and wondered if somehow he had been drugged.

Aishal didn't think he was going to be allowed though the doorway. The Sequoia fey said he had an odor of darkness about him and they were already having problems with a traveling band of Eilibear. But since the Eilibear had finally moved on and Aishal had a pass, they allowed it. He worked hard at keeping his wits and temper in check as he had to grovel before forest fey. They were a gentle folk, tall and thin, swaying as they moved like trees in a soft breeze. He felt a pang of jealousy at the tranquility of their lives. Their Meadhan was bursting with the bouquet of magic…it almost overwhelmed him. It had been a long space of time since he had felt renewed. He breathed the magic in gratefully, as it was free for the taking, and was soon ready to go on the hunt for the shifted one.

Once he left the Meadhan and entered Alainn, the trail the Eilibear had left behind was easy to find. Their pungent stench was unmistakable; it reeked of death and decay. They were on the move, fast and filled with the balm of magic they were gleaning from the one they followed. The demon's presence in the area was disrupting the balance and he had seen mortals who had been affected by it all along the route. There were multiple car wreaks and the sound of sirens seemed common placed. The mortals he saw were agitated and fighting with each other and the air was filled with tension. He took all that as a good sign, not caring about the mortals that might be hurt.

The Eilibear were traveling swiftly up the coastline towards the forest. At first it was just their odor he could track, and then a more tangy smell came to him, like a mixture of spices and hemlock. It could only be the shifted one. It had a bit of fey in it, like a recipe gone wrong. He blinked his way up the coast, as far as he dared to push his newly revitalized powers. Then he would search until he found the smell again and blink on.

He overtook some of the slower Eilibear as night was drawing on. The things were little more than shadows to him, shades of mist. He used a bit more of his store of magic and cloaked himself. Never before had he been so close to Eilibear and it scared him. But he didn't need to worry; the things were intent on following the shifted one and didn't notice him at all. He was able to hear them as they called out to her and it was disturbing even to him.

Aishal was glad for the trouble the demons were giving the one they followed. As they trailed after her, they left a stream of their foulness that was easy to find. He was able to blink, search, blink and search, making his travel quick and precise. At last he caught up. He could see her, smell her, feel her pulse of power. The area was filled with fog rolling in from the ocean, the forest closed in tight to the road save for a bare spot for cars to pull off. There was a table and a water faucet where the figure was kneeling.

As he crept closer, he saw she was washing herself in the cold water. When she stood and turned, he saw her for the first time ever. A young woman with long golden hair. She would have been considered beautiful even in the fey realm. Then the vision blurred and for a split second he saw what he had expected to see. A hag...with cuts and bruises on her face, her arms covered in oozing sores. Then she blurred again. Her skin glowed with power in the fog and he was taken aback by it…he'd never known a shifted one who radiated with that much enchantment. Around him he could see the demons closing in on her, doing their very best to torture her. Their calls were taunting as they whipped banes of distress and anguish at her. He expected her to fold, become weak and thereby an easy target for him.

Taking a step forward, he was about to bind her with a quick glamour when she did the unexpected. Standing straight she coolly waved her hand out towards the demons, and him, and declared "Get lost."

He was literally blown away from her. The force was so great that he watched in shock as the threads of space whirled past him and he found himself standing on a lonely beach with the water lapping at his feet. Dazed, he moved from the water and stood, trying to compose himself. His magic had been suffocated; he was stifled, barren of power as he threw a temper tantrum with no one there to see.

It was useless and there was nothing he could do about it. A fey without magic was a pathetic sight; he had never been this hopeless, this low. He had to walk and keep walking. It was cold, he felt it and his anger mounted at the one who had done this to him. When he reached a road he had to decide which direction to go in. He had no idea where he was, but the air smelled of hemlock, telling him that he was close to Marshfield.

A car passed him and the wind it created pushed him away from the side, but he made the decision, the right one, to go in the same direction as it. After the third car passed, he began to feel a glimmer of power tingle in his fingers. He allowed it to build until he could snap a glamour of clothes on himself. Blue jeans and a wool cardigan sweater with pure white loafers displaced his normal forest garb and he was instantly warmer and more at ease.

As the traffic increased, he found himself marveling at the mortals and the advancements in Alainn. They might be disadvantaged without magic, but the wonders they had created impressed even him. He still thought blinking was a more efficient means of travel, but found himself wondering what being in a car would be like. Firinn always remained the same…year in, year out. Sometimes magic would grow in a different way, but overall it remained as it always had.

For the first time he started to understand why so many found Meadhans and Alainn more appealing than Firinn and he wondered what it must be like to be an Alltha. To live out here all the time, never going back to Firinn... never allowed to go back. The Druids seemed to be okay with it; they were the first to choose to use their magic to help the mortals. But look where that got them. Some mighty warriors they were, almost killed off by the same beings they were trying to help.

The ground under his feet changed from dirt to gravel and he spotted a sign that said *Welcome to Coos Bay*. In the years since he had last traveled here, they had changed the town's name. And although he knew that they had, it still affronted him that the mortals would do that. The fey would never even have thought to do such a thing; once something was given a name, it was that name forever. That the mortals could do something as simple as changing a name of a town was offensive.

Grumbling to himself he kept walking and it wasn't long before he was in the town; it had grown and matured over the years. Clean smooth sidewalks made the path in front of the stores a rather pleasant walk, though he was anything but pleased. His power was building…he could feel it. Soon he'd be able to blink to where the shifted one had been and continue following her. He had lost track of time and hoped that she had not reached the path into the forest yet.

His mind worked out how he was going to get her to take him into the Meadhan forest as he walked and he almost missed it. The prickle of magic. At first he was confused, thinking it was his own, and then realized it was something different. Standing still, he closed his eyes and felt for it. There it was, behind him.

Enticed, he turned around and looked for it. The sidewalk was empty and the stores still closed. No mortals, neither fey nor demon were near. It was something other than a being. He started to move slowly, searching, and ended up in front of a window of an antique store. The window display was full of beautiful furniture, mixed with baubles and cheap trinkets. The magic was coming from inside that store.

Looking around to make sure no one was about, he used what power he had to blink. He found himself standing in the dark of the store, the only light, a glow from a glass cabinet near the front counter. Excited, he moved closer. The glow was coming from above the cabinet, from a framed box that held a necklace.

He hunted around for something to stand on and, not seeing anything to use, ended up just jumping onto the counter. The framed box was just within his reach. With one hand he used the glass cabinet to balance himself and touched the box with his free hand. The magic that shot up his arm into his being was unexpected and he lost his balance, falling, taking the glass cabinet with him. As the cabinet hit the floor the glass doors shattered and the contents from inside the case scattered around him. Pulling himself out from the wreckage, he scrambled back up onto the counter to look closer at the necklace. There was nothing special about the necklace itself, just some twisted vines, but hanging from it was a small hemlock heart. The heart glowed with power and he yelped with surprise.

There in front of him was a talisman. One of the Woodsman's talismans. How it got here, he didn't know and didn't care. Making a fist he slammed his hand into the glass of the frame and reached inside the box to take hold of the necklace. As he made contact with it, he almost choked, drowning in the deluge of energy that ripped into him. It engulfed him and his body went rigid from the intensity of it, the overflow radiated out from his pores, a hot white light of power. When it finally settled into him, he was weeping and gagging, then he started to laugh. He had it, the forest's power, or maybe the Sumair stone's, he wasn't sure which…but never had he felt this way.

He knew instantly what this meant. He didn't need the shifted one to enter into the Meadhan. It was his now. They could take the forest back. He slipped the necklace over his head and let it fall against his sweater. When he looked up, a car screeched to a stop in front of the window, bright blue and red lights flashed on its roof making the fog outside glow. In a panic, he realized that the mortal who owned the shop must have somehow known he was there.

Calming himself, he watched as the blue-clad men jumped out of the vehicle, started yelling and pointing little sticks at him. Aishal smiled, then blinked...and was gone.

CHAPTER 28 - Ivy

After I had walked only a short ways, I stopped and almost slugged myself. I could blink! Why in the world had it not dawned on me? Well maybe because this *new* little trick of mine took some time to get used to. I felt stupid for not thinking of it sooner and blinked down to the first thing I thought of, the start of the rock part of the path.

Maybe I should have thought of Granddad's tree with the marker on it, but I didn't. I wasn't sure if it would work outside the veil, but I had just shaved hours off of my trip. Rather proud of myself, I thought of the big hamburger just waiting for me at McDonalds and smiled to myself as I knew where I was going to try to blink next. I closed my eyes and opened them to a large green trash bin at the back side of McD's.

It was mid-morning, the sun was shining, and a breeze was blowing in from the ocean. The air was filled with yummy smells coming from the restaurant. I didn't care what I looked like. The blinking thing worked and I was hungry. I dug out a couple of bills and walked around the building until I came to the side door. The place wasn't too full. I went in and headed first to the bathroom. I caught a view of myself in the mirror as I went into one of the stalls and noticed that my new little plant life was now just green lines on my face. Cool, I thought, realizing I hadn't given any thought to what people would say about vines growing on me.

After I used the toilet, which was a wonderful change from the outhouse, I washed up the best I could and went to stand in line. Everything on the menu looked good to me and when it was my turn, I ordered a huge bag full of food and an iced mocha. There was no way I was going to sit down inside with all the people so I took my bag outside and sat on the curb devouring a couple of hamburgers in no time flat.

I pulled the large order of fries out of the bag, then put the bag with the rest of the hamburgers in my backpack, put it on, grabbed my mocha and started off to Margo's shop, munching the fries on the way. As I got close to the sidewalk with all the shops, I noticed a commotion up ahead. A police car was parked in front of the antique shop and an older woman, who could only have been Margo's grandma, was standing on the sidewalk talking frantically with the officers.

I slowed my pace and got as close as I could without drawing attention to myself. The officer's voices were calm and sounded patronizing to me.

"Winnie, you need to file a report. Someone broke into your shop and made a hell of a mess. Whoever it was had to have taken something," he was saying, but Margo's grandma cut him off.

"Nothing was taken, how many times do I have to say it? The cabinet was old and a leg must have broken and it fell over," she said, obviously frustrated with the man.

"Okay Winnie. I don't believe it for a moment, but if that's how you want to spin this, I'll leave it alone," the officer said as he closed his note pad and motioned for his partner to follow.

Grandma Winnie watched silently as the officers got back in their squad car and waited until they pulled away from the curb before she went back inside. There was a small crowd off to the side and I went and stood next to a pimply faced kid.

"Hey, what's going on here?" I asked him.

"Someone broke into the old lady's shop this morning.

Broke a glass case, then disappeared," the kid answered, excited that he had someone to tell.

"You mean they didn't catch him?"

"No, I heard the officers say they saw him and everything, standing right there inside." He pointed inside the shop. "But one second he was there, and then he wasn't. They had to wait for the lady to come unlock the door before they could go in and look around. And get this, all the doors were still locked and the guy was gone. Like he did a vanishing act."

Another couple of people had come up and were listening to the kid also, asking questions and the kid kept talking about the guy that had vanished...I moved away in slow motion. I had almost choked on my fries...someone vanished...like blinked out? No, it was impossible. Why would a fey be in Margo's shop?

Oh crap! I dropped my fries and what was left of my mocha and just stared at the front of the shop. The necklace. It *had* been one of the necklaces that Granddad had made…and it wasn't just a necklace, it was the lost talisman. Could I be any more stupid? Why hadn't I known that's what it was when I first saw it? And now someone had it, someone that had blinked out. It had to be a fey...or an Eilibear thing maybe. I didn't know enough about how all this Eilibear business worked. Could they have found it and be on the way into my forest now. I felt on the verge of a complete melt down. Could my life get any more bizarre?

"Ivy," a voice whispered urgently from behind me.

Yes. Yes it could. I knew that voice. I'd even had a few pleasant dreams about the voice and the face that went along with it. Turning, I found myself looking straight at Zack. He didn't look very happy.

"Hi Zack." I looked around us at all the other people on the sidewalk, confused. What was he still doing here? Wasn't he supposed to be hiking, and how did he find out my name? "Uh, what are you doing here?"

"We need to talk," he replied, and I felt a stir of uneasiness in the area around us. That was new. I didn't remember ever being able to feel emotions in the air.

"Uh, sure, but I was going to find my friend. That's her grandmother's shop and it looks like something happened there. I need to check to see if she's okay," I hedged as I backed away from him.

"She's not," he answered nervously.

"Who's not what?" I said, still moving away.

"Margo, your friend. She's not okay...and it's my fault and we really need to talk," he said as he looked around anxiously.

I stopped my backwards motion. Zack looked pale, frightened, and totally freaked out. In the last few weeks I'd come to know that look; I'd seen and felt it a lot on my own face. I quickly put two and two together. The talisman had been stolen from Margo's store and here was Zack telling me something was wrong. I had to overlook the fact that I had absolutely no clue why or how he was involved in all this, but he was.

"Okay, where?" I asked, looking around us. The sidewalk was packed with people, and if he was going to talk about anything close to what I guessed he might want to talk about, I didn't want it out here in the open.

He pointed down the street at an old rusty jeep. "It's Margo's." He took me by the arm, rather roughly I should add, and forced me to walk with him towards it. He relaxed his hold when he realized that I wasn't going to bolt on him and we ended up at the jeep with him opening the passenger side door for me. The thing had a soft top and even the door was little more than canvas on a frame with an odd smoky plastic window with a zipper. Yep this had to be Margo's; I could just see her in it. I sat stiffly as Zack came around the other side and got in. He didn't say anything as he turned the key and the beast roared to life.

He wasted no time pulling out, whipping a U-turn in the road and heading back the way I had just come. The noise from the jeep drowned out everything else and it gave me time to think. This didn't help much, since I was only thinking of questions.

I wasn't the least surprised when he pulled into the parking lot of the motel I had stayed in and cut the engine in front of the last room. My old room, it turned out, but I didn't think he needed to know that information. Without saying anything, he got out and went to the room door and unlocked it, only then looking back at me to see if I was coming. I hesitated for a moment before I got out and followed him into the room. He lost no time closing and locking the door behind me.

"So, what's all this about? Where's Margo?" I asked looking around and deciding to sit on the edge of the bed. He took one of the old chairs and sat facing me with his head down as if he was about to lose it or start crying.

"I don't know," was his curt answer. He looked up at me with those fascinating almond-shaped, green eyes, worry written all over his face.

"Why do you have her jeep?"

"Because when she vanished, I didn't know what to do. I hunted for her for an hour, then gave up and decided to come find her grandma. I had the keys so it seemed the fastest way. When I got there, I saw the police and panicked, thinking something horrible had happened and the police had found her. But it turned out to be a break-in and then you were there," he said in a rush. He had stood up partway through his explanation and was now frantically pacing up and down at the end of the bed, wringing his hands.

"Whoa, start from the beginning. Where were you when she vanished?" I asked, wondering how this could be connected to me.

He stopped and faced me, his eyes focused intensely on

mine. "We were looking for you. Yesterday we had searched all the areas around where I last saw you, but it got dark. So this morning we got ready to tackle the hill with the blackberries, where I found your tire tracks. We were standing there in the fog when this weird lady showed up. She looked like a bag lady you see in the movies. There was a smell that came out of the fog with her, like raw sewage. It was revolting." He scrunched up his nose. "But that wasn't the odd thing…she looked bad, but if you moved even an inch you could see a different version of her. It was like there were two of her, like a mirror and one side was disgusting and the other side was breathtakingly beautiful. It was really disconcerting. She kept staring at my coffee, like she couldn't take her eyes off of it. She asked what we were doing and we said we were looking for our friend.

"When we asked what she was doing out in the fog, she answered that she was looking for someone too…her daughter. Can you believe it? She was looking for her daughter on the side of the road, in the fog. And the way she said, it was chilling."

I couldn't say anything, not that Zack was giving me a chance. He was talking a mile a minute, and I think I was speechless anyway, so I just let him talk.

"Margo moved behind me and started pulling me backwards with her. She was scared and I guess I was, too. So we started to back away from the lady, and then we turned and started to run. I lost Margo in the fog somewhere on the bridge; I think the lady was running after us. Then I heard Margo's phone go off. She must have stopped; I think she was getting her phone out of her pack when I heard a scream behind me. I turned back and saw the blonde being tackled by some preppy guy. Margo suddenly appeared out of the fog, and rushed the guy, knocking him to the ground. I think she thought she was helping the lady." Zack was breathless from his rant; his eyes had gotten wider as he recalled what had happened.

"What happened then Zack?" I asked softly.

"The lady screamed that she had to find Ivy. The guy yelled back that he knew where she was, and then they all vanished right in front of me. I mean they disappeared right there. One second all three were fighting, and then they were gone." He was yelling now, I think he was in some kind of shock. I knew the feeling.

I closed my eyes, fighting down the panic that was rising in me. One of us had to stay sane and since I thought I knew what was going on, I figured it better be me.

"What did the lady look like when she was pretty?" I asked very softly as I patted the bed next to me. He hesitated, and then sat down hanging his head, but he looked up at me when I spoke.

"She was beautiful. I mean drop-dead gorgeous. Her face was like a porcelain doll, with these huge blue eyes and really long blonde hair like you'd expect to see in a fairytale." He looked at me with pleading eyes. "Ivy, you've got to believe me, I'm not making this stuff up. The blonde lady and that guy took Margo."

"Skyler, her name is Skyler," I told him wretchedly. That was my *mom* alright. One second she was the prettiest thing, and then she was a creature from nightmares. Skyler was here and I didn't have to go looking for her. I really wasn't surprised. She probably knew everything about me and always had…and the forest, and the cabin, she had to have known where I would go. She followed me.

"You know her? She was looking for you. Who is she, *what* is she? What did she do with Margo?" He demanded as he grabbed me so tight it hurt. I yelped out in pain, but he held on tighter. "What's going on?" he screamed at me.

"You're hurting me Zack!" I cried out and pulled away. Luckily he let me go. I stood and looked down at him.

"She's my mom...or was...or people thought she was. That's a long story. What did the guy look like?"

He looked skeptically at me as he answered, "I don't know, it was foggy. Tall, dark curling hair, really pale features like he was made of stone. He looked like he should be in some tight-ass boarding school."

"Aishal," I said more to myself than him. Aishal had to be the one who had broken into the shop and taken the talisman. That meant he could get into the forest, and he must have blinked. I didn't think Skyler could, so it had to be him. He must have taken Skyler and Margo with him. *Crap!* I didn't know how a mortal became a shifted one, but if she was pulled into a Meadhan realm, that could mean he shifted Margo.

"I've got to go," I said as I hurried to the door. Zack grabbed me roughly by the shoulders and pulled me back.

"No! You know something. It's my fault Margo is gone, she might be hurt and it's my fault. I dragged her into this and I need to find her."

"I can do this Zack; you don't need to be involved. It wasn't your fault. Now let me go," I said, struggling against him. But he wouldn't let go this time. He whipped me around so I was facing him, but kept his hands on my shoulders. I realized how much taller he was, and as he looked down at me one of his rough lengths of hair swung and hit me in the face. It smelled good. I'm such an air-head to be thinking that right now. I forced myself to look up into his eyes.

"You're right. It's not my fault, it's yours," he said, his voice dangerously low. He glowered at me.

I yanked myself out of his grip and took a step back. "My fault? What the hell are you talking about? Why were you even looking for me?" I screeched in anger.

"Because you vanished in front of me and I had to look for you," he fired back.

"Wait a minute, just how did I vanish in front of you? Last time I saw you, it was at McDonalds and you were stealing mustard for me." I was so confused. Who was this guy?

"That's the last time you saw me. But I saw you pulling that damn wagon off in the middle of the night. I followed you and then you disappeared on the other side of the bridge."

"You followed me?" I gasped, appalled. This guy had been following me?

"Yeah, I had been since you stepped off the bus. I thought you were cute and different and then you started doing bizarre things. Like buying all that stuff and keeping yourself apart from everyone. I had to know what you were up to."

"Well, aren't you the Sherlock Holmes…who asked you to be my keeper? Who the hell do you think you are?" He thought I was cute.

"You seemed all alone and someone had to watch out for you," he replied, finally calming down and for the first time looking a little discomfited.

"So all this time you've been running around looking for me? Who else did you tell? Did you call the police and put flyers up, too?" I didn't think it really mattered at this point and I was wasting time standing here with him when I should be out looking for Margo.

"No...I went on the hike...with my group. I thought you maybe got confused before you found the trail, or were part of a surprise for our group, like an entertainer. I figured I'd find you up at camp doing something for us. But you weren't there," he said, twisting his mouth in irritation.

"No I wasn't," I snapped.

"You disappeared."

"No I didn't."

"Yes you did," he insisted.

"No…I didn't," I shot right back at him.

"Yes you did. You were there and then you weren't, therefore you disappeared," he argued. "So where did you go?" he demanded, his face rigid.

"To my cabin."

"You have a cabin? Where? How'd you get there?"

"I walked, you moron."

"Oh. Well how was I to know that? You were gone, and it was a mystery and I couldn't get you out of my head, so I came back early to look for you."

"I've been gone for over three weeks. If you came back early, just how long was this camping trip of yours?"

"Uh, it's only been a little over a week, Ivy," he said looking oddly at me.

I knew it had been three weeks. I could account for all the days and it was three weeks.

"No it hasn't, I've been gone…" Then I stopped and thought about that. Marmaw's diaries said they always brought me back so I could grow. I was stuck in some time warp and needed the forest to make me mature. I didn't age in this realm. *Crap*, I thought again as I looked up into his green eyes.

"You were saying?" he asked, relaxing his posture somewhat as he waited for me to gather my thoughts.

"I...oh nothing." What was I going to say? It's not like I could tell him that time worked differently in the Meadhan. Right…that would go over good. "It really doesn't matter how long I've been gone. Why was it so important for you to find me?" I demanded.

"Don't ask me," he said throwing his hands in the air. "I don't really know." He flopped down on the bed. "I'd been traveling all over the world with my dad. He worked for this big company and we were always on the move. I've been to just about every country you can think of, some that you've never heard of and I've never done this before." He sounded exasperated with himself, but it didn't explain anything. "There was just something about you, you smelled good." He sighed and looked over at me. "That doesn't make much sense, I know...but you *were* different. I saw you in the bus station and couldn't wait to talk to you on the bus. You had this thing about you, and you kept putting me off, which made it all that more important that I get to know you. I couldn't get you out of my mind." He saw my look of skepticism and he waved his hand in a gesture of giving up.

"You followed me because I smelled good?" I raised my eyebrows and smirked just a little bit.

"Okay…it sounds dumb even to me. Maybe I was stalking you a little bit, but you made it so fun. You were doing all those crazy things. When I got back, I went and found the one person I'd seen you talking with."

"Margo," I filled in for him, growing serious again.

"Yeah, she was so adorable and bouncy. All manga like, decked out in wild clothes, with that cute little hair thing, and she knew you. She was so excited to have someone else to talk to about you, like you did the same thing to her. We both had to find you." I liked his description of Margo. She was adorable and fun and a friend after only one meeting, and now she was probably shifted and in danger and it was my fault for talking to her in the first place.

"Why did you have to look for me?" I cried at him, frustrated that he had gotten himself involved in my strange life *and* brought Margo into it. "I just wanted to be left alone. It's not like we were friends or anything. I wasn't even nice to you." Okay, that sounded mean even to me. "That didn't come out right…but you know what I mean," I finished a bit lamely.

His face got all serious on me, and for the first time I could really see his features. It was like his hair and bangles always distracted me from seeing *him*. He looked like a rugged manly-man sort of guy, tan, with hard features and thick brows. The dread locks and his almond eyes seemed to overpower everything else about him. I had to admit it; I felt a pull to him also and couldn't explain it. Just like I had felt a pull towards Margo. I had hurt him; I could see the pained look in his eyes.

"You are right, I will concede that point. We aren't friends...but you seemed all alone and, I don't know...I just couldn't stop," he admitted curtly.

I mumbled as I stood and headed for the bathroom. This was outside my experience. No one just instantly cared about me, worried about me. He was making my head hurt. I needed to get to the forest, but if my protections worked, then they couldn't enter the glade, couldn't leave through the doorway. I had time to go to the bathroom.

"Ivy, you seem to know what happened and who those people were, and that lady at least knew you. We need to go now and find her," he demanded fervently. I stopped and looked at him. I felt for him, but I just couldn't tell him anything. I couldn't get him tangled up in this. He got up and came over to me, standing close enough that I could smell him. It wasn't a bad smell. Weird, here I was thinking about how he smelled, when he had done the same with me.

"Whatever you are mixed up in, I don't care. Just tell me where to go to find her," he pleaded with me.

We stood there staring at each other, me trying to figure out what to say, him just waiting for me to say something, anything.

"I need to use the bathroom," I finally announced and started to turn away when my eyes were drawn to his necklaces. Most were just natural cords of different types with pendants of crystals, weird Chinese coins, a shark tooth and other things. One was just a green speckled rock with a hole drilled in it. I looked down at his arms; I couldn't count the number of different types of handmade bracelets that hung over wide leather wristbands set with the same colored stones. All of his rings were silver, they looked old, handmade. I got the same feeling I had when I saw the necklace in Margo's store.

"What are those?" I asked captivated by them.

"These?" he asked holding up his arm. "I picked some up when I was traveling with Dad. When I came back to the states to go to school, Dad started sending new ones to me." He held up one of the necklaces. "This one he got off the coast of Africa, and this one is from Scotland." I reached out and touched the simple rock. My fingers tingled as they made contact with it.

"How about this one?"

"That? Dad told me I found it when I was a toddler and wouldn't let it out of my sight. He finally drilled a hole in it and strung it on a shoelace. I've worn it ever since. Why?"

"No reason. Sorry, need to use the bathroom," I answered, evading his question. The stone had a bit of magic in it. I was new to feeling it, but now that I knew what it was, I had a feeling it was hard *no*t to recognize it. I wondered if Zack even knew. I turned and walked towards the bathroom.

"Ivy, make it fast. We're wasting time."

I looked up at him and forced a smile. "I think we have time for me to go pee," I said as I entered the bathroom and shut the door.

CHAPTER 29 - Ivy

I locked the door behind me and leaned back against it. I just needed time to think. What the hell do I do now? I looked longingly at the shower, but knew I didn't have time. I did some deep breathing and attempted to work through it all. I wanted to just blink out, but couldn't bring myself to do that. That was the easy way out…besides I had to stop running from my problems sometime and maybe I *did* need his help. When I came out Zack was standing by the room door with his pack on and a determined look on his face.

"Look Zack, I appreciate that for some reason you feel responsible, but you aren't. You can't come with me," I said as I started to walk towards him and the door.

Zack's eyes were glued to mine. His face was set and I knew he wasn't going to drop it and let me leave.

"Where were you?" Zack asked again, his face was serious. Nice face. I still wasn't sure what had motivated him to worry about me, but maybe I *was* just a bit peculiar and he knew it, and…what? Liked it?

"If I told you, you wouldn't believe me."

"Try me," he responded.

"I went on the path to the forest, to the cabin where my Granddad and I used to stay."

Without blinking…not the vanishing kind like I do…he continued to stare at me. Then he got up and laid the map on the table. Pointing at it he said, "Show me."

I looked down at his map; it was a really good one. It was easy to see where the river snaked down out of the mountains to the ocean. The town and beaches and camp grounds and all the roads and bridges were laid out very nicely. It looked similar to the one Granddad had shown me when he was trying to make sure I knew how to find Coos Bay. I didn't have to look hard to know the forest wasn't on Zack's map. I don't know why I had never thought to look closer at the map that time with Granddad. I was bored I guess and just followed his finger as he showed me how to get to the town. Maybe if I had paid more attention, I would have discovered it then…and asked questions and got answers that might have made the last few days less of a shock.

I looked back up at him, miserably. "It's not on your map."

"Why not? Is it some secret place your family owns? At least point to the area it's in," he demanded with a slight plea to his voice.

I looked down again at the map. Where I knew the forest to be, the map showed only rugged mountains, impassable ravines, sheer cliffs and all of it was loosely populated with trees. Even the most daring and experienced hiker wouldn't want to go to the areas that were on this map. There were no roads, no hiking trails and it looked desolate.

"No, not like you think. I don't even know if I can show you or if you would even be able to see it if I did." Okay, I knew I had said too much, but his response was totally unexpected.

"Like I haven't been able to see it all this time already?" His voice was slightly irritated as he pushed his dreadlocks back out of his face. "What, it's like some secret garden that only you can see?" he snapped at me sarcastically, and then snickered as if it were a joke.

"Yes," I admitted, dropping my pack in frustration.

"Is that where Margo went? Is this some kind of put-on, are you just making stuff up as you go along?" I didn't like his tone, or the look on his face. He was angry at me and his voice had risen to almost a bellow.

"No, I'm not making it up. I think that's where Aishal took her, although maybe he didn't mean to. He probably only wanted Skyler. I think the fey have been after her for a long time and he finally got his hands on her and Margo just got in the way," I yelled back at him.

"What's a fey?" he asked, "Are they a gang? What are you mixed up in?"

I had to laugh; the thought of anyone ever mistaking Laven for being part of a gang was just too funny. Zack grabbed my shoulder. "Stop that! This isn't funny. Don't you care that Margo is missing?"

I pushed his hand away and glared at him. I had to work at keeping my temper under control; I could feel the little ball of fire on my tongue and didn't want to let it loose here. When I finally could speak, it was between clenched teeth.

"Yes I care. I think I know where she is, and I don't think she's in any danger like you are thinking. The danger is in where she is, what the forest might do to her. I don't know really how a mortal can shift, but if she does, it will change her forever and if she comes back here, her life will be hell! You can't go there, or it might happen to you too. I've got to go and find her before Aishal figures out a way to open the doorway. And who knows what Skyler is up to. She's nuts most of the time 'cause the demons won't leave her alone. For all I know, she let the Eilibear in and now I have to deal with them too." I knew I'd said too much. The look on his face told me he thought I was insane.

Then he started to laugh, and it wasn't a nice laugh. I felt my face getting warm and was sure it was a glowing beet red...I really hated being ridiculed. I might as well go the full distance.

"Zack, you just don't get it. We are not talking about normal stuff; I wouldn't even have believed it a few weeks ago. I just found out myself, it was kept from me. But there's more going on than you can even imagine."

"Tell me," he ordered.

"You really want to know? Do you? Fine, I'll tell you. There's these fey running around in the fey realm gathering up all the Frìth they can find, their leader Laven is sleeping at my command in the forest and chances are he is going to be pissed at me when I wake him up. Aishal hates me. He and all the other fey want the doorway back. Someone called Shivf is hanging out in the fey realm, wanting to get his hands on the Sumair stone and kill the tree, Willow. I thought Skyler was my mom, and she turns out to be a shifted mortal, the daughter of the people who found me in the forest and raised me. I think I'm called an Alltha. She hates my guts, and you have no idea what life has been like with her, since Granddad and Marmaw died. I have plants that grow on my face, I've lost most of my memories, discovered there's something called Eilibear, that are kind of demons, that can suck magic out of anyone who is shifted. I've got to figure out what to do with the Sumair stone, and Willow, and the doorway, and now Aishal must have gotten his hands on a talisman, blinked out with Margo and Skyler, and I don't know what the hell to do!" I threw up my hands in surrender. "There, now you know!" I grabbed my pack and started towards the door again.

Zack jumped in front of me, blocking my way. "You can make up all the outrageous stories you want, but I'm coming with you. I'm not letting you out of my sight again, and it is my fault Margo got involved. Nothing you can do or say will change my mind," he declared through tight lips. He crossed his arms and stood there, daring me to try to get past him.

I still could just blink out, that would show him. But then I really would be disappearing in front of him…on purpose. No matter what a pain he was being, I couldn't do that.

"You might be hurt…bad…forever. Is that a chance you are willing to take?" I asked him.

"And you won't? Look at you, you are half my size," he sneered down at me.

"I can take care of myself." I was insulted that he thought it was all about size, like I couldn't take him down right now.

"You said Margo might already be hurt, what about her? Can she take care of herself? What kind of a man would I be if I hid here and she was out there hurt?"

"A live one!" I screamed at him.

He crossed his arms even tighter and opened his stance as if prepping himself for me to try to run over him.

"Fine. But we do this my way," I said as I narrowed my eyes into slits. Let's just see how well he handles a bit of my weirdness. "Get your pack on," I ordered and watched as he reached down and put it on without taking his eyes off me. I walked up to him and put my hand on his arm and blinked…

"What the hell?" he called out as he discovered he was standing next to the rail by the river. I had let go of him and he swung in a circle, looking around himself quizzically.

"I said we were doing this my way. This is the way I get around. You like it? It's called blinking," I snapped at him. I did the hands on hip thing and gave him a smug look.

"How'd you do that? It's like some magic trick, right?" he asked as he struggled to understand how he was now outside, standing by the side of the river gorge.

"Yes, that's what it is, magic. I'm a fey and I do magic, okay?" He glared at me. I took his shoulder and turned him around until he was facing the river, then I made sure I wasn't touching him before I said, "Look over there. What do you see?" I asked pointing across the river.

He looked down at me, still stunned, and gradually

looked to where I was pointing. "A steep mountain, blackberry bushes, rocks, a couple of tall sickly looking trees and the cliff down to the river... nothing, there is nothing over there, Ivy."

"See what I see Zack," I whispered and touched his arm while I pointed with my other hand out across the open space again. I didn't know if my words would work or not. If they didn't, well he was really going to think I was a kook. He glared at me as if I was wasting his time and looked up once more.

"Holy shit!" he exclaimed, grabbing the rail to keep from falling over and I had to move fast to keep contact with him. "There's a forest over there! I can see a trail winding up the mountain." He turned and looked at me, and out of the corner of my eye I could see his turmoil. Yep it can be a real headache playing around with realities, just ask Skyler. "This is some weird hallucination, it's an illusion. How are you doing it?" he demanded as his eyes kept going back to his newly adjusted view.

"No illusion...now. The illusion was what you were seeing before. It has a veil on it so that mortals can't see it. It's called a between realm, Meadhan. That's what I've been trying to tell you. That's my path into my forest and up to my cabin," I said with just a little bit of pride. I couldn't help smiling. I really did love that forest, and the only things I missed when I was there were fresh meat, and a real bathroom, and maybe someone to talk to, completely discounting Laven. He was still on my shit list.

"That's where you went?"

"Yes"

"Why couldn't I see that? How could I have missed that, how could anyone?" He asked.

"It's veiled, I told you that. Granddad hid it so other mortals wouldn't just happen onto it, it's not a very safe forest right now. Only the fey he lets in, and my family can go there...and we only could because we have something that lets us in. It's another realm, Zack, another dimension I guess. Do you really want to go in there and maybe not be able to come back? And if you can get out, you might be terrorized by your worst nightmares come to life every minute of every day. Are you really willing to take that chance?" I didn't know how to get it through to him that this wasn't just a nice little hike where he could go home when he got bored, or if things went bad.

He looked at the view of the forest and back at me, then again at the forest. I could tell he was arguing with himself. That I understood, and I wondered who would win this argument. I could see him clenching and un-clenching his fists, thinking it through then coming to a decision.

"No trickery?" he asked sincerely.

"No trickery, Zack. That's real."

I watched him take a few deep breaths as if to steady himself, then he stood just a bit straighter and proclaimed. "It doesn't matter if it is or isn't. If you know where Margo is, then I'm going. Whatever the consequences are, I will accept them. I'm going with you," he stated firmly, as he straightened his pack onto his back and looked at me.

He'd made his decision; I'd tried but couldn't change his mind. Granted he really didn't know what he was getting into, what form of reference would any normal person have for this sort of situation? But I had to accept the fact that he wasn't going to stop unless I left him, and I couldn't do that. Besides, part of me really wanted him to come with me.

"Okay then. I'm going to blink us to the start of the path. I have no idea where Aishal blinked them to in the forest and I think it's best if we start at the tree."

"Sounds good to me," he answered with a fake light voice. I wondered if he really did believe or if he was going along for the ride, thinking the truth would be more mundane. I really didn't like the thought that maybe he did think I was off my rocker and he was just playing along. Who would blame him though? I don't think I would have believed it at all a few weeks ago. In fact, I could have probably ran the other way as fast as my legs could carry me if someone had said the things I had to him.

I held out my hand, and he took it in his bigger rougher one. I blinked, and we found ourselves staring up at Granddad's tree with the mark on it. I loosened my hand from his, wondering if he'd still be able to see the path, I didn't need to speculate long.

"It's gone," he stated as he looked once more at the steep hillside covered in blackberry bushes.

"No it's still there," I replied as I looked at the path before me with my fey eyes and saw all the stately trees and ferns that lined it. "Are you really, *really* sure Zack? You can still back out," I said, giving him one last out.

"Not a chance. Let's get this show on the road and find Margo."

I took his hand and held tight. I wasn't sure just how a mortal could go through the veil, but if Aishal had taken Margo, then it had to work by touch. I started forward and he came behind, the path too narrow at this point to walk side by side. As we neared the tree I could feel a drag, a pull of resistance that I had never felt before. Zack was walking with difficulty, having a hard time moving his feet. He was clutching my hand tightly, holding on for all his might. His face was dripping sweat and he was almost leaning forward pushing against something I couldn't see, when, like a balloon popping, the resistance was gone and he slammed into me and we both went crashing down. He landed on top of me and rolled off quickly. We weren't touching now and he was still here. I had been worried that no matter what, the realm would just dispel him. I hadn't figured out what I would do then, knowing that it might have done the same to Margo and I wouldn't have a clue where to find them. But it was all good, he was still here, still alive and breathing.

"Whoa, that was weird," he managed to say as he got to his feet and helped me up. "It was like I was walking through tar. Are we in now? For real? In this place you say is another realm?" he asked looking up at me with a weak grin, and then his face went all shocked like. "Ivy I don't want to scare you, but there's a plant on your face and it's started to bloom."

I put my hand up and felt for the vines. Yep, forgot about those. "It's okay, it's kind of part of me now." He looked closely at them, even touched them and tried to pull a leaf off. It was like someone was plucking my eyebrows. I slapped his hand.

"Stop that or I'll start with your nose hairs." He leaned back and forced himself not to gawk at me, trying to change the subject.

"So, this is where you live?"

"Yes. This is my real home," I said as birds started chirping around us. The air was clean and filled with summer.

"Cool," he said looking around, a smile playing at the corners of his mouth. He was enjoying this I realized, and wondered if he was like insane. Who in their right mind just accepted this and wasn't freaked out by it? He patted my shoulder as he surveyed the area around us. "It's amazing, Ivy. It reminds me of the Redwoods, or maybe a tamer Amazon jungle." He looked up at the tall trees that loomed above us. "You could make an awesome tree house in those." And he grinned wider. Great, now to add to everything else, I had *wild boy* who probably saw himself as Tarzan.

We started up the path, Zack still a bit dazed. At first he had trouble walking, as if his equilibrium was off. He said it felt like he had been on the water for a long time and was just coming onto dry ground. I'd heard of *sea legs*, but that was one thing I'd never done. Granddad and I both avoided being on large bodies of water, I'd never been on a boat before, and hoped I'd never have to.

We walked in silence, with me in the lead. I wasn't sure what to make of him. In all my life, that I could remember, I'd kept myself apart from boys. Most of my girlfriends were dating, while I'd just stayed on the edge of every friendship. Maybe I was just too scared to get close to anyone…closeness meant explaining things. I didn't want to give my life over to someone else to control; not to a boyfriend, or however well-meaning, an adult. My life may have been shit, but it was my life and I had wanted to work it out myself.

Now I had this guy following me around. I'd read enough books to wonder, for about a second, if I had thrown a spell on him. But that was ridiculous and I knew it. Zack just found me interesting enough to want to solve the mystery of me; the only problem was he had gotten himself thrown headfirst right smack dab into the middle of a thriller-mystery.

I resented him forcing the responsibility for his well-being onto me. I could barely take care of myself and I had all this stuff I had to figure out…how to keep everyone happy or at least safe…and all I wanted to do was to lock myself in my cabin and brew a cup of tea. Okay, I was being a bit of an ass, but really, I didn't ask for all this. I walked, deep in my own thoughts, while I listened to the birds and felt the sun on my face. I found I actually missed the weird bugs that had always greeted me and traveled the path with me.

I was feeling sorry for myself and I knew it. I could hear Zack trudging along behind me. He didn't try to talk to me, which I did appreciate. After about an hour, we got to the part of the path with the cliff and boulders. I looked back to see Zack had stopped and was sitting on a boulder, drinking from his water jug and looking out at the view.

"I am still having a hard time believing it," he admitted

as I came over and sat down next to him and he passed his water bottle over to me. Gratefully, I took a couple of drinks before handing it back. I hadn't thought to bring one with me. "Does this sit on top of what I could see; is it like on a different plane or something?" he asked as he continued to look over the cliff to the far horizon of the forest below us.

"You know, I never thought of it. You've got to realize that until I came this time with-out Granddad I thought everyone could see it. I had no idea it was *veiled*."

He looked down at me sitting there next to him with an incredulous look. I could see he'd started to say something, then stopped and waited a minute before he said, "I'm sure there's a whole story here, about you and your life. Maybe sometime you will tell me about it."

"It would be nice to tell someone," I said before thinking, and then realized how pitiful that sounded. Self-consciously I stood up and busied myself with my pack. I could feel his eyes on me and knew he had risen too. The silence seemed to hang around us.

"How far are we from your cabin now?" he asked. He was standing close to me and it made me uncomfortable. Without looking at him I looked up the path, considering what he had asked. We hadn't seen anything that would lead us to believe they had been here. There was really only one place I could think of that Aishal would go.

"Uh, well about a couple of hours, but I'm wondering if we shouldn't just go to the doorway. If Aishal was going to blink anywhere it would probably be there. What do you say, blink or walk?"

Zack really did give it some thought, before he answered me. "I'd love to continue the hike, mostly because I enjoy hiking. But we didn't come here for me to enjoy myself. Do your blink thing and let's get to where you think Margo might be. I just need to find her and make sure she's okay," he said, pulling his hair out of his face and tying his dreads in a knot on the back of his head. He adjusted his pack and held out his hand to me. I took it and for the first time, it felt like we were holding hands instead of me grabbing for him. It felt more intimate and made me even more self-conscious. I blinked before I had time to think about it.

CHAPTER 30 - Ivy

We opened our eyes to the little hollow by the large tree roots that held the doorway to the fey realm. We heard Margo before we had time to adjust to our new surroundings. There was a loud joyful shriek and then I found myself in a bear hug with Margo. She was screaming and crying and hugging me so tight I couldn't breathe. When she was done with me, she started in on Zack, who returned her hug with a tight bear hug of his own.

"Oh, I knew you would come for me!" she cried into his shirt.

"Are you okay? That guy didn't hurt you?" Zack asked as he gently pushed her back and started to look her over.

"No, I'm fine. Just a bit scared. The guy disappeared the minute we got here and the lady just dropped and is asleep and I can't wake her," she said as she hugged him again, pulling me in as well. Zack and I found ourselves being pushed very uncomfortably together until she finally released us.

"And you found Ivy, where was she?" she turned to me and pointed her finger at me. "Where were you? You had us scared that you had fallen down a cliff and got yourself killed," she said as she wagged the finger at me.

I was looking at Skyler, lying peacefully in the ferns. She was in her pretty form and looked like the picture that Marmaw had painted of her. She really did look beautiful and seeing her like that made me wish she really was what the picture made her seem. I started to go over to her, when Margo attached herself to my arm.

"I'm so glad you came back. Really where did you go and how did you know where to find me? I don't even know where I am," she said pulling me to a stop. I had no choice but to answer her.

"I'm sorry Margo, but I told you where I was going, to stay at a cabin in the mountains. You and Zack didn't need to be worried about me. And this..." gesturing around me, "…is my real home. But I'm sorry that you were worried and got all mixed up in this," I said looking over at Zack. His face was more relaxed than it had been since me had found me on the sidewalk. He was looking around the hollow with interest and I saw his eyes land on Skyler and stay there.

"So, sleeping beauty over there hasn't been a problem?" I jested, looking at my fake mom. She really did look unreal, like a doll posed in the flowers and ferns.

"Naw, she staggered around a bit, then fell down and went to sleep. She looks nice like that, can we let her sleep?" she asked innocently. She didn't know what a wise statement that was.

"Where's the guy?" Zack questioned, as he scanned the area.

"Yeah, where is Aishal? I'm shocked that he would have gone to all the trouble to get Skyler and then just leave her here," I stated as I started looking around. The doorway was closed, and except for us, the area didn't look changed or disturbed at all.

"Is that the guy's name? The one that was beating her up?" she asked pointing to Skyler.

"I think so. From what Zack told me it sounds like him, and I think he was the one that broke into your grandma's shop and took the necklace. That's how he could get in here."

"Someone broke into Grandma's shop?" she screamed, "Is she okay? What happened?" She started firing questions at me so fast that I couldn't keep up. Finally I just had to take her by the shoulders and shake her a bit to get her to stop.

"Margo, she's okay, the shop is okay. Everything is okay now…sort of. I need to know, where is Aishal? "

She took a couple of deep breaths before she could talk, and I could tell she really would have rather found out more about her Grandma than answer my questions.

"I don't know. We kind of popped in here. She staggered and fell and I got really dizzy and started to fall myself when I got hit in the face with this," she said, pointing at the necklace hanging around her neck. It was the one from her Grandma's shop…she had the talisman. "And then this bug started to attack me. Like a big bumblebee gone nuts. It kept dive bombing me as I bent to pick up the necklace. It's that one of grandma's, you know. I don't know how it got here, but I picked it up and put it around my neck and the dumb bug stopped hitting me, but it still wouldn't leave me alone so I wacked it good," she informed us, doing a little pantomime as she did.

The only weird bugs I knew of were the Wisps, which meant that Aishal must have changed back into a Wisp when he entered the forest. Maybe he thought having a talisman would negate the hex. Uh…he was wrong apparently. Boy he must have been pissed off, blinking in with Skyler and Margo only to discover that he was a Wisp who couldn't wear the talisman anymore. And to make matters worse, he had to watch as Margo picked it up and put it on. Geez, I would have loved to see his face while all that was going on. Then to be swatted like a fly…that would have been priceless.

"So where is the bug now?"

"It was over there. After I wacked it, I made sure it wouldn't come back. I stepped on it and smashed it good. It won't be bothering us again."

"You did what?" I screamed and started to frantically

look around where she had pointed. "Where Margo, where did you step on him?"

Margo looked at Zack with confusion and I heard her whisper, "Why is she so upset about a bug?"

Before he could answer I yelled at her, "It wasn't just a bug, Margo, it was a fey…like me. You know, a person? Only in the forest, the fey turn into Wisps, unless I let them be in people form. He must have thought that having one of the talismans would let him be whatever he wanted, or maybe he didn't even think about it. Granted, Aishal was kind of an ass, but I didn't want him hurt or…oh geez…killed." I had started to cry.

I started searching around in the moss and ferns, making more noise than anything else. "Where Margo, where was he?"

She was still dazed by what I had said and started mumbling that, really it had just been a bug. But she came over and pointed down at a spot in the ferns. I could see where they were broken and smashed into the loam of the forest floor. I could even see her heel mark, ground back and forth. He must be dead, I've seen what happened to flies when I swatted them, all blood and guts. I got down on my hands and knees, Zack and Margo looking with me. I could see them giving each other odd looks over my head, but I didn't care. I was desperate to find what remained of him.

I didn't know when they had stopped looking, but I felt Zack's hand on my shoulder and I looked up at him through tear-filled eyes. "He was a real pain, but he didn't deserve to be smashed," I sobbed.

"Ivy, you aren't making any sense again. How could a bug be a person?" I looked at his concerned face, then at Margo standing behind him. She was standing on one foot, looking like a lost little girl, and suddenly I realized how I must look to them. Maybe Zack had started to believe in my little world, maybe he had even come to believe in *blinking*, but it was more likely he thought I had some sort of mind control over him.

Either way, I could see the concern for me on their faces, and maybe just a bit of concern for themselves, now stuck in this forest with a maniac. I glanced over at Skyler. She was still peacefully asleep, but I didn't know for how long, or what I should do with her before she did wake up.

I stood up and looked around. The doorway wasn't open. The air was still. I had two friends with me who didn't know anything and even though both were heroic in their own ways, neither could help with me this. I needed another fey.

"Ivy?" Zack started, but I held up my hand. I didn't have a choice, I needed him. I needed Laven. I took a deep breath, let the fire build, and then yelled as loud as I could.

"Laven wake up and come here, I need you!" Birds burst out from the underbrush in a loud profusion of noise and before their cries had died down, or Zack or Margo had time to recover from their shock at my scream, my little familiar bug flew into the glade, hovered around us, then popped into form.

Margo screamed and then collapsed in a heap at Zack's feet. I was a little glad someone else had that reaction. It proved I wasn't that abnormal. Zack knelt to take care of her, while taking in the sight of Laven. And boy was he a sight.

He was as perfect as always, from his blond wavy hair to his toes. Seeing him next to Zack, it really was comparing night to day. Everything Laven was, Zack wasn't and vice versa. Two sides of a coin. Although Zack didn't do what Laven did next, thank goodness.

"My lady, you return," he proclaimed and knelt in front of me, bowing his head.

"Get up Laven; I don't have time for this. I'm sorry I did that to you, but you really left me no choice," I snapped at him, trying to be nice and failing horribly.

"My lady, it is I who must apologize. I demeaned myself and the clan by supposing to tell *you* what to do," he replied keeping his head down. He sounded like he really meant what he was saying and I felt like an impostor…I had no idea what I was doing.

"Laven, stop it. Please? I said I needed you and I do. Aishal has been causing problems…anyway I think it was Aishal." I heard a little squeak behind me and realized I had forgotten Margo and Zack. She had come around and was standing holding onto Zack's arm, staring with shock at Laven.

"Zack, Margo, I would like you to meet Laven. He's a fey also." My two friends looked from Laven to me. They just stared at the pale god-like creature. Even Zack looked shocked and maybe a bit awed. Laven was having his own reactions to my two friends. He took one look at Zack and stumbled back a step, his face twisted up in alarm. He shuddered and then stood straight and steadied himself. I guess it was a surprise for me to have friends other than fey.

"Fey?" Margo said, and Zack looked at me as if expecting me to tell them more.

I had some more explaining to do. This was getting so complicated. "Margo, you kind of missed what I told Zack, I'll have to fill you in later. But short story is that I am a fey."

"A Frìth fey, my lady," Laven corrected, keeping his eyes trained on me.

"Okay, a Frìth fey and so is Laven. You are in another realm, called Meadhan. This is my forest, and I guess I'm the owner of that doorway that leads to the realm of the fairies," I said pointing at the tree roots.

"Firinn of the fey," Laven corrected again.

"Stop that!" I snapped at him.

"Yes, my lady."

"Anyway, other fey used to own this forest and doorway. A really bad thing happened and it hurt the everything. The original owners of the forest left and it ended up being given to my Granddad…and now me. My granddad put a hex on the area so that any fey that came here turned into a Wisp, unless I let them be in their fey form, like Laven here is." Margo was staring at me like I was nuts. "That's the weird bug thing you hit, Margo. Anyway, there's a bunch more to this story and I'll tell you all of it, but first things first." I had to take a breath before I turned to Laven. "Laven, would you please do something for me?"

"Anything my lady." Geez it was like having a puppy dog and a servant all rolled into one. I really wished he would stop it.

"These are my friends and they are under my protection. No harm is to come to them. I want you to be nice to them, okay?" I asked in my normal voice.

He bowed at me, then at each of them. Margo actually giggled; Zack looked a bit put out. "Also, could you become a Wisp, fly nicely over to them for a second, maybe go up and down and then change back so they know what you look like as a Wisp?"

"Of course Ey-vey," he replied...then he was a Wisp. Both Margo and Zack called out in alarm. I seemed to be shocking them right and left today. He slowly flew over to Zack and hovered a moment, then flew up and down. He repeated this for Margo, who looked delighted with him. When he was finished, he came back to where he had begun and once more converted into a fey.

"Thank you Laven."

"Anything, my lady."

"Stop calling me that."

"Yes my la…yes Ey-vey," he said, correcting himself.

I looked over at Zack and Margo. "So do you believe me now that he is a fey *and* the bug thing?" Margo nodded yes, but Zack glared daggers at Laven, then he turned his gaze on me.

"He lives here with you?"

Boy that was unexpected. Of all the questions he could have asked, that was not one I had expected.

"Uh, no, not with me. He lives in the forest and only when Granddad would let the fey in. I lived…live in the private glade in my cabin. No fey are allowed into that glade or the cabin, not since it was built, a long, long time ago."

He seemed to relax as I spoke, but he still eyed Laven with distaste. Interesting, but not important right now. I turned back to Laven.

"Back to what I was saying. Somehow Aishal got into the mortal realm and got ahold of one of my family's talismans. He found Skyler," I pointed at the still-sleeping form and Laven glanced over at her with disdain. "And brought her here. He wasn't very nice to Margo and she didn't know he wasn't a bug. I'm afraid she stepped on him and hurt him and I can't find him. Can you please?"

"He has a talisman?" he asked in a level voice as his eyes narrowed.

"Not now. I have it!" Margo called out cheerfully, holding the necklace out for him to see.

Laven's face scrunched up and for a second it looked like he was going to cry. He looked over at Margo, composed himself, and then was fine again. I wondered if he was upset that Aishal didn't still have it. But he had collected himself and started considering what to do.

"Ey-vey, if Aishal is hurt he will have gone somewhere to heal. Fey cannot be that easily killed," he stated more to Margo, than to me. "He will heal, but he would heal quicker in Firinn. First though it is exceptionally dangerous having *it* here." He said pointing to Skyler.

The frantic pounding in my heart had calmed down when he informed me that Aishal wouldn't die. But I looked over where he pointed. Skyler didn't look dangerous to me…now.

"Why? She's asleep Laven. She can't hurt us."

"*It* will not be sleeping for long. I've heard what the shifted one can do and there are no fey that will dare be around it. *It* is filled with evil magic...can you not feel it?"

"But that's impossible. She has a talisman, and you said they couldn't touch her."

"It does not matter if the shifted one has a talisman, which she does not. I would feel it. If *it* did have one, the talisman would only protect *it*, not us. It is soaking up magic as we speak, can you not feel it? Look at it."

So saying he went over and laid his hand on her, and then looked back at me. "It is filled with evil from the Sumair stone Ey-vey. We must put it in the tree fast." He picked Skyler up and looked expectantly at me.

I could see that he was serious. But I just couldn't put her somewhere. I had made a promise to myself that I'd look after her for Granddad. But he was right, she was asleep now, but she had always caused trouble. I didn't want to just have her wake up on me and try to kill me or my friends.

A rotten smell was coming from her, and I looked up at Laven. He had almost turned a sickly green. He was holding his breath, and to his credit, was still holding on to her.

"The evil thing smells my lady, and it's draining me quickly. Please let us hurry." He pleaded with me.

"Nasty," Margo said from behind me and I agreed. Mom…crap…Skyler, smelled nasty.

"Let us go Ey-vey. The hemlock tree will hold her while she sleeps. The shifted one will not be able to take magic and the evil will not be able to be released on us."

"What tree?"

"I will show you my lady," he declared as he shifted the weight of the thing he was holding, his face full of disdain.

"You will need to touch me Ey-vey so that we may blink, since you do not know where we go."

He was right, and I started over to him.

"Oh no you don't. You aren't going anywhere without us," Zack said as he grabbed my hand and reached out for Margo's with his other one. I had to admit I didn't blame him one bit. I would have probably done the same thing. I touched Laven on the shoulder and he blinked, taking a trail of people along with him.

We arrived in a remote part of the forest I didn't remember ever being before. The trees were monster in size; three, four and sometimes five trees had twisted together forming gargantuan looming giants. There was no sunlight, but there was a faint glow from the vegetation. It was another surreal moment for me. Laven walked over to one of the massive trees and looked back at me, as if waiting.

"You need to open it Ey-vey. I believe you can. The Woodsman always said, 'open' and it did." He was turning his head to the side and I could see his eyes were starting to water.

"Are you okay, Laven?"

"It is siphoning my magic. Please hurry Ey-vey, it does hurt," he admitted, looking even more uncomfortable. "The shifted one cannot harm us in there. This is what the Woodsman always did, when he brought her."

I didn't hesitate a moment longer. I ran to the tree and yelled "Open." The bark of the tree cracked away and began to swing outwards. Laven had to duck to go in. I followed him, amazed at this new discovery. The tree was hollow, from what I could see. It was pitch black inside except for the light coming in from the opening. There was a raised flat root that created a bed of sorts, and Laven dumped Skyler onto it.

He turned and, pulling me with him, exiting the cave of the tree. "Close," I yelled, to the shocked stares of Margo and Zack.

As soon as the hidden door was shut tight and it looked like nothing more than a tree again, I turned back to Laven. The air was still filled with the stench from her. I wanted to jump in the pond and wash myself and I wasn't even the one who had carried her here. Laven still looked a little green and he had gone over to another tree and leaned against it with his palms flat on its bark. His eyes were closed and he was saying something under his breath.

"Laven?" I called out to him.

"Sorry, my lady. I need the power of the forest," he whispered weakly and remained still for a few moments longer as three of us looked on. When he opened his eyes, they looked clearer, but I was alarmed, and went over and touched his arm.

He put his hand over mine and his face broke into a weak smile. "I am well, my lady."

"Good, well I think Margo needs to sit down." Zack said roughly as he came over and yanked my hand away from Laven's and didn't let go of it. Zack was right, Margo looked done in. But there was still the issue of Aishal.

"Laven, what can we do about Aishal? If he's hurt we just can't let him be alone, and at the same time I don't want a pissed off Wisp attacking us," I said looking back at him, and catching him glaring at Zack. Could he be jealous of a human boy being in the forest? But he answered me in his normal silky voice.

"I have given it some thought, my lady. Our forest has been drained of some of its already low portion of power by the shifted one. Also, you and I and the dr..., your friend, do not have enough combined power to restore it. I would humbly suggest that you allow the other fey in through the doorway and at the same time expel Aishal. No matter where he has gone to hide, your magic, and I believe you still have enough, will push him back through. He will heal quicker in the fey realm also. We can even request one of the brothers, possibly Rayni since his special talent is regrowth, to stay with him to speed his recovery."

I looked at Zack and Margo. They looked like they were at the end of their endurance for more weirdness, but I had to agree with Laven. We needed other fair folk, people on my side, especially if Skyler was going to be a problem. I thought about the fact that I didn't feel sorry for her right now. She was safe in the forest, asleep, and the Eilibear couldn't hurt her here. I just hoped she wouldn't wake up and hurt us.

Laven was waiting patiently for me to make up my mind and Margo had come over and was leaning against Zack, looking like she might fall over. Zack was still holding onto my hand like I was going to disappear on him.

"Fine. Okay, we will do that. Go wait for me at the doorway. I'll take Zack and Margo to the cabin and grab the axe and meet you there," I declared, growing more confident in my decision as I spoke the words.

Since the three of us were already touching it made it a simple thing to quickly blink us into the glade, remembering at the last second to call out to unlock it for them and myself only. I didn't want to blink in and have them hit some barrier and bounce to India or someplace.

Zack scooped up Margo the moment we opened our eyes. She had swooned, probably from the motions of blinking. I wasn't even used to it yet and it was supposedly part of being a fey. I hurried to unlock the door of the cabin and waited while Zack carried her in. I couldn't give him time to stop me. I'd never met the other fey, not really, and I needed to let them in. I grabbed the axe and then blinked out before Zack knew what I had done.

I ended up in the middle of the hollow. Laven was standing next to the doorway extremely still, looking up at the top of the trees.

"What is it?" I asked following his gaze.

"I do not know, but the air feels different to me. Let us

bring in the other fey, the older ones may know what it is, I'm thinking it's the Druid though. This forest has never had one enter it before," he said as he smiled his beautiful smile at me, as if all would be wonderful if he had more fey to play with.

"Uh, okay. What's a Druid? Is that something that came in with Aishal and Skyler?" I asked, thinking that when I found the time, I really needed to write a dictionary for all these fey words.

"No, my lady, you brought him. Granted he is heavily protected, but he is full Druid."

"Whoa! I didn't mean to bring something in with me," I said frantically looking around in circles, as if whatever it was must be hiding from me.

"The boy you brought with you, Ey-vey, Zàc. He is a Druid," he said with heavy contempt.

"Noooo!" I exclaimed. "You mean, he's shifted right? He and Margo are now shifted and they might become like Skyler did." I felt the tears starting to well up in my eyes. I had done this to them.

"My lady, your friends are not shifted. The little one, Mary-go, has a talisman that protects her from magic, I do not know what she is, but she is *not* shifted. Zàc is of fey blood. He is a Druid and you should not have him near you. He is wearing Celtic charms to hide what he is from you, I beg you to get the Druid out of our forest as quickly as possible. A Druid's only purpose is warfare and no fey wishes to be near them."

I started to say something...and stopped. Then started again...and stopped. I had to keep telling myself to stay focused. Aishal first, good fey in next to heal the forest...then I would deal with this new information.

"The doorway, my lady?" he asked me again, snapping me out of my thoughts.

I walked up to the tree roots with the axe. "Ready?"

"Yes, my lady. Dispel Aishal first; I will follow him to

seek out our kin. After I leave, you should ban Aishal from returning, but leave the doorway open please. I know that you still have the Wisp hex on for everyone but me and for right now that would be good. But I would ask that you allow Aireen, Myste, Whisper and Bryear be free of it so that we can talk to you when we return," he said respectfully.

I thought about what he asked and knew it probably made sense. What use were they to me if I couldn't talk with them. I nodded my agreement and spoke the words for the hex to not affect Laven or the four he named when he came back.

"Thank you, my lady, I will return shortly." His voice was just so pretty, just too pretty for a boy, but it fit him without a doubt.

"Can I trust you, Laven?" I inquired, looking steadily into his violet eyes.

"Always and forever, my lady. I have seen and felt for myself what great power you have; the Frìth will be strong once more with you here."

"You don't think I need to worry about bad fey coming through if I leave it open?"

"The Frìth will know if a foul one tries to enter." His answer really didn't do much to dispel my qualms about leaving it open for any to come and go. But wasn't that why the fey were upset... a mortal had controlled the doorway? I wasn't a mortal, and I gathered that the doorway now belonged to me in whatever the legal system was in the fey world. I guess I could always tell someone to leave if I didn't like them.

I gently held the heavy axe up and touched it though the opening. I felt a quickening vibration from the axe down to my fingers as the doorway appeared. Letting the axe drop…it was rather heavy…I looked around. There was no sign of him coming on his own.

"Aishal, I ask you to leave this forest," I said, then

quickly added, "I am sorry my friend harmed you, get well soon." I finished just as a tiny flash of light soared out of the foliage by the old fallen tree and seemed to hit with a splash into the film covering the doorway, and then was gone from sight.

"That was Aishal…he lives," Laven informed me, before he bowed regally, then entered the doorway and was gone.

CHAPTER 31 - Ivy

I was getting sort of used to this blinking thing, but I wasn't seeing much of my forest. When Laven left, I stood there for a short time, wondering if I had time to have a good cry. Nope, there wasn't time…I still had to deal with Zack and Margo. I wasn't sure what to do with them now, but I needed to get back and I would take it from there.

Blinking took me to the glade. The axe was heavy and I hadn't even picked it up before I blinked. And now I just sort of started dragging it towards the cabin door when it opened and Zack stood there in the doorway. His face said it all.

"You disappeared on us again," he accused me.

"Right you are," I said with a weak smile. He looked like he was considering whether he should be mad or not. I was glad when he chose not to be. He walked over and took the axe from me and walked me back inside.

As we entered I heard the sound of the axe being placed on the bench in the entry and the door closing behind me.

"Were you planning on chopping wood or fighting off more of those things?" he asked as he came in and went over to the stove. I looked around my darling little cabin and pointedly didn't answer him. It looked the same as when I had left it this morning. Wow, was it really only this morning? Margo was nowhere in sight and I sat on the bench at the table and watched as Zack poured hot water into a mug that had a tea bag string hanging out of it. He sat down across from me and slid it over.

"Where's Margo?" I asked as I sipped the tea before it

even had time to steep.

"Up in the loft. I made her a cup also, she drank it, yelled 'ooh a loft!' climbed up and I haven't heard a sound from her since." I had to smile when he did the impression of Margo's cute way of exclaiming at everything. I smiled down at my cup.

"Soooo?" he asked quietly.

I looked up and he was watching me. Nothing had changed about him; still the wild crazy hair pulled back from his face. His jewelry was in place and his pretty green eyes were trained on me. I didn't know what Laven's problem was with him, but I trusted Zack a lot more than I did the slick fey.

"You must have tons of questions."

"You think?" he asked with a slightly crooked grin.

So I started to tell him. All of it. About my early life that I remembered…about Skyler, Mom, and my life with her. About Granddad and Marmaw. I got out the fairytale books she had written, and he flipped through them, as I told him about my last few months at home. The hardest part was telling him about coming here...running away to the cabin and what had happened when I got here. I left the stuff about the Sumair stone out. That was my secret and needed to remain so. He nodded a lot, or frowned, or smiled, but for the most part he didn't say anything as he let me get it all out.

"So these notebooks, can I read them?" he asked when I was finally finished. I thought about it…someone else needed to. Maybe he would find something I had missed. I went over to the bed and pulled the box out, opened the lid, letting it fall back.

"There they are. The one on the top is the story about Willow. The rest are Marmaw's diaries. I put them back in order so start with that one," I said pointing to the top one on the right. "I need to use the outhouse," I walked to the door, leaving him gathering up some of the items and sitting down in one of the overstuffed chairs.

When I came back, he was deep into the Willow story. The sun was setting outside and I gave thought to whether any of the fey and Laven had come back yet. There had been no sign of Wisps when I had gone out. I put more wood in the fire and started another pot for tea and the large one to make a stew in. As I busied myself with making a meal, Zack read quietly on, and Margo slept. It was pleasant and my uneasiness decreased...somewhat.

Aishal was livid. He had completely forgotten about the Wisp hex. Finding the talisman and then the shifted one right at the entry to the forest had been providential. He had blinked into the heavy fog and the thing hadn't seen him. He had stood there listening to the shifted one speak with the mortals, and then the mortals had left. It was an easy thing to go up to it, and take it by the shoulders. He had planned on blinking with it to the doorway.

But when his hands had made contact with the shifted one, he had almost fainted. He had never come in contact with a shifted one before, and hadn't known it would feel like this…dark and spinning. His mind felt like it had been caught in a whirlpool as the shifted one attempted to wrench his newly acquired power away. He had no choice; he had to hold onto it. She had turned on him, screaming and punching him awkwardly in the chest. He'd landed one good blow to her head, and it had started screeching. Abruptly, out of nowhere, he was attacked on his other side. A small mortal had pounced on him and was clawing at his face. There was no time.

The shifted one kept screaming unintelligible words, but he caught a name…Ivy. She wanted to find Ivy. That startled him. He pushed the little mortal roughly away from him and kept his attention on the shifted one. Over her shrieks, he told her he knew where Ivy was, and could take her to her. The shifted one had calmed down then, enough for him to take a firm hold of her arm. He blinked, and realized too late that the little mortal had attacked him again, making contact with him at the moment he'd blinked and had ended up coming with them.

He didn't know what he was going to do once in the forest, but at least he would be in his own realm and not standing by the side of a road in Alainn where more mortals could come at any time. The instant he completed his blink the forest hex hit him and he transformed into the hateful little Wisp. The talisman didn't change along with him. It pulled him down to the ground in a wild spiral, where he landed with it on top of him. He wasn't harmed, but now he had to figure out how to hide the thing while in this tiny body.

Before he could figure out what to do, the little mortal had started to pick it up. He'd zoomed at her, hit her with everything he had to drive her off. It worked for a little while, but she had seen the necklace and wanted it. He dived and hit and dived again, but to no avail. She picked it up, looked at it and put it on. He couldn't touch her after that, but he could annoy her and that's what he did.

The mortal seemed to have quick reflexes though…she had actually hit him, sending him sailing across the glade and before he could right himself she had stepped on him, pushing him into the ground. It hurt, his wings were smashed and torn and one leg was shattered. He lay still and waited for her to leave, then blinked to a low branch dense with leaves and tried to heal himself. He didn't have much magic left; what the shifted one had taken coupled with the magic needed to blink all of them here and now blinking again to the branch left him empty...and enraged. How? How had Ivy done this? How had she somehow put in place magic to stop him?

He could see the hollow from where he sat and the

shifted one had gone to sleep. That he had expected. Only once had he been inside when the Woodsman had brought *it* with him, and *it* was fast asleep then. The little mortal girl had called out for help, but hadn't left the hollow and finally had sat and cried and braided some flowers and looked around. She didn't seem all that scared to him.

He didn't know how much time had passed; he had closed his eyes and continued to try to pull magic from the forest. The forest did not wish to give it to him; it was like something else had a hold on its magic and none was left for him. A sound opened his eyes and he saw Ivy standing in the hollow, with a huge Druid and the little mortal was hugging them.

That's how. The shifted one and Ivy had help; they had called the Druids in. The Druids didn't help just anyone and had kept to themselves for years. He couldn't even remember the last time he had come across one, but they were powerful magic, strong warriors who fought great battles. He didn't know how Ivy had managed to get one to help her, but he needed to tell Shivf. Shivf would know what to do; he was from Scotland and probably knew more about the Celtic fey than most.

He watched them and heard them discussing him. In amazement, he observed that Ivy seemed upset that the mortal had hurt him, and even shed tears for him. It confused him; how could she care, and at the same time be the one taking everything from him?

Then she called Laven. Laven had betrayed him, he was helping her also. He fumed and shook and was irate that these two were working together to get the forest and the doorway and the Sumair stone and keep it all from him. In his feverish thoughts, he missed Laven picking up the shifted one. His mind pulled in with the pain and he only heard the voices of Ivy and Laven, the ones taking everything away from him. His body was too broken to engage them and before he knew it, they had all left.

Laven came back first and only stood there, smelling the air and muttering to himself. Then the Alltha had returned with the iuchair, opened the doorway, and ripped him off the branch and sent him back into Firinn and Rootmire.

His body reverted to the fey form as he landed. It hurt…every inch of him hurt. His last thought was that he didn't think Rootmire held enough magic to help heal him and he collapsed.

He woke to Myste kneeling over him. "Aishal?" Myste asked as he opened his eyes, "What happened?"

Aishal couldn't speak, his body was broken and he didn't know if it would ever heal. He couldn't move and when Myste jumped up and yelled out Laven's name he could only lay there in agony.

"Laven, did Ey-vey do this thing?" Bryear bellowed out as he saw his brother emerge from the doorway.

Laven didn't answer but instead made his way through the crowd of fey over to where Aishal lay crumbled on the ground. Leaning close, he whispered, "I'll take care of you and this situation my brother."

He stood and faced the others standing around. The meadow was filled with fey, most he didn't know, but it was apparent that they were not pleased that Aishal had returned in this condition. He could hear them muttering amongst themselves about what could possibly have happened.

"No," Laven called out, and then yelled out louder, "No, the Hemlock forest did not do this to our brother, nor did Ey-vey, the owner of the doorway. Aishal found a talisman and the shifted one attacked him. Aishal fought a good fight."

"Aishal found a talisman? Where is it now?" Whisper asked eagerly, keeping her voice low.

"In the Meadhan, I could not retrieve it...yet," Laven answered quietly, then looked up at the others standing around him. The meadow outside of Rootmire was teeming with fey. He recognized a few of them from Meadhans he had visited. Most were forest fey and mixed in with them there were some doorless clans and a good number of wanderers, like him and his siblings.

"You have done well, so many are gathered. Is Rayni here?" he asked Bryear, as he scanned the meadow.

"Here I am brother," a voice called from the other side of Aishal's fallen body.

"Could you take Aishal some place safe and help heal him? We will need him. The Alltha is actually worried for him and has begged that he return as soon as he is whole once more," he explained loud enough for all to hear, then under his breath added for only his clan's ears. "Ey-vey will be easy to handle, it's what she brought back from Alainn that may give us some problems."

Other fey had come closer to see what was happening. As they closed in, he forced a joyful smile onto his face again as he turned to them. "Fair folk, a fey has come back to the Meadhan, our forest belongs to the fey once more. The fey Ey-vey welcomes you and asks you to come visit the forest."

A voice from his other side called out, "Has she opened the Meadhan to Alainn?"

Turning towards where the question came, he bellowed out so all could hear. "Not as yet, there is powerful magic to be unwoven, but she can do it."

"What about the Sumair stone and Willow?" another yelled out.

"She wants the forest to be free from them and will help us rid it of both," he shouted and a cheer went up around him.

"Really Laven? She is willing to give us the forest and the stone and Willow? What does she think she will get in return?" Myste questioned her brother, leaning close so others could not overhear.

He looked at his sister fey, "Don't worry; she will do as we say. Let us get back through the doorway and we will speak in private then."

Rayni picked up Aishal, who moaned pitifully. Rayni nodded to his brothers and sisters and blinked out. Other fey started to crowd in on Laven yelling out questions. Myste moved to stand next to him and whispered in his ear.

"They are unsure whether we are telling the truth. You need to speak with them, convince them," she told him.

Laven looked around and spotted a stump nearby. He blinked to it and now was standing high enough for everyone to see him.

"My brothers and sisters!" Laven called out, raising his arms high. "The new owner of the Meadhan has invited you to come make a new home and enjoy the magic the forest has to offer us."

A cheer rang out among the crowd and the feeling in the meadow shifted. Joy and harmony radiated from them.

"The doorway is open! Ey-vey has said it may remain so for a time. She wishes to work with Aishal when he is whole, and make things right with the Hemlock clan, and keep the honor of the elders. There is but one request. May the elders of this gathering that have knowledge they wish to impart find me in the morn. We have matters to consider and Ey-vey has asked for your wisdom."

"Laven…really?" Myste asked in a hushed tone.

He motioned for her to wait and called out to the crowd again, "Go now into your new home!" He finished with a flourish and motioned towards the doorway. The crowd moved gently like a slow rolling wave towards the doorway and one by one they entered.

Laven waited until all the other fey had left the meadow and he was finally alone with his remaining brother and the girls.

“You made all that up didn’t you?” Whisper said with a sly grin.

“Of course I did. We need as many fey as possible to take their magic into the Meadhan.”

“What was that about elders being needed?” Myste asked moving up to stand next to Whisper.

“The elders needed to know that their knowledge was desirable and sought by the new owner of the doorway; it would dispel any doubts about Ey-vey. The older fey will bring a stronger older magic with them, we need them more than we need the other fey,” he said putting his arm around Aireen’s shoulder and walking towards the doorway.

When he was almost there, he stopped, and looked back towards the woods. He knew Shivf was there watching and figured the old fey would be following soon enough. Feeling very pleased with how everything was working out, he continued through the doorway and back into the hemlock forest.

CHAPTER 32 - Pengal

Pengal was extremely satisfied with the little enchantment he had placed near the doorway. It allowed them to know when Rayni, Bryear and the girls had come through from the forest. He was a bit mad that the five hadn't seen fit to tell him, meaning Shivf, that the doorway was once again in use. But he knew that Laven was smart and was moving the plan forward.

He also knew when Aishal had come through and had been able to begin the joining with his brothers into Shivf to be able to meet the young fey as soon as he had entered their dwelling. At least that young fey had come to tell them the goings-on in the hemlock forest and as disturbing as some of the news was, it still mattered not as new fey started to blink into Rootmire the very next day.

More and more had been showing up every day since, filling the meadow with their voices and magic. The young ones that aligned with Laven had been busy, going into every inch of Firinn and through what doorways they could gain access to, telling any fey that would listen about the newly opened doorway and the new owner, a Frìth fey.

It worried Pengal that some of the fey might recognize the odor of Boggarts. But even more worrisome was that the elders might catch the scent of the Eilibears and sound the alarm. It was a simple thing to pull a bit of magic from the incoming fey and use it to seal the area around the dwelling they lived in and redirect any fey that might venture too close.

They took to staying outside, watching and saw when

Aishal had been expelled from the doorway ripped and broken. There was no way for them to know what the lad had done and how he had ended up back in the Meadhan. He was supposed to be out looking for a talisman and the shifted one. Pengal seethed, not wanting to hear Ganee tell him, again, that he shouldn't have trusted Aishal with anything or given him their only pass into the Sequoia Meadhan.

Before he had time to figure out what to do, Laven himself walked out of the doorway. The three crept closer so they could hear what the lad was telling the others and threw an eavesdropping spell at Laven so they could hear all of his words. Staying in the shadows, they watched and heard all.

"Aishal done messed this up," Tubaw bawled when Laven shared the news about Aishal finding a talisman and the shifted one. "The lad be finding a talisman and then lost it?" Tubaw hissed. "Me poor ole mam could have done better."

"Hush, listen tae me. The doorway is open and the shifted one is there. That is all we be needing. We will cloak ourselves and go see what there is to see."

"I want tae stay, me toads need me," Ganee stated looking shyly at his brothers. They knew for all his talk, he was scared of the fey and what they would do to them if they were found out.

"So be it. Ganee, feed the thing. Don't ye be forgetting now," Pengal said to him. "Remember, in three days, Ganee. Open the portal fer our friends in three days and then come join us. Bring the body, and the Eilibear in with ye."

"I don't remember when I last did give it anything," Ganee wailed and Pengal slapped him smartly on the back of the head.

"Well you go now an feed it. I not be having everything ruined cause of you," Pengal snapped angrily.

Ganee yelped and jumped away. Shooting Pengal a sorrowful look he scampered away towards the ruins, rubbing his head as he ran. Pengal watched him until he disappeared and hoped his brother hadn't messed this up for them.

"Tubaw cloak us now," he said turning to look back to his remaining brother. Tubaw did so and the two started forwards, mingling in with the unsuspecting fey.

When the two reached the doorway, they could feel the power surging on the other side and triumphantly pushed through the veil. Turning into a Wisp was a new experience. They were disoriented for a moment before they came to their senses and found each other. Moving low to the ground, they sought out shelter, then continued until they were deep in the forest, away from the others.

Both could feel it, the foul tang of Eilibears. Pengal and Tubaw had flown haphazardly towards the odor. It was so strong it was almost visible, and they couldn't believe none of the fey were smelling it. The tree and the surrounding glade were as Laven had described in their prior meetings. They could see the outlines of the door in the largest of the tree. Even though it was covered by moss, the opening and closing of the door had left a faint outline of itself in the greenness.

Pengal hunted for a way in, not able to do anything in this form except fly around. Tubaw was having too much fun defecating from the air, eager to see where it would land. Pengal thought it looked like fun, but they needed to get inside. He inspected the tree from top to bottom, then again, this time with Tubaw's help. At the very top fork of the main trunk they finally found it, a tiny crack, but big enough for them.

He entered, leaving Tubaw to stay by the entry just in case the boy Laven was able to get the Alltha to un-hex the forest. He didn't want to be stuck inside and depend on Laven or one of the others to let them out. He traveled down through the hollow tree, till the dirt floor could be felt and found the sleeping shifted one. The void in the trunk was lightless and he had to move by smell and touch. He was having a hard time flying as the finger that he had gleaned from his brother in the last shifting had given him an extra leg that kept making him want to fly in circles. Flying into the dirt floor and then into various sides of the tree hadn't helped his mood at all. He could smell the Eilibear but could not see the shifted one that they were housed in. After a lot of mishaps he finally landed on the flesh of the once mortal girl.

The shifted mortal was unconscious, close to death and was full of shades. He wondered just how many of the Eilibear had crammed their way inside her, and wondered how she could still be breathing. A pale yellow glow started to shine out of the nose of the shifted mortal, as a line of shade broke free of its host. It wasn't long before the entire horde had come out, leaving the mortal body deflated, crumpled and very much dead. He gave the body a once over and decided it would still work for incubating new Eilibear even in this shape.

The Eilibear shades that had come from the body had filled up the small cavity in the tree trunk. He was sure they were crying out at him, but in this form he couldn't seem to understand anything. He was reduced to flying at the crack in the door and up to the ceiling following the route he had taken before and attempting to show the things the way out into the day light. Eilibear were pretty stupid for the most part and only wanted magic, which they could detect all around them. When the things finally calmed down, they merged together and pushed out, flinging the door open to the waiting forest full of magic.

Pengal flew out after them and settled on a tree branch along with Tubaw. They watched as the Eilibear called to the crawling creatures. They came, hopping and slithering along right up to the green mist of the Eilibear. It was interesting to watch the Eilibear shades break apart once more into small minute separate pieces and push their way in through the mouths of the unintelligent creatures, instilling a bit of themselves into a new host.

The two Boggarts now had only to wait for Laven to come through for them and get this hex turned off, and then the final part of their scheme could be set in place.

Laven went through the doorway with Bryear, Myste, Aireen and Whisper. Looking around he could see the fey, now in Wisp form, flittering around in the trees. He found he felt superior because only he and his tight clan were free from the hex and stood a little taller with pride.

"Did he come?" Bryear asked nervously as soon as the hollow cleared of the Wisps.

"I did not see him, but that does not mean he was not there. Shivf has the ability to shift; we have all seen a couple of forms he likes to use. He may have come up with another for the entry. Also, he would have turned Wisp when he entered," Laven replied unconcerned as he started to walk into the forest.

The others followed, none of them speaking until they came to the small pond deep inside the grove of giant trees. The giant tree Laven had shown Ivy was close by. Laven chuckled at how easy it had been to get her to do as he'd asked, and deposit the shifted one inside.

"Bryear, look around and make sure we are alone," he whispered to his brother, as he and the girls made themselves comfortable on the soft moss around the pond. They waited quietly as Bryear did as he had been asked. The twins, Whisper and Myste, took turns brushing each other's long crimson hair and had started to braid flowers into the strands by the time he came back.

"We are alone," he announced, as he sat by Aireen,

lying down, putting his head on her lap.

"I don't like her," Whisper announced suddenly in a surly tone. "She is too small, like a brownie or pixie. What Frith is small and dark like that?" The others laughed nervously in agreement.

"We do not need to like her, my dears. She is young and alone and has been easy to manipulate." He decided not to tell them that she had been able to force sleep on him when she had left. It worried him when he did awaken, however he had made some useful discoveries. One was that she was more powerful than she knew, more powerful than even they had originally thought when she had first released them from the hex. And second, that she had the mind of a youth, accepting what he told her. Sweet talk seemed to offset her to his advantage, for the most part.

"She returned with allies," he advised them casually, tracing his finger down Whisper's arm.

"What? Other Allthas or mortals? Please don't tell me that the Woodsman has returned. I was quite pleased that we did not need to deal with him after all." Aireen grimaced as she stroked Bryear's hair.

"Well one is indeed a mortal, she will be no problem. The other may be, though," Laven said nonchalantly, keeping his worries out of his voice.

"Is he an older Alltha who knows the laws?" Whisper asked sitting up straighter, clearly troubled.

"No he is young, very young, close to Ey-vey's age," Laven informed her, still trying to figure out what to do about him.

"So what is the problem then?" Bryear questioned disinterested, as he rolled over onto his elbows and looked at Laven.

"He's a Druid."

All of them sat up and stared at him startled. "A real one?" Aireen asked, her eyes growing wide with excitement.

"Yes, a real one."

"I've never seen one before. I've heard they are very…delightful," she purred, leaning into her sister and giggling at her little joke.

"Yes…that may be. However, if we were truly from the Meadhan in Scotland you would have already met some of them. So if I were you I would not be saying that too loudly."

"Hasn't she realized that we are not Frìth? She can't be that stupid…or maybe she can," Aireen laughed vindictively.

"That is why I wished to spend time with her alone, to see what she knows."

"I am sure there is more to the story than you are telling us. Was the Druid really the one that battled with Aishal and not the shifted one?" Whisper questioned him, but Myste broke in.

"Just how did Aishal get in? The last we saw of him, he was standing there with you in the hollow. Did he not go back into Firinn after us?" The others nodded agreement, asking their own questions of him, until Laven put up his hand to stop them. He didn't know the answers, but he was very good at surmising what might have happened.

"Yes he went through the doorway and I expected him to come back with you. But Shivf must have planned it all out. Aishal somehow went into Alainn, found the shifted one and a talisman. He brought them in, after that I don't know what happened, except that Aishal was hurt."

"Were you not waiting for them when he came back?" Bryear asked the question that Laven had been trying to avoid. He smiled his sweetest smile at his brother, but it didn't reach his eyes. Maybe it would be a good thing for them to know the truth.

"The Alltha child may not know all there is to know about fey, but she is not entirely stupid. Before she left to retrieve them, she returned the hex to the forest, and to me." He had their full attention and renewed their distrust of the new little owner of the forest. "Aishal and Shivf could not have known. Shivf must have found where the shifted one was. Aishal showed great honor to us by going into Alainn to retrieve *it* and finding a talisman," he answered, wishing that Aishal was not coming out the hero in this. "But he did not know Ey-vey had renewed the hex, he lost control of what he had gained."

"So he had the shifted one and a talisman?" Bryear asked. "And he managed to lose both?" And Laven grinned to himself. It was so easy to distract his siblings.

"No, he only lost the talisman; however it did get him in and he was able to get the shifted one inside the forest before the hex overtook him." He watched while his brother and sisters pondered this information. They had heard tales of shifted creatures, horrible creatures that normal fey did not wish to be near, as they may suck their magic away from them. They had only come in contact with one, the Woodsman, and he was very powerful.

"So how were you able to subdue it?" Bryear asked, leaning forward with interest.

"The young Alltha couldn't even control it, and called me back to assist. I was able to make it go to sleep." He replied, puffing himself up in their eyes. Bryear relaxed and leaned back again, nodding approval at his sisters.

"What happened to the talisman Aishal lost? Does the Alltha have it back?" Myste asked, looking sideways at her brother.

Laven sat there silently, not responding to his sister's question. He knew he needed to use the truth. Myste had the annoying ability to comprehend situations better than most. He couldn't just say another mortal now had power. He and Aishal would both look like buffoons. He was digging a hole and needed to come up with a plausible story for them. He had a quick mind and it wasn't long before he figured it out, pretending to be more interested in creating a new garment from a nearby flower. When he had formed it to his satisfaction he had also re-worked the story in is mind.

"No, the shifted one gave it to the Alltha, who then gave it to the mortal." They all gaped with shock at that announcement. "Do not worry, we will get it back. Remember that this was a two-part plan, get in and open the doorway. This we have achieved. Not being able to keep the talisman for now is not an issue. First we, or rather I, need to convince Ey-vey to remove the Wisp hex completely from the forest. I believe I can do that." And they nodded agreement to that statement. "I will also try to get her to leave the doorway open for us, as I am unsure if Shivf has made it in yet."

"Does it really matter if he has not?" Whisper asked with a smirk. "The deal was he would help get us our own Meadhan and we in turn would help him find the Sumair stone and give him Willow. But if she locks the doorway, do we not already have our own Meadhan?"

"No...no we don't. She is still here and lords it over us. If she has control of the doorway and the entire forest and the hex of Wisps, then it is not ours. It's hers and she can still remove us whenever she wishes. We need Shivf. He has guaranteed us that he has a way to take control of the doorway from her, open the Meadhan for good and set us up as the owners."

"Do you really think he can?" Aireen asked dubiously. "I've never liked him, or trusted him. He stinks and is so very vulgar. I would rather not have to deal with him anymore. I'd be glad if he couldn't come into our Meadhan," she declared, looking at the others to see if they concurred. They did; the other two girls were making faces like they agreed that he was dreadful and hoped he didn't show up.

"Enough of that now," Laven rebuked them. "He was able to find the shifted one, and get Aishal in with it. It may not have gone completely according to his plan, but it still worked." He was glad he had thought to have Ivy lock Aishal out of the Meadhan. This way he needn't worry about keeping his story straight or having his power-hungry brother mess things up for them. Although, he was sure he would stay mad at his brother for quite some time for going and losing that talisman.

"So you will be convincing the Alltha to un-hex all the fey and keep the door open; what would you like us to do?" Myste asked sweetly as she came over and snuggled with him.

"I would like you girls to flirt with the Druid, glamour him. He is young, though he has protection. Get him to take the pendants and amulets off, keep him beguiled and turn his alliance from the Alltha to us. Do not even attempt to harm him. I do not know what triggers his Dywel, and we do not wish to find out unless he is 100 percent on our side. It would be interesting to have our own Druid." The girls smiled mischievously at the thought of seducing the Druid.

"I've heard stories about the Druid's Dywels. It just seemed impossible that magic would alter a fey in that manner. I do not think I would wish for a sword to immerge from my arm," Bryear said as he held out his arm and looked at it.

"But it's true none the less. The Druid's magic was formed to fight the Eilibear. A Druid must always have his weapon ready and I would think that having a sword appear whenever you need it would be a good thing...but personally I do not wish to see one since to do so would mean the Eilibear were near," Laven said giving his brother a stern look before continuing.

"Bryear, I would like you to round up some of the gentler, but still devious fey and glamour away the mortal. Do not scare her or harm her, just entice her away," he said as he wriggled his fingers through the air like a butterfly taking flight and they all laughed at their cleverness.

Pengal heard the sound of voices drifting to them through the trees, and he and his brother followed the sound until they were perched on a tree limb above Laven and his clan. Although Bryear had checked the area, the two brothers had hid deep in a knot of a tree and waited till it was safe for them to come out. The stupid fey never did find them and gave the all clear to his little clan. The two flittered out and got as close as they dared...and spied on the unsuspecting fey.

It was interesting listening to them, and if Wisps could cackle jubilantly at the new knowledge they had, they would be doing so. Maybe there had been just enough goodness remaining in the Boggarts to be kind to these fey, but not anymore. The little clan had sealed their fate and didn't even know it.

CHAPTER 33 – Elsie

July 23, 1986 –

It's a big day for me. My first book is published! I've been writing the stories off and on for years and they have been printed in papers and magazines. But I really wanted to do something with my paintings. When I put this book together and sent it off to the publisher's I expected them to reject it. I was surprised a few weeks later to get a contract in the mail, along with a nice little check. Milton was happy for me and made the mistake of telling one of the Uncles about my achievement.

The Order was not happy. They knew about the little stories I wrote for the papers, just short cute little tales. So I was shocked when I was informed by Milton that I needed to have their permission before I wrote anymore about the fey. I'm outraged that these men, and it was the men, the Uncles, that really think that I have to get their consent before I do something as innocent as writing a story. They informed Milton that I was to turn over all my notes and send any future stories to them before I try to have more published.

These men do not know me. Really, they know nothing about me. Milton and I have worked very hard at keeping that information a secret and I know more than they could ever imagine. How dare they! I will not give them anything and Milton, though worried, says he will take care of it.

April 3, 1987 –

Well it's been a fun year. I've gained a bit of notoriety for my fairytales and two more of my little books have gone to press. The Uncles have backed off now that they see my stories are children level books and more pictures than story. Besides I write of the type of fairies that mortals feel comfortable with and stay away from any real facts about the fey.

I'm still having the dreams and I dare not tell Milton about them. I know where it is to be found. I called Winnie from a pay phone and told her. She promised me that she would start looking today.

May 24, 1987 –

I received a nice note from Winnie in the mail today. She is such a darling woman. Her message was so sweet and so very clever, "Elsie, my dear, I miss you so. It has been so long since we had a chance to have tea together. I found the perfect little heart tea set and wish you could come visit and have a spot of tea with me."

I showed the note to Milton and he said that he couldn't go with me this month, but if I wanted to I could take Ivy and he would take care of Skyler so I could spend some time with my friend. I called her this afternoon and told her when she could expect us.

CHAPTER 34 - Ivy

Zack was still poring over the notebooks when dinner was ready. I left him to it and went to wake Margo. She was curled up in a cute ball with Marmaw's quilt, wearing a peaceful look on her face.

"Margo? Dinner's ready," I said, shaking her shoulder gently. The sunset was hitting the window perfectly and colors played off the small area making it bright and cheerful. She stirred but didn't open her eyes.

"I'm comfy Ivy, I like your home," she mumbled from under the quilt.

"You look it, but you've got to eat and I cooked so you need to try my food," I replied with a smile. She rolled over and looked at me with bright eyes. Her little pony tails were lopsided and she looked like a child waking up on Christmas morning.

"This is such a wonderful place...even the weird bugs are pretty cool now that I know what they are." She sat up and tried to arrange her shirt before she crawled out of the nest and stood up. Leaning over the banister she looked down on Zack.

"Hey Zack!" she called down.

He looked up at her with a grin. "Hey sleepy head. Come down and eat. Ivy's food smells good and I think maybe you should start reading these too."

She looked down with interest at the box and the pile of notebooks around Zack's feet, and then gave me a quick hug before she maneuvered down the ladder, hopping past the last couple of rungs. "What ya got there?" she asked him, picking up one of the notebooks.

"It's Ivy's life. You will not believe it," he said, then looked at me, realizing that it really wasn't all that great and gave me a weak smile. "It will explain a lot. Here, you need to start with this one." And he took the one she had picked up out of her hands and handed her the story of Willow. She looked at it and flipped through the pages.

"Looks like a fairytale," she mused as she read a couple of lines.

"Yeah, but this is a real one, it turns out," he said as he got up and held out his hand to help me get off the ladder. "You go ahead and start and I'll help Ivy set things up for us to eat." He said with a pat on the chair he had just left. She flopped down into it and opened the notebook to the first page.

I went over to the shelf and started to get down plates and cups and the basket with silverware, when I felt Zack's presence behind me.

"Here, let me reach that," he said, easily taking down the large bowls that I had to stand on my tippy toes to reach. I turned and found myself blocked by him. "Ivy, I'm sorry. I really didn't know," he whispered to me.

"How could you, Zack? Would you even have thought this up in a nightmare?" I asked as I ducked under his arm with the cups. He turned and followed me the couple of steps to the table and set them down next to the cups.

"No, I don't think I would have. Do you remember any of it?"

"Not really, just bits and pieces and in my mind they all happened in a normal span of time," I said not looking at him. I went to the stove but he beat me to it and grabbed the pot of stew before I could. Instead I dug around in one of my baskets until I found the ladle and put it on the table.

"Amazing," he said to himself as he watched me mix up some instant lemonade. I wasn't sure if he was talking about my cooking abilities, the cabin, my store of items, or my life. Any of them could be described as pretty amazing though. I was rather proud of my cabin and how I had arranged everything.

I pointed to the other side of the table and Zack scooted down onto that bench while I sat across from him. Margo joined us, bringing the book along, her nose stuck in it while we put stew into her bowl, then ours.

"Sorry I don't have any bread or fresh meat," I apologized as I started to blow on the stew while I opened a packet of crackers.

"Why didn't you do that thing and just go grocery shopping and come back?" Zack asked nonchalantly

My head jerked up and I stared at him. I could, couldn't I?

"I only learned I could blink yesterday," I said. "But that's a great idea. I could have meat and bread and eggs..."

"And a mocha now and then," Margo added, looking up with a grin.

"Yeah, a mocha!" I agreed, wishing I had one right now.

"Ivy, is Willow really still here, in this forest?" he asked between mouthfuls.

"Yeah, he's by the doorway." At his questioning look, I realized he didn't know where the doorway was. "In that hollow. The tree roots are the doorway." He nodded as if this made sense and continued to eat. "I haven't gone looking for him. I only saw the top of the branches. But it's the only willow tree I've seen in the forest, so it must be him."

"What are you going to do about him?" he asked as if it were just a simple question. His jaw had tightened a bit and it was very apparent that he was giving this a lot of thought. I wondered if he really was Alltha like me and didn't know his own history. There was no way I was going to muddy the waters of my own problems by bringing this up right now. Besides, he's right…this needed thought.

"I've been thinking on it, when my mind wasn't busy dealing with stalkers and creepy fake moms," I teased and won a curling up of his lips as he looked up at me.

"Touché."

"The fey...or I should say the fey from Scotland want to kill him I think."

"I thought you guys couldn't be killed?" Margo stated with wide, innocent eyes, looking up from the book.

"I guess not like normal *dying*. Laven said if our magic is sucked away, we become empty and can die then...or something like that."

"Like a vampire sucks blood?" she asked, looking at both of us. "Hey, are they real too?" It should have been funny as they both looked at me like I would really know.

"I don't know!" I exclaimed in reply to their questioning looks.

"Kind of cool if it was, you know. I bet a lot of starry-eyed girls would love to know one of their favorite movies might be real." Margo smirked at us, showing her cute dimples.

"I didn't like the movies," Zack announced looking annoyed. We both laughed at that, most guys didn't. It was a girl thing for sure. Zack huffed at us and continued to eat. Margo and I shared a look of complete understanding and couldn't keep the giggles away.

Zack finally had enough and laid down his spoon. "Okay already. So fey can't normally be killed, like the Sumair stone did to them…just drained of power into nothingness, right?"

Trying to keep the smile off my face, I redirected my thoughts back to our reality. "Yeah I think so. I think Skyler was so messed up because she took her talisman off, and they must have been really getting to her." I felt a little guilty that I had just stuck Skyler in a tree. "We probably should check on her, you know." They both gave me a questioning look. "We....I....just should. Anyhow, back to the Willow problem. I got the impression from Laven that Allthas and mortals and anything that isn't fey is like beneath these guys. The fey I've met so far seem really territorial on their magic and don't want anyone to have it; even if the person didn't take it on purpose or even want it in the first place. I think these fey haven't been around mortals...ah humans...very much. It's like they were brought up with everyone telling them that tomatoes taste bad so they believed it and never ate one to see for themselves." I wasn't sure if that made sense, but it was the best I could do.

"Prejudice, like racism," Zack responded thoughtfully. He got it.

"Yeah. Take Laven," at the sound of the fey name, Zack's face went rigid. "He speaks about mortals and shifted ones as if they are nothing. He has never known them, so he just thinks, if they aren't fey, they aren't worth anything or even worth thinking or worrying about."

"So he doesn't like Margo and me?" Zack stated, as his face grew dark. "Well I didn't exactly like him either. He was too wishy-washy, too perfect for my taste, something's not right with that guy."

"Well I don't know many fey yet, but the others are like him. Except for that guy Aishal, they were all over the top nice to me. I think he's a little bit fake, myself," I said, making a face the others understood. "He thinks I'm his queen, since I guess, the forest supposedly belongs to me," I said rolling my eyes.

"So what *are* you going to do about Willow?" Margo asked. We both looked at her then back at each other.

"Well, I'm thinking he needs to be released and not given back to the fey for them to continue punishing him. I've been wondering if I can, like, pardon him."

"Does he still have the Sumair stone?"

"Uh, no. Granddad got rid of it. It isn't part of the puzzle at all now. No one, not fey or mortal can get their hands on it now."

"How about those demon things?"

"No...they can't either."

"You sound pretty sure about that," Zack stated, looking hard at me. I could feel his eyes boring into me, and I had to look down before I answered.

"I'm sure. The Sumair stone is out of the picture now and forever."

"So that's why your grandma never talked about it again."

"Uh huh," I said, feeling a little guilty about lying to him.

"If you gave Willow a pardon, where would he go?" Margo asked, pointing at the book. "He sounds like he was really young…has he aged?" Well that was a good question. I hadn't thought about that. Did he know what was going on around him or was he just frozen inside the tree? Or was he just a tree? Crap, I didn't know. Looking at them, I shrugged my shoulders.

"Couldn't he go back to the normal world?" she asked quietly. "You could live there, maybe he could also. The fey wouldn't care about him then." Okay, Margo was not stupid.

"Margo that's a great idea," I said jumping up and looking excitedly at both of them. "If I can reverse the magic of the Sumair stone and bring him back, then I could expel him from this realm into Alainn." I looked around my cabin, not seeing it, but thinking hard. "I could give him money even, for him to take care of himself. I don't know if he would have magic, but he could learn to live without it."

"Are there lots of fey out there?" Zack asked pointing really to nowhere. I looked hard at him, he really didn't know.

"Um, I think there are more fey living out there in that realm than we could imagine. Laven says the fey that live in Alainn are called Alltha, it means wild ones. Some, like me, probably don't even know they are fey." I watched him, and either he was a really good actor...or Laven was lying. I decided Laven was lying and I wasn't sure why.

I sat back down and finished my meal. That was the answer, Margo had it. I couldn't wait to tell Laven that a mere mortal had figured out a plan. I wondered if she could come up with what to do about Aishal too. The meal progressed in a lighter mood, with Margo exclaiming over what she was reading. We discussed the stupid Sumair stone, at least the parts they now knew and all the other things they were learning about.

After dinner they helped me clean up and Margo went and used the outhouse for the first time. When she came back she hurried to wash her hands, pushing us out of the way as we washed the dishes.

"You really need to get a real bathroom here Ivy," she chirped, winkling her nose.

"I know...I want a shower really bad. But I have no idea how to do it. It's not like I can hire a contractor to just put one in," I said agreeing with her.

"Well you know..." Zack said as he dried off his hands. "I think maybe we could add on fairly easily." He looked at me as if I might be upset that he was even thinking of how to change my cabin. But hey, I was open to ideas. It did seem a bit cramped with the three of us. I wondered how Granddad and Marmaw had handled it with all four of us here.

"Go on, how?" I encourage him.

"Well since you can bring other things in, like you did me, maybe we could figure out a way to get the materials here to do it," he finished looking around the small space.

"If she could do that, why not just pop an RV or a trailer...or, I know...one of those manufactured homes?"

Margo said as she bounced over to one of the chairs and took up the book again. "Don't they have ones all built that look like log cabins?"

Zack and I looked at each other shocked, and then we both started to laugh. I was not ever going to discount anything that Margo said again. She was undeniably brilliant.

We popped some popcorn, built up the fire and Zack and Margo read the notebooks. It was after midnight when they finished and now they knew almost everything I did. Margo wouldn't stop hugging me. She would get up to get something to eat or go use the outhouse or grab a quilt to wrap around her and hug me each time. I guess it was her way of telling me she understood what a crappy life had been handed to me. As the early morning started, I needed sleep and bid them goodnight and went up to the loft. Margo joined me soon after and we both quickly fell asleep. I didn't know how long Zack stayed up, but I heard him put more wood on the fire, then nothing more.

I woke to the smell of coffee and pancakes. Food that I hadn't cooked myself…yummy. I hurried to find clean clothes and changed before heading down the ladder. Zack was finishing up flipping a pancake and grinned at me as I walked over to him. He pointed to the table and handed me a cup of coffee. It wasn't mocha, but it smelled just as good.

"Thanks," I said taking it and sitting down at the table. "Where's Margo?"

"Oh she took off a little while ago. She took a pancake with her and said she was going to explore. Is there anywhere that is dangerous?" he asked, growing concerned.

"Nope, not as long as she is wearing that necklace. I think I need to tell her about it. I forgot all about it last night," I said, as I poured syrup heavily over my breakfast. The door flew open and a whiff of the forest wafted in, followed by Margo carrying a large bouquet of flowers.

"I hope it was okay to pick them?" she said, looking panicked. "I had a handful when it dawned on me that I might be destroying something's home." I had to tighten my mouth not to smile… she really was concerned.

"Those are ones from the yard, aren't they?" I asked, sure that they were.

"Uh huh," she answered with wide anxious eyes.

"Then you have nothing to worry about. The fey aren't allowed into my glade at all."

"Oh thank goodness," she said, flopping down across from me.

Zack had pulled down one of my big mason jars, turned green from age, and filled it with water. He set it down in front of her and she arranged the flowers very nicely inside, and then moved it to the center of the table. It was a nice cheery sight and the fragrances made me feel good all over.

"Margo, you are still wearing the necklace, aren't you?" I asked.

"Yeah, see?" she answered pulling it out from inside her shirt. I reached over and inspected it. The moment my fingers touched it I recognized the feel of the talisman. I wished I had touched it in her shop. Maybe I would have known then. I smiled with warmth at her as I let it drop.

"Remember how I told you your grandma's shop had been broken into?"

"Crud, I had forgotten," she cried, getting all worked up again. She stood and started to race to the door. "I've got to go see if she is okay."

"Margo, stop," I yelled at her. She turned in mid-stride and looked back at me. "She's fine. Aishal found my mom's...I mean Skyler's missing talisman. Remember in the notebook? Skyler cut it off herself on the beach. Granddad could never find it. I think somehow your grandma did and knew it wasn't just some random piece of jewelry. I can't believe I'm saying this, but your grandma must really have the ability to see auras. She knew it was important. And so did Aishal. He found it and used it to bring you guys here."

"The necklace is the talisman?" Zack said coming over to look at it.

"Not the necklace, but the little wood heart hanging from it."

"Really?" he asked, in a rather dubious voice.

"Really…look at mine," I said pointing at my own vine-braided necklace. "See it's not the vine, it's that little wood heart. The magic is in it." Zack leaned down and looked closely at mine and then looked at the one Margo wore. "Okay, they do look the same."

"You realize what it does, don't you?" I asked Margo, who shook her head no, then at Zack who stood looking at the notebooks. When his eyes focused again on me, I could see he had dredged up the right thing.

"It lets you come and go through the veil doesn't it? And it keeps the fey away, they can't hurt you."

"You got it. They can't even touch you with magic from far away. Margo when you are wearing that, you can come into this realm and be safe from everything. Nothing can hurt you. Please do not ever take it off, not even to shower or change clothes. Make it part of you," I said as seriously as I could.

"Really? Wowzers," she said and I had to smile at her choice of words. "So I can go home whenever I want to?"

"Laven assured me that you are not shifted. No magic has transferred to you, or to you Zack. You are protected by the talisman and Zack you seem to have protection also, but I'm not sure what it is," I said, wondering if I might have said too much.

"Me?" he questioned suspiciously.

"One or maybe more of the pendants you are wearing. Laven said they are Celtic talismans," I replied cautiously, watching his expression.

"Celtic?" he said looking down at his multitude of

necklaces.

"Yes, Celtic."

"Really? Celtic talismans?" he said again, this time to himself. I'd learned in the short time I'd been around him that when he was nervous or thinking hard, he played with his long hair. He did it again now, taking the front hanging parts and pulling them back, though they just fell forwards again. He turned and walked over to the chair and sat down, mumbling *Celtic*? to himself.

I watched him for a while, then went and sat in the other chair. I started to gather up the notebooks and return them neatly to the box. Trying to seem disinterested I asked, "So does that mean something to you?" He didn't answer. I looked up to find him just staring at me, a shocked expression on his face.

"What Zack?"

"My dad always said these were my protection. He'd laugh each time I'd find a new item…a ring or one of the bracelets. He really would," he said looking at me as if I didn't believe him. "I'd find one that I just had to have…I'd tell him it called to me and he would laugh and slap me on the back and say 'so it does'." He looked down at the rings on his fingers and the bracelets with their stones, then back up at me. I could see him taking a deep breath, distress was written on his face. "Ivy, I know now why I couldn't stop looking for you, why I was...stalking you..." he said with a weak attempt at humor. "You called to me the same way these did," he said, holding up his hand. "It felt the same." I opened my eyes wide at him and twisted my mouth. Hmmm...I *called* to him. Laven could be right. I considered telling him more, but Margo had come over and was standing in front of us.

"I think I need to go home and see if Grandma Winnie is okay with my own eyes. I really like it here Ivy and I'd love to stay, but I need to make sure first. Hey do you know you have vines growing on your face. A pink flower just opened…it's pretty. So can I go see her?" She seemed to have missed the whole *you call to me* thing, and didn't care that plants were growing on me. Who wouldn't like Margo?

I considered her question about going back to town. There was a lot we probably needed to do if all of us were going to stay here. I really didn't want them to leave me now; they knew everything and I liked having friends around me. Zack still looked a bit dazed and had zoned out with his thoughts again.

Looking up at Margo, I nodded agreement. "Let me go see what Laven is up to. Why don't you write a list of things you might need if you do want to come back. Zack..." no response, "…Zack?" I said a little more forcefully.

"Yeah?" he said, finally hearing me and shaking his head to clear it.

"I'm going to see what Laven is up to. Why don't you make a list also of what you might need, that is if you want to go with us and then come back here?" I said, as I stood and went out into the morning. The sun was just starting to rise, and the mist in the air was still heavy enough to feel a slight wetness. I walked over to the arch leading to the forest path.

"Laven are you back?" I yelled out into the void. Birds flew up at the sound of my voice and I scared a squirrel that had been sitting motionless on a branch. It chattered at me for disturbing it before it scurried away.

Instantly Laven popped in on the path and bowed at me before he started to walk down the path to be closer. His color was good and I was amazed to see he had changed clothes. Now he was garbed in leggings that looked like leather and his vest was a bunch of crushed flower petals. Manly and girly all at the same time. It looked good on him.

He stopped a few feet from me and bowed deeply again.

"My lady," he said with adoration, then his eyes left mine, and traveled to behind me. I turned and wasn't really surprised to find Zack standing there. But Laven wasn't done, and to both our stunned surprise he bowed to Zack also. "My lord." I turned back to Zack and mouthed, *what the heck*? but he looked as shocked as I felt. Okay then, something else to ask Laven about when we were alone.

"Laven are the fey here, did they come? And is Aishal all right?" I asked, trying not to let the odd greeting to Zack throw me off.

"Yes Ey-vey. They all came, everyone who could. The forest is filled with our Frìth kin and many other fey that our sisters allowed to join."

"Lost me, Laven. You mean Myste and Whisper?"

"And Aireen, my lady. Any fey who wished to come had to pass their inspection."

"Really? Bryear and Rayni didn't have a say?" I asked, kind of joking, but my words made Laven uncomfortable. My eyes narrowed at him. "Spill it Laven."

"Our brothers seem interested in only one criteria. Our sisters looked at other things," he stammered, and for Laven that was alarming. I had no idea what he was talking about. Behind me, I heard a chuckle that grew into a belly laugh.

"What?" I asked Zack as I turned and found him laughing for all his worth.

"They're looking at their, uh, bodies?" he asked Laven, trying to find a nice way to say it.

Laven hung his head and nodded. Really, were guys the same everywhere? I looked at Zack, who was still finding this hilarious and then back to Laven who was humiliated.

"Enough," I said to both of them. "Laven, tell the sisters thank you and I hope they did find some who the brothers would like also." Laven looked up at me and grinned sheepishly and I knew they had.

"I told the clan that you may wish to speak with them

today in the meadow," he said, once again shy. I didn't like that he was telling fey what I was *going* to do; it was as if he was telling me *what* to do. Wasn't going to work that way, but I didn't want the fey to feel I was dissing them.

"No, today would not be good. Tell the fey that before we speak I think they need to feel comfortable in the forest, to decide for sure if this is where they wish to live."

"They do Ey-vey..." Laven broke in and I put my hand up to stop him. I wish I had a picture of me, just barely 5 feet tall, less than 100 pounds, with red and purple hair, holding my hand up to this god-like personage who towered over me. Who would believe that he actually conceded to me? Amazing.

"Laven, I've decided. I want them to be sure. I want them to look around the forest, inspect it and get comfortable. I would like to speak with each one, and I'm sure, eventually, I'll get the chance, but for now could you please maybe organize them into groups with a spokesman?" Laven was smiling brighter and brighter. "I'm sure there are some extremely wise fey out there," I detected a twitter in the trees above us and had to smile to myself. "Ask them to speak with the other fey and pool together their greatest concerns and maybe have some advice to offer on how to address those concerns. Since I'm leaving I'm going to close the doorway..." Laven moved forward, concern written over his pretty face.

"My lady, there are still fey coming. Can we not leave it open for a few more days?" I looked back at Zack and he wasn't any help, as he only shrugged at me with a crooked grin.

As far as I had read and learned from Laven, Granddad had never left the doorway open when he wasn't here. But this was different, these were fey that wanted to live here and acknowledged I was the owner. Really I had no clue what to do, but I decided since I had sort of froze Laven the last time I left I could do this for him…this one time.

"Okay, until I get back. Then it will be locked until all issues are decided upon," I finished, pretty proud of myself. I even kind of sounded like I knew what I was doing.

"Yes my lady, they will be pleased to hear all your words." He beamed as he bowed again to me.

"I need to go see how Skyler is but I don't know how to find my way back there. Can you take me now? I asked.

"And me," Zack said coming to stand next to me.

"I just checked on her my lady. She is still sleeping peacefully…the same as she always does. It will be many days before she wakes. I will let you know immediately if there is any change. I will see to it that a fey is with her at all times," he said and bowed that annoying bow of his.

"Well okay. I'm going to take Margo and Zack back to town until tomorrow morning," I said and Zack tapped me on the shoulder.

I turned and he leaned down and whispered in my ear. "That's what, 3 or 4 days here?"

He was right and I had forgotten about the time difference again. I thought about what Marmaw had written about Skyler and she had always seemed to sleep for long periods. I didn't think I needed to be worried.

"I think she will stay asleep for the time we are gone," I said to Zack and then turned back to Laven. "When I get back I'll need you to take me to her, okay?"

"Of course. It is very impressive the love and concern you feel for the shifted one. It is my honor to be your servant," he said bowing again. "My lady, I have a request if I may…"

"Yes?" I asked, knowing full well he was giving me compliments just to butter me up for what he wanted.

"The fey would be more comfortable in their natural forms. Could you not release them, as you have me, and my brother and sisters?"

I looked at him and thought about it. I wasn't sure if I felt comfortable with little Wisps all over the place who I didn't know and couldn't see. Like now...I knew we were not alone. Granddad had done it; the diaries had told me that. So I waited for the fire thing to build on my tongue then called out loud enough for any close to hear my words, if not feel them. "All fey in the forest of hemlocks may be in their natural form. I would like to see who I am dwelling with. The glade and my cabin are still off limits, even in Wisp form, but everywhere else, be as you wish to be."

Laven smiled broadly and bowed yet again. I turned to see Zack looking at me oddly. "What? I want to see them. Granddad used to do it," I stated, as I grabbed his arm and pulled him back to the cabin with me.

"You think that was a good idea?" he asked once we were inside.

"You think it would be better to be spied on by bugs?" I smirked back at him.

His response was to give me a quick hug, "No you did well. Laven looked...happy."

"No, he looked like the cat that swallowed the canary," I snapped back, before looking at Margo, who was still sitting at the table writing. "You ready?"

She jumped up, almost knocking the bench over in her excitement. "Yeah, I got a good list of necessary items." I rolled my eyes at her, then picked up my pack and made sure I had money and went up the ladder to grab another change of clothes. When I came down the ladder, I saw Zack rummaging around in the baskets on the shelves.

"Hey, you have a measuring tape around here?" he asked without stopping his search.

"Bottom shelf, silver tool box."

He left off destroying my baskets and bent down to retrieve the little box. He opened it and searched in it for a second. "Got it! Be right back," he declared and rushed out. Margo and I watched him for a moment, then grabbed up our packs and hurried after him. We found him walking around the outside of the cabin and measuring the spaces between it and the fence. “Can we take down this fence?” he asked, as we came over to him.

“No it’s what makes the barrier to keep this part private.”

“Damn. Okay, there’s room on this side, or in the front, and it looks like your Grandpa put leach lines in for the outhouse. If we find something that has the bathroom on this side I can connect it. Wait.” Finally he stopped his musings and looked at me. “Water. Where does the water come from?”

“I don’t know. Granddad put that hand pump in.” Zack was off again to that side of the cabin. He found a small plank of wood that leaned up against the side of the cabin and when he removed it, we could see it was covering a hole that went underneath. He got down on his hands and knees and looked inside. “Okay, it looks like he rigged a pipe line somewhere. Is there a river or stream nearby?”

“Uh yeah, down that way,” I said pointing to the other path.

“I’ll have to check that out later. This will work. I really think this will work,” he said as he stood and grinned at me. I guess he had decided I was getting a home make-over and a bigger house meant more people. I assumed he, at least, had decided to come back with me. I wondered how long he would stay.

“Are we ready now?” I asked, itching for a hot shower.

“Let me get my pack,” he said, walking rapidly around the side of the cabin to the front door. He went inside and was back in a second, holding onto his pack. I touched their shoulders and blinked us to the back side of the motel parking lot.

CHAPTER 35- Laven

As soon as Ey-vey and her friends left, Laven hurried to gather together his siblings. It took longer than he had hoped as the freed fey all wished to stop and speak with him of the wonders of this forest and how great the new owner was. He bobbed his head and made sweet sounds, but hurried as quickly as he could.

The girls were easy to find as they had huddled down near the glade in hopes of a look at the Druid. It was their laughter in the trees that Ey-vey had heard. He was upset with them for showing a bit of their hand by watching unseen and allowing Ey-vey and the others to know they were being watched. But it had worked in his favor; he just wasn't sure how it had. It had been too easy of a thing and it concerned him.

Bryear was found with a group in the meadow and it was hard to draw him away. He had been fairly honest with Ey-vey about what the male fey were looking for. When the hex was taken down for the first time, the males could spend real time with the other fey.

They joined up in the same little hollow as before, cheered that Laven was so easily able to get the Alltha to do what they wanted. The plan had been put in place in regards to making friends with the mortal and the Druid, bringing in a few more of their closer friends in the fey to help. There was no need to tell them why. The female fey were interested enough in the Druid, and jealous enough of the little Alltha fey to join in; the same with the boys in regards to the mortal girl.

None of them could wait to tell Shivf how far they had already progressed. Though now that the hex was gone, and *if* he had been able to enter the forest, he wouldn't already know. Laven was fairly sure where to find him if he had come through the doorway. Laven had given him a map of the Meadhan and the tree where the shifted one had always been kept. It was to be their meeting place. None of them had figured that the shifted one would actually be *in* the tree, however that was a nice bonus.

As a group, they blinked into the secluded glade of giant trees.

"Shivf? Shivf are you here?" Laven called out, wondering if he had somehow gotten lost. The fey was quite old.

"Ah be here, young Laven, ya can stop ye bellowing." Shivf's voice came from behind the tree. Laven and the others started to walk towards his voice, but they discovered that their feet were stuck to the ground.

"What kind of trick is this Shivf?" Laven asked as he frantically tried to remove his feet. This was a new spell, not the type fey would normally use.

"It not be aw trick," Shivf said as he came from around the tree. But it wasn't Shivf who came with the voice, but an ugly little fey.

"Boggart," Whisper hissed as she crouched down like she was about to leap on it and tear it limb from limb.

"Aw, ye be knowing about me, do ye?" the Boggart laughed a raspy deep laugh, as another one of the creatures came out from behind the tree.

"They be looking good enough to eat," the other crackled as he came close and pinched Aileen on her rump. "Nat much meat on this one." He continued to laugh as Aileen swatted at him.

"There is no need for this," Laven stated in his overly silky voice. "I had wondered about you, Shivf. You have a great knowledge of Scotland, the history of the Sumair stone and a visible hatred for Willow of the Wisps. I entertained the thought you might be other than you had said."

"Ye entertained the thought, did ye now?" Pengal said in a sneer.

"Yes, and it does not bother us in the least. You kept your promise to find a talisman and open the doorway. We will keep our promise to help you find the Sumair stone and release Willow so you may do to him as you wish."

"Well that be aw well and good, but me be thinking a bit more permanent-like would be the thing," he scoffed as he held up a large, plump toad. It was still alive and they all watched in revulsion as he twisted its head off and moved towards Laven.

"Open up now, me lad. Just a wee bit tae make ye mind," Pengal crackled as he motioned for Tubaw to hold Laven's arms. Laven fought, twisting and turning, but to no avail. The Boggarts were stronger than they looked. He ended up tightening his lips as much as possible and moving his head away from the disgusting remains of the toad that was being pushed into his face. His struggles were only making the uglier of the two Boggarts twist his arm almost to the point of snapping bones.

For the first time, Laven felt he was in over his head. All the ruses and pranks his little clan had pulled in the past had only gotten them booted out of larger clans, or other Meadhans, but they had never really gotten in trouble. This was to be their greatest adventure, taking their own Meadhan. It was supposed to be fun, a lark. They hadn't planned on physically harming any fey; just tricking them out of what they owned.

Now here he was, being held by what could only be the darkest of all magic. He knew what the toad meant…Eilibear. The demons were behind this. The damned Boggarts had joined forces with the demons, and now were going to enthrall them with frog blood tainted with Eilibear shades. This was not good, and Laven didn't know if they would survive. The one with the toad came close and reached out to Laven, roughly pinching his nose shut. Laven held his breath as long as he could, before there was no choice. He opened his mouth, and the slime from the toad was squeezed in.

His brother and sisters were screaming and trying various spells, none had any effects on the Boggarts or the Eilibear evil the Boggarts were forcing inside them. Laven watched as one by one they were subjected to the same abuse as he had been. He could feel the tiny shade dig into him and he fought against it, but the darkness came. His mind was still his, but he knew his actions and words would not be. Now their only hope was the Alltha that they had been trying so hard to manipulate. She had to be more than he thought her to be or all of them were lost.

"There now," Pengal said when the last of them were contaminated. "We be liken your plan. But we want the Druid killed, get the protection off of the lad and kill him! And find the Sumair stone!" He patted the face of Bryear, feeling the tears the fey was shedding. He turned to find Tubaw pinching the breasts of one of the females. She didn't even seem to notice, gone away into herself to try and survive the horror. He walked over and slapped Tubaw smartly on the head.

"Leave them be," he snarled as he dragged his brother away to the tree that they had made their home in, leaving the fey stuck there and giving the Eilibear poison time to set in.

CHAPTER 36 - Ivy

"I thought you'd like your jeep," I told Margo as we blinked in and she realized where we were. She hugged me and bounded off, then came back and held out her hand to Zack. I wasn't sure what she wanted until Zack dug in his pocket and pulled out her key ring.

"Your pack is in the back seat," he called out after her.

"Thanks," she called as she took off again. "I'll be at the shop or back here if you don't come for me…don't you leave me behind. I'll walk in if I have to," we heard her yell as she started her jeep and pulled out.

"Zack, I don't know what day it is. We need to find out. Remember, there is a time difference between the realms," I whispered to him as we started to walk towards the motel room. He thought about that, and then changed directions. I followed as he walked purposefully to the motel office. The little bell clanged as we entered and the large woman I had seen before looked up at us.

"Hi," Zack called out cheerfully. "I couldn't remember how many days I paid for."

"That's okay sweetie, you are paid up until day after tomorrow. Did you need it for longer?" she asked looking around him at me with a lecherous smirk on her face.

"No, but my girlfriend is going to stay with me tonight and tomorrow. Do I owe you more?"

She waved him off. "No, you two go have fun, just make sure you have protection," she said with a disgusting wink. To my dismay my face turned beet red and Zack sounded like he was choking as he pulled me out of the office.

We walked back to the room in silence, and I waited as he opened the door. When we got inside and had the door closed, he started laughing again until tears were running down his face. I wasn't sure what embarrassed me more, that Zack had told the lady I was his girlfriend or the comments the lady had made. Okay I was pissed at both. I stood there glaring at him.

"Have protection?" he managed to say, and then held up his necklaces. "We've got protection all right." Then he was laughing again. Sheesh, he found that funny? Really? Weird sense of humor this guy had. I didn't say anything; instead I gave him a look of annoyance before walking over to the bathroom and closing the door on his laughter.

After I undressed I got in the shower and let the warm water flow over me. Eventually I washed my hair, then just stood there some more. I didn't want to get out, but Zack starting banging on the door and demanding the use of the toilet. No way was I going to share; we weren't that good of friends. I finished up and wrapped a towel around me, then opened the door. He was standing there waiting, not very patiently I should add. I ducked under his arm as he hurried in. I caught a look at myself in the mirror; my vines were now the little green lines again. Cool. No one would be looking oddly at me.

I pulled on my jeans and a sweatshirt and dug around for some cash. I only had 5 bills with me, hundreds of course. We could get some food, and I was thinking some lawn chairs might be nice to have in my glade. After I finished at the post office, I'd stop in at the hardware store and see what they had.

By the time Zack was done, I was ready to leave.

"Where are you off to?" he asked as he washed his hands.

"Post office, hardware store, library and food," I called out as I opened the door.

"I'll be at the library, look for me," I heard him shout as I closed the door. I blinked and stood in the alley behind the small post office. It was deserted, except for the blackberries that were threatening to take over the side fence. I retrieved my new driver's license from my bag. I had never used it, but thought it wise to get it after drivers' ed last semester. Mom wouldn't let me use the car, even though she never did. I stopped midway through that thought...she wasn't my mom. When would those memories go away?

An older man stood behind a set of security bars when I entered the post office. I wondered when they had to start locking postal workers up, then snickered at my own bad joke. I was as bad as Zack. I went to stand in line and when it was my turn, I moved up close and smiled sweetly at the old man.

"Hi. I don't have a box, but this is the address my parents gave me to use while I'm staying with my aunt. I'm supposed to ask for general delivery?" I asked in an innocent voice.

"Sure miss. Do you have any I.D.?" He inquired, trying to look all important-like. I handed him my license and he looked it over, looked at me, then back at the picture. Come on, how many girls have purple and red hair? He handed it back and disappeared around a tall shelf.

An older woman came in and stood behind me, complaining about having to wait. She talked endlessly about her feet, the wait and getting no respect from young people. I decided it was best to ignore her, but she insisted on just talking to my back. I was extremely happy when the guy came back. He was holding a small manila envelope and a brown box. He handed them to me and I could see right off they were from Uncle Geraint.

"Thanks," I said without looking up and turned around to leave, bumping into the old crab of a lady. I mumble apologies and hurried out as she told the next person in line that she didn't think my hair looked normal. Nice. Well at least I didn't bore perfect strangers with stories about my feet.

There was a little wooden bench in the entryway of the post office. I took off my pack and sat down. The envelope was flat, so I figured it was a letter. I opened it and pulled out a folded up piece of white paper. A small paper sleeve holding a plastic card fell out onto the ground. Picking it up fast before someone walked on it, I could see it was a credit card. I sat there looking at the thing… I'd never used one before nor had anyone in my family. I wasn't sure what I was supposed to do with it, so I stuck it back in the envelope and looked at the paper. It was a letter from Uncle Geraint. It was written in fancy longhand, so I knew it was his…he never typed anything.

"Dear Ivy,

I received your letter and I have to admit I am distraught, but not at you dear. I am upset with myself and the other Uncles.

It is our duty to watch and protect and we failed you. I will apologize to Milton later, but I am going to break his trust and the Alltha's canon. I have a feeling that the veil is already coming down for you even though you have not achieved the age.

I got that far and stopped. How could he apologize to Granddad later if he was dead? And what other uncles? I only knew of one, him. I'd just learned the word *Alltha*, that's what I was. A wild fey. So there was a gun thing for wild fey?

People kept coming and going, opening and closing the door and I realized this might not be the best place to read this. I folded it back up and without looking at anything else, put it in my pack, picked up the box and went out.

Standing in the chilly sunshine, I tried to think where I should go and kept coming back to the same idea. The library. Zack would be there and it might be nice to read this and have him to discuss it with. I blinked over to it, not caring if anyone saw me pop in or not. The library here was sad; an ugly flat topped building with peeling paint. It looked deserted. There were only a couple of cars in the far parking lot, but the lights were on.

I went in and the librarian looked up and nodded at me. It wasn't hard to find Zack; it was a really small library. He sat at one of three computers. I walked over and stood behind him, trying to see what he was looking at.

"Hi," he said without turning around.

"Hi. I've got mail," I said like a computer voice.

He looked up then and gave me a *really, you just said that*? look.

"I mean it. At the post office, there was a letter and this box." The box was under my arm; his eyes moved to it before he turned back to the computer.

"Hold on, let me write this down and then I'm done for now," he said as he wrote a couple of notes on scratch paper then logged off. The library had one reading nook with two old but comfy chairs where we could sit and talk privately. I opened my pack and got out the envelope and the letter. Zack leaned close so we could read it together.

"Dear Ivy,

I received your letter and I have to admit I am distraught, but not at you dear. I am upset with myself and the other Uncles.

It is our duty to watch and protect, and we failed you. I will apologize to Milton later, but I am going to break his trust and the Alltha's canon. I have a feeling that the veil is already coming down for you even though you have not achieved the age."

I stopped reading it over again and pointed that out to Zack. "See that's what Laven said I was; a wild fey, an Alltha. I don't understand about the cannon though, what does a weapon have to do with this."

"Ivy, look at how it's spelled. Not cannon, like boom!

But a canon…like a law," Zack said and I felt kind of stupid. Chalk one up for the older guy.

"I gathered from your letter that you are under the impression that your grandparents are deceased, and that Skyler has been living with you for this past year and taking the funds that were meant for you. My dear, this is not the best manner in which to tell you, but your letter has prompted me to take some action and I cannot be with you at this time.

Your grandparents are not deceased, at least not to my knowledge. I can only assume that Skyler informed you incorrectly, no doubt on purpose. Skyler herself was supposed to be in a lock-down with another Uncle, however I have just now discovered him missing, as well as Skyler.

Again, I made an oath to Milton that we would keep the veil on for you until his return, but since you have gone to the cabin it has no doubt already started to come down.

As you know, Skyler has never been right in the mind. To say that she has been a handful for all of us is an understatement. Last year she mutilated herself, cutting out her protection. Elsie was unaware and how the girl hid it no one knows. We can only put together the pieces by conjecture now, but we believe Skyler led Elsie to where the Eilibear were waiting and gave them her mother, probably thinking the things would then leave her alone. When Elsie and Skyler did not come home, Milton went to find them, discovered Skyler close to death and Elsie gone. Milton brought Skyler to me and I put her in the lock-down.

He and Uncle Rōber left to retrieve Elsie. We knew it would take some time so the trust was set so that you would be taken care of until his return.

My dear, I am so sorry that Skyler got away from us. I can only assume the worst, please watch out for her. She cannot enter the forest, but I believe she may get help from the Eilibear and be able to find a way in. She means you and the forest great harm.

As for your trust fund. I myself may be gone for a time and did not wish to leave you without means. Enclosed you will find a credit card. It is in your name and your pin is the name Elsie gave you before we knew you as Ivy. It is unlimited, whatever you need my dear.

Stay safe. One of the Order is aware that you are in the area and will be checking on you soon, and with luck, your grandparents will return shortly also.

With my deepest love, Uncle Geraint.

To say I was speechless was putting it mildly. I re-read the letter a couple of times, then looked up at Zack with tear-filled eyes.

"They're alive? Oh my goodness, they're alive," I mumbled as I slumped back in the chair. Granddad and Marmaw had been alive all this time and Skyler had purposely told me that they were dead? She had been locked up by Uncle Geraint and got away and wasn't even supposed to be with me? And it was her fault that they were gone? I was almost screaming in my head at her. If she wasn't already locked away, I'd find a way to make her pay.

"Ivy, are you okay?" I heard Zack's voice as from afar, and turned to it with vacant eyes. "Ivy, come on snap out of it." He took my hand and squeezed it. I looked down at his hand holding mine and didn't feel anything; my emotions were on overload…anger, joy, fear, rage and mostly shock.

He reached over and touched my face where the vines lay hidden. "Come back here, Ivy, there's more in this letter than your Grandparents being alive. More than Skyler being an ass-wipe." And he leaned in even closer, almost blowing into my ear, "My father's name is Rōber. He left about a year ago with my Uncle Glenwood."

Well that seemed to do it, another shock was just what I needed.

"That's our last name, Glenwood. We're cousins!" I screamed, not caring about the stares of the librarian and a couple of young kids who had come in with their moms and were in the little kid book area.

"Shhhh..." he said as he put his finger to my lips. I sat up and mentally shook myself. I had to get a grip. I refused to ask the question that I had been asking myself for weeks. The whole *can my life get any more weird* thing had taken on a whole new dimension. I was starting to worry that if I kept asking that question, the answer would always be *yes*.

I leaned close to him and whispered between clenched teeth. "You think we are cousins?"

"No I don't…not blood ones like you are thinking. Milton and Elsie aren't your blood Grandparents, but they adopted you…made you family. Tell me, is Uncle Geraint really old, with pure white hair and does he wear bow ties?"

"Yeah and he drives this really cool old car, it's a..."

"1939 fully restored Crosley..."

"It's red and tan," I finished looking expectantly at him.

"Ivy, I have a lot of *uncles*. They were always coming around and then Dad would take off and I'd have to stay with one of my aunts, and there were bunches of them also," he whispered with eyes as wide as mine. "Was your Granddad tall and really big and solid looking, always wearing checkered flannel shirts?"

"Yeah," I said, slumping back in the chair again.

"Wow," he said and slumped back in his own. "I think there's this group of Allthas with laws and our families are part of it. Your Grandma's diaries said they had met other Allthas that they had become friends. If my dad is part of it then that might mean...." he left the statement unspoken. I already knew, only since Laven had kind of told me. Now I had proof and Zack was just finding out. I guess I should have told him what Laven had told me.

I don't know how long we just sat there in silence, staring off into space, but it dawned on me that the little credit card was still in the envelope. I sat up again and picked the manila thing up and emptied it into my lap. The little sleeve holder fell out. I pulled out the card and found myself holding a gold card with my name on it. I knew what the pin was...Ruth, and Zack probably had figured that out also. I held it up at him and mouthed 'unlimited', as I raised my eyebrows at him, grinning impishly like only a teenage girl could.

"Cool," he said, his lips turned up in a grin.

I picked the package up next and took a look around the library. Other people had come in and we already had created a little scene as it was. I glanced at Zack and whispered, "Motel?" and he nodded. We gathered up everything and started to walk out the main door. Just as we exited I blinked us both back to the room.

We dropped everything and I hurried to open the package. Zack had to take over when I couldn't get the tape off the cardboard box. He was able to rip up one flap and I upended the box. A smaller box dropped out onto the bed.

I recognized it. Granddad had made a box for each of us a few Christmas's ago. This one looked like Skyler's. Wrapped around it was a thin blue cord, and it was really wrapped around it. Several times one way; then again, several times the other way. I tried to pull them off and they wouldn't loosen. Zack pulled out his knife, but it had no effect on the cord. I ended up sitting on the bed holding this little wooden box wrapped with cords, wondering what I was supposed to do with it. As I touched the cords I noticed that weird tingle of heat at the back of my throat. I hadn't told Zack about that either. Looking down at the box, I wondered if magic was the key.

When Zack went to use the bathroom, I held the box close to my lips and whispered, "Please open," letting the heat come out. The blue cords seemed to melt off and I was left with just the box as Zack came back in.

He stopped walking as soon as he saw the box void of

the cords. "How'd you get them off?"

I looked up at him, and rolled my shoulders up, "I asked it to please open."

"Okay," he said making a face and sitting down next to me. I guess that wasn't any weirder than anything else. I lifted the lid of the box and we both looked inside. It was empty except for a small brown heart.

"It's one of your talismans isn't it?" he asked.

Yeah. I think its Marmaw's…the one she gave Skyler after her first one was lost. This is Skyler's box that Granddad made. It's made out of hemlock wood." I tried not to think about the fact that this little heart had been inside Skyler. I just hoped Uncle Geraint had washed and sterilized it. Yuck. But it had been Marmaw's first and I kept thinking that thought as hard as I could.

"Is that like the one Margo has?" He said pushing it around with his finger.

"It's a slightly different color. I think the one Margo has is the first one Skyler had that was lost on the beach," I said as I looked at it. If it was still a working talisman maybe Zack could wear it for protection, and come and go to my forest also. He must have read my thoughts. I watched as he moved a bunch of smaller bracelets off of the larger wristband on his right arm. It was a really cool wristband. The leather was little more than a rough cut of hide and three polished stones were inlaid into it. I watched as he pushed down hard on the center stone and turned it. When he let loose, the stone popped up on a hidden hinge.

"May I?" he asked, pointing at the tiny heart.

"Sure," I said with a sly grin, not wanting to bring up where it had been before. He gingerly picked it up and dropped it inside the hollow the stone had left. He pushed the stone down over it and twisted it again.

"Never had anything that I wanted to put in there before," he said with a crooked grin. I smirked at that, wondering how he had even known the thing would open.

I picked up the credit card, waved it and looked at him with a devious smile.

CHAPTER 37 - Ivy

"I know what to do with that first if you are game," Zack announced as he eyeballed the credit card.

"Sure," I answered, wondering what he had thought up.

He started to pick his stuff up. I followed suit, pushing the trash aside and closing up my pack. "Ready?" he said standing and holding out his hand. I took it and he didn't let go as he walked me out into the late morning sunshine. It was finally starting to warm up a bit, but the wind was still blowing, making me glad I had a sweatshirt.

"Look down the road, way down. See that blue and red sign?" he said pointing away from town to a car lot and a few sparsely placed businesses.

"Okay, I see it."

"Blink us somewhere around there." I didn't ask why, I just did as he asked and found we were on the other side of the car lot. I remembered seeing this place when the bus went by, but thought it was a trailer park. Now I saw it was a combination RV and manufactured home place. Zack looked at me with a smug secret grin and walked me to the office. Once inside he pulled out a paper from his pack covered with figures and notes and proceeded to talk to the salesman.

I was impressed; he had worked it all out. What size would fit, where the rooms needed to be and what sort of rooms. He told the man that we owned a piece of land where there was no electricity and we wanted something prefabricated and ready to place. The salesman listened and looked at his notes, then eyed us. I could see what he was thinking, we looked like rejects from a bad all-night frat party, and how could we afford this?

"Zack?" I asked innocently, pulling out my gold card. "Why don't we just order on-line like Daddy said, and have it delivered? Then we wouldn't need to take up this man's time?" Zack rolled his eyes at me.

The man jumped up, grabbing fliers of the manufactured homes they carried and assured us he had some models that might work. We looked over a few of the fliers and then followed him out to the lot.

Zack put his arm around my waist and pinched me playfully, "That was quick thinking," he whispered.

I have to admit, it was fun. We looked in several model homes, most looked really contemporary and already furnished for showing. I fell in love with one of the models, not because it was so great, but the furniture inside was awesome, country and old farm house looking. The dining room table was like a large butcher block with padded chairs in red and white. I got stuck in the bedroom; I couldn't stop looking at the bed. Zack finally had to pull me out of that one to see yet another.

And there were some really cool ones, but in every one, Zack would shake his head, it was too big, wrong shape, bathroom on the wrong side, or something. We had almost given up and both of us were feeling a little let down when we exited from the back door of one and found ourselves at the very back of the lot. There, sitting on large beams as a base, was a log house, well really part of a log house.

"What's that?" I asked, pointing at it.

The salesman looked where I pointed and sighed. "Some rich dude had ordered a log cabin built from a kit. They built it in three parts and were moving it down the coast. Some trucker coming the other way lost control and hit the first hauler. It was a huge accident; the two front haulers lost their load. This is all that's left." It was a sad story, I felt sorry for everyone, but I couldn't stop looking at the odd house.

It looked like it had been cut from another piece; two stories angling down to one on the other side, kind of, the roof lines were all strange. Someone had put plywood and plastic up to cover the open side and the logs must have never been sealed, because they were a dull faded brown now. One side had a stone chimney. I'd never seen anything like it.

"We haven't figured out what to do with it. It's been sitting there for a couple of years now," the man said as he tried to have us follow him to yet another of the pre-fab models. Zack and I just stood there looking at it. It was almost square, at least five times bigger than my cabin and was two stories.

"Hey, we want to see that," Zack called to the salesman who was walking away.

"Kids you don't want that. It's a mess," he said looking at us like we had lost our minds.

"We would like to see it," Zack repeated and grabbed my hand as he started walking towards it. The man followed and he gave us this speech about it not being stable up on those beams as we came up to it. He really didn't want to show it to us, and kept trying to discourage us, but we were seeing something he wasn't. It was perfect, at least on the outside.

The salesman had to climb up, and then tried the door, which we thought was funny since he could have just gone in though the plastic. But the door was unlocked and he motioned us up. Zack easily picked me up and placed me on the deck, then climbed up after me.

It was amazing. The lower floor was open, with the kitchen on one end and the other looked like half of what was meant to be a lot larger room. The fire place was complete with the rocks, and it was off center on the wall. Back by the kitchen was half of a bathroom, only the toilet part remained. A staircase sort of cut the room in half and went up half way and turned two directions. One part went to nowhere, but the other lead to three rooms. A small room cut by the open side, it might have been a sitting room for a larger bedroom and then a long room with windows that at least two beds would fit in. The last room was a large bathroom with a walk-in shower. It was missing one wall, but other than that was complete. There was a railing that ran the length of the hallway and you could look down into the living room section below. The whole thing was odd, misshaped and unfinished. It was perfect.

We went back down the stairs and stood in the kitchen. A large butcher block counter sat in the center, with open shelves for stuff on the walls. The coolest wood burning stove I had ever seen sat against the wall, all chrome and black cast iron. It had a baking drawer and a top warming thing and I couldn't stop playing with it.

Zack was going through all the miscellaneous stuff piled around. It just looked like cans and metal boxes to me. There were coils of wire and tubing and flat panels and parts of windows leaned up against the walls. Zack finally finished looking at that stuff and came over to look at the stove. Off the back there were two stove pipes going up. One angled towards the outside wall, while the other went up to the second floor.

"What's this about?" he asked the salesman.

"The man that designed this was trying to come up with ways to heat the upstairs. That vents to the bedrooms. Supposedly when the damper is open, it carries the heat from the stove up there and will heat the rooms," he answered with a shrug, like he didn't think it would work.

Zack wandered outside and around the structure and took notes. When I joined him he was already telling the man we would take it, but that it needed to be worked on first. I just followed along behind the guys as they discussed what contactors the salesman knew and we ended up back in the office with the man on the phone.

Both of them pulled out paper and were discussing building plans and I was bored. I asked for a pad of paper and some post-it notes and told them I was going to go look at the furniture in the model I liked. As I left, a man in a beat up white pickup pulled up. He looked like someone who built things; his truck was filled with ladders and paint cans and tools. Zack was going to have fun.

I ended up back in the model with the country furniture and went around with my notepad and wrote down the numbers of the stuff I liked and put post-it notes on the pieces. I really took my time, and filled out a couple of pages and went through several models until I knew I had enough to furnish our new home.

By the time I went back to the office all the paperwork was filled out, and the contractor had a list of what to do. Zack informed him that everything needed to be completed by tomorrow night. Everyone agreed, signed the paperwork and I used my credit card for the first time, trying not to think of what I was spending. It was a large amount for the house, the work and all the furniture I had listed. The salesman looked like he was gleefully figuring up his commission when we left.

CHAPTER 38 - Elsie

June 1, 1987 –

It was a very fun trip on the train and then on the greyhound bus up to Coos Bay. Ivy finds the funniest things to do and say. She looks about 12 now and really has a mind of her own. A woman at one of the stops had a little yappy dog that would not stop barking. The woman was trying to calm it, but it was not minding. Ivy walked up to it, not caring that the woman said it might bite, in fact she didn't pay the woman any attention at all. She focused on the dog, telling it was insufferable and making too much noise. Then she told it 'stop being a brat and be quiet'. The dog yapped once at her, curled up nicely in its stunned owner's lap and went to sleep. "She has a way with animals." was all I could say and hurried Ivy away. It was funny.

We got into Coos Bay in the late evening. Milton had booked a room for us in a nice little motel close to Winnie's shop.

June 4, 1987

It has been a busy few days for Ivy and me. We spent the first day with Winnie and walked on the beach. Ivy played in the sand giving us time to talk. The dear really did find it and has agreed to help me in any way she can. I gathered that she too has had run-ins with the Uncles and dislikes their sexist attitudes. She is one of the few that 'know' me well.

It was odd to put a talisman on again after all this time. I packed all the notebooks, writings and drawings I had prepared into a backpack and then took Ivy for a walk to the cabin.

She was thrilled to be back and I let her run and play, feeling a bit sad knowing she wouldn't remember any of it later. I went through the diaries again and ended up needing to tear out only the last few pages. She wouldn't need that information. Then I emptied out my chest that held my art supplies and put the other items in, laying some of the art supplies on top. Milton never bothers with my stuff so I know everything will be safe until it is needed.

Milton would be very upset with me if he knew what I was up to, but it doesn't matter to me what the Uncles nor what Milton thinks at this point. This is about Ivy and she will need any help I can give her.

We stayed only a couple of nights and then went back to town. I helped Winnie put the talisman in its new home until it is needed and I gave her the other little book to keep for when Ivy comes. She doesn't fully understand everything I'm doing, but helps me anyway.

I do not know when or if I will ever be able to return here. There is a horrible darkness ahead. I have done all I can.

CHAPTER 39 - Ivy

We walked down the road holding hands gaily, like little kids. As soon as we were out of sight, Zack had me blink us to the hardware store. He took off and I didn't see him again for quite some time, but I didn't care. I had time to find outdoor chairs and some other stuff that I thought was fun, I purchased them and had them loaded onto a large dolly. When the sales clerk turned his back, I blinked it all back to the glade of the cabin, leaving the dolly behind of course. I just left it all there in a messy pile in the middle of my pretty glade, then blinked back to find Zack.

He had been just as busy. I found him in the lumberyard of the store with a long list of items that he and another salesman had worked up, along with a pulley cart of even more stuff. With him grinning beside me, I paid for everything and told the sales clerk we would be back tomorrow with a truck to pick it up.

Next stop was the bookstore, which we walked to in the normal way. We were having fun and I could see people reacting to our smiles and silliness. This was the kind of adventure I'd always dreamed of...a cute guy, friends and the feeling that I had a family again and a home and a life and ...geez everything.

In the book store, Zack found so many he wanted to get that I wondered when he'd have time to read all of them. There were building books, masonry books, and books on solar power, ones on living in the woods, survival and on and on. I found some for just plain enjoyment and a really cool one on the most famous songs of the 1960's.

Granddad would have loved reading it with me and in the back of my mind, I was kind of hoping that someday we might have the chance to do just that.

After we bought all of them, I blinked us to the motel, we made a pee stop, then headed back to the parking lot behind Grandma Winnie's store. Not wanting to seem too familiar, we walked to the front of the store and went in with the cute little chime declaring our entry.

"Ivy! Zack!" Margo yelled when she saw us. She was standing in the back aisle with Grandma Winnie, who looked up with a worried expression as we entered. Margo pulled her grandma reluctantly towards us, then gave up and ran up to us.

"I showed her I had the necklace and told her sort of where I went and she didn't say anything," she whispered to us. I didn't blame the poor lady; she probably thought Margo had lost her mind. Your store gets broken into, then your own granddaughter shows up wearing the only thing that was stolen, and I could just imagine Margo trying to tell her about Meadhan and the fey. Good grief, this should be real interesting.

The little lady looked like every grandma should look, small and white haired with delightful wrinkles that played over her face. Her eyes were a light, murky blue and they locked onto mine as she hesitantly came closer.

"Hi, we haven't met before, but I've heard a lot about you," I said putting out my hand and smiling gently at her. She looked at my hand and I could see her lips moving, then she reached out and took mine in a soft grip. Her face seemed to clear, as she looked at our hands together, then up at me. "Alltha," she whispered.

Margo looked from her grandma to me, then to Zack. We were speechless. Zack recovered first.

"Madam, you know the Alltha?"

Grandma Winnie pulled her eyes away from mine and looked at him. She released my hand, then reached out towards Zack and placed her palm against his cheek. He hadn't shaved and I wondered how the stubble felt. She held it there for a moment, and then did a soft slap thing against his cheek. "Curious," she declared as she turned and started to walk towards the back, gesturing for us to follow.

"Grandma?" Margo called out, hurrying after her. Zack and I gave each other a wide-eyed look and followed quickly.

She had stopped at the little table in their break area and motioned for Margo to make some tea and for us to sit down, while she gathered a used looking candle. Placing it in the center of the table, she lit it with a match. Then she sat and studied us, her face changing from that of a sweet grandma to that of a serious-minded business woman. She looked like she knew how to be in control of any situation.

The candle was burning oddly, making more smoke than flame and she waved it around at us. I coughed, but Zack just sat there watching her. No one said anything until Margo had finished with the tea, set cups down for everyone and took another chair.

"Grandma?" she started again.

Grandma Winnie reached out and patted her granddaughter's hand. "Shhh now Margaret, it will all be explained." Then she turned to us again, looking at me first. "Tell me Ivy...who are you?" she asked as she took a sip of her tea.

I looked questioning at my friends and they weren't any help. "Uh, I'm Ivy."

"Yes dear, I know you know that. But do you know *who* you are?" she asked in a gentle voice. I gathered that she was asking more than my name; she knew something about the Alltha, so this must be a test.

"I'm Ivy, of the Frìth fey and I am the rightful owner of a Meadhan doorway?" I said with a question. She humphed at me, then looked at Zack.

"And who are you dear?"

"I'm not sure. I think Dad is working with the Allthas, with the Uncles and maybe I'm some sort of fey like Ivy," he replied not taking his eyes off her. She sipped her tea a couple more times, giving herself time to think.

"Grandma Winnie? I think he might be something called a Druid, one of the fey told me they thought he was, but I didn't know if I should believe him," I added hesitantly, thinking I had better come clean about knowing.

"Wait, who told you?" Zack asked looking at me miffed.

"Laven, when he told me about the pendants. I thought he was trying to make me not like you. Sorry, I didn't want to tell you because I thought it would make you mad."

"Yeah, you should have told me, maybe the letter about my dad being mixed up with your Granddad might not have been such a surprise," he growled.

"Well, sorrrry," I snapped back. "I didn't know, and still don't know what a Druid is. I thought he might be calling you yucky fey slurs. Give me a break, Zack, this is all new to me too, remember?"

"That will be enough, you two," Grandma Winnie said curtly, slapping us both on the hand. "It is not time for either of you. You, young man, have at least 2-3 more years before you were to be told and then your training would have begun. And you, my dear, should have been allowed ten or more years. This is not the way, but it has happened, and everything happens for a reason…and to be truthful, the Seer spoke of something like this occurring."

"Seer?" I asked and all three of us waited for her to reply.

"A Seer, someone who sees the future. She's the one that told me where to put the necklace, that it would be needed. She also told me that Margaret would end up with it," she said looking over at Margo.

"Cool," Margo said cheerfully.

"Did the Seer say anything else we should know? Can

we speak with her?" Zack asked hopefully.

"Even if she did, I cannot tell you…and no, you may not speak with her," Grandma Winnie said ending that discussion. "Tell me Ivy, who told you about the Alltha?"

"I heard the term first from the fey in the forest," I confessed. "And saw it in some of Marmaw's writing. Then again in the letter from Uncle Geraint." She 'humphed' at me, again.

"And you?" she demanded of Zack.

"I guess from Ivy and the letter. The term keeps coming up, and the Uncles. It appears that the man I called Uncle Glenwood is Ivy's granddad. He and my dad are off hunting the Eilibear and looking for her grandma," he said as he took a drink of his tea, looking a little silly holding the tiny cup with pink roses on it.

"Too much, and not enough," she proclaimed and set her cup down, looking at Zack with hard eyes. "How did you find Ivy?" For the first time during the questioning, she seemed bothered.

"I guess we bumped into each other. I was going to college in Ashland…well wait, I *was* going to college back east, that's where Dad enrolled me, but it was a bore, so I transferred to the one in Ashland. I liked it better there, and anyway, signed up for a summer hiking program at the end of the school year. I saw Ivy on the bus trip here and...well..." he didn't finish and looked over at me, clearly uncomfortable.

"He was stalking me, Grandma. He said I smelled good and he couldn't stop following me," I finished for him with a smirk.

She 'humphed' once more, and this time chuckled. "Yes I'm sure you do smell good to him." With that odd statement, she seemed to revert to just a sweet little grandma and looked at Margo.

"My dear, could you get me my glasses, please." Margo jumped up and went over to the counter and came back with a purple case. Handing it to Grandma Winnie, she sat down again.

"Are you going to do the aura thing?" she asked as we all watched the little lady take her glasses out and perch them on her nose.

"I think it would be a wise thing," she said and turned to me. "Hmmm, I see green, bright green in fact around the edges, with a bit of red around the mouth. There's a hint of blue near your heart," she announced.

"Is green good?" I asked, leaning closer.

"Yes dear...it means you have a strong ability to heal, to fix things. It's an earth color; you are part of the earth and have an abundance of new growth in you," she said, warming up as she spoke. "The red is not...normal...for a Frith. Have you discovered any interesting things you seem to be able to do?"

"I get this weird feeling in the back of my throat and on my tongue and if I like…push it out when I speak, my words kind of happen." Both Zack and Margo looked at me with shock, and I made a face like *weird huh*?

"Give me an example dear," she asked quietly.

"Um, if I let it loose, I can lock a door with it or make a fey go to sleep," I admitted, feeling mortified and not sure why.

"A very different magic," she mused. "Must have come from the stone."

"How about Zack? What color is he?" I asked, wanting to change the subject.

She turned to him and looked him over from head to toe, then leaned closer and felt his hair and handled some of his pendants. When she sat back, she seemed captivated by him.

"I've never met a Druid before in person. His colors are very vivid. They start out pure blue at his center and move to a darker hue of the same. Around his head there is a crown of maroon and at his feet is a dark earthy brown.

The right arm is deep blood red; it pulses as if it wants to escape. That must be his Dywel," she said as if it worried her.

"So just what *is* a Druid and the dry well thing? Does it have something to do with the stories about Stonehenge? I am a fey right? Like Ivy?" he asked, and I couldn't tell if he liked the idea or not.

"The Druids were once common fey; they started out that way at least. But they became warriors, and in the land of Firinn, that was useless. There are no wars or battles to be fought there. The Druids moved up into the Meadhans and Alainn and found a way to use their gifts. No one crosses a true Druid…they are Allthas, dangerous ones that still have fey honor. The Dywel is your weapon, all Druids have them. Yours is there, almost mature and it is bright red."

"So I'm a warrior and I have a weapon in my arm?" he stated smiling at me. Okay, he was liking this. So was I, really. Pretty cool that this wild-haired guy had turned out to be as weird as me and little Margo's grandma was part of it, which made Margo even more part of it. "Does that mean Dad is one also? And how do I use this?" he said looking at his arm. It looked just like a normal arm with lots of jewelry on it.

"Like I've said, I've never met a Druid before. I don't know how it works; you were supposed to have training. I don't know about your family; do you know where they are from?" She asked as she reached out and took his hand, rubbing her thumb over the top of it.

"Mostly Wales, but I've traveled a lot with my dad. I've been to many places, but the U.S. and the British Isles mainly."

"Most Druids originate from those areas, as well as Scotland and some from Ireland," she said. "Now give me both of your hands."

Zack did so and she took hold of them, closing her eyes.

She swayed a little, then started to speak in a low almost trance-like voice.

"Your feet are rooted, very firm. You are still trying to find what you are meant to do, but you like yourself and you have balance." It was silent in the room as we all waited for her to continue. We could see her eyes moving around under the closed lids. When her voice came again, I saw Zack jump a bit. "You are very independent. It's your head that gives you problems, you take everything to its full level; anything physical, hate, love...passion. There is no middle ground for you…it's either one or the other. Good or bad, right or wrong. Because of this, you have a hard time connecting with others; you stand apart but are searching for where you belong."

I watched the emotions play across Zack's face as Grandma Winnie seemed to read him down to the slightest detail…like he wasn't sure if he believed her or wanted to believe her. He tightened his lips and nodded agreement to her.

"You say Milton Glenwood is with your father?" she asked Zack, opening her eyes to look at him.

"I think so," he answered, looking at me to confirm.

"Wait, how did you know my Granddad's name?" I cried out, interrupting them.

"We are old friends, my dear." And she turned back to Zack. "Just who is your father?" she asked.

"Rōber Edsmond," he answered. I hadn't known his last name, hadn't even thought to ask it. It sounded like a nice name.

"That explains quite a bit then. You must be Zaccheus Quade Edsmond."

"Yeah, that's my full name. Quade is the family name, but we go by Edsmond. How did you know that? Do you know Dad?"

"No, I've never met him, but I've heard of him...and of you," she said quietly.

"Why? What's so special about me that you would have heard here in a little town in Oregon?" Zack probed. I had to agree with him; that was pretty peculiar.

"We talk. We older ones don't have much else to do, so we talk about the young ones coming of age. Both of you are interesting. That you found each other is even more so, then add my Margaret into the mix...well remarkable," she ended, not really explaining, but we did know more than we had before and seemed to have found someone we could trust to ask questions and get some answers.

Margo had remained rather silent during this, which must have been hard for her. She got up and started some more water for tea. The silence wasn't at all uncomfortable; we had a lot to think about. When the tea was done, Margo refilled our cups and I picked mine up gratefully. It smelled wonderful.

"Grandma, tell them about me," Margo requested with a shy grin at us, as she sat down.

"You, my dear, are ever changing. You have been a bright purple marigold since the day you were handed to me. You radiate all spectrums of purple out from a tiny gold center," she declared patting her granddaughter's hand.

"Yeah, and tell them what that means," she chirped merrily, grinning at us.

Grandma Winnie turned to us with a proud smile. "It means her center is wisdom combined with a vivid imagination. She is full of vibrations, of energy, new ideas. It's like her thoughts are always growing, developing. It means she can't sit still for a moment and needs adventures and escapades, needs to see new things..." Her face grew serious and she looked at Margo with a woeful face.

"Grandma Winnie, you are fey like Zack and I, aren't you?" I asked, thinking I had it all figured out.

"No dear. I'm a shifted mortal, with very weak powers. However I am an Aunt and good friends with your

Grandparents and the many of the other Allthas. My job is to keep watch and help fey that come into the area seeking the Meadhan. Since this one is closed, there are times fey need my help."

We all digested this. Margo didn't seem upset at all by this information. On the contrary, she seemed very happy and jumped up to give her Grandma a hug.

"You're not crazy or losing your mind. That's awesome."

"No dear, I'm not. But what better cover for the odd things that happen around me than for mortals to believe I'm a bit eccentric?" she asked, looking none too embarrassed being found out.

"Grandma, it's obvious that *you* are not who we thought you were, is Margo?" I asked hesitantly, worried that I might not like the answer. Grandma Winnie turned her face from Margo and looked at me sadly.

"This wasn't supposed to be the time, and I still do not think it is. However it seems to be out of my hands now. The threads are reworking themselves," she looked at her grand-daughter, then got up and hugged her tightly. "Oh, my dear little Margaret. Forgive me for telling you like this. You were only a tiny little thing when the Uncles brought you to me.

"So I'm like them?" she asked with her eyes going all sparkly.

"That remains to be seen. You are a blend, more mortal than fey, I'm afraid. Unfortunately there are a few of the Allthas that like to *interact* with mortals in ways that are not approved and you are a result of one such interaction. But you do have fey blood, just this delightful tiny bit." Grandma Winnie held her hand up and pinched her fingered together. Her face was worried, as if she expected Margo to fall apart at the seams.

Instead Margo jumped up and hugged her grandma with all of her might, then started to hop around in circles, yelling out that she was a fairy and it was great and wasn't that cool that we are all like special things, and then stopping and asking herself what kind of fairy, then hopping up and down again. She couldn't hold still; it was like a bee was in her pants, stinging her over and over again. I'd never seen anyone get so excited about anything before.

"She's handling that well," I said, trying not to laugh. Grandma only smirked and rolled her eyes at me.

"It's the Sprite in her," she whispered to us, and then she called out to Margo who was now dancing up and down the aisles. "Calm down Margaret. You are way too young to come into anything yet. Come here so I can see." Margo skipped back and held out her arm. She must do this a lot and Margo saw me looking at the odd business.

"She does this, checks my pulse. She thinks I have high blood pressure," she mouthed at me.

I didn't think that was what Grandma Winnie was doing. It might look like it, but I had a feeling she was checking something else entirely. The little old woman put two fingers on Margo's wrist and held still for a minute with her eyes closed. When she opened them, she looked sadly at Margo, then at me. "Well I believe I need to let things just happen now. Her levels are rising; it might be from wearing the talisman. Interesting how she got that," she said looking accusingly at me, as if it were my fault somehow, "But it's probably more from being around you two and going to the Meadhan…it jump-started her. You three will make a very interesting trio of friends," she declared siting back heavily in her chair.

Something was bugging me. "If Margo is fey then why didn't she turn into a Wisp like Aishal did when he took her and Skyler into the Meadhan?" I asked.

"To be honest I don't know much about the hex Milton put on the forest or how it works. It could be that Margo has enough mortal blood that the hex overlooked her."

"That makes some sense I guess," I said, then thought of another question. "Why did you leave one of my family's talisman out there, by the front door? Everyone could see it and anyone could've taken it," I asked, rather miffed that she had put it in such an unsecured place.

"I was told I had to put it there…exactly in that spot. There are always reasons even if *you* don't know, understand or even agree with them." I felt chastised and could feel my face turning red.

Grandma Winnie reached out and patted my hand. "Now are you three full up on tea, or should Margo make us another pot?" she asked sweetly and I knew I had been forgiven.

She had reminded me of a something that had been bothering me. I didn't know who to ask, I had been thinking about bringing it up with Laven but really hadn't wanted to. Maybe she would know. She seemed to know quite a bit. "Grandma Winnie, why do I sometimes feel like I am, well, I guess *full* and other times *empty*?"

"Ah, good question, child. The Alltha have power, but each one is different and gains their energy from different places. Water, air, nature, sometimes rocks, or minerals. It's different for everyone. I pull mine from the ocean's tide, but I've grown weaker and see only auras now. I like it better this way...not nearly as stressful," she admitted to us. "What seems to help?"

"When I'm in the forest," I stated honestly.

"Then yours must be nature. Try looking at a tree or plant here in Alainn and see if you can draw any magic from it."

"So it is like a battery that I have to charge?"

"I believe that would be a way to think of it. Ivy, the protective veil on your memories is coming down. Going into the forest without Milton might have initiated it, but I am thinking that your new friend here had more to do with it than you might think. Your...*battery* is now functioning, it will be interesting to see what you can do when it is fully charged," she said smiling at me.

"And if it gets drained? Do I just recharge from a tree? It won't hurt it, will it?" I asked.

She started to stand up and patted my shoulder. "No dear, you pulling magic doesn't harm the thing you pull it from. In fact, it gives back another type of energy. All things work together, it's the balance. Now if you pull from other fey and only Eilibears are known to do that, *that* would cause great harm to a fey. When we draw from something, we leave a part of us there for the other thing to use, but if we pull from a sentient form we only *take* and that is not good."

She paused, then went over to a bookcase and pulled out a large book from the bottom shelf. We watched as she mumbled something, then opened it and removed a smaller book from it. Leaving the empty shell of the larger one behind, she came back to me and placed the little book in my hand.

"Elsie gave this to me to hold for you the last time I saw her. She said I would know when to give it to you." Her voice was forlorn, as if she missed her as much as I did. "I think you should have it now." She looked over to where Margo was starting to twirl in circles. "You might need it to help understand Margo also," she sighed deeply, and then looked from Zack to me. "Go now, I'll have her ready to leave by tomorrow. It might take me that long to calm her down. I'll be here if you need anything," she said, walking over to Margo.

"Margo? Tomorrow…at noon?" I called out. "We'll meet you at the motel." She waved and giggled as she pulled away from her grandma, then leaned back and kissed her robustly on the cheek. Zack and I left then. Margo's story sounded like it might be as interesting as ours was turning out to be.

Zack and I walked over to a seafood restaurant and

enjoyed a dinner among normal people. The noise of tired kids, young people out for the night and families was just what I needed, along with the food. It had been an interesting day and we whispered our conversation over our meal. We had learned a lot, about ourselves and this new life. It had been a good day, though Zack was quiet about what he had learned about himself and his dad. He wanted to talk more about the house we had found and how to get it there and set up.

It was almost dark by the time we found ourselves back at the motel. I felt self-conscious for the first time with Zack. He was being too quiet and the silence between us continued to grow. I was beat and knew we needed to get some sleep before our early morning blinking party to get the rest of the stuff back to the glade. I shut myself in the bathroom and put on a pair of loose shorts and a tee before I went back out. I'd never seen Zack without his heavy neck full of necklaces, so it was a shock to see him in his undershirt and jeans, void of all the neck jewelry and most of his bracelets.

"The bed is yours," he said pointing at it as he took his turn in the bathroom. I was glad he didn't want to share; that would have been just too uncomfortable for me. Pulling the blankets back, I snuggled in and pulled them up around me. It felt good to be in a real bed. I must have fallen asleep because when I woke with a start, it was dark in the room. I could hear Zack breathing on the floor next to the bed, and as I rearranged myself, I tried to do it quietly.

"Are you awake?" His voice came to me slowly.

"Yeah," I said as I turned back to face the side of the room he was on.

"Did you really not have any idea?"

"I didn't know...really. I felt something in your pendants, and then what Laven said and you just seemed to be able to accept it all. There were lots of clues."

"Right in front of me all the time, huh?" he answered and he sounded miserable.

"I guess."

"Dad should have told me."

"Granddad should have told me," I responded sinking a bit into my own sorrow.

"We're quite a pair, you know?"

"Yeah..."

"I wonder if it's the age thing and something to do with all the Uncles," he mused. I heard him shift below me, like he was sitting up. His voice came from closer to me. "How old are you Ivy?"

"Sixteen," I answered without much thought.

"Really?"

"No, I don't think so." I really didn't want to think about it. I felt sixteen, wasn't that enough?

"I'm nineteen."

"Really?" I asked, with a chuckle.

"No, I don't think so." He laughed nervously as he answered. "I seem to have too many memories of places I've been. I keep trying to put dates and years to them and they get all mixed up, like there wasn't really enough time for all of it."

"I know what you mean."

"Ivy?"

"Yeah?"

"It shouldn't, but it scares me a little bit. I keep thinking about Dad, how he had all those people I called uncle and aunt hanging around all the time. Coming and going, how he'd disappear for long periods. Every time he'd come back I'd ask where he was and his only response was 'fighting the good fight.' I thought he was like a secret agent or special ops."

I lay there thinking about that. He went with Granddad to find Marmaw, maybe he was some special type of agent or warrior. Laven had called Zack a Druid warrior and so had Grandma Winnie, and then there was the thing in his arm. "Maybe he is...just not the kind we normally think of."

"We don't know much, do we? Like what the Order is and what they really do. Now that I know I have something in my arm, I wonder how it works," he mused in the dark.

"Just more questions, Zack. I don't know. I seem to be going day by day. Just a few weeks ago, I was in high school and came up with this great plan to run away. I wonder if I would have if I had known all this."

It was silent in the room for a while and I thought Zack had fallen back asleep. Would I have run away if I had known? Maybe I could have helped find Marmaw or known to call someone and get Skyler locked up again. I could have finished school, taken care of myself there and waited for all this till Granddad came back.

I heard rustling below me, then the sound of him walking towards the bathroom. The light came on for a split second before the door closed.

When he came out, he came over to the bed. "I can't sleep," he announced. "May I?"

"Yea," I said as I moved over and make room for him.

He climbed in next to me, pulling a pillow up behind him.

"I'm not sure what to think about everything…it's rather unnerving."

"I know," I said as I turned to him. I felt his arm reach out for me. "Come here." Whatever qualms I'd had about sharing the bed dissipated with our shared uncertainties. I scooted over and curled up next to him, letting him slide his arm around me. His hair kept getting in my way and I leaned up and pushed it back. It smelled good, but was weird to lean against.

"At least we have each other, Ivy. I was kind of glad to find out we weren't really related. I'd be feeling really lost right now if you weren't here."

"Sorry I was such an ass to you."

"I was being a pain."

"Yeah, you were," I chuckled, as I moved his hair again as it fell in my face. "Why the hair Zack? It's kind of different," I mumbled against him.

He chuckled before he said, "Dad and I were in Jamaica when I was about 10. I had been growing my hair out, more from just not having time to get it cut than anything else. There was this old Jamaican lady who wore her hair like this and I asked her why. She told me it was to protect her, that it kept evil confused and it couldn't settle on her head. I thought that was cool and Dad seemed alright with it, so I let her do my hair. It was only a couple of inches long and stuck out all over. I must have been a sight. I've kept it this way ever since."

"Another protection," I stated.

"Yeah, another protection...but protection from evil or to keep me from gaining knowledge?" he snapped with a bit of resentment. I snuggled closer and lay there feeling safe and listening to his heartbeat. The steady rhythm lulled me into a peaceful sleep.

CHAPTER 40 - Ivy

Zack woke me up at three in the morning. I sat up, rubbing sleep out of my eyes and waited until he had used the bathroom and was ready to go before I did my own thing. I started to ask where he wanted me to blink us to when he stopped me.

"I'm supposedly a type of fey also, right?" he asked, all dressed once more with his assortment of jewelry.

"Yes, I think we have that one figured out," I answered wondering where this was leading.

"So I should be able to blink also, right?" That brought a smile to my face. I hadn't thought of that. I nodded yes and he grinned impishly.

"So teach me, what do I do?"

"Laven just told me to close my eyes and think of where I wanted to be. You have to know you can do it, then just do it."

He raised his eyebrows at me and then pointed at a spot near the door. He closed his eyes and appeared where he had pointed. "Whoa, I did it," he said grinning widely.

"Yep, I think we just have to know what we can do before we can do it. Maybe someday someone will tell us what else we can do," I said.

"So true. Come on, I'm going to blink us this time."

Zack was in an even better mood than the day before. It was like all the dark and depressing doubts and questions had disappeared while we slept. The moon had risen, shining through the fog, sending a soft illuminating light down to us. We blinked into the lumber yard Zack pointed to the staged items he was supposed to pick up with a truck early in the morning. We started blinking loads back to the glade and I felt a sense of dismay as ferns and flowers were crushed under the heavy items. I could feel a weak sigh of pain each time we blinked in and wondered if I now was going to have to deal with feeling every little disruption in plant life. That would get old real fast.

Zack took the last load by himself and we met up at the all-night laundromat. I wondered anew just where Laven and the other fey got their clothes. I was sure there were no clothing stores or washers and dryers in their world. We both had gathered all the clothes we had, and brought them back with us. While we sat waiting for four washer loads to get done, we realized our own silliness. We could have just blinked to a mall somewhere and gotten new ones. Oh well, I liked my clothes and we could always do it another time. Besides, mall shopping was not my thing. I liked thrift shops and odd little stores that carried unusual clothes. Looking at the way Zack dressed, I figured he was like me. Except for his jeans, his attire was as abnormal as his hair. Anything from silk dress shirts in bright colors to an old man's vest, mixed with hiking boots, high tops tennis shoes or sandals.

When we finished, we blinked to the model home lot and Zack made sure the work on the house was going as planned. It seemed like the contractor had his act together. He had the open side framed and the insulation, windows and door installed. We got there as his workers were using a loud nail gun to put up slabs of raw logs to match the other three sides. There was no doubt the contractor would have it done by tonight.

We got back to the motel just as Margo showed up. All three of us cleaned up the room and then Zack went to check out. We figured it was wise to stay on good terms with the lady at the motel…who knew how often we would want to stay there? When we were set, Zack took hold of

Margo's hand, winked mischievously at her and as she gave me a look of surprise, he blinked them out.

She reacted the way we thought she would…enthusiastic didn't come close to describing the hug she gave him when they opened their eyes to the glade. She even oohed and aahed at all the stuff sitting in heaps long enough for it to get old. She stuck around for a little while before she disappeared into the forest, saying she wanted to play with the fairies. I figured since they couldn't harm her, she was safe enough and watched as she skipped excitedly down the path and out of sight.

Zack and I set about to readying the area for the house that we still hadn't told Margo about. We let her assume that Zack was going to build it. I was glad Zack seemed to know what he was doing as he marked off the area with orange thread, then leveled it expertly. I worried when he climbed the roof of the cabin and started up the nosiest battery powered saw I had ever heard. But he made quick work of trimming the eave so that the addition would fit snug. By the early evening he had set the beams in for the foundation, mixed mass amounts of concrete in a large wheelbarrow and poured it into the frame. It really was the coolest foundation I had ever seen. Granted it was the only one I had ever seen built, but Zack was extremely pleased with himself when he was done.

My chores seemed to be to follow behind and clean up his messes, hand him tools that I didn't know the names of, or what they did, and tell him how awesome he was. It was a job I could handle.

When he was finished for the day, we walked down to the pool for the first time since he had come to the forest. I couldn't wait to show it to him and enjoy a swim in the cool water. As we came down the path and out of the thick blackberry bushes, we found Margo sitting at the water's edge with Whisper and Myste. They blinked out as soon as they saw us, but soon returned sitting on the rocks, eyeing

Zack and whispering together. He gave them no mind as he stripped down to his shorts and dove in. I had planned on following, but Margo wanted to show me the flower garland the fey had been teaching her to braid.

By the time I turned to undress and join Zack, I saw that Myste had beat me to it and was swimming playfully with him, and Whisper was splashing them from her spot on the rocks. Both were beautiful beyond description, with their pale smooth skin and flowing hair. Even their bodies were perfect and the water left little to the imagination once it soaked through their flower petal clothes.

Zack didn't seem to mind at all that the sisters were paying him attention and as I stood there, more females popped in and joined in with the fun. One had found a large tuber and was playing keep away with it over Zack's head. He looked like he was enjoying himself and I decided I really didn't want to be part of the party. I felt small and ugly compared to all of them.

I turned to talk to Margo and found that in just the few seconds I had been watching Zack a couple of boy fey had shown up and were picking berries for her. The biggest argument seemed to be who had found the best berries for her to try. She looked like she was enjoying herself also. It was obvious that they didn't need me around, so I trudged back to the glade and looked for something to do.

It started out fine. I untangled the pile of stuff I had brought and dug out the new lawn chairs. They were really cool, all twisted metal like a vine gone nuts, covered in a deep green patina. I had even switched out their plain cushions for ones with bright cheerful flowers. I sat them around on the trampled grass and looked around, wishing someone would come see what I had done.

I plopped down in the closest chair feeling a bit let down. Maybe it was childish, but I had bought all this stuff, brought my friends here and they had, well, deserted me. My poor glade didn't look anything like it had before;

the flowers and ferns looked wilted and sad. One little flower lay on its side next to the chair, its stem limp and the flower crumpled flat. I touched it gently and told it how sorry I was and that I hoped it would get better. I sat there absently stroking it, feeling sorry for myself. A gloomy melancholy seemed to have enveloped me. I couldn't stop thinking about how I looked next to the other fey. It wasn't fair; why couldn't I be all perfect and gorgeous and voluptuous like them?

Even the air around me seemed to grow heavy with shade and I realized it was just the sun starting to set. I went to stand up and happened to look down. The tiny flower was standing straight and in full bloom again. A memory erupted in my mind. Marmaw worrying over her tomato plant…it had been dying and the tomatoes were small and misshapen. She had called me over and asked me to work 'my magic' and make it happy again. I remembered playing along with her, leaning close to the dying plant and talking to it. Telling it to get well and grow big to make Marmaw happy. And the next day it was so; big red ripe tomatoes hanging in abundance on a tall healthy plant.

My magic. I looked around at my glade and snickered to myself. Why not? I had vines growing on my face, why not try? So I went around the glade, talking to the plants, telling them how beautiful they could be, asking them to grow strong for me again. Shrubs that were past their blooming time started to bud and then blossomed before my eyes. Everything perked up and by the time I was done, the glade looked even more wonderful than before.

Cheered, I started digging out the other treasures I had brought back with me. There were yard statues and bird houses of every type and make, with little hangers or shepherd's hooks to push into the ground. I arranged them among the flowers and ferns and stood back smiling at how pretty it looked. The last piece was a huge sun dial. I just needed a really big interesting rock for it to rest on, but for that I needed help from Zack...or someone. I had thought about putting in a pond, maybe one with a fountain and wanted to talk about it with Zack, but, well, he was busy with his new friends. I sat down and waited for them to come back and see all that I had done, but as the light faded, it became apparent that no one was going to be seeing anything today.

Sulking, I walked back to the cabin, stopping to see if the concrete on the foundation had dried. It seemed to still be goopy wet in places and in a huff I cried, "just dry, will you!" and wiped my fingers off on my jeans and made my way inside, alone. I was cold, more than I had been since I first came back to the forest and went and found my biggest, warmest sweatshirt. Pulling it on, I grabbed my MP3 and put the earbuds in. Music would help...it always did when I was alone.

Building up the fire, I made a casserole of canned chicken, noodles, mixed with mushroom soup, canned mushrooms and peas. It was one of my best concoctions and I couldn't wait for them to try it. By the time it was cold, I found I'd lost my appetite. With tears threatening, I climbed up the ladder and curled into a tight ball and cried myself to sleep.

CHAPTER 41- Ivy

I heard sounds down below when I woke up. I was unquestionably upset with them. Crying last night hadn't helped, especially because once I started to cry, I had to think of all the reasons I had to cry. I missed Granddad and Marmaw, I missed being normal, I missed my pretty forest where I could walk and find joy and now I felt like the outsider. I was ugly and little, hated my hair, my clothes and the dumb vines on my face. It had been a long night, filled with unresolved feelings of desertion and I didn't know why or how it had happened.

Forcing a smile on my face, I went down the ladder. Zack was making coffee and Margo was washing dishes and both were laughing and talking. They didn't even notice I was there until I sat down at the table.

"Hey, you missed a great party! They built a big bonfire. We danced and sang and they had food and gosh, I wished you had been there," Margo bubbled rapidly at me. Zack meanwhile poured himself a cup of coffee and straddled the other bench and looked at me when Margo had run out of words.

"Really, where did you go? You could have told me you were leaving. The girls said you would be at the bonfire but you never showed. The least you could have done was clean up after yourself last night," he snapped at me.

As he spoke all pretense of smiling left my face and I could feel my lip starting to tremble. I gulped a couple of times trying to control it, then gave up. I stood, facing away from them, trying real hard to get my emotions under control. I was failing big time.

"Ivy, what's wrong with you? Oh, the concrete dried during the night. We can get the *you know what* tonight if you think you can stick around for it, and there's work to be done first. We wouldn't want to stop you from playing, but work first okay?" he said. That was it, I couldn't take it anymore. I picked up my pack and climbed the ladder to the loft. I heard them talking about me down there, how I was acting strange. Then they started talking about the bonfire and Zack was recounting things the girls did and I couldn't listen. I put on jeans and a t-shirt and pulled the sweatshirt on over it.

"Hey Zack?" I called down, but he didn't hear me. Something about hanging from a tree branch and swiping the hat off some fey's head was more interesting. "Zack!" I yelled, probably too loud. Both of them shut up and their heads jerked towards me.

"I'm going for a walk; I'll meet you here at 7:30 okay? It's what, about 6 now?" I asked.

"Yeah I'd guess that, I'm not sure where I put my watch," he replied with a straight unreadable face.

"So 7:30, here, we will finish the work and get the *you know what* tonight?"

"Sure, see you then," he said turning back to Margo and they resumed their conversation.

I watched them for a while, and then whispered in a flat voice. "Sure...see you." And I blinked outside to the start of the forest path. Maybe it was like my time of the month or something and I was just being over-sensitive.

I needed to check on Skyler and still didn't know how to find that tree. I decided to walk off my anger and hoped I'd find Laven or one of the others that could take me to where Skyler was. I started up the path and took a side route I hadn't been on in a while. It was peaceful and my heart rate was slowing. I was being dumb; it wasn't their fault I kept telling myself.

As I came around a small bend I saw three fey I hadn't met…I hadn't really met any except for Laven and his three sisters and the brothers. I smiled and walked towards them, getting ready to say hi, when they blinked out. I stopped and looked around. That was kind of rude.

"Hello? I'm Ivy; I'd like to meet you," I called out and was met with silence. Well maybe they were shy. I continued my walk, and now was looking for them. I got a glimpse of others a couple of times, but every time I got close enough for them to see or hear me, they were gone. It was kind of creepy, like they were watching me. I'd had times before in my life when I'd felt eyes on me and turned to find some boy staring at me, or some old person ogling my hair or clothes. But this was different; it was like there were eyes all around me.

I thought about turning around and going back, but I really wanted to find out why they were acting so strange. The path took me deep into a grove of tall hemlocks where little sunlight filtered down. At first I could hear birds and other critters in the underbrush, but after a time it was mostly frogs, which I found different. I didn't remember ever hearing this many. I started looking for them and soon my eyes were picking them out. Big ones, little ones, yellow ones, green ones; hopping over the forest floor and clinging to the trees. Okay, I was getting creeped out now. I stopped and looked around. It was dark and felt dank and menacing. I looked at my watch and it was close to 7:30, so I gave up the hunt to meet any of the newly arrived fey or see Skyler and blinked back to the glade.

Figuring that Zack and Margo must be inside, I hurried, wanting to tell them about the strange actions of the fey and all the frogs. I knew the minute I opened the door though that they weren't there. The cabin had never felt empty before, but it did now. I went back outside and looked around, hoping that maybe Zack was working on the bathroom plumbing. He had said he needed to dig a trench to connect the sewer line. But he wasn't there or anywhere in the glade.

Going back inside, I made some coffee and sat and waited. No one came. This was not the way I thought it would be having friends in my forest with me, or letting the fey in for that matter. I straightened up the cabin that had become packed with everyone's belongings. Margo seemed to have brought her entire wardrobe with her. Boxes and bags sat piled on Granddad's bed. Zack, at least, still only had his one large pack. I picked it up and heard jingling in an outside pocket. He must have a bunch of coins in it, I thought as I shoved the pack under the bed. It wouldn't make sense to try to find places to put Margo's stuff when, hopefully tonight, the addition would be placed.

By the time the sun was high in the sky I gave up thinking either would return. I didn't know what they were doing and didn't know how to find them. I was getting tired of waiting around and I needed to be outside. It was a pull on me to be in the air of the forest. Deciding that maybe I could try out my growth trick in the forest, I started to get ready to leave. I still didn't know just how the fey gave a forest health, although from the diaries, it sounded like that's what happened.

I changed my undershirt to a tank top, considered for just a moment putting on a bra, then decided against it. I really never wore the things; there wasn't much there and it seemed silly to be uncomfortable for no reason. The sweatshirt was still a must, I discovered when I went outside. It had warmed up a little, though it was still cooler than I wished it was, so the bulky shirt went on again. I strolled down different trails and tried to enjoy being in the forest.

Now and then the sounds of others would come to me, but I never saw anyone. Sometimes I'd get a chill and feel eyes on me and forced myself not to look around. One path led me to the wide open meadow and I could see the fairy rings growing plainly in several places. Granddad would bring me here and point them out, telling me stories of the cheerful fair folk who danced in the glow of the moon. The rings had always been brightly colored tiny flowers like pansies, pinks and purples and shocking bright blues. Today I was met with more shades of fall, tiny yellows, golds, and oranges, mixed now and then with purples. It was a wonder to see the place where the fey had danced and I wished I could show it to Margo and Zack. Then wondered if maybe they had already seen it, even been here for the dancing.

I knelt by one and was saddened to see the little flowers were wilted, like they needed watering. I reached out and called to the little things to grow and be healthy, then stood back to watch as they perked up and spread. The meadow was alive with butterflies and little birds and now and then a small garden snake would pass in the grasses near me. I found myself standing in the center of the area with my eyes closed, just listening to the sounds and trying to catch all of it. It was amazing how much I could hear, the wind, the leaves moving, a cricket chirping on a blade of grass.

A shadow rolled over me and I looked up to see billowing white clouds had floated in front of the sun. It turned the meadow into a mixture of lights and darks. Across the meadow was a line of trees that looked like birch. Their leaves were small and delicate, swaying in the wind that was picking up. They looked content and I chuckled to myself for thinking that a tree might have emotions. I walked towards them and saw a newly made path in the grasses that led into the small wood.

I followed it in and soon heard the sounds of water and splashes and laughter. The path seemed to end when it came to a grove of larger trees surrounding a pond I had never seen before. It was glassy smooth and sparkled when a bit of the sun's rays touched it as the clouds broke. No one was around and I was disappointed since I had hoped I had found where everyone was. A splash made me jump and turn to see only a ripple on the water and the large eyes of a toad pop up and look at me. I had to smile at the silliness of it and moved around the pond to see if the path maybe continued on the other side. It didn't, not really. Instead there continued a series of ponds, connected by a cheery little stream flowing down tiny waterfalls into each pond. I followed the edges of them, wondering how I'd never seen this place before.

Again the sound of the laughter came to me, and I followed it up along the side of the ponds. Some had giant water lilies in them, with pads larger than a dinner plate. Toads seemed to like this area and they were everywhere, their buggy eyes following me as I walked and hopped on the rocks and climbed over logs. They really seemed to be all over the place. The splashes and movements in the pond and in the trees made me edgy.

"Hello?" I called out when a sound came to me again from up ahead, but no one answered. "Uh, hi, I'm Ivy," I said, trying to sound pleasant. It didn't make any difference, no one returned my greeting. I knew they were there; I could feel them rustling in the trees and just out of sight in the dense wood of birches. It seemed dryer here, surprising since there was so much water. The underbrush was almost dried up, dead blackberry bushes creating nothing but walls of thorns. Why were they dying? Didn't having more fey mean it should be healthier in the forest? A sound of voices came from my side and I whirled around to see and caught a glimpse of a form as it blinked out.

I have to admit I was feeling very slighted. Was I that different? I gave up and, in a huff, wondered where I should go, then picked the doorway. I hadn't been there since I had opened it, maybe Laven or some others of the fey were hanging around there. I blinked and discovered I was correct. Laven was standing just off to the side of the doorway. I caught sight of the back side of a line of fey hurrying through the film under the roots. Laven was arguing with another older fey who, when he saw me, turned towards the doorway and rushed to leave. Why were they leaving? I looked around at the lushness of this area…it seemed fine.

"Laven what's going on?" He actually jumped at the sound of my voice.

"My lady...nothing, just old feelings. They are unreasonable," he answered with a pompous air.

"Like what?" I asked, and backed up as Bryear and a couple of other male fey came out of the forest to stand behind him. They didn't speak, only stared at me with what looked like loathing.

"The older fey say they feel drained, that the Sumair stone is still at work and taking their powers. They are leaving, we need to get the Sumair stone and take it away so the fey will not leave," he announced as he moved backwards towards the other fey, keeping his eyes on me.

"Laven, the Sumair stone is not even here in the forest," I snapped at him, telling myself that the statement was just on the verge of a lie, but not really.

His head jerked up at me with wide eyes and the others behind him started to whisper amongst themselves.

"Not here? Where is it then?" he asked just a bit too concerned with its whereabouts for my liking. I thought he didn't care. That's what he had told me just a few days ago anyway.

"Granddad took it from the forest a very long time ago. He put it somewhere safe, where it couldn't work at all. As far as I'm concerned, it is dead... gone," I said with conviction.

"That's impossible Ey-vey...it must be impossible," he said as if to himself.

"No it's gone. I'm sure of that. Tell the fey they can come back, it's safe. I thought they wanted to live here?" I said looking questioning at the fey behind him. None of them would meet my eyes.

"Ey-vey, even I feel the pull of something on me. If not the Sumair stone, then it is something else," he said as he looked sideways at me. "It may be that the Sumair stone gave its full power to another and that is what is draining us and the forest."

I really didn't like his tone or what he was hinting at; I narrowed my eyes at him.

"My lady," his voice had changed, softer like he had always been before, warmer. "Do not concern yourself with the ones who deserted us. They have lived long and are set in their ways," he said trying to console me. He must have thought I was worried about them leaving. I was, but I was far more concerned with the fey standing right here. One of the fey behind him was sneering at me.

"Are they still gathering tomorrow so I can talk to them? Zack and I..." I stopped; we hadn't really talked anymore about Willow and our plan to set him free into the mortal realm. I needed to talk to him about it and I wasn't sure this was a good time to be freeing someone that even Laven seemed to want to harm. "I mean, where are Zack...and Margo? I haven't seen them today, except for when we first got up."

"They come," he said and gave me an odd look. I heard giggles from behind me and turned towards the sounds. Zack was strolling up the path with a female fey on each arm and a number of others trailing behind. I recognized Aireen, but none of the others. The two holding onto Zack had their long flowing hair filled with braided flowers, and were clothed in the now familiar floret garments. Aireen's outfit looked like rose petals that had been glued to her, the other had one large fern leaf with tiny white flowers molded to her frame. They were both breathtaking and each was more voluptuous than the last. I felt like I was looking at a line-up of Playboy bunnies. They were hanging on Zack's arms and he was giving all of his attention to them. Aireen stopped and tried to pull him back when she saw me, her face twisting in something akin to hatred. Unfortunately for her, he saw me and tried to move forward, almost dragging her along with him.

"Ivy, where have you been? The girls said they went to find you and you weren't at the cabin," he said as the other one leaned up and whispered into his ear, giving me a sly look. Zack laughed at whatever she had said, then came into the hollow and stood there smiling weirdly at me. It was like he was high or toasted. Did fey drink alcohol? He sure seemed drunk or at least not himself. His face was flushed and I watched astounded as one of the girls said something and he started to tickle her...and chase her, stopping only when he got his arms around her as she laughed. He looked at me then and grinned with that weird dazed look.

He looked different to me somehow. Granted his face had a dorky look on it, and then I noticed it. I felt like I had picked up one of those books at the doctor's office that had a page of 'find what's different with these pictures', I just won the prize. All of his jewelry was gone, save for the large leather wristband with the talisman. Now I knew what the jingle was when I moved his pack. One of the girls pulled him down to her as she gave me a smug look, and then whispered to him. He shook his head playfully at her and said 'no,' as if he meant yes and just wanted her to beg some more.

I heard giggles from behind me and swirled around again to see Margo and a young male fey erupt out of the tall ferns. He was playfully chasing her and she started to play a game of hide and seek between the other fey and Laven. They paid her no mind and continued to stare at me, now with creepy forced smiles. When she finally spotted me, she bounced over and took my hand.

"Ivy this is Warren," she said pointing at the boy, who

now had joined with the other fey and was staring at me with that odd look. Margo leaned over and whispered, "Isn't he cute?" I smiled at her and looked at the boy. No he wasn't, his face was hard and long, with mean-looking eyes. Not the type I could ever see Margo with.

More laughter and giggles came to me, seemingly encircling me. I glanced to the edges of the hollow and more fey came out, male and female, all with strange little smiles looking at me peculiarly. I heard a guaaaap and looked down. Toads and frogs were coming out of the ferns now, gathering around the feet of the fey. Okay, I'd had enough. I felt surrounded and really creeped out. This is not how I expected my first meeting with the other fey to be. I pulled Margo in to me, in a nice sisterly hug, as I smiled sweetly at everyone and moved over to where Zack was.

The girls were touching his face and petting his arms familiarly as he stood there looking like that wasn't weird at all. As I moved closer, they tried to pull him back, but I was faster and got to him, taking his arm with my other free hand and pulling him close to me as I pushed Aireen back.

"Hi Ivy, when did you get here?" He asked me with a tilt of his head. His breath was vile, like dog poop. Gross.

"I've been here Zack," I answered softly as I pulled him towards me in a tight, one armed hug. The other fey tried to keep a hold on him, but he yanked his arm away and shook her off so he could sloppily hug me. I blinked.

CHAPTER 42 - Ivy

The cabin felt cold, and Margo looked up at me, then got an odd look on her face and let go of my hand. She ran to the sink as quick as she could. The vomit came fast and furious, she sounded like she was throwing up her guts. Zack staggered back, an amazed look on his face as he scanned the cabin, as if he couldn't figure out where he was. He started towards the door and I reached out and stopped him. He pulled his arm away and gurgled out, "I got to go, we're gonna cut my hair."

I yanked on his arm with all my might. "You are not going to cut your hair!" I yelled at him in shock.

"Yeah, we..." then he looked at me, really looked at me, his eyes questioning. "They said I had to cut my hair or they couldn't play..." His eyes got wide and he just stood there for a minute and looked around the cabin some more. "They wanted to cut my hair?" he said more in his normal voice and staggered sideways.

I pulled him over to the chair and sat him down. He slumped back and closed his eyes, then started to snore. That was quick. Sounds of gagging were still coming from the sink and I went over to Margo and started pumping water into it to clear it out. I couldn't help but see what she was spewing. It was nasty, and I almost lost my breakfast seeing it. When she was finally done, her face was pale and dripping with sweat. I helped her to the chair next to Zack and found her some clean clothes after I gave her the best washing I could. She just sat there letting me while she was busy moaning. After I had her dressed, somewhat, and tucked a blanket around her in the chair, I pulled down my teas and started a pot of water.

Marmaw used to mix fresh leaves in when I got sick and I tried to remember which ones she had used when my stomach hurt. Finally I just went out to my garden and looked at the little herb plants, gathering ones that seemed right. When I went back inside, both were in a restless sleep, as if bad dreams were plaguing them. I brewed two cups of the tea and, feeling a bit like a witch from some bad movie, started to talk to the floating leaves, telling them to heal my friends and kill whatever was in them. Who knew if I was really doing anything, but it made me feel better at least.

When the tea was ready and cooled a bit, I took a cup over to Zack and woke him. He took the cup without complaint and drank it all in one long gulp, then sat there looking drained. I forced the tea on Margo next; she fought me a little bit, but I got most of it in her. Afterwards I cleaned off Zack's bed, remembering his jewelry. I didn't care what he thought as I opened the pack and removed all the items. I put the pendants around his neck and he gazed up at me with murky eyes. He let me lift his hands and replace the rings and then the bracelets without complaint.

I led him the few feet to the bed and helped him lay down and tucked him in like a child. Margo, I had to blink up to the loft since I couldn't exactly carry her up the ladder. Only when they were all settled did I allow myself to think about what had happened. I didn't know anything about the fey; maybe this was normal. Not normal for me though, thank goodness. I told the house to lock itself, so they couldn't leave without me knowing and pulled the chairs together in a make-shift bed. It was comfortable enough, but I couldn't fall asleep. The only light was now from the stove and it had finally warmed up and felt cozy again.

I had no idea what I needed to do, and didn't even know

if Zack or Margo would want to talk about it in the morning. I don't know when sleep finally overtook me, but I must have slept a long time as I woke to birds chirping outside and the sun shining brightly through the windows. Zack and Margo didn't wake for another full day. I stayed in the cabin with them. If I had to use the outhouse, it was a very quick trip and I blinked there and back.

I thought about pushing all of the darn fey back out the doorway and locking it tight, but then pondered whether my forest would die. Then wondered if it mattered as I looked at my friends and speculated what they were dreaming about. Zack looked like he was enjoying himself; he chuckled a lot, maybe too much. It made me mad that he could be dreaming about being with them after what they done to him. Of course then I had to wonder what they *had* done to him. I was new to the whole jealousy thing, but I wasn't so dumb that I didn't recognize it. I knew I was being a bit territorial…Zack was *my* friend. He thought I was cute and different, and he had told the fat lady at the motel that I was his girlfriend. I knew he didn't mean it, but that didn't stop me from liking the sound of it. We had even spent one night in each other's arms. It sounded so romantic, but really we had just used each other as pillows and I'd tried to sleep over his snores.

No matter what spin I put on it, I ended up coming to the same conclusion. I didn't like the female fey hanging all over him or *him* liking them hanging all over him. I watched him as he slept. It was wacky, I know, but I couldn't stop. I loved his hair and his eyes. I liked the way he made sounds when he moved, all the jewelry becoming his own little chorus of noises. It was Zack. I looked in on Margo also, making sure she was okay, but I didn't sit watching her. I saved that strangeness for him.

When Zack started to stir, I made another pot of tea and readied it for him and remembered to unlock the cabin just in time. He woke and bolted for the door as soon as he could and I could hear his violent heaving from where I was. When he returned, he looked a little green and without saying a word, sat down and took the tea I handed him. I sat down across from him and waited.

"Must have got a bug, I guess," he mumbled, holding the mug between his hands and looking at me feebly.

"Must have," I answered and waited. The silence grew uncomfortable, for me at least. There were so many things I wanted to say and questions that needed to be asked, but I wasn't sure where to start.

"We're going to get the *you know what* today, right?" he said when he finally spoke.

"If you are up to it,"

"Hey, I'm fine. 7:30 right? Sorry I must have fallen back asleep. What time is it now?" he said looking around as if trying to find a wall clock. There wasn't one.

"Sure, if you add about 48 hours," I said seriously, taking his empty cup and refilling it.

"Wow, I've been out that long? Where's Margo?" he asked, just realizing she wasn't here.

"Still asleep, same...bug."

"Oh," he said closing his eyes. "My head really hurts, got any aspirin?"

I got up and went and found my bottle and handed it to him. He downed a couple, then got up and changed his shirt. I realized he planned to go out and I couldn't put it off any longer.

"Zack I don't think it's a good idea for you to hang out with the fey, there is something going on with them," I started to say, but he turned to me with an indulgent glance.

"Now Ivy, I know you have a thing about the fey. They want to get to know you. If you would only talk to them and not run away every time they come close, it would be better. They want to be friends."

What? I didn't know what to say to that odd comment, so I just stood there as he came over and patted me on the shoulder like a big brother. “I promised Myste that I’d help her catch a fish this morning, I’ll be back and we’ll go get the house and get it all set up.” He was talking to me like I was a simple-minded child. The gall.

“You think I hide from the fey?” I asked through tight lips. My eyes narrowed into slits as he continued to talk, my anger barely held in check.

“The girls told me all about it. It’s okay,” he said in such a condescending tone that I wanted to slap him. Maybe he still wasn’t *well*, he seemed to really believe what he was telling me.

“Uh Zack, you took your protections off and they were going to cut your hair,” I said slowly, deciding being mad wasn’t going to help this situation and waited for his response.

He started to laugh. “Right, look they are right here,” he said wiggling his ring-covered fingers at me and then holding out his necklaces for me to see. “And wow, look at that, my hair is still long,” he said in a mocking voice. “Really Ivy, you’ve got to stop this. They are worried about you.” He lowered his voice to a whisper. “I’ve been sticking up for you, but you have to stop your little games.” Then he actually tried to hug me. I stiffened up and did not return the hug. Instead I let the power come and roll on the tip of my tongue before I whispered into his hair.

“You can’t be cut, nothing can cut you.” When he pulled back, my eyes went to each piece of his protections and I whispered, “You can’t come off, not by Zack or other magic.” Only then did I look up at him.

“Come join us this morning, you’ll see.” My face went rigid and he must have some reasoning left because he read it right. “Okay, have it your way. I’ll see you here in a couple of hours.” And he left. I hoped my voice thing had worked, or he was going to be one bald puppy when he returned.

I never even saw Margo. After I composed myself, I

went up the ladder to check on her. She was gone. Crap, I'd really led my friends into something bad and I didn't know what to do about it. I went looking for them when Zack didn't return, and except for the giggles and sounds of movement in the trees and the stupid frogs, I saw nothing. Not even a bird. My forest was having some problems.

I wandered the paths and called for Laven. I was growing very concerned for Skyler as well. She was somewhere in this forest, but I had no clue how to find her. Laven never even answered me…there was only the laughter from the trees. I wasn't sure now if he had been answering before because he wanted to or because he was compelled to. Either way, I was getting upset with him.

After a few hours of roaming the different paths, trying without success to find the right grove of trees that I had placed Skyler in, I gave up and went back to the cabin…alone again.

They returned late that night. Zack was still in one piece, just moving very slowly. Poor Margo was sick to her stomach again and I gave them food and my special tea and spoke words of protection over them as they slept. I kept trying to get them to stay the next morning; even begged Zack to help me get the house when Margo was out of ear shot. He'd say the words I wanted to hear, but there was nothing behind them. I was losing them to the fey and didn't know what to do, or if I even had a right to do anything. Maybe this is what they wanted to do. If they were in their right minds, then they had the right to make their own decisions.

The next day I'd had enough of Laven ignoring me. If Laven and the damn new fey weren't going to answer me or leave my friends alone, I had only one choice. I stood at the edge of my glade and let the power build on my tongue until it started to hurt, then yelled out into the forest. "All fey in this forest, I demand you all return to Wisp form!"

I waited, knowing that Laven would be upset and would

come find me in his Wisp form. But nothing happened and no Wisp showed up. I was growing extremely apprehensive when Laven still didn't appear and perturbed that my plan hadn't worked the way I'd thought it would. I stood there a few minutes more before I gave up and turned to go back to the cabin. From the edge of the forest, shill laughter erupted and I turned towards it. Wisps didn't laugh.

"Who's there? Show yourself," I screamed, but no one answered. The forest grew quiet and I shivered with fear.

After that I hid in the cabin. I didn't know what to do. My power didn't seem to work, the fey wouldn't show themselves to me and I couldn't stop Margo or Zack from leaving each day. I tried to follow them, but Zack would take Margo's hand and blink out, leaving me alone time after time.

We settled into this pattern of me begging, them leaving, me taking care of them when they returned, and when they woke, it starting all over again, day after day. I hunted and called for Laven to no avail.

Finally I stopped looking and, instead, just wandered. I didn't try to find them or see anything or anyone, the need to be in the forest was overwhelming, so I walked. It was then I came upon him. Zack. He was leaning against a tree and was holding tight to a fey I'd never seen before, but this one wasn't gorgeous, in fact she wasn't even that pretty...and they were kissing. I must have made some sound and they both turned to look at me.

Zack just stared at me, as if it was interesting that I was there, but not the fey. She hissed at me. I mean she really hissed at me, like a cat. I had to look away as she turned back to him and continued to kiss him. I thought I was going to be sick as I noticed the frogs clinging to her hair. Whatever the attraction was, it was pretty yucky as far as I was concerned.

I didn't care what Zack thought, or how awkward it felt,

Zack wasn't acting like Zack. I broke out in a sprint towards them and shoved the girl away with all my might. It must have been a pretty good shove since she sailed a good ten feet before a tree stopped her. She just laid there not moving and I didn't care that I might have hurt her. Instead I turned to Zack who grinned at me with vacant eyes and held out his arms as if he wanted a hug.

I touched his arm and blinked us into the glade. Then watched as his eyes started to clear and he glared at me for a moment before a look of surprise came over his face and he started to throw up. I left him to it while I went inside for a bottle of water and a towel. When I came back he had left again and I heard laughter in the trees. I poured the water on the mess he had made and then told it to take its foulness out of my glade. I didn't want to know what the crap was that he and Margo kept throwing up; I guessed it was some weird fey thing. What really scared me was that maybe that's what I was supposed to be like, and it sickened me to think about it.

Enough, I'd had enough.

I walked over to the start of the path, staying safely inside my protected glade and yelled with all the power I could gather.

"Laven!" This time he appeared on the path and the look on his face wasn't happy. In fact, he looked annoyed with me.

"What do you want?" he asked in a tone that was completely different from any other time we had spoken. A cloud moved in front of the sun and it was suddenly dark where he stood, his form a mere shadow on the path, his eyes glowing at me in the darkness.

"What the hell is going on?" I demanded of him.

"I know not of what you speak."

"Give it a break Laven. The fey are playing some weird keep away game; they are turning my friends against me and making them sick. Why?"

"We play no games...my lady," he smirked at me, his teeth white and perfect. I heard a chuckle nearby and pointed at it.

"Really, what was that? Why are some of the fey leaving and why are the rest of you acting all weird?" I asked frustrated at him and myself for having no one else to ask.

"I do not know...my lady." That smirk again, then a look that I almost missed. A blur of ugly, then it was gone. The forest had gone still, the silence hung around us. Suddenly frogs started to croak, one, two, tens, hundreds, everywhere. I heard them and decided I did not like frogs...and right now I didn't like Laven or the fey.

"Laven, I allowed the fey to come, I allowed the hex to be dropped."

"But you tried to put it on us again," he sneered at me.

I felt terror down to my bones and started to shake. "I did and it didn't work. Why not Laven? What's going on? I thought you were my friend. I thought you didn't like mortals and thought Druids were dangerous. You even told me to get Zack out of the forest as soon as possible. Now you are all like the best of friends," I had started to cry and couldn't control it.

"I was wrong…you are weak, unfit to be the owner of this Meadhan," he answered, flashing a really irritating blank smile.

"Really? Wow, *you* were wrong," I repeated back to him. It was like I was talking to a completely different person. I didn't like the first version of him all that much, but this version I absolutely hated. "Listen closely to me now Laven. If Margo and Zack are not released from whatever weird spells you are putting on them, I will shove you back through the doorway so fast you won't know what hit you." I kept my voice low and spoke very slowly and clearly.

He looked at me with those violet, stunning eyes and

sniggered, as if he found my threat funny. Raising his hand at me he started to say something, but no sounds came out. His face twisted as if in pain. Then as if forced to do so, he bowed to me. “As you say my lady.” And I found myself alone.

CHAPTER 43 - Aishal

Rayni blinked with Aishal into the meadow of Rootmire late in the afternoon. It had been four very long days. Aishal had watched as Rayni used every bit of magic the fey had and could find and pushed it into him to help him heal. Aishal knew that Rayni was now drained and he wasn't even close to being restored. His brother had begged other fey to help, but the fey did not wish to, turning their noses up at Aishal who had allowed himself to be injured.

His brother Rayni had done all he could and at least Aishal could walk on his own now. Painfully and slowly, but at least he *could* walk. The two had come back to the doorway and Aishal thought it meant that both would be going back into the hemlock forest. Rayni had other plans and as soon as they arrived at the meadow, his brother bid him farewell and blinked out.

Alone now, he wasn't sure if he should allow himself to heal more or go through the still open doorway. He was angry at everything, and everyone, but didn't know what he would find if he went into the Meadhan. Laven had probably used this time with him away to take over everything. It was *his* idea first to take the Meadhan and Laven had just taken over. He wanted to be the owner of the Meadhan and to do that he needed that talisman back. He could taste the power it had given him and nothing was going to stop him from regaining it. Also there was the issue of that mortal who had hurt him...he needed to get his revenge on it.

He considered the doorway for a moment, before turning and hobbling down the path in the other direction to the old ruin. If Shivf was still here, he could help heal him some more…if not, then he'd just have to follow in this damaged shape and hope he would heal fast once in the forest.

The sounds of the frogs could be heard long before the ruins came into sight. It looked the same as it always had, broken down and beaten, like how he felt. He entered the door that was hanging open, disgusted again at the wreckage. His dreams of renewing this place into a grand domain had not dwindled in the least. If anything, he was more determined.

"Shivf! Shivf are you still here?" he bellowed out with what little strength he had. Only the sounds of dripping water and the toads answered him. He made his way into the remains of the kitchen and it looked exactly like it had before. Even the mess on the table of the frog guts and blood was still visible, now dried to a sickly brown color.

The door to the cellar was open. He had never ventured down, but this seemed like as good a time as any. He hesitated at the opening, listening. The sound of something could be heard, maybe moaning, but he wasn't sure.

"Shivf? Is that you?" he asked and received no response. He started down the darkened stairs; a faint glow from a flittering flame came from below, his only light. "Shivf are you down here?" he called again as he reached the last step. The place was a disaster, broken furniture, moss growing on the stone walls and more frogs everywhere, watching him. Moans came from a far corner shrouded in darkness.

"Shivf, answer me. What is going on?" he called out gravelly.

"It be dead. I done and kilt the thing," a voice he didn't recognize answered him from the shadows. He moved closer and then, taken aback, stopped and looked at the sight in front of him. A small man knelt by an open crate.

He could only see a foot, but it looked like a mortal's. "Pengal told me tae feed it and I'd be forgetting tae." The thing whimpered. It turned its head and looked up at him with mournful eyes. It was the ugliest thing he had ever seen.

"Who are you?" he whispered hoarsely to it.

"Ganee. I be Ganee," it replied, staring up at the fey youth standing over him.

"Where's Shivf? What are you doing here? What are you?" he demanded, confused. Shivf hadn't ever mentioned having a servant.

"I be one of three, we be Shivf," it responded, standing up and wiping a long line of snot from its face. Aishal noticed it was missing a finger as it started towards him, pointing a remaining one down at the figure in the crate.

"You check the thing, maybe it not be dead." Aishal looked from the small man to the form in the crate. His mind was working overtime trying to figure out what 'one of three' meant. The creature kept pointing at the crate, and not knowing what else to do, he moved over to it and looked in. It was an older mortal female. She was long dead, wasted away, from not being fed, no doubt.

"It's dead. Who is it?" he asked standing up, forcing himself not to move back from the little man. The thing was repugnant. Aishal stood to his full height and glared down at the little man. If this was Shivf's servant, and Shivf was gone, then Aishal was the one in control now.

"It just be a mortal," he answered as he started to wail again. "Me brothers told me tae bring it tae them, it be the body fer the shades," the thing's eyes grew big as its mouth opened even bigger before a long wail erupted from it. "Ah be opening tae door." He screamed as he looked behind them to the opposite wall.

Aishal saw where he was pointing. There was an outline drawn on the stones with brown paint. His eyes traveled downwards and he spotted the headless dead frogs at the base and realized it wasn't paint he was seeing, but dried blood. His mind was whirling; this creature, blood on the wall. He could feel blood rushing to his face as he turned to look down at the small man.

"Dark magic. You've been using dark magic to bring the Eilibear into Firinn," he growled out at the thing fiercely. "What have you and Shivf been doing?" he screamed, grabbing its arm and shaking it violently.

"Ah been trying tae tell ye, Shivf is all of us. The three of us make the one!"

Aishal was stupefied, how could three become one? He studied the little man; his long nose turned down almost past his mouth, which looked like it had been stretched across the expanse of his pock-marked face.

"How is that possible? Shape shifters cannot join with each other," he challenged.

"Ah…now ye be listening ta ole Ganee. Ah tell ye a secret…" he lowered his voice as if others might hear. "We's made a deal with the underworld things, we did. They be given us the Willow and our magic back, and we be given them back *their* magic the fey done stole from them," he finished with a little jubilant clamp of his hands.

Aishal was almost too stunned to ask, almost in a stutter, "How were the…" he found he couldn't say it. He felt chilled to the bone and getting colder by the second. He hadn't wanted to know what Shivf had been up to. Didn't want to ask, always afraid that Shivf would tell him and it would be something like this. No fey in their right mind would want to unleash the…the Eilibear.

"Ah be telling ye, the stone, the Sumair stone. Me brothers they be in the Meadhan, letting loose the wee devils now, but I don't have the body to give them.

"No. I can't be a part of this," Aishal started to mumble to himself in panic. "No." He had to leave, hide, and go somewhere where no one would know he had been a part of this. He wondered if Laven had known all along, then decided he didn't care. For once Laven would be beaten at his own game; almost gloating to himself, he backed away from the thing that called itself Ganee.

Suddenly the thing passed gas, a long, drawn-out smelly discharge. A green misted vapor seemed to rise up from its backside. The fumes about knocked Aishal out as he struggled to back away quickly, stumbling over discarded debris.

"Aw do ye see? The wee one with me wants tae play." The little man grimaced and started to cackle as Aishal fell backwards over something. He was instantly up and racing up the stairs. His power was just about gone, but he blinked as far away as he could and started to run as fast as his injuries would allow. If he was lucky, no one would find out he had a part in this mess.

CHAPTER 44 - Ivy

I stood there in shock that Laven would just leave. The frogs had stopped croaking and the normal sounds of crickets had returned. The sun came back also, throwing cheerful rays down on the path, as if Laven had taken the gloom with him. I started to turn when I saw Margo and Zack walking towards me.

"Hi," they both said together in childlike sweetness, stopping just outside of the fencing of the glade.

"Are you two okay?" I asked them looking closely at their eyes. They seemed clear and all there, sort of.

"Of course we are," Zack answered with a little titter and turned to Margo. "We're just fine." Margo looked at me and grinned happily and nodded. "Laven said you wanted to see us."

Zack didn't mention me shoving the girl or popping him back here. Okay, he didn't want to talk about it so I didn't need to bring it up.

"Uh yeah, I did. I'm worried about you. You keep saying you want to help with the...uh surprise, but you take off every morning and don't come back," I said looking from him to Margo.

"Well, I've got things to do, people to see. But you're right! I completely forgot," he said slapping his forehead. "I'm sorry, give me um, let's say an hour, then I'll be here. I'll meet you here in an hour," he said looking down at Margo and tilting his head towards her, like he didn't want to say more.

"Why can't we go now, all of us? In fact why don't you

guys come into the cabin and I'll make some lunch, then we can go together, okay?" I felt like I was trying to coach a five-year-old into doing something he didn't want to do. But I knew I'd said the wrong thing when his face changed and drew tight, so I switched tactics. "I don't think in an hour will work. There will be people around you know; it needs to be done in the morning or at night."

"No Ivy, I said in an hour. If you want to do it so badly, it has to be then. I have plans tonight. Right now I'm going to go tell Pearl that I can't spend time with her today…it wouldn't be right to just leave without telling her. Stop acting like a brat and grow up. I'll be back here in an hour," he snapped as he took Margo by the arm and they disappeared back up the path.

I watched their backs and fought back the tears. What had happened to *we're in this together* or *I'm glad I found you,* I wondered. Now that they were here, I was all but forgotten. They couldn't have gotten in if it wasn't for me. I felt used and thrown away. I went back inside and waited and knew he wasn't coming. I waited a couple of hours before I decided that I needed to do something.

Grabbing my sweatshirt, I blinked back to the meadow. I liked it there, even liked to see the fairy rings. Of course I had to push my new knowledge about the fey out of my mind, but I could still remember how wonderful it had been to be here with Granddad and that made me feel better.

As I stood there attempting to find a peace that seemed out of reach, I spotted tips of trees rising above the others in the far off distance. They were taller than any of the other trees nearby; towering over ones I knew to be huge. That must be the grove of trees where Skyler was imprisoned. I stood there, debating with myself. I really didn't like her, and although I'd called her *mom* for my entire life, *I'd* never really thought of her as such. She was the thorn in my side, what my nightmares had been about. Everything in my life that had been negative had come from her, and her alone.

Still, I owed it to Granddad and Marmaw to care. I didn't know how long she would sleep, but knew from the writings that she would wake up eventually. It had been less than a week, but I should have checked on her by now. The fact that Laven didn't seem to think it was important…he didn't seem to think anything I wanted right now was…didn't mean that I should stop trying to find her and make sure she was okay.

I focused on the largest branch I could make out and blinked to it. I had never before tried to blink to a position other than standing on the ground, and wasn't sure how it would work.

When I opened my eyes I had to reach out quickly and grab a nearby smaller branch. I was way high, higher than I had ever been in my life. The trees swayed in the wind, giving me motion sickness. I had to close my eyes and white-knuckle the branches, waiting for the dizziness to pass. When I was finally sure that I wouldn't fall backwards or lose my breakfast, which would have been bothersome to say the least, I opened my eyes.

I had a breathtaking panoramic view of my forest. For the first time I could see the expanse of it and it took my breath away. I had to peer through the lattice of leaves, but still I was able to see far and wide. Butterflies in the millions flew above the canopy of tree tops, each a bright radiant color, creating a kaleidoscope wave of movement. I couldn't take my eyes from it and knew I had discovered my favorite place in the entire Meadhan. There were birds up here, and once they got used to me being in their domain, they came back, twittering and chirping.

I don't know how long I sat there, peaceful in my hidey hole, when I heard the faint echoes of voices below me. Feeling somewhat venturesome, I focused on a branch a bit lower and blinked to it. The sounds were still unintelligible, so I blinked down lower still. The foliage gave me complete cover as I peered down on an odd sight. There were fey down in a small grove between the giant trees. They appeared to be playing some sort of game, jumping, falling, and calling out to one another in a cocky manner.

Inching down the branch, I positioned myself for a better vantage. They were still just shapes; I couldn't make out genders or faces. I had to see what they were doing, even though I felt like a peeping tom. I had never really been around fey before and I didn't know what they really did, or how they lived. Maybe this is where they settled and I was really curious about them. Hoping that no one would look up, I chose a place I thought I would be concealed, but where I was still be able to see. I blinked down to it, hoping that I wouldn't disturb a squirrel or something and have it make a ruckus. I was in luck, nothing was disturbed and I remained hidden and unnoticed.

I made myself as steady on the limb as possible and moved around until I could see down through the leaves without moving them. There were five, no six, fey in the area and it took only a second to see that they were not having fun. Two little men were with them, both looked like midgets to me, the word *troll* came to mind. They were two of the ugliest things I had ever seen. The one with the fat belly was holding on to a fey, talking slowly to him, coaching him to do something. He must have done as the little troll man asked, because the thing let out a wicked snort and called out. "That be a good lad. Ye feel better soon." And he slapped the fey on the back before moving over to a line of small trees deeper into the shadows. I lost sight of him and started watching the other troll guy.

The other one was trying to catch something on the ground and looked like a weird kid playing leap frog as he jumped from place to place. The fey were trying to help him. They did this strange dance, hop, jump, hold still, leap, then cry out in frustration when they hadn't achieved what they were trying to do. One thin fey with brown hair tied back in a ponytail let out a cry and held something up.

A frog, he was holding a frog. That's what they were trying to catch; I could see them now, hundreds of the things all around their feet. All types of frogs in a vast array of sizes and colors covered the ground. I couldn't believe I hadn't realized it before. Now I could hear them. It was a mixture of sounds; guaaaap, guaaap, rib-bit, cwaak-cwaak-cwaak. The air was filled with their croaking and chirping.

The fey holding the frog hurried over to the tree and something I hadn't seen before moved. It looked like a slug about the size of a person, huge and nauseating. It wiggled and bent itself in half. I watched in horror as the fey bit off the frog's head then said something and the slug thing wiggled some more and I could see a shape of a head. The fey held the frog out over the thing's head and squeezed the frog's insides out onto it. Yuck, the fey was actually feeding the thing, and I felt bile starting to rise in my throat. The fey was enjoying himself, crushing the headless frog like a tube of toothpaste, trying to get the last little bit out. The slug thing turned a bit more and I could see it *was* a person. Deformed and bloated, covered with a gray slime, but none the less, that was a person laying down there.

I didn't want to, but I had to get closer so I could see who it was. I started saying silent prayers that it wasn't Margo or Zack, then realized it didn't matter who it was down there that these trolls were using in this manner. This was nightmarish and I had to do something.

Across from me, closer to the ground, was a thicket of vines that had climbed one of the trees. I scanned the tree until I found a spot that I could blink to while remaining hidden and then blinked myself over to it.

Instantly I wished I had never come here. Closer up, I

could see the face…Skyler's face. Her eyes were gone and as I watched, a toad climbed out of one of the empty sockets. I couldn't help it, I screamed, clapped my hand over my mouth and blinked back to my glade.

I was throwing up before I had even opened my eyes. I wished I had thought to blink into the cabin, with my head over the sink. Instead I found myself barfing on the foxglove and clematis growing by the cabin door. Really gross I know, but I couldn't stop the heaves. The tears came next, as I made my way into the cabin and over to the sink. I think my brain shut down for a while, the overload of emotions had *turned me off* and I was just a body, who knows where my mind went during that time.

When I finally came to myself, I was curled up in a ball under Granddad's bed. All I could figure was I must have not only tried to crawl away mentally, but physically also. I was pathetic. My understanding of what it must have been like for my family was complete. I didn't want to think about Skyler, not then and not as I had seen her today. Some things just don't need to be relived in any way, shape, or form.

I found a water bottle and filled it from the pump. Adding one of the little lemonade packs, I stood in the open doorway looking out on my glade as I shook the heck out of the bottle. The glade was still beautiful, peaceful, but a dark cloud was settling in on my forest and I wasn't at all happy about it. I really needed to talk to someone, anyone. I thought about Zack and knew that whatever Skyler had turned into was somehow connected to how he and Margo, and the other fey were acting.

Winnie came to mind. I didn't want to pull another person into this mess, but I needed some guidance. Still undecided, I downed the lemonade as I tried to figure out a plan.

My brain wouldn't focus…I just couldn't think here. I put the empty bottle on the table and found some paper.

No matter what an ass Zack was being, I'd promised I wouldn't just vanish on him again. I wrote a note, making sure I put the time on the top of the page.

"Zack, I waited until 2pm. Maybe you decided tonight would be better, like I said. I'm going to go do some stuff first and I'll be there at midnight. We really need to talk. I saw something really awful in the forest today. I need your help. Ivy."

They had gotten back before midnight a couple of times, so even if he completely forgot, the note should remind him. I hated just leaving them out there, but was at a loss as to how to get them back. If what I had seen was dangerous, it didn't matter, since I had no idea really what I had been seeing or how to stop it.

I got my pack and blinked to the first place I could think of. McDonalds. I got myself a hot coffee then wandered down to the beach. The fog bank was heavy; it was cold and slightly windy, which meant I had it all to myself. I walked and walked, listening to music, picking up rocks and shells. I found a large piece of drift wood and sat down to finish the drink, wondering if anyone cared, and figured they didn't even know I had left.

My mood wasn't helped when a Roy Orbison song about being lonely started playing in my ears. I sang along with it, making myself feel even more depressed. After the first few lines I couldn't even mouth the words, tears were falling again. Stupid I know. It was my fault,

I didn't know either that well, and I let them have my family's talismans. I let them in. Let them into my forest, my glade, my cabin, my life. It was my fault. Whatever had happened to Skyler was probably because of me. Crap, there was a reason I liked being alone. I shouldn't have let anyone in, not the fey and not Margo and not Zack. I shouldn't have left Skyler alone…it was all my fault.

The need to talk it all out with someone was strong and there was only one person right now that I could talk to. I turned off the offensive song and wiped my tears, then walked a ways more before blinking to the back of Winnie's shop. I tried the back door and it was unlocked, so I let myself in.

"Grandma Winnie?" I called out as I walked through the back storeroom and peered into the shop. "Grandma Winnie?" I called again.

"Up here dear," I heard her answer from the front of the shop.

I ran, and to her surprise, hugged her tight. She pushed me away looking down at me concerned, then behind me as if she expected the others to be with me.

"Where are Margo and Zack dear?" she asked with a voice full of uneasiness.

The story exploded from me. I told her everything, how they were spending time with the fey and didn't want to be with me. I guess I really was wallowing in self-pity. I didn't mention the frogs or the gross things I had seen, only that my friends didn't seem to want to be around me anymore. No doubt about it, I was only sixteen at that point and was acting very self-centered. When I had got it all out, I wiped my tears and snotty nose with the back of my hand and looked at her pathetically.

"Can't you come back with me and talk to them?" I whined out a plea.

"No dear. I can't travel to a Meadhan. But not to worry dear, they are just enthralled," she said giving me a hug.

"Enthralled?" I asked, wiping away more snot that had started to run out of my nose. I'm never a pretty sight when I cry.

"Dear, you've been around fey quite a bit in your life, even if you don't remember it. I know Margo has not and I would venture that Zack has not either. They are young and weak against the pull of the fey. Just jolt them back."

"How do I do that?"

"Do something that will scramble their minds for a bit.

I'm sure you can think of something. A good shock of reality is what they need."

"Could I blink them back here?" I asked, wondering if I could.

"That would not be a good idea. They need to be where the fey are, but see clearly what is around them. Maybe get something from here that would remind them of who they are. Margo's jeep or something big that will really shock them," she said. "Even if you aren't able to, the enchantment will run its course, they will come back, dear." She smiled gently as she led me to the little table and made me a cup of tea.

I calmed down as she puttered around, cleaning up the area and thought about what she said. Something big to remind them. I knew what the something big could be. I still hadn't told her what I had seen in the forest, and to be honest I really didn't want to talk about it. She might know what was happening to Skyler though and know how to fix it.

"Grandma Winnie, there's something else I need to ask you about." I started to say, just as the door chime sounded at the front of the store. Grandma turned, dusted off her hands and started to walk towards the front. "Grandma, really I have something else I should tell you. It's about someone else that came into the Meadhan, Sky..."

"No!" she yelled, suddenly very upset. I watched as she worked to composed herself and forced a smile on her face. In a quiet voice, she came over and took my hands. "No Ivy, do not tell me. The Seer said you had to do without help from me. Whatever it is, it will be just fine, I'm sure of it. You think about what I said. I think you need to spend the rest of today away from there, calm your mind."

I shook my head and started to argue, but she put her hand up to stop me.

"It will be fine…there *is* time and it will all work out in the end," she said as she turned and walked away to the front of the store.

I was left there completely confused. Maybe I should have told her about the frogs and Skyler first, though she clearly didn't want to know about it. I wondered just who this Seer was and why on earth she would tell Winnie she couldn't help me.

I debated trying to talk with her again, but maybe she *was* right. Everything was fine, maybe I hadn't really seen what I thought I had seen. Besides she had given me an idea on how to get my friends back.

I left the way I had come, by the back door, standing there for a moment making sure no one else was around before I blinked to the back side of the log house's small porch. The door was still unlocked and I let myself in. I could hear cars on the road, and once in a while someone's voice would drift to me. No one came close to where I was. I wandered through the rooms, trying to bring back the memories of the excitement that Zack and I'd had when we'd found this.

I finally sat down in the middle of the floor and imagined what it would look like with the furniture and decided what the hell. I knew that the salesman would keep the furniture in the other model homes until I came for it. It was late afternoon and the lot was empting. Only a couple of cars were in the parking lot. I blinked into the first house and inspected the stuff I had purchased. It was still there, in exactly the same places.

I started blinking the items, piece by piece into the half section of the log house, placing stuff in the right rooms. It still looked bare when I was done. There weren't any real big stores in Coos Bay, not the kind I needed to find the stuff I was thinking about. Maybe in that town the bus had stopped at. I knew the bus terminal and really didn't care if I surprised someone by blinking in. If a shock was what was needed for Zack and Margo, then I was going give them a big one.

Deciding the bus terminal bathroom would be my best bet, I popped into it. It looked deserted, but for the first time since staying in the motel with Zack, I saw myself in a mirror. I didn't look good. My hair was a mess, my face looked drawn and tired and a frown seemed permanently stuck on it.

I tried to smile at myself and just couldn't. Instead I winked. "*Love you Granddad.*" It felt like I was back to where I had started, alone. I cleaned myself up as best I could and went out.

Turned out there was a mall in Medford, some lady pointed towards the other end of town. I couldn't see it, but I'd pick something I could see down the road and did a blink hop thing until I found it. The next few hours were fun, as fun as it could be doing things alone. I got bedding and kitchen stuff, large rugs with bright flowers for all the rooms. I came across a frame shop and picked up several that Marmaw's pictures would fit in. Each time my arms got full I would find a safe place and blink back to the log house to drop the stuff off. The rugs were interesting. I paid, and then asked for help carrying them. When the gal turned her back to speak in her little walkie-talkie thing, I blinked out with them.

I went nuts with the house stuff, adding more chairs and bookcases. In one store there was this huge fish hanging on the wall on a really cool wall hook thing. I could picture the axe in place of the fish and brought it, leaving the fish behind. I even got curtains, light breezy sheer ones and the rods to hold them. Lastly I got some more clothes. I hated mall fashions, but I needed clean clothes…I was beginning to look like a reject. I got some items for everyone, and stocked up on aspirin and toothpaste. I hadn't planned on having two other people using my stash, and they had been using them a lot the last few day.

Those purchases I put in the upstairs closets when I blinked in and the house was starting to fill up nicely. I discovered that I was having a blast, even without them being with me and blinked again, feeling hungry and a bit drained. This time I went outside the large mall after getting a huge bag of food. I sat on the ledge of a concrete flower box and watched the normal people coming and going. Life was going on, and the fey and the forest and the heavy dark cloud seemed not so important. Across the wide street of fast moving cars, I spotted a sign for an antique mall.

I'd gone to some of those with Marmaw and although it was always more fun with someone else to look through all the stuff that was always jammed into those places, I decided to check it out. I walked, even waiting for the light to change, and crossed the street with a couple of other people. The place was huge and just like the other ones I had been to, had stalls filled with a variety of things. I discovered loads of stuff that I could envision in my house, a long side chair, and a cool antique fainting couch in purple velvet, an old kitchen cabinet and side tables that looked like they were from the Victorian age. In the same booth, I found two tall matching lamps with glass at the top that looked like golden flowers about to open. When I stood on a stool to see what kind of light bulb they took, I was pleasantly surprised to see they weren't electric, but instead were little kerosene lamps. I had to have them. The place was so cool. I must have picked out fifty items, big and small, and happily paid for them, telling the man behind the counter that my dad would come with a truck.

Then I wandered and blinked each piece back when he wasn't looking. I guess I could have just taken them without paying, but that never really crossed my mind. By the time I had blinked the last of the items back to the house, I was worn out. I laid down on one of the mattresses upstairs and fell into a restless sleep. Images of frogs and fey wouldn't leave me alone until I used a bit of magic and told the house to be locked, only when I felt nothing, human or otherwise, could get to me, did I finally fall asleep.

CHAPTER 45 - Pengal

Pengal was agitated. No matter what the fey did the Alltha wasn't breaking and giving up the Sumair stone. Laven's plan to isolate her from her two allies was working, to a point. For some reason he couldn't understand, every night they were drawn back to that glade of hers and expelled the Eilibear vapors they had worked so hard all day to get into them. Each morning they were starting over again and the brainless fey had even allowed the Druid to stay protected.

He didn't understand how it could be so difficult to cut the thing's hair off. He had tried himself to gnaw at it with his sharp teeth; he hadn't even left a mark. The mortal was just as perplexing; she should have been the easier of the two, but no matter how much Eilibear poison they forced into her, it did nothing more than enchant her for a time.

He was pacing now, waiting for Tubaw to return from spying on the Alltha. Tubaw enjoyed being in the Wisp form and he was always announcing that he wanted to keep this form when they went home. Pengal wasn't sure just why he liked it so much; maybe the flying, but more likely the ability to be small and go anywhere. A squeal made him jump and turn. One of the dumber fey had caught another frog and brought it over to him. Holding it out like it was a piece of gold ore. He snorted as he snatched it out of the fey's hand and waved her away before going over to where another fey was bound to a tree.

Without giving it much thought he twisted off the frog's head, punched the fey in the gut to make it open its mouth and squirted the frog's juices inside. Another of the bound fey squealed and started to squirm hysterically. He knew his brother had returned.

"Tubaw, git out of the girl's knickers."

He waited until he saw the Wisp appear from a hole in the girl's leg coverings and convert back into his rightful form. Tubaw was grinning ear to ear, which wasn't all that hard for a Boggart.

"What did ye see? Did Laven find out any more abit the stone?"

"Nay, but the Alltha looked like she was fit tae be tied. It will not be long afore she will do as we demand," he snickered as he ran his hand up and down the closest fey's leg.

"We are needing the other mortal body…and Ganee. Ganee should have bin here by now. I'm worried abit him," he grumbled out loud. Ganee was the youngest of the three and Pengal missed him more than anything else. "The body of the shifted one wilt not be lasting much longer. Go git him and the others, be back afore nightfall. We need tae start sealing the doorway."

Pengal discovered that Tubaw wasn't listening to him at all; instead he was poking various places on the tied up fey. Pengal was weary, and had no patience for his brother's mischiefs. He reached out and slugged his brother hard on the head. "Mind me, go fetch Ganee and the others…now!"

Tubaw grumbled, but he changed back into a Wisp and took off. His brother had set a fey guard by the doorway and the dumb thing had fallen asleep. He changed back into his normal form and whacked it across the face. It woke with a scream, and he was through the doorway and gone before it knew what had hit him.

The meadow of Rootmire looked the same to Tubaw,

desolate and boring. He had to walk the rest of the way and wished, once more, that he could keep the Wisp hex. It was the finest thing he had been able to do his whole life. He continued to grumble as he made his way up to the ruins and through the mess to the cellar. Then wished he hadn't.

His brother's body was hanging upside down from the rafters, sliced and diced right nicely. Green slime dripped in pools from the remains. A glance around the room told him what had happened. Ganee had never been too smart, maybe he'd lost too many parts from all the joining they had done over the years. The body of the mortal lay lifeless and the portal was open. He snatched up the first toad he spied and hurried to close it back up. The job wasn't a pretty one, but no more Eilibear should be able to come through.

He sat down on a box and tried to figure out what to do. Ganee must have let the mortal die and the Eilibear in. They must not have been too pleased to find their vessel had been rendered useless. He wondered where the shades had got off too. He doubted they would have gone back into Ifrinn once released and they couldn't pass through a fey doorway unless they were in some sort of body. There seemed to be fewer frogs, so maybe they had taken their forms and hip-hopped through. Pengal would not be pleased with this bit of news. Deciding to keep his brother company, he made himself a nice cup of tea and sat down, delaying having to go back to face his older brother.

Nightfall came and went with no Tubaw or Ganee in sight. Pengal could only call his brothers foul names and torture the bound fey as a release to his anger and frustrations. The Eilibear were gathering in droves about him, he could feel their presences multiplying with the smaller creatures, into any larger forms they could find.

Already they had filled up quite a few of the fey and if he didn't act quickly and find that stone, it would be all for naught.

He didn't believe for one moment that the Woodsman had taken it out of the Meadhan. He could feel it, as could the Eilibear. It was here somewhere and the likely place was that private home of the Alltha. It was time to seal the doorway into Firinn and force the Alltha to give it up. The Eilibear had been working on draining her power and that of the Meadhan. Unless she had an influx of new magic, they should be able to bring down her barrier to the glade and ransack the little hovel she lived in.

He whistled shrilly, calling the frogs and creeping things in, then directed them to the doorway to begin the sealing. That at least they would have no problems completing.

CHAPTER 46 – Elsie

May 12, 2011 –

It has started, my dreams are dark and confusing and the terror I feel is about to tear me apart. I find I can't even look at Skyler now. I know too much. No person should have to go through this. My odd new friends are ready and promise me it will be well. I hope so. Dear Milton is clueless and that is for the best.

It will happen this day and my dreams do not tell me how it will play out for me. I am not a main character in this story and know it. I have spent the day with Ivy, loving on her as much as I can. God give me strength for what lays ahead.

CHAPTER 47- Ivy

I woke up to complete darkness and for a moment didn't know where I was, then I remembered. The log house. I looked at my watch and saw it was after midnight. I left the *lock* on the house and blinked back into the forest right into the cabin. A soft fire was glowing in the stove and Zack was snoring in the bed. I peeked up into the loft and found Margo curled into a tight ball. Her hair was matted and she smelled horrible.

I glanced back at the table and found the note I had left for him was gone. I looked at Zack and wondered if he had read the note, but the sight of a crumbled piece of paper in his fist told me all I needed to know.

Well, they had come back, and that was a good thing. It would be a super big shock when they opened the door and tried to go outside in the morning. Smiling a little wickedly to myself, I closed the door quietly behind me, and told it to keep them inside. I really didn't want to blink a whole house back and smash one of my friends who might come out and stand in the way.

I went back into Alainn and gathered all the power I could. I was finding it easier to fill my reservoir with power from tons of things. I pulled in from the ocean and the woods behind the lot, and even from the weeds in the parking lot. When my battery was charged, I stood on the deck at the corner of the log house and blinked to the corner of the foundation Zack had constructed.

It worked like a charm…funny I know, worked like a charm, I'm a real comedian…and I really wished that Zack had been there to see how well he had figured it all out. The doors lined up perfectly, creating a short hallway between the two structures. I realized that the little alleys now created outside on either side of the new hallway would be wonderful places to put more ferns and flowers and maybe even that fountain I'd been thinking about.

I didn't bother blinking, but walked around to the new front door and entered my new home. It was a disaster. I hadn't noticed it when I was bringing stuff in, but a couple of years sitting on that back lot meant a lot of dust and cobwebs, add to that the sawdust from the workers and I had a real mess on my hands. It didn't help that I had put so much stuff inside.

I opened the door the workers had installed and then unsealed the cabin and went in. I built up the fire in the cabin's stove as quietly as I could, and put both of my large pots filled with water on to heat. Then grabbed the broom and went back over and started to clean. I had to move a lot of stuff around, and I cheated with some by blinking it out of the way.

By the time any hint of light was coming in the windows I had the downstairs pretty clean. I had retrieved the pots of hot water and blinked them from one stove to the other. I washed all the shelves and discovered a little door I didn't know about, on the kitchen side of the stairs. It was a large closet, perfect for storing more food.

When I could pull myself away from the kitchen, which I really liked, I started on the floors. I even squirted wood polish all over it and mopped like Marmar used to do. As the sun rose over the trees, rays started to filter into the room making the floor glow a rich deep red brown color. I had never heard of Brazilian cherry wood before, but I really liked this.

I had to let it dry before I could do anything else and ended up back in the little cabin waiting for them to wake up. A bunch of groaning and moaning accompanied their waking, and I started the pot for tea and mixed up the herb combination that seemed to work best on them. By the time both were up, heads hanging down like the worse hangover ever, I had their tea made and a couple of aspirins sitting by each mug.

They followed the same routine as every day this last week. Drinking the tea, taking the aspirins, mumbling to me while they washed and dressed, refusing any breakfast, and then going to the door together to leave. The only thing absent today was my arguing with them.

Zack opened the door with Margo behind him. I stood back, trying not to smile as he just stared at the open door into the log house. He hung back as Margo looked around him, then they looked at each other before they turned to stare at me in confusion.

"It's the house Zack. Margo, we meant it as a surprise for you but...well I guess it's a surprise for both of you now," I said as my smile slipped from my face.

Zack's face went from bewildered to furious, his eyes darkened and he turned and walked straight through it out the other door leaving it hanging open. Margo watched him, looked back at me, and then peered into the new addition with amazement. Her face started to glow with her smile and suddenly I was tackled by her.

"You got a house! You got us a house!" she yelled, hugging me wildly while pulling me around in a circle, and I couldn't help but smile as she let go of me and ran into it. She stood and looked around, her eyes wide as her smile, and then she started running from room to room screaming with excitement as she found new things.

"Why didn't you wait?" a cold voice came from behind me. Turning, I saw Zack standing in the outside doorway glaring at me.

"I did wait, for days and you never came," I answered honestly.

"You said 7:30. I would have been there," he snapped at

me. "You didn't have to go and do it early."

"Early? What are you talking about? That was close to a week ago. Every day, when you would talk to me you'd say the same thing. 'I'll see you at 7:30, be there at 7:30'," I said. "Well after eight days, I figured you weren't going to show no matter what you said." The nerve of the guy.

"That's just like you Ivy. You make things up. When you came back you told me you'd been gone three weeks and it had only been a week. Now you are trying to tell me that something we decided last night was really over a week ago? You are insane!" he screamed back.

"Last night? Who's the one that's insane? Since the first day we came here you and Margo have been taking off every day, going who knows where, doing who knows what with the fey. You come back to the cabin at night and barf your guts up, then do it again the next day! I haven't had a normal conversation with you since we got here!"

"Well the fey are right, you are crazy! You are a malevolent spiteful little bitch! All that talk about wanting to open up the doorway was your little vindictive way of sticking it to them. You've been lording it over them, forcing them to do what you want," he screamed at me, his face twisted up in anger. "I've seen you sneaking around the forest, spying on them...on me. They were right...I tried to tell them they had it wrong, but they weren't. You let them in only so you could steal their magic!"

I had to let him say it. It hurt, but I wasn't surprised, though maybe I should have been. It's what I had thought the fey were doing, turning him and Margo against me. I didn't know why or what the end game was, but there it was in all its sickening glory. If this is what fey did to people with their *enthralling* thing, I didn't like them one bit. I'd never do something like this to someone. When I was sure he had finished, I asked one question.

"If you haven't been spending time with the fey for the last eight days when did they tell you all this and when did

I have time to 'sneak' around?" I asked as I crossed my arms over my chest and tried to stop the shaking. "You and Margo have been enthralled, enchanted, call it anything you want. But you haven't been you."

He did a really good impression of a goldfish for a moment. Opening and closing his mouth as he started to answer me. His fury was replaced by bewilderment that ran rapidly across his features, as his eyes darted from me to around the house. He turned and stomped out, only to stop and look around outside. He was swaying a bit. He would start to walk in one direction, then stop as if disoriented. That must have gone on for a good ten minutes. When he finally turned back to me, his eyes had opened wide in panic. I could see he really was trying to gain focus.

He walked slowly back into the house and stood a couple of feet away from me. I could only look up at him and hope he was snapping out of it.

"They glamoured me?" he finally stammered. "Why would they do that?"

"I don't know, but after those girls tried to get you to take off your jewelry and wanted to cut your hair, I kind of put a lock on you, as much as I could," I admitted.

"They wanted to cut my hair?" he said putting his hand up to his head as if to ensure it was still all there.

"Yeah, and you were all for it. Telling me that I was jealous of the attention they were paying you. You wouldn't listen to me. You had already taken off most of your pendants and rings. I put them back on you. I did a whammy thing and well, now your hair can't be cut, not by anything and your jewelry won't come off."

His face said he didn't believe me, and he tried to pull a ring off. It wouldn't budge; he tried a necklace, also to no avail. Pulling a pocket knife out of his jeans, he opened it and tried to cut the cord. His knife wouldn't cut it. At last he took a long piece of his hair and tried to cut it…and discovered that his knife was useless. I was worried that he would be upset, but his face showed he was more amazed than anything else. When he finally looked at me his face was serious and I didn't know what he was going to say.

"You protected me from myself? I remember…" he said looking down as he tried to remember more. "They said you kept hiding from them and wouldn't talk with anyone. You decided not to meet with all the fey like you promised." He looked up at me with puzzlement. "I called you names, damn, I called you a bitch. I've been calling you some really bad names," he admitted.

"Yes, yes you did and you have," I agreed.

"Yet you still protected me from them."

"I couldn't do anything else. For some reason, I couldn't stop you from going to them. Not you or Margo. I did what I could; made sure you couldn't be hurt. You must have remembered something since you both came back every night. I finally went to see Grandma Winnie. She said I had to shock you back to reality."

"I don't remember what I was doing." Alarmed, he started pulling his hair back away from his face and looking around as if he could find his memories if he looked hard enough.

"I…well, I saw you once…you were kissing this really ugly fey and I…well, I kind of slugged her. You just stood there and laughed at nothing. I blinked you back, but you just took off again."

"I kissed one of them? And you saw me do it?" he sputtered.

"Yeah, and she was yucky."

"Well, make me feel better, why don't you?" And he smiled for the first time. His eyes left mine and I saw them grow wide as he looked at something behind me.

Turning, I spied Margo on the stairs. I didn't know how long she had been there, but it was apparent that she had heard enough. Her face had gone pale and she looked like she was about to throw up. I ran over to her and I could hear Zack following me.

"I…I did some really gross things," she said as she looked around wildly at us. And then she started to gag. Zack picked her up and hurried her into the cabin where she was violently sick in the sink.

When she was done I put a pot of water on for more tea and then sat down next to her putting my arm around her shoulder. She was crying silently and Zack looked like he just might follow suit.

"Why would they do this to us?" he asked, shaking his head.

"I don't know. Maybe the fey are just like that, mischievous."

"More like evil little creeps," he spat, jumping as the tea kettle started to whistle. He got up and went to grab the normal tea bags. I stopped him, handing him the mixture of teas I had made. He looked at me questioningly.

"I concocted this. You both kept throwing up and were having bad dreams. This seems to settle your stomachs and calm you." I looked over at Margo who had put her head down on the table and was still crying. "I think she needs it." He nodded agreement and helped me make a cup for her and then made one for himself also. I just put instant coffee in mine.

When we placed it in front of her, she sat up but couldn't meet our eyes. After a couple of sips she started to hiccup so hard she had to put the mug back down.

"I can't believe I did what I did. I can see myself doing things, saying things, as if it wasn't me. Oh Ivy, was it only to make us do things we normally would never do? Oh, geez I think I'm going to be sick again...I feel sleazy!" And she started crying again.

"I don't know why…maybe because they couldn't hurt you physically, although I think they were trying. They found another way to hurt you, and me. But then again, maybe they are just raunchy, rowdy people and didn't realize the harm they were causing."

"I don't believe that. I can remember what they were saying about you, and shit, I was buying every word," Zack snorted, annoyed at himself.

"But why?" she pleaded.

"Yes…why? That guy Laven seemed to be fawning all over you, so happy that you had opened the doorway and let all the fey in. I thought he was a little bit too slick," Zack mused as he drank his drink.

I couldn't help but feel like smiling. Maybe what had happened to them had been kind of depraved, but I had my friends back. Grandma Winnie had been right, shocking them had worked. They were here, really here, with their minds intact. Now we just had to make sure they stayed that way.

"You guys hungry?" Both looked at me as if I had lost it. "As far as I know, you haven't eaten any real food in days, and you've been throwing up a lot at night. You must be hungry." They looked at each other and I could see they were dumbfounded that they weren't. "Well, even if you aren't, I think you still need to eat." I stood and began looking over what I had. Deciding that maybe they needed solid food I used some of the breakfast meals that had eggs and potatoes and opened up a can of spam. It smelled good to me and I noticed that soon both of them were getting in the spirit of it and had started to organize the table for a meal. It was nice to see the table being set and both of them busy and talking.

By time it was done, everything was ready for us to have a good meal. Once they started to eat, neither seemed to be able to get enough. We went through all of the breakfast packs and all my cans of spam and one of corn beef hash before they said they were full…for now.

We cleaned up and then Zack announced he was going to start figuring out what we needed to do to get the plumbing connected to the house and Margo really wanted to start working on organizing the items I had purchased. I was glad that the surprise had jolted them out of the glamour thing, but I still had a concern.

"Uh, guys?" I said as they started to leave. Both looked back at me, thankfully really looking at me. "After all that has happened, are you sure you want to stay here? I would understand if one or both of you wanted to get away from this mess and go home."

Zack stared at me for a moment, cocking his head to the side as he considered me before he spoke. "Do you want me to leave?"

"And me?" Margo asked, looking like she might cry.

"No, of course I don't. But this…" I waved my hand towards the door, "isn't your problem and it hurt you. I don't want you guys to get hurt," I answered hoping that they would stay, but at the same time really meaning what I said.

"Ivy, Grandma Winnie was right about me. I've been searching for what I'm supposed to be doing and looking for where I belong. I have no doubts now…this is where I belong and I'm not leaving," Zack said and now I felt like *I* might cry.

"Me too," Margo said as she came over to me and gave me a hug. "This feels like home already, like I was supposed to be here and have just been waiting for you to show up. I love Grandma, but somehow I think she would understand."

The tears came then and embarrassed I wiped them away, trying not to make an idiot of myself. "Thank you," I mumbled and glanced outside. I still was worried about them and what the fey might try next. "Could I put some protection on you both so you can't just take off with the fey now, maybe seal you in? I couldn't seem to do it to you when your minds were *gone*, but maybe it would work now."

Both answered without hesitating, “Yes!”

“I don’t know about Margo, but I want to know what I’m doing and be the one doing it.” Zack said. “Seal away.”

“I agree. The zombie thing is not for me,” Margo said making a face.

I did my *thing*, feeling the power go out to the barrier and this time I knew it had worked, like a latch going down and shutting them in. Neither would be able to leave the glade until I unlocked it.

Each one of us, for our own reasons, kept ourselves extremely busy that day. Zack went and found his discarded tools and all the notes he had done on how to connect everything and got to work with gusto. He was a man driven and we were happy to drop whatever we were doing and run to help him if he called for us.

In between being his helper, we cleaned the upstairs and organized the bedrooms, deciding who was going to go where. Margo thought I should get the private bedroom, but I didn’t want to be alone. I didn’t care if I shared with her or Zack, but there was no way I was going to be isolated again. We put Zack in the small room and we took the larger one.

It was like being in college and having roommates. I gave the choice of the bedding over to Margo and she was very happy dividing it up for each of us. We probably should have cleaned and organized the main living rooms first, but it seemed that the together time in our own room was what we really needed.

We did trip after trip into the cabin and gathered up our clothes and personal items and arranged them in our room. I waited until I knew that Zack wouldn’t call for help for at least a couple of minutes before I brought out the bag of clothes I had gotten her. I’d never seen anyone have as much fun as she did with kitty cat pink knee socks. It seemed I did pretty good on sizes and picking out odd enough stuff to suit her. It didn't matter if any of the new stuff matched anything she already owned since nothing she wore ever matched anyway. She was clipping on these cool hair things I had found when we heard Zack yelling for us.

We ran to the back window and looked out to see him standing in the ditch for the septic line.

"About time!" he said with a frustrated smile.

"Sorry, uh, we were trying on clothes," Margo answered with a huge grin.

"That's nice, but do you want a working toilet or not?" he asked raising his eyebrows at us. "Go flush the upstairs toilet. See if anything happens."

I ran to try it. This was the funniest bathroom, a combination of modern and turn of the century, but for us it was perfect. I pulled the hand cord and heard the water we had filled it with…one of the chores he had given the two of us earlier…empty into the bowl and we both clapped when it flushed like a normal toilet. It was amazing how excited you can get just by seeing the swirling in a toilet bowl.

I ran back to the window and did a thumbs-up at him, but he was looking into the ditch seeming to follow the sound of the now flowing water until it went into the septic tank. Only then did he look up and grin at me.

Margo and I had moved on to figuring out the kitchen when we heard loud banging outside again. We opened the new back door to find Zack manhandling the large black barrels that somehow were supposed to give us hot water. All this stuff was out of my league, and maybe Zack's also, since he'd spent as much time reading as he had doing anything else for a while. But we helped him put the things where he wanted, and held the ladder for him to climb onto the roof of the cabin and then handed the flat panels up to him.

It was more than my brain wanted to know, but he was

sure enjoying himself. Every now and then we would look out and see him connecting pipes, or wire, or reading a manual while inspecting something in his hand. He was a lot like my Granddad I'd discovered, as he was apt to come up with some very interesting language when he dropped something from the roof, or hit his thumb with the hammer. The best was when he discovered he had mounted two of the solar panels upside down. Margo and I would grin at each other as another torrent of cursing could be heard and go on with what we were doing.

It was late afternoon before he had finished with the plumbing and hooking up the weird looking battery to the house. He said it would take about a week for it to be charged and ready to use for the water heater and pump and also have enough juice for the small refrigerator and freezer.

None of us cared that we had to wait; it was exciting in itself that this was even possible. So Margo and I gladly helped him put together the stove pipe for the kitchen stove and fiddle with the one for the weird fireplace. We were outside, Margo and I standing down at the base of the ladder, with Zack up on the roof putting the vent roof on, when the fey started to appear.

The girls came first, standing as close to the barrier as they could and called to Zack. He ignored them, which only made them get louder and rowdier, all to no avail.

I climbed the ladder up to where Zack could see me. He motioned with his head towards where the fey stood and then looked back at me. "Please turn them into those bug things."

"I can't. I've tried, but something is wrong. Just like I couldn't keep you inside the glade, I can't call on Laven or change them into Wisps," I answered sadly. "But apparently they still can't come into my glade, so that's a good thing." He digested that and then smiled weakly at me.

"It will be okay. Let's get our work done and we can try to figure it out later."

The girls continued their badgering of him as I made my way back down to where Margo stood at the base of the ladder. She looked scared and I understood the feeling.

After a few more minutes, the girls gave up and the guys took over. About ten of them stood where the girls had and called to Margo, their voices low and enticing, probably more so than the girls had been.

She gave me a look of *I'm sorry* before she ran back into the house to hide. The guys didn't give up, but they changed tactics, now they were calling out insults to me. They covered everything from my bodily functions, to my looks and something about a dog I didn't understand. I had no problem pretending they were not there. It was when Laven and Bryear appeared that I almost turned to them. But the first words out of Bryear's mouth stopped me.

"Sorceress! No fey has the magic you do. Give us the Sumair stone," he jeered at me as he leaned oddly sideways. I disregarded him and Laven. The name calling continued for a time, before their voices changed and the pleading began.

They took turns asking me where the Sumair stone was, telling me what they would give me, or do for me if I'd tell them. Their voices were silky and sweet, pleading, begging, offering up themselves and special treats if I'd just disclose where it was. Zack was almost finished and started down the ladder as I held it when they changed tactics again, and the insults started again.

They called us cowards, Allthas, defectors, traitors, deserters and names I didn't know the meaning of. I heard I wasn't a real Frìth since I couldn't shape shift. I wasn't sure if that was true since I hadn't tried, and really didn't want to anyway. Laven told Zack he was not a real Druid since real Druids lived in Alainn and not in a Meadhan with other fey. Yet here he was with me, the worst of the worst, and on and on it went.

Zack and I locked eyes as he came down the ladder, giving each other much needed support. I cleaned up the area, while he put the ladder behind the small cabin, then holding hands we went inside and closed the door on their slurs.

Zack read us the manual on using the fireplace, while trying to drown out the voices from outside. When I couldn't take it anymore I let the heat build in my throat and then yelled out that unless the fey had something nice to say, and mean it, *we* couldn't hear them. I guess I should have thought of that sooner, to work my magic on us and not them, since it was quiet after that. I guess they had nothing nice to say and I knew as soon as I had built up some courage I was going to blink to the doorway and get rid of them.

We went back to reading the manual and it sounded easy enough. You just built a fire in it, turn the dampers a certain way and the heat turned a fan that forced it out to the front room, or if you closed the glass doors and closed one set of dampers and opened the next one, the warm air would heat parts of the upstairs. Pretty cool.

Zack disappeared out the back door and soon the sound of him chopping wood could be heard. Within the next couple of days we would need to go out into the forest for more logs, but we would deal with that when we had to. And I needed to tell them what I had seen in the grove of trees. I just didn't want to bring it up now, Margo would just end up barfing some more.

I watched as Zack brought in armfuls of wood that fit in the little alcove and he filled it to the brim. I lit the lanterns that looked like flowers and all of us were delighted by how much light they gave off. As the sun started to set, we went around and lit all the copper-backed wall hurricane lanterns that were already set in the walls. Margo found the packing box that held their matching glass globes and gently placed them on the lanterns after I lit them.

When we were done, the log house had a cozy soft glow going on and together we tackled starting a fire in the new stove. In no time we had it nice and hot enough to make soup and put a pot of coffee on. We ate at the new antique table and spoke of nothing but the house. The elephant in the room loomed over us, but none of us wanted to bring up the fey just yet.

Margo and I had put items around the house that needed Zack and his hammer to put in place, so while Zack puttered around taking care of that I looked for something to do. I still had a lot of nervous energy and decided to do something I had been telling myself for weeks I would do. I made bread. You might think this was easy. It seemed like it was when Marmaw had done it, but I found out differently. I followed the recipe as best I could. I didn't have butter so I had to use lard, and by the time I had a nice large ball of goo I wondered if I ever wanted to do this again.

Flour covered me and the kitchen, my hands hurt from kneading and I couldn't see how this could ever taste good. But I divided it into two bowls that the sales lady had said were made for this, and put both in the little warming tray of the stove, with cheese cloth on top. If this worked, then all I had to do was divide it into the pans before I went to bed and it would be ready to bake in the morning. We would see.

The night ended with us sitting around the fireplace, drinking hot chocolate and wondering if the fey were always like this. I pulled out the notebook I had created, with my outlines, and we went over everything I had pulled from Marmaw's stories and notebooks. The results were that we didn't know any more than before.

In frustration, I threw the notebook down. "I just don't know enough about all the different types of things. We have a list of names, but what are they and what do they really do?"

"We know that Margo is part Sprite, you're fey and I'm a Druid," Zack stated the obvious as he tried to get a handle on it. "We know what we are like."

"Yeah but we are all wild, remember? We're Alltha," I said irritated. "They all should have told us more."

"There's the book," Margo said as she pulled a melted marshmallow out of her cup of hot chocolate and tried to eat the sticky mess off her fingers.

"What book?" Zack asked her, looking at the partly filled book shelves around us.

"The one Grandma gave Ivy," she answered as she dove into the chocolate again for another marshmallow.

"Crap, I forgot about it!" I cried jumping up and dashing for the stairs. I found my backpack next to my new bed and hurried to open it, retrieving the little book. When I had it, I retraced my steps and ended up out of breath holding it out to Zack.

He had found a washcloth and was trying to get Margo to wipe her hands before she got the mess on the couch. I had to laugh; she even had it all over her face. It was so good to have her back. Zack gave up and took the book, opening it as I sat on the arm of the chair and looked over his shoulder. Marmaw's pretty handwriting covered the front page. Zack scanned the page for a moment, then began to read out loud to us.

"The Fey"

"To my Ivy – All the things I've wanted to tell you and couldn't. May you never forget your Marmaw."

I found myself starting to cry and wiped my tears with the back of my hand. I didn't care whether they noticed or not. If they did, neither said anything, and Zack turned the page and continued to read.

"I set myself to write this log as we find ourselves in constant companionship with folk we know nothing of. It has been many years and we have developed friendships

with the Allthas and fey in both realms. This notion of realms was once hard to wrap my mind around, however now I wonder how others live without the knowledge.

Our home is Alainn, The Beautiful Land – This is the mortal realm, where mortals live, work, play, sleep and go about their mortal lives. It is Earth and all the planets and any area of knowledge to the normal man.

The folk are from Firinn, The Real Land – This is the fey realm. It is just as large and unending as Alainn, but does not have other planets. It is one plain, long and wide and unending which has openings into yet another realm.

The middle realm is Meadhan or The Middle. These are delightful little pockets of space set in Alainn, unseen, veiled, but quite nice for the most part. Meadhans and Firinn are connected by doorways. The folk can live quite nicely in any realm, but have a need to pass through into Meadhan and thus into Alainn quite often. This need is not unlike the need a mortal has to draw a breath, the folk need to draw and expel their magic.

There is yet another realm, one no folk would ever wish to find themselves in. Ifrinn. Mortals know of this realm and seek to hide from it as much as the folk do. It is called Hell in Alainn, and the demons we be so afraid of, are Eilibear. Any may travel there, but who would want to?

This all made no sense to me when first I found myself living a shifted life, just another thread in the weave of the folk. And weave they do; they weave the life into all realms, they weave the stories and nightmares and daydreams; they weave the hopes and dreams and the desires of the heart. I have seen that the mortals believe they have no need for the folk, hence they refuse to see them; and the folk think themselves better than the mortals, and yet would have no magic if not for that which the clueless mortals create and give back to the creatures. The weave of life bears all realms, all creatures, and if one was to disappear so would they all.

My eyes are open and my heart is full – may this writing bring you joy. Marmaw"

"Ivy this is fantastic!" Zack said after he read the opening out loud to us. "I wish we'd had this book days ago." Then he realized what he had just said and looked up at me with puppy eyes. "Sorry."

"It's okay. Maybe we needed to go through all of this for a reason; Grandma Winnie said there was a reason for everything. I don't know about you, but I can't wait to find out what the reason was for the last few days."

"Agreed. There must be a reason; we just need to figure out what it was," he said as he flipped through the pages of the book. "Look at this, your Grandma has cataloged all the folk she's met. Wait, here's something about Allthas.

"Milton came across the Alltha Order when he had to go on a hunt for Skyler again. We had thought ourselves all alone up until that time. They are a very nice group of fey, very diverse in types and skills. It seems there is a large amount of fey that for one reason or another have decided to make Alainn their permanent home. The Order keeps the peace; helps when there is a problem and generally are there to talk with.

I find it endearing that they greet each other as Uncle and Aunt, bringing us together as a family. In a life without end, a constant family is a necessary thing as our mortal ones do seem to leave us quickly and frequently.

Uncle Geraint seems to have decided that the 1930's were the best of times and has stopped his life there. I understand his thought, as Milton does so seem to love the 50's and 60's. Milton took to the music of that time and to my dismay will keep that music alive in our home forever."

I had started to laugh and couldn't stop. Marmaw was so right about Granddad. He did love that music. It was like having her here in the new house with us. Weaving her story like she said the folk did. Zack was happy to hold off reading anymore until I could control myself, and I finally gestured for him to continue.

"As the years went on Milton found his place in this Order and he and his new friends found many that were in need of their help. Uncle's Darby and Afon keep him busy traveling around in between taking Skyler and Ivy to our Meadhan. I find that I have made friends myself with many of the Aunts; Elisabeth, Carlian and Winifed are some of my favorites and I was so pleased when Winnie agreed to the post in Marshfield. Many a time when Milton would take the girls I would stay with her in town. Milton called it our girl time, I miss those times.

I would have to admit that Uncles Henson, Eann, Eddie and Traveon are a delight when they visit, even for a short time. I wish it was allowed to bring the young ones together, but I do understand the Order's rules and the reasons behind them. What with the caring for Skyler and Ivy, I find I cannot travel as Milton may, to greet them in person, but I do always send my love."

"Do you think she knew me?" Zack asked, looking up at me.

"You knew Granddad so I would suppose so."

He flipped through more pages and came to one titled Druids and I wasn't surprised when he stopped there and silently started to read. I left him alone and went to check on my bread. I found it had outgrown the bowls and wondered what I had done wrong. Pulling the bowls out, I dumped the mess out onto the floured block. I watched with dismay as the goop deflated and spread. I picked up the cookbook and found my place in the recipe.

I discovered that was what it was supposed to look like and decided I was pretty awesome. I floured my hands and punched the heck out of it. When I was finished, I divided it into loaf pans and then put them in the warming drawer to rise a second time. Hopefully we would be able to bake the things in the morning and have something resembling bread.

When I got back to the front room, I found Zack putting another log on the fire. He took hold of my arm and pulled me down onto the larger chair with him.

"You've got to read this part Ivy. If I don't say so myself, I'm supposed to be pretty amazing…if I can ever figure out how to do it." I smiled at that, since I understood his feeling. I was finding the things I could do with my tongue kind of amazing and pulling power from things even more so. I made myself comfortable with him and started to read where he pointed.

"Druids – The history of these particular fey I find incredible. The most intelligent of all the fey, Druids are. A large number were scholars, others following whatever way their particular magic led them. As all fey, they began their life living mainly in Firinn. Out of the clan of Druid, there developed a line that leaned towards the art of weaponry; their powers and abilities are amazing, although in Firinn there was no use for their brand of magic. The other fey found their magic a disturbing thing for a fey to have. This did not set well with any of the Druid clan.

The Druids as a whole migrated to a Meadhan in Scotland, and from there found their way into Alainn. Even the scholars discovered that Alainn held more resources and avenues for their knowledge. The Druids branched out over the British Isles, becoming known as the Celts. More is known about this branch of Druids than the warriors, although it is the warriors that have achieved the most balance.

In the time of weave, the doors of Ifrinn were not yet closed and the Eilibear and their various cousins took to invading Alainn with great abandon. It was during this time that the Druid warriors found their Dywels, the magic of the sword, and with it fought back the creatures that threatened to overtake Alainn. As time moved on, the Druid warriors became known in all the realms for their strength and range of magic. There are none more renowned for their training, dedication and purity of character, nor feared by those from Ifrinn.

Zack looked up at me and smiled. This was pretty cool and I wondered how Marmaw could have known how much we needed this sort of information. Maybe it was a rite of passage ritual and all Alltha kids got something like this when they were finally told the truth. I smiled back at him and he continued to read.

Others of the Alltha joined with the Warriors, shape shifters of strength and courage that found the good fight against the Eilibear to be an honorable use of their skills. Milton tells me that he had seen great bears and wolves fight alongside them all, only at the end of the struggle to return to the shape of a mild fey with twinkling eyes. I would like to see that, as well as the great Dywels that the warriors wield. They are described as glowing swords that erupt from their arms in times of need, or when-ever the Eilibear threaten.

Milton tells of cords of fire that ensnare the Eilibear and bind them back to Ifrinn. 'T'is a great power these Druids have to go head to head with demons, even to the point of seeking them out to keep the mortals and fey safe. The Druids' travels take them far and wide in search of the very dangers the rest of us run and hide from. What great adventures they must have, though tis a pity there are not females of their kind.

Zack stopped reading there and closed the book.

"Don't stop, at least finish the page." I exclaimed. I wanted to know more about this *Druids not ever being female* part.

"Maybe later," he said nervously and started to get up, laying the book down on a side table. My curiosity was piqued at his manner, so I picked the book up, found the page and read the rest to myself. I noticed he had stood with his back to me, but hadn't moved away.

Milton does tell of how each Druid is sired by a joining of a Druid and a fey that compliments and completes the Druid's own magic. It is a long quest to find the 'one' and many spend their weave of time alone and only have the fighting of great battles to keep them warm at night, as it is rare for the right mate to be found. That being said, the birth of a Druid child is a rare and wondrous thing. I have seen pictures of the new child and understand why Rōber and Elisabeth are so proud of their son."

"Your mother's name is Elisabeth?" I asked when I had finished reading the entry.

"I don't remember. Dad never spoke of a wife or me having a mother. I only remember being raised by Aunts," he replied in a strangled voice. I gave him a minute, knowing this had upset him. When he finally turned, he looked down at Margo.

"It's late; let's get sleepy head up to bed." I looked over at Margo. She was curled up into a small ball of bright colors, the purple tutu she had put on over the white leggings and kitty cat pink socks was sideways, and her t-shirt with the smiling turtles was scrunched up around her arms. She looked darling.

I went around and turned down the lanterns and put a lock on our home, then followed Zack up the stairs as he carried the still sleeping Margo. He put her in her bed and I tucked her in like a child. We whispered goodnight, but Zack stopped as if undecided about something. He walked over to me and pulled me into a tight embrace.

"I'm sorry," he whispered to me.

"I know. I'm sorry I wasn't able to pull you out of it sooner," I mumbled back, enjoying being held by him. He was so solid and it felt safe and right.

"You did good, thank you," he replied as he loosened his grip and bent down and gently kissed me. I'd had some pretty nice dreams about him doing just this very thing. I should have been excited and happy, but all I could think of was him kissing that gross fey. I pulled back and looked at him, feeling very uncomfortable. He misread my look of distress and gently hugged me again before releasing me. He smiled weakly and walked out. I heard him go into his little room and make sounds like he was getting undressed for bed.

Sleep didn't come for some time. I lay there thinking about the kiss and what Marmaw had written. How a Druid had to find the one that fit with him. I guess Druids didn't have much say in who they ended up with and it left me feeling discouraged in some odd way. I liked him; more than any other boy I'd ever met and wondered what it all meant.

If I could just get the picture of him and the fey out of my head, I knew I could enjoy the fact that he had kissed me. I wanted to. He was the first boy that had ever even tried and here I had pushed him away. Crap. The stupid fey were even ruining my first kiss. I lay there for a long time thinking about it. When Margo started to snore in a very unladylike manner, I found the constant rhythm calmed me and eventually I slept.

CHAPTER 48 - Ivy

The day started good. My bread did its thing and I was able to bake it into something that looked like bricks. To all of our amazement, once Zack was able to slice it, the insides were soft and smelled yummy. Margo flitted around the kitchen dressed in red pajamas with elves on them, and Zack tried his hand at cooking. Overall we laughed a lot, got some food in us and felt like we had a handle on our day.

Silly us.

Margo left me to get dressed and I started trying to figure out how I was going to wash the dishes without running water, since the water pump wasn't charged. I started by building up the fire in the new stove. Then I had to pump water into my pots from the older section of the cabin. I set them on the new stove to heat and began climbing the stairs to get dressed myself.

Our little Sprite met me half-way, coming down the stairs wearing a green jumpsuit with a fluffy pink undershirt and combat boots. Her outfit today was polished off with a hat that looked like a large daisy. I just loved her. She announced that we needed flowers in the house...lots of flowers...and took off with my bucket and kitchen scissors to cut some large bouquets.

I could hear Zack pounding away, installing the lower panels, as I pulled on a pair of jeans and one of my new tees with a picture of a unicorn. I had just finished pulling it down over my head when all hell broke loose. I heard Margo let out a blood curdling scream, and I bolted down the stairs and outside, slamming into Zack who was coming from the back of the house. I barely registered that I had knocked him down as I yelled 'sorry' and continued to run. I figured he'd get up and be right behind me. I could see Margo across the glade. She was screaming and pointing out towards the forest. She didn't look hurt, only scared out of her mind, as I ran up to her in a panic.

"Margo, what's wrong?" She didn't answer. She just shrieked louder and gestured out to the forest. I looked and saw them. Fey were standing like weird zombies, with frogs and slugs crawling all over them. They were just standing there, glaring at us. It was beyond hair-raising and I could see why she had started to scream. I pulled her away, trying to turn her and force her gaze elsewhere, only to discover it was impossible as they were lined up everywhere outside the hemlock fencing. Just standing there, covered with gross things, watching us. There were so many that I wondered if they were blinking along with us, following us as we hurried back to the house.

I heard a sound from near the house and spied Zack. He was lying on the ground moaning for all he was worth, holding onto his right arm. With Margo still sobbing in the background, I hurried over to see what was wrong with him. He looked up as I came near, rolling just a bit so I could see. His arm was bright red and about twice the size it should have been.

"Zack? What happened…did you break it?" I yelled as I ran over and knelt down, trying to touch it.

"I don't know, but it hurts like hell," he moaned. I'd seen some gnarly things; cuts, broken bones, even someone who had caught their hair on fire in chemistry class once and burnt the side of her face, but his arm looked like nothing I had ever seen before. I touched it and could feel heat coming off of it, and I did the only thing I could think to do, I found the little heat in the back of my throat and rolled it to my tongue and whispered, "Be well, don't have time for this now."

Still kneeling, I looked past the fencing again. The fey had gathered there and were watching us with dead eyes. Turning back, I saw Margo standing in the doorway of the house, her face white.

"Margo, come help me get Zack up and into the house," I called out. She looked at me, then at the fey. I could see the terror in her eyes, but she moved towards us. We both helped get him up and moved towards our shelter.

"Ey-vey," a dead sounding voice came from behind me. I stopped and turned. Laven, along with Bryear and a couple of other fey were standing at the fence. I motioned to Margo to take Zack inside and turned to the tall fey, taking only a couple of steps towards him.

"What Laven?" I snapped, irritated at everything.

"Do you feel it? We are taking it back. Your little spell of silence was easy to break." I looked at him with alarm as I realized that I had muted them all last night and now I *could* hear him.

"Taking what back?" I asked cautiously.

"The power you are stealing from us. You may have thought that bringing in magic from Alainn would overpower us, but you are mistaken. It will not be enough, we will still be able to break the barrier and take back what is ours," he snarled.

That stopped me. What the heck was going on here? "Laven what are you talking about? I'm not taking anything from you, and I didn't bring in magic from Alainn."

"You deny it, yet it sits behind you," he said with a scowl, his arm aiming out toward the new addition. That was magic from Alainn? Well maybe it was, but that would mean I was bringing magic in, not taking it out.

"That's just a house, Laven. Just a bigger house for us to live in," I tried to explain to him, but he wasn't listening.

"You are taking the magic from Meadhan; you are

taking it from us. We can feel it; that is why the other fey left," he growled, paused and then his voice changed. "Just give us the Sumair stone Ey-vey, that's what we want." He purred at me in a honey-sweet voice, which made the whole business even eerier. I didn't think I was taking anything from him or the forest, but then again I'd never had this tongue thing before. Maybe I was and it was hurting them. Maybe they had reason to be mad at me. But even if I was hurting them somehow, they were not getting the Sumair stone. It seemed they had been smart enough to figure out where it was, but I wasn't going to admit to it, not now, not ever.

"Laven something is wrong. Don't you feel it?" I asked pointing around.

"Yes...my lady." He almost sneered at me as his misty, violet eyes narrowed. I didn't like the tone he used when he called me *my lady*, it sounded like he was mocking me. "We are taking back the power you are stealing. You have the Sumair stone, or you have taken its power and are using it against us. We want it back…it doesn't belong to you." The others behind him moved closer, threatening. "You cannot stay in there forever; we will get in and take what is ours." It was then I noticed the multitude of frogs again. Their chant of croaks and rib-bits brought back the memory of the glade. I really needed to tell Zack about that.

I was beginning to get scared. He was right; I could feel the barrier weakening, myself weakening. I needed to sit down something awful. My head was starting to hurt, and I felt dizzy. I took a deep breath and looked down for a second. Around their feet were slugs and frogs and a bunch of other slimy things. Some were clinging to their pants and the bare skin of their feet. That shocked me back and I remembered who I was supposed to be. Even he had told me.

"Why is it you think all the power is yours? This is my forest, remember? I let you in, them in," I spat indignantly at him, pointed at the other fey. This guy had always seemed off to me and now maybe he was just showing his true colors. Maybe that had been the plan all along, to be nicey-nice to me so I would open the doorway and then I would be alone against all of them. Maybe that was why they had tried so hard to turn Margo and Zack against me. It was like high school where the cool kids always pushed the others around, and the others let them, because, well, they were the cool kids. Not me...I didn't care.

He only smiled a really weird smile at me and whispered something to the others just before they vanished.

"Come back here, Laven!" I screamed at him. No one came and I tried to find the power in my throat to force him, but it was just a tickle. That was it, I was going to lock the doorway and push them all out. Maybe Granddad would show up soon and be able to tell me what was going on. In the meantime, I needed to get the forest back.

I turned and walked into the house, closing and locking the door behind me.

"I wasn't much help, was I?" Zack said from a chair.

"You were here. I wasn't alone," I said giving him a quick hug and noticing that his arm was back to normal. "They're gone for now. Let's leave off working outside and dig into the weirdness around us." He nodded quietly.

Margo was huddled on the couch, her eyes showing how scared she still was. "Are they gone? I never want to see those things again. I can't believe what I did with them, or what the other fey were doing. I thought I had buried the memories until I saw them standing there," she whimpered.

I looked at Zack wondering if he knew what she was talking about, but he wasn't even paying attention. He had retrieved the little book and was looking through it, flipping pages as if searching for something.

I sat down next to her and put my arm around her shoulder. "I should have stayed in my jammies," she whined as she huddled tightly to me.

"Maybe, but if you hadn't seen them, we wouldn't have known they were even there. Margo, do you know what they want? I mean, I think I know that Laven and the fey just really wanted my forest all along, but what's with the frogs?"

"Don't want to talk about it," she whimpered into my arm pit. I pushed her up and forced her to look at me.

"Margo, I think you are going to have to. What you know may help us. How can I fix things in the forest if I have no clue what is going on." I turned to Zack who was reading intensely. "Zack?" I called out and he looked up. "We are going to have to talk about this. You guys have to remember as much as possible about what was going on."

"I'm with Margo, I don't want to remember. But you are right…and I found something. I remembered when we were reading last night seeing something about frogs. I didn't think anything about it until I saw all of the fey standing there with frogs and slugs all over them." He started to read out loud from the page he had found.

"Eilibear are as bad, if not worse than anyone could imagine. They do have limitations in the realms. Milton and I have discovered that they can take many forms; drifting like smoke, almost unseen, they can travel to and from, in and out, without a person taking notice. It is when they form into a 'thing' that they be dangerous in Alainn. A form can give voice to insults and find the ways to crawl inside a person. I do mean that literally, as the creatures like to creep into small things; flies, earwigs, nits, tree frogs and slugs. The snail seemed to be a form they do not like, I think it is due to the hard shell that does not travel well. Once one of these new little forms finds a way in, be it an ear, nose or any other opening a body does have, then they can form into creatures of your nightmares, and mortals do seem to think up a full range of horrid things. The Eilibear have learned each time and these forms can be used collectively to haunt and disrupt a person's life.

I remember when Milton first told me that the things I'd been seeing were of the netherworld of Ifrinn, I was much afraid. But soon discovered they have no power in Alainn that we do not give them. It's the learning not to give in that is hard.

Firinn and the Meadhans have been free from the creatures for many a year, the Druid warriors do a fine work of keeping the pests down and away from all doorways. There is always the worry that some shifted one or Alltha will take one in either willingly or unwillingly, knowingly or unknowingly, into a Meadhan, thereby allowing one to find its lost magic and come into full being once more.

Only once in the history of the fey has this occurred. One very silly fey allowed himself a pet, of all things, a newt, and took it back to Firinn with him after a visit into Alainn. The newt carried the poison of the Eilibear and the Druids had a right hard time ridding Firinn and the affected Meadhan of the things. They do tend to grow and multiply at an amazing rate, spewing their vile poison to any fey unfortunate enough to be near.

They do not eat like other creatures, but spew a bit of themselves into a thing, usually an anura, and then eat the thing. It does give them energy and life. Vile and despicable the Eilibear are. I must admit after hearing this story I do hate all anura and once frog legs were a favorite, now I will not abide any form of anura, alive or dead, in my home or garden."

Zack raised his eyes from the book and looked at us. "Anurans are the family of toads; there are thousands of types; frogs, toads, newts, salamanders and so on. I remembered seeing this entry about frog legs last night and my stomach turning over." He looked at Margo. "I remember why now."

I looked from one to the other, both looked a bit pale and neither spoke. The silence kept growing and I knew I had to tell them about Skyler, but before I could, Margo started to gag as she tried to speak.

"What?" I pleaded, encouraging her.

"They fed me frogs, frog legs, frog eggs. I remember watching as one tore off the head of a toad and handed it to me. I sucked it out," she cried, then gagged and ran through the doors into the cabin and I could hear her throwing up in the old sink.

That was disgusting. Not the throwing up part; that I understood. But sucking out a raw toad? It was a bit unbelievable, until I glanced at Zack and he was pale and green and nodding at me. And he wanted to spend time with them? I could tell he was fighting down bile, and I understood when he got up and dug around for a bottle of water. I really had to tell them what I had seen. I knew it was connected and they were not going to like it one bit.

I went to look in at Margo and she was still heaving. It was a while before she was able to come back and sit with us in the front room. I went and retrieved her happy pajamas and helped her change first, then bundled her up in front of the fireplace with the softest, fluffiest blanket we had.

"It's gross, I know, but I have to tell you something that I saw. You won't like it."

They both looked at me like there wasn't anything I could tell them that would make them feel grosser. So I told them about going into the high trees, seeing the fey and the troll men. And seeing what had become of Skyler. I didn't even want to think about it, let alone talk about it. As I spoke, both of them turned the palest I'd ever seen a living person get, and by the time I was finished, Margo didn't look like she would recover anytime soon. I was worried about them, but they had to be strong and help me. They had been out there with the fey, had dealings with the frogs and it was all connected. They had to remember and talk about it.

"Where did they all come from? What were those things and what happened to Skyler?" I asked them both.

"Do you really want to hear what I remember, Ivy? I'm not proud of any of it," Zack said and he hung his head down, resting his arms on his knees.

"Pride has nothing to do with it Zack. You were enthralled," I said, coming close to him and putting my hand on his back. "Zack, if it had happened to me, what would you do?"

"I think I probably would have gone out and killed the fey that had you," he said looking up at me suddenly, as if accusing me of not protecting him as fervently as he would have me.

"Really, you would have killed fey? Fey that up until a few days ago seemed to be friends? I'm sorry, but no matter how weird they are all behaving, I have to believe that something else is pulling the strings here." He leaned close to me for a second, and then his expression changed. He mouth twisted in concentration before he looked at Margo.

"Margo, do you remember anything about the little men?" he asked her.

"Yeah, who are those weird troll guys and what did they do to Skyler?" I asked looking at both of them in turn.

"The fat little men with the long noses," he said hesitantly. "One tried to eat my hair." He shuddered next to me.

"I like what Ivy calls him, troll. That's how I see him in my dreams. A little fat man with a huge mouth and the longest nose I've ever seen."

Wait a minute…I knew that description, I'd read it, even written it down. I jumped up and ran over to the bookcase and snatched my notebook. I walked back to my seat while frantically flipping through the pages. I had listed all the variables in Marmaw's books and I knew that something she talked about she had described that way. I scanned each page as quickly as possible and couldn't find what I was looking for. I went and retrieved the Willow of the Wisp story, thinking I must have missed writing it down, when I saw the picture sticking out of the back of the notebook. I pulled them out and let out a shriek.

"Crap!"

"What?" Zack said, coming over and looking down at the picture I held in my hand

"Boggarts…that's what they are. Look, does this look like the little troll men to you?" I asked holding it out to Margo.

"Yeah, that's them. There were two of them for a while, and then I only saw the one. But even he wasn't around the last couple of days. Only the frogs."

"How would a Boggart get here?" Zack asked.

"Or why would it come here. Don't they live in the ground in Scotland?"

"Crap, crap, crap, crap, crap," I yelled standing up. "Don't you remember? That last part of the Willow story. I told you I didn't read it cause I hate history, but you did, out loud to me. Marmaw wrote that the Boggarts were suspected of opening a door to Ifrinn and letting the Eilibear have some of their magic. How much do you want to bet the crappy little things really did that and somehow got across Firinn with no one noticing. I left the doorway open; they could have just come in!"

"Or…" Zack said thoughtfully, "The ass-wipe Skyler could have brought them with her. Remember how bad she smelled. I bet that's why she went all slug-like. She would never have gotten in on her own, right? She didn't have a talisman, but Aishal brought her in. I wonder if he even knew about the stuff she had inside her."

I had to really compose myself now. It was horrible what had happened to her. I guess I had kind of pushed it aside, not wanting to believe that the thing I'd seen really *had* been Skyler. I felt a mixture of revulsion and pity for her. She had sure screwed things up for everyone, but no one deserved how she had ended up.

"We've got to go back to the large trees and see what's happening," I said under my breath. I didn't want to, who *would* want to?

"That's where the little man was," Margo squeaked from her nest of covers. "I'm not going back there, please don't make me," she begged.

"What do you think?" I asked Zack, who was already up and looking like he was ready to go.

"I think we better let her stay here. I'm not sure how *I'm* going to keep from going all enthralled on you as it is."

"Think about sucking frogs; that will keep you focused on how gross they are," Margo suggested.

I had to keep from laughing; she always did seem to cut to the heart of the matter. Even Zack saw the humor in it.

"Sucking frogs; got it," he said doing a thumbs up at her.

"Margo, you stay in this house. You are safe if you don't go out and don't let anyone in, okay?"

"Got ya; stay inside, and no unwanted guests. I'm going to sit here in my jammies and start this day all over again." The color was returning to her, and I knew she was going to be okay. Sarcasm always was a good sign. "You ready?" I asked Zack.

"Yes, I just wish I had a weapon." I bobbed my head in acknowledgement of that. I wished he did, too. I looked up and saw the axe. It had worked well for Granddad. Zack saw where I was looking and quickly reached up and took it off the hooks.

He balanced it in his hand and looked at me with an obnoxious grin. I didn't want to imagine what he was thinking of doing to those things.

"Let me blink us, I can see a place in my mind where we can see the tree but hopefully won't be seen ourselves. I just want to check it out," I said taking his hand. He squeezed my hand a couple of times to either tell me he was ready, or to give me encouragement. I didn't know which and didn't care. Just having him with me was good, the trick would be to keep him thinking about sucking frogs so he wouldn't think about beautiful fey girls.

I blinked.

CHAPTER 49 - Ivy

The glade was dark. A heavy thick fog hung low in the trees. It had a greenish tint to it, and the smell was foul. The area was dry and brown. The tree I had put Skyler in looked dead. The upper part had broken off and fallen, and had wreaked havoc as it had crashed down. Broken branches and smashed trees lay along its path. What was left still looked like a tall tree, with a wide gaping hole in its hollow center. There looked to be some life in it still as a soft moss was covering it. Then I saw the moss was moving and realized it wasn't moss. Frogs by the hundreds were crawling out of the opening.

I heard a croak nearby and spotted the largest toad I'd ever seen, sitting on a pile of rags. It croaked again and spewed out green bile that the other frogs were lapping up. Slugs were everywhere, clinging to the trees and the dried remains of the bushes and brambles. Things that looked like slimy green lizards were mingled in with them; the ground was swarming with creepy green and yellow things. I saw the pile of clothes that Skyler had been wearing, but there was no sign of her body, thank goodness.

The space felt *empty* and I knew that meant there wasn't much magic left in the area, whatever these things were, they were sucking it dry. I moved my mind over to a far tree and asked for its help and felt it give its magic to me freely. I brought it in and rolled it around my tongue a few times before I whispered. "Cover us in protection, they can't see us or hear us, nor take from either of us." A little burst of heat came out from my mouth and I felt the protection cover us. I turned to Zack who was staring off to the side of us, I didn't even know if he had seen the dead tree. I looked where his eyes were trained and at first I didn't see anything. Then I wished I still couldn't see anything.

A group of fey were sitting or lying on the ground. I could barely see them through all the slimy things covering them. I thought them dead at first, until I saw a hand twitch, then a knee jerk from one. Green slime almost completely covered him. Sludge was dripping from his eyes and nose, while a lizard popped its head in and out of his mouth. I thought I was going to be sick. All of the fallen fey were writhing in agony. The little men were nowhere in sight. I started to whisper something to Zack when I heard his moan. His hand had let loose of the axe. As it slipped from his fingers I grabbed it quickly before it fell on his foot. Him cutting off his own foot right now would not be a good thing.

He moaned again and pulled his arm in tight to his body. It had turned bright red and as I watched, shimmering ripples ran down the length of his arm to his fingertips. We had to get out of here. I looked at the axe in my hand and knew.

"Hold on Zack. I'm going to the doorway to get rid of these things," I said as I blinked.

I wasn't prepared for what met us there. Luckily I had kept the protection on us and the fey and the little man didn't notice our arrival. They were standing at the doorway and it was covered with frogs and slime. I didn't know what it meant, but didn't like anything that I was seeing. Laven and the girls were standing frozen off to the side, a look of terror etched onto their faces.

"Zack, I have to unprotect us so I can pull in more power." He didn't answer me. I felt weak and quickly looked around for something healthy to pull from. Everything was looking pretty dead to me, almost dying before my eyes. One tree stood the proudest and I wondered how it was possible. The Willow could be clearly seen now, as the other foliage had wilted down. I took a deep breath, steadied myself and dropped the barrier. I instantly focused on the willow and pulled with all my might. I got enough; it felt different, but the tingle was there. Before the fey and the Boggart realized we were standing there, I screamed as loud as I could.

"Leave this forest now!" I felt the power surge and expel out, but nothing happened. The little man sneered at me and started to laugh.

"Aw, the lassie be thinking to get rid of us, does she now? Too late for that we be thinking," the ugly Boggart bellowed. I didn't know what to do and tried to raise the axe to protect us. Zack screamed beside me and I looked at his arm. It all happened as if in slow motion.

I watched in fascination as his fingers elongated, then spread wide as the tip of a sword began to emerge from his palm. The blade grew in size and length until it was a full three feet long and three inches wide at the center, tapering to the tip that had first appeared. Zack's face glistened with sweat as the blade kept emerging from his palm, now the start of the pommel could be seen, and as it expanded from his palm, his leather wristband seemed to blend with it, wrapping itself around the pommel. It stopped as the brackets reached the three stones and I remembered that in the larger stone, the talisman was hidden. The stones merged together and formed an ornate guard of solid malecite with my little heart of a talisman set in the center, the wristband continued to emerge until Zack stood there holding the most awesome sword I had ever seen.

"Ivy, I can't hold it any longer," he cried.

"Don't," I screamed and watched as he lifted it high and red ribbons of lightning burst out from it straight at the ugly little man. The little man screamed and ran, but not nearly fast enough. The ribbons attached themselves to his feet and coiled around them, dragging the thing down to the ground. It tightened and squeezed, as the man screamed for mercy. The cords continued to wrap and intensify their hold, until there was a sickening crunch of bones and the Boggart was popped like a water balloon. Bits of his body, blood, and innards splatted over us and the surrounding fey and foliage. A thick, unusual mist rose up from the various remains, hovered for a moment, then rocketed towards a fey or a frog. We watched terrified as the mist entered the unlucky recipient, by way of their nose or ear…or mouth, if they were unfortunate enough to have it open.

"I can't control it," Zack yelled and I felt for him, but he needed to try. What had happened to the Boggart was gross beyond belief, but the fey were closing in on us now, as were all the frogs and things. The Dywel's cords loosened itself from the mess on the ground and started to reach out to the closest of the fey rushing at us. It connected, making short work of taking it down. A quick 'pop' and vibration in the air around us, and we were greeted with the vomit green mist shooting out from that body. And then the mist went on to seek another.

I watched in sick fasciation as the mist converged on a large toad. It was like the toad sucked it in, expanded to twice its size and then exploded on its own. That's when I knew…we were really seeing the Eilibear. Zack and I were standing here, alone, fighting Eilibear. How the hell did this happen?

One of the fey came up behind me, only a croak of a frog informing me it was there. I turned and swung the axe with all my might, just about dislocating my shoulder. I hit it in the hip and it went down. More of the cords of red ribbon had emerged from Zack's sword and were whipping all over the place. He may not have been doing much damage, but he was sure scaring the shit out of all of them. The Eilibear were pulling together and then pulling apart, trying to stay out of Zack's way as he aimed at them. The damn things were hard for him to get a fix on. One second the air was clear of the revolting mist, then Zack would pop one of the creatures and the mist would be released to only instantly seek out something, or someone, to hide inside of.

I was feeling really weak, physically and magically depleted. I looked around for something else to pull some power from. I needed a good scream to help push these things back. My energy was just about gone, and that was not a good thing. I turned my back to Zack and pushed up against him, looking frantically around. I saw a range of pine trees and sought it, though it was farther away than anything I'd ever tried before. It was fresh and clean and almost jumped into me, then moved out and into Zack. Crap, I thought; I hadn't realized that he might need lots of juice to keep that sword thing going. I had a little bit left and tried to put the protection back up around us. I didn't have enough.

I noticed that Laven and the girls and some of the other fey had come around and were looking with terror at Zack, the sword, and the things that were attacking us. The cords reached out for them, and squeezed just enough to force the Eilibear out. Zack must be gaining some sort of control, since the cords loosened before the fey were damaged and then found another target.

I watched as Laven and the girls tried to go through the doorway, and were stopped by the slime stuff. I was glad they were free and were as scared of these things as we were. I hoped that meant they hadn't really been in cahoots with them all along. They gave up trying to go through and took off into the forest, running as if their lives depended on it. Wimps, I thought, as they left us to battle alone.

I saw another drove of thick pines in the distance and pulled again. Zack took it from me as soon I had it. I felt like little more than a charger for Zack's battery. He was screaming out words I didn't know the meaning of, but the Eilibear sure did. Every time another group of the slimy things would join together, the red cords from the sword lashed out and grabbed them, and squeezed.

Suddenly Zack was moving, chasing after a large form. I had to struggle to keep up with him, not knowing if he even understood that I was the one providing him the energy. I lost him in the deep forest. He ran on and I tripped, and went down hard. I tried to blink, but there was no power left in me. Something tickled my leg, I looked back and had to swallow my scream… no time for that now. The newts were swarming over me; I looked down at the ground and saw a tiny sliver of clean dirt. I clawed at it with my fingers and felt the power down deep in the ground. I yanked on it and pulled it in, not even giving myself time to play with it as I screamed for them to be mush. It felt like red hot flames shot out of my mouth and turned the things to nothing.

I had my new source, which meant Zack did too…if I could get to him. I got up and sprinted as fast as I could, lugging the axe. I followed his path through the forest and ended up at the start of the path to my glade. Zack was now backed up to the protective barrier; the things were forming and reforming into different creatures around him. I heard a roar and saw a giant bear erupt out of the foliage and charge right at Zack. His attention was focused on another creature to his left and didn't know it was coming.

"No!" I screamed, pushing my anger at the thing. It stopped, turned and started towards me when my power hit it. A shadow of ash took its place, and then it dissipated and fell to the ground. I dug my foot into the ground and felt the dirt and pulled again, thankful that I wasn't wearing shoes. I threw the power towards Zack. His back arched as it hit him, and he turned to look at me. I moved until I was almost against his back again and continued to pull from the ground. It seemed like an unending supply.

I felt a disruption in my bones and saw that my barrier had come down around the glade. For a second, I worried about my glade, then Margo, then I remembered the big picture and kept on fighting the things. I needn't have worried. I heard her before I saw her. She came running outside with the largest frying pan I owned and walloped frogs as she went. I could tell she was getting all her anger and those memories out, smashing them into pulp as she did. We were outnumbered; it was only the three of us against the Eilibear and all the other living things in the forest.

I couldn't help her and I knew it. I had dropped the axe by my feet and my hands were palms down on the dirt pulling magic as fast as I could. I had to keep the energy coming to give it to Zack. It was futile and I wondered when he would realize it…the things just kept coming. He'd take one down, only to have three more take their place. Fey and frogs and even a couple of deer were coming at Margo. She couldn't smash them fast enough. The air around us was vibrating, like small earth quakes over and over again.

Suddenly an amazing thing happened and I took hope from it, for Margo at least. Margo shape shifted. One second she was a wild girl in red elf pajamas and the next she was a thing from Marmaw's little fairy drawings. I heard a yelp, a peal of a tiny bell, and a clank as the frying pan hit the ground. She flew upwards, and I hoped she could fly far enough to get away. I underestimated her though; the little red dot that Margo had become, descended, landing on my head and started screaming instructions to Zack.

CHAPTER 50 - Milton

The cellar wall exploded in a spray of rubble and gore. The Shade's green mist streaked out of the opening into the dark chamber. It was followed closely by two large forms, one wielding a flaming white sword.

"Come back here ye vermin!" the tall blond man bellowed as he chased after it. His weapon brought light to the dismal chamber and they knew they had finally broken through into another realm. The warrior swung the sword with all his might and a red cord of power whipped out from it and snared the tiniest bit of the green mist. It wrapped and coiled and collected the shade back into a reasonably solid form, then tightened as the thing screamed obscenities at them, in between screeching and howling. The screams turned to high pitched squeals as the cord continued to tighten until there was a squishy pop and the creatures dissipated into nothingness.

The chamber was almost a dungeon, dark stones covered in green moss made up the walls. Large metal rings were set high, their use apparent by the hanging dead forms of fey in various stages of rot. Off to one side was a living area of sorts, with a broken table, a couple of chairs and a box pulled up to sit on. Next to it were a few old crates piled on top of each other, holding spoiled food. In a darkened corner something was hanging from the ceiling, newly killed. It was still dripping, making the plop…plop…plop sound echo in the chamber. A couple of blankets and what looked like a pile of rags completed the grisly scene.

The blond continued to hold his sword up high, providing them a light source and they looked around.

"Where do you think we are? This doesn't look like Ifrinn; there is too much structure to it," the other man finally spoke. He was a large man, with unruly hair and a full beard. His face was strong and strained, with deep dark bags under his eyes. He wore a thick flannel shirt and carried a small hatchet as his only physical weapon.

"It feels like Firinn, but I can't be sure. There' a lot of contamination from the Eilibear. They have been here a while. This has to be where they were keeping Elsie."

"Were? You do not feel her life force now, Glenwood?" The blond man asked, looking about the room.

Milton went over to where the blankets and rags were and kicked at them. The unmistakable sound of bones came to them.

"What ye find there?" Rōber asked, walking over to where his friend was looking down with disgust.

"Don't rightly know. It's not Elsie, that's for sure. It's too small and uglier than a pig's behind," he replied. Rōber watched as Milton moved the thing with his foot, turning it over. They both jumped back in horror.

"It's a Boggart," Rōber snarled between gritted teeth.

The thing must have been hit by the wall as it exploded. The back of its head was crushed and as they looked on, it began to melt until only a misshaped skull and a pile of small twisted bones was left. A small vapor of green mist lingered around the skull's oddly shaped nasal cavity. Milton stood back and watched as Rōber's sword flamed again and caught the Shade as it tried to escape. It was a small one and popped quickly into nothingness.

"How did a Boggart get here?" the blond man asked as he allowed his sword to retreat into his arm.

"I believe we need to know where *here* is first to answer that," Milton said as he studied the rest of the chamber. Looking up at the thing hanging, it was easy to see it was another Boggart, this one ripped to shreds. They only gave it a quick glance, and continued to inspect the area. In the corner was a large crate, one side askew. Milton pulled on it and looked inside only to fall to his knees, letting out a wail of anguish.

Rōber came over and looked over his friends shoulder.

"Are ye sure it be Elsie? I hate to say it, but there's not much left of the face."

"That's her dress…it's her," Milton said.

"I'm sorry my friend, we were too late. It does not look as if she was tortured; she looks rather peaceful, in fact."

Milton shook his head like a large dog, wiping his silent tears with the back of his hand. "I knew she would probably be gone, but I couldn't leave her with them. I guess what hurts the most is that, as hard as it was for her to say the words, she *had* asked me to take Skyler away. And I was just too stubborn to do it, thinking I could handle her." He looked down at what remained of his dear wife. "And she's the one who paid the price," he finished with more of a sob than words. "What will I tell our Ivy?" he lamented. "She will never forgive me for losing her Marmaw."

"You tell her the facts Glenwood, just the bare facts. She died and sometimes there is nothing you can do about it."

Milton searched for a way to take her remains with him and the only thing he could find was some old dirty blankets. He had no choice since to leave her behind would be worse than wrapping her in rags.

"Well we know now why they kept her. Those Boggarts must have let the Eilibear in," Rōber said motioning to all that was left of the Boggart. "Had a bit of one inside him. Since the Eilibear have no shape of their own, they would have been needing a full-sized fey or mortal to hold a complete demon."

"You think that's why they kept Elsie? To be a vessel?"

"I believe so. She must have passed before they had time to get to her, and by the looks of that fellow," Rōber pointed up, "they weren't too happy about that."

The two friends made sure nothing was left alive in the chamber before they started up the stairs, Milton carrying the remains of his wife in his arms. They found themselves in a ruin of what must have at one time been a grand house. Rōber's sword flamed out once more and he picked off the bits of Eilibears hiding in the frogs and toads. Milton stood back and allowed his friend to finish it, holding on to Elsie with all of his might.

It took some time to clear the structure and then the courtyard. Milton finally found a safe place to lay the bundle and helped finish the things off. It was almost night fall by the time Milton had retrieved Elsie's remains and they started to follow the scent of the creatures. They ended at a doorway covered in Eilibear slime.

"Well, that be it. We are in Firinn for sure. That would be a doorway into a Meadhan and the Eilibear have gone through. They used a might of magic trying to seal it," Rōber said as he scratched his head.

"Do you know which doorway it is?" Milton asked as he cradled his load.

"Naw, but I need to be trying to take that magic off. Stand back a ways there, Glenwood," Rōber said as he released his Dywel. Milton backed up and watched as Rōber zapped the doorway with all of the might of his Dywel. At first nothing happened, the red coil of frames hit it and smashed outwards in a wide red circle. Rōber kept forcing his Dywel to attack the doorway entrance and after a time, a small crack could be seen. "Throw whatever power ye have left at it Glenwood, I'm about drained," Rōber called out over his shoulder.

Milton closed his eyes and looked deep inside himself for his special magic. He didn't have much, being gone too long from his forest, but what he had he sent as a bolt of energy straight at the doorway. A loud boom snapped his eyes open and they were looking at an open doorway.

"There she be. I'm thinking we'd be finding a ton of the creatures on the other side. Look smart Glenwood, we'll go through and high tail it out to Alainn to gather the Uncles for a mighty nice battle," Rōber shouted as he ran towards the doorway.

Milton followed, holding tight to the bundle with one arm and his little hatchet with the other. When he popped through he almost bumped into Rōber who had stopped, startled, taking in the scene.

"We're in my forest!" Milton yelled, looking around at the mess of dead creatures and fallen fey. He lovingly sat his load down in a clear area by the roots and looked up at the battle scene.

"It's still going on. Someone is giving the things a mite run for their money," Rōber said as he took off down the path towards the screams and shouts. Milton followed close behind, trying to figure out how or why the Eilibear had ended up here. Rōber stopped short on the path and Milton all but ran into him. He pushed around Rōber and found he was at a loss for words. He knew now why Rōber had stopped so suddenly.

Ivy was standing just outside their glade with her back to a wild-haired young man. She was radiating so much magic that she looked like a light bulb with too much wattage. The young man wiped his head as he swung out at another large Eilibear. Milton recognized his friend's son, Zaccheus. He stood with his back to her, wielding a Dywel so powerful its heat could be felt from where they stood. It was bright red and was shooting out multiple lines of cords at the Eilibear that were surrounding them.

Something was screaming in a high, wild voice and they saw a tiny Sprite sitting on top of Ivy's head, surrounded by the power and pointing out creatures to Zaccheus. There was a bolt of power radiating from Ivy straight to

Zaccheus's back; it was a sight neither of them had seen before.

"She's powering him," Rōber whispered in awe. "How's that possible?"

Milton had seen something else; *his axe* lay at her feet! "Doesn't matter my friend. The kids are fighting a battle even we wouldn't have taken on alone and doing a mighty fine job of it. Power up there, Edsmond, the fight is on," he yelled as he barreled down to where Ivy was and snatched his axe from under her feet. Her eyes were closed and she was calling out to the ground to give up it's magic.

The two men joined in the battle. Milton was a powerful shifted mortal with or without his axe in his hand, but even a Druid wouldn't dare cross him when he had hold of the enchanted axe. He started swinging and charging, cutting down everything close by, while Rōber's sword joined his son's, and together they whipped and coiled the things, pushing them back into the forest and away from the glade and the cabin.

CHAPTER 51 - Ivy

I felt the change in the air around me. My mind had been so focused on pulling energy for Zack that when he pushed it back to me, I found myself staggering under the weight of it and fell, shutting off the connection to the source of magic under my feet.

Breathe, I told myself, *just breathe.* I knew that others had joined the fight, and didn't care who it was. I was satisfied to know that whoever it was, was here and on our side. The area around me was clear of the things. I stepped back into the space that should have been my protected glade and called the barrier back into existence. A few croaks of frogs came from the foliage near the house. Turning, I pulled energy with my toes and allowed it to travel up to my throat. When the tingle rose to a burning fire of pain, I threw my head back and screamed.

"Only clean creatures and my friends can be inside this barrier. Anything else, get out!" Okay, I've never been good at writing speeches. I knew it wasn't the most eloquent way to say it, but it worked. It was quite satisfying to see frogs and toads and a skunk and two little foxes flung from my glade. I added a second barrier around the house and cabin, just to be sure, before I took off after Zack.

As I ran, I had to jump over several fallen fey. Some were shrunken down to flattened rag dolls; others looked like they were well again and struggled to stand, looking around in panic. None challenged me, but rushed into the cover of the nearby foliage. If I spied any wild-eyed creatures, I would yell at them, *be gone!* Like an invisible hand had plucked them up, they would be flung back and my path was cleared. Maybe I could have been saying *be dead*, or *go back where you came from*, but to be honest, that never occurred to me.

I had no idea where I was going, only followed the trampled vegetation and the sounds of the battle up ahead. I found Zack at the glade where Skyler had been held and where the ugly Boggart had been holding the fey. It was probably the last place I wanted to be, but it seemed to be the epicenter of this weirdness. It's hard to explain how strange this battle was. Zack was fighting with his new found Dywel as if possessed, while Margo whipped around him calling out when creatures came close.

It may have been easier or made more sense to me, if we had been fighting creatures from the black lagoon, or zombies, or anything that was scary. But we weren't. The enemy was the beautiful fey and normal creatures found in my forest. There were cute little bunnies, deer, and chipmunks, all the creatures that had always lived peacefully alongside Granddad and Marmaw and me. Even the birds seemed to have turned against us, dive bombing down through the strange green mist. Margo had found a twig and was attempting to whack anything that came close to her and Zack.

At first my brain could only process that everything had gone nuts and hated us now. I watched as Zack lassoed a large hawk with the strange cord of flame that burst out from the Dywel. It coiled itself around the beautiful creature and squeezed it until there was a sickening *pop*. There was a reverberation in the air as the bird fell to the ground. When it hit, more of the smoky green mist rose from its beak, and joined up with the rest of the green haze that was beginning to look like the shadow of a giant.

The hawk lay there for only a moment before it moved its wings, then took flight, racing away from us as quickly as possible. The Eilibear were being driven from their hiding places inside the creatures. I thought back to the flattened fey and realized that the Eilibear must have taken too much from the poor folk. They had been sucked dry…that's how a fey could be killed. It was not a fate I wished on anyone, no matter what they had done.

I joined in the fight, changing my tactics somewhat. I would find a cluster of frogs or birds, and focus on them as I waited for the tingling to build. When it was strong enough I'd yell "Get out of them!" The first time I was pleased to see the creatures cease their attack; fall and the green mist leave them from various points of their bodies. I waited to see if the creatures would recover, and some did, scampering or hopping away as fast as their legs could carry them. The others added to the piles of deflated repulsive shells littering the ground.

I really tried hard not to look at the tree where Skyler had been put or at the ground by the opening in the tree. After a while though, I didn't have a choice. I had worked on clearing away the layers of live frogs and lizards and newts, while Zack kept the Eilibear mist and the larger animals and fey back. Every so often I would send Zack a recharge on his magic and even though it seemed to hit him like a sledgehammer, he never complained.

The hole into the tree was gaping wide, and coldness more intense than I had ever felt, was coming from it. I focused on the door of bark and yelled for it to close. It was hard…so much debris was in the way…and it fought and pushed as it tried to obey me. I kept at it, watching in fascination as it shoved against everything until finally it closed. I continued to focus on the tree, telling it to heal and hold back whatever had been coming out from it. The tree seemed to swell, along with all the other trees that were curled around it. The bark grew before my eyes; new branches erupted from the trunk, covered with new growth. The ground moved under my feet as the tree started to grow, then shuddered violently one time and went still.

The Eilibear mist stopped breaking off and trying to attach itself into other living things. Now it was pulling itself together making it easier for Zack's Dywel to grab on to larger parts and dispel it away. His face was tense as he almost effortlessly swung his sword with both hands. Any motions he made with the sword would make the cord of red respond in kind. Like a computer mouse moving a curser around on a screen, he controlled it. Each time he would connect with the thing, a squeal of agony would rip through the forest, just before the *pop* and disruption in the air around us.

I could hear the voices of the others who were helping, coming towards us, yelling as they drove the Eilibear our way. Over the tree tops, a cloud of avocado green mist could be seen rolling violently in our direction. It looked like someone had pushed fast forward on a movie of a storm cloud. Margo whacked Zack on the side of his head to get his attention. Pointing at it, and screaming for him to stop it.

Zack looked back at me, his face filled with a new maturity and sense of purpose. "Ivy, I need more," he yelled. A wind had come up, brought along with the fast moving cloud. My short hair was whipping around my face, stirring leaves and probably a bunch of yucky dead things around me.

I nodded at him, and he turned back to face it with determination. Planting my feet firmly, digging them down until only bare clean dirt met the soles of my feet, I pulled from down deep. I could feel the energy surging up to me and told it to travel out to Zack. The power radiated through me, making me feel frozen in place, as it found its route to him. It was a really awesome sight. The pure white bolt of magic shot out from me to him and hit him hard. He arched his back in pain as the magic connected, then he held his sword up high pointing at the cloud.

A primal scream erupted from him as multiple cords of red exploded out and found their target. The cords wrapped and looped around the greenness as it convulsed and twisted trying to get away. More cords appeared from the tip of the sword, corkscrewing up before curling down, pulling the cloud together. Margo had left Zack's head to come over to me, grabbing handfuls of my hair and hanging on. Her screams combined with Zack's and the wind and the screeches spewing from the Eilibear. I was in sensory overload and barely heard the roar of the newcomers as they crashed through the forest towards us.

I saw the white flame just before it turned red and joined with Zack's, coiling tightly around the thing. The air crackled with electricity and flickered wildly with sparks. The Eilibear struggled and pulled, all to no avail, as the two joined cords constricted, strengthening their hold. The roars and cries intensified, coming from all of us, the forest and the creatures. Suddenly there was a sonic boom so deafening my ear drums felt like they had burst, as the air around us wrinkled in on itself…. and the thing was gone. The world around us went dead silent as a shock wave of pressure burst outwards and slammed me backwards.

Zack lowered his sword as his Dywel retracted into his arm; sweat dripped from his face as he turned to look at me. I didn't even have the strength to smile. Whatever that thing had done to the air had made me dizzy and I started to fall. Someone caught me from behind, and I felt myself cradled in large, strong arms. I knew the feel of the arms, the odor of sweat and sawdust.

I looked up and saw familiar eyes staring down at me. "Granddad?" I whispered dreamily, as I fainted away and my world went black.

CHAPTER 52 - Ivy

I woke slowly. The feel of new sheets was my first sensation. They were so soft. I rolled over and enjoyed the wonder of fluffy pillows and the smell of newness. The next thing I noticed was sunlight on my face and I opened my eyes to stare out the long panel of windows upstairs in our new addition. I could hear birds singing along with the most off-key rendition of "This Old Heart of Mine" I thought I'd ever heard. Then I realized that was familiar, I'd heard it before, sung just that way. I jumped out of bed and raced down the stairs.

I skipped the last two steps and bolted into my kitchen. He turned just in time to catch me. I jumped up into my Granddad's arms and wrapped my legs around his middle. He caught me easily, embracing me for all he was worth.

"There's my girl. I love you-ou-ou, yes I do," he sang as he swung me around. I was crying so hard I couldn't see and just kept saying, "You're here, you're really here."

"I sure am. You can't get rid of an old fart like me that easily," he said with a chuckle, as he fingered the vines by my eyes. "That's a right nice little plant you got there." He chuckled as he hugged me again.

"Now that be a lovely sight." A loud booming voice came from behind me. Granddad set me down and turned me to face the voice.

"Ivy, my darling, I'd like you to meet my best friend, Rōber Edsmond. You can call him Uncle Eddie," he informed me. "Eddie, this here's my wonderful granddaughter, Ivy."

I would have known that he was Zack's dad, even without the introduction. They looked so much alike it was chilling. At first I didn't know what to say, but words didn't seem right anyway. I leaped from Granddad to him and hugged him around the middle.

"Thank you, thank you for bringing him back to me," I cried.

"Oh, my little lassie. He done brought me back. I was just along for the fun," he said gently holding me. I released him and stood back, grinning ear to ear and wiping my tears away. My darn nose was filling up again, just like always and I found I needed to blow it something awful. Granddad knew me well and handed me a napkin. I blew it, none too lady-like and laughed at my own discomfort.

I looked around for Zack or Margo and didn't see them…that worried me. I didn't remember much after falling down.

"Don't worry. Zack is out playing with Margo in the glade," Granddad said. How the heck was *Zack* playing with Margo? I had to see this and ran out the front door to find them. I saw them before they saw me. Margo was standing in front of Zack and he was in a football player's position as if getting ready to tackle her.

"Okay, I'm ready. Try it again," he called out.

Margo seemed to shimmer, then popped into a Sprite and flew straight at him, while he tried to catch her. She had no problems zooming right over his head and then popped back into a girl.

"No fair! You didn't say you were going to change that time." He laughed, and then saw me. His face changed, got all serious-like, and then I found myself being tackled by him in a huge bear hug.

"You're awake," he murmured into my hair.

"'Bout time, I'd say," Margo said running up and joining in on the hug. Then she let loose and started yelling that I was awake as she ran towards the house.

"I missed you," Zack said, as he pulled back and looked at me. He moved some hair out of my eyes and leaned down to kiss me. This time I had no problems forgetting all about the gross fey and just enjoyed it. When he pulled back, his eyes were twinkling. "You saved us, you know." I just shook my head at him. "You did. Dad said that my Dywel was just too powerful for me yet, and it would have drained me and probably killed me along with it. You kept me going. It was pretty amazing. Thank you." And he kissed me again, just a sweet peck, before draping his arm around me and started walking us back to the house.

"How long have I been out?" I asked, still a bit dazed. I liked being kissed.

"Long enough for us to clean up the mess in the forest. We found Laven and what remained of his clan. That's a story; they had planned on tricking you into giving the Meadhan to them, but instead ended up releasing something even they were scared shitless of," he answered as we entered the house. There was so much more I wanted to ask, but I could smell food and wondered what Granddad had been cooking up. It smelled so good…like home and Sunday mornings making breakfast with Granddad and Marmaw.

A question I didn't want to ask loomed and I had to.

"Granddad, where's Marmaw?" The laugher in the room quieted as he came over to me. Zack didn't release me though; he seemed to pull me in tighter.

"She didn't make it, dear. Those things never got into her though; she went peacefully. She just allowed herself to fade. It's what she'd been wanting to do for a long time," he said gently, coming close.

"So she's gone? Really gone?" I asked, starting to weep.

"Now don't cry, sweetie. I found her and brought her back. She has a nice resting place with the flowers she planted."

I hiccupped a couple of times, and looked around at the faces of my family. Weird huh, that I thought of Margo and Zack and my Granddad as my family. They looked worried and I sucked it up. I'd find time to cry and mourn for her later. I'd done a lot of it this last year, crying over her death anyway, so maybe I didn't need to do it now that it was real.

I forced a smile on my face and hugged Zack tight, before I released him and went and put my arm around Granddad.

"I'm okay," I said taking a deep breath and worked at changing the subject. "I smell food, I'm hungry."

The heaviness cleared and we went to sit down at the table. Margo, Zack and I got to tell Granddad and Uncle Eddie about our adventures; the house, how we met, about Grandma Winnie and what had happened to Skyler. Zack had already told Granddad about her, but he still looked sad as I told my part of the story. I told them about finding the diaries and the stories and then about Grandma Winnie giving me the little book from Marmaw.

Rōber asked a lot of questions about Marmaw's writings, wanting to know what all she had revealed to us. The three of us cheerfully told what we remembered from them, glad to share how helpful they had been.

Margo and Zack took turns telling their part of the story and it hit me again how much these two had been worried about me. Margo was thrilled to show Granddad the necklace she wore and he confirmed that it was indeed the one that Skyler had lost on the beach years before.

Zack told about meeting me on the bus and his dad stopped him, wanting to know first just how he had come to be on *that* bus, when he was supposed to be back east at school. It was fun to watch Zack get a royal chewing out for changing schools without telling him. No matter what his dad said, Zack would only nod, grin and bump me with his leg under the table.

Margo couldn't seem to stop showing off and had to keep running upstairs to change clothes. She had discovered that whatever she was wearing gave her different colored and shaped wings as a Sprite. I was a bit jealous. Here I was a fairy and I didn't get wings. Bummer.

After a very long extended meal, Zack pulled me away to show me the most amazing thing. Our pump and water heater were working. Okay maybe not the most amazing thing looking at my present life, but it was still awesome. He turned on the faucet at the sink and hot water came out as if by magic. We raced to the bathroom next and everything in there worked also. I must have flushed that toilet a thousand times before he pulled me away to race upstairs.

There he stopped at the large bathroom and kissed me on the forehead and said I stunk, then pointed at the shower. We were going to get along just grandly. Laughing, I shut the door in his face and stayed in there for almost an hour.

When I finally came down, smelling good and dressed in something other than my sweats and a tank top, I found everyone outside helping to attach the lower panels on the house. We spent the day playing, working, talking and laughing.

As night fell we found ourselves preparing and sharing dinner together, staying up until Margo started to fall asleep. Zack carried her upstairs and put her on her bed, gave me a quick hug and left me alone with my thoughts. After pulling off Margo's shoes and tucking her into bed, I readied myself for the same. It was as I started to get under the covers that I remembered that I hadn't kissed Granddad goodnight.

I hurried out of the room and started down the hall to the stairs. Most of the lanterns had been put out, it was dark, but a faint glow was still coming from the one on the dining table. As I started down the stairs I could see that Granddad and Uncle Eddie were still sitting at the table talking.

I started to call out, but stopped as Uncle Eddie's voice came to me.

"I thought we told *you* to tell her to *not ever* write anything down about the fey," Zack's dad whispered in a rather angry tone.

"I did. She told me she understood," Granddad responded. I couldn't see his face from where I stood, but his voice did not sound pleased.

"Well she pulled one over on us, didn't she now," Uncle Eddie snapped with annoyance.

"It turned out okay in the end. What is the use of being upset now?" Granddad asked as he got up from the table. I moved back a step up the stairs so that he wouldn't see me.

"That is not the point. We told you that we would take care of it and you said *you* would instead. Now these kids have knowledge they shouldn't have. Elsie helped them, knowing it was not allowed…and to top it off, Winnie was in on it. Something will need to be done," Uncle Eddie said firmly and I got the feeling he was used to being obeyed.

"Rōber, you listen to me. This is our children we are speaking about…and my wife. We are *not* going to do anything. Ivy and Zack are safe because of what was done, Elsie is gone and Winnie helped one of her best friends make sure the kids came to no harm. That part of the story stays between you and me. *Do I make myself clear*?" Granddad said heatedly as he pounded his fists on the table to make his point.

If Uncle Eddie thought that he could tell Granddad what to do, then I knew he didn't know Granddad as well as he thought. Granddad's words sent shivers down my spine. I would not want to cross him on this and hearing no response from Uncle Eddie, I gathered that he understood that too.

I crept back up the stairs and went to bed. There was a lot to process from overhearing that bit of conversation, and I tried to put all the pieces together, but my body had other ideas. I fell into a deep peaceful sleep and all my worries faded away.

That next morning Uncle Eddie left and when he returned later that day, he had Uncle Geraint with him. The three adults banished us from the house for a time while they discussed how to handle everything that had happened. I told Zack and Margo about the conversation I had overheard while we sat out in the garden and they were worried that something horrible would be done to Grandma Winnie because of the part she had played in helping us. I wasn't too worried about any of it though, as I knew that Granddad would take care of everything like he had always done for me. My feelings proved right in the end.

Fey law can be a good thing at times, I discovered. The Uncles and Granddad had decided how to handle everything which was fine with me, but it turned out that now that I was officially the owner of the Meadhan and doorway, they couldn't do anything without my permission. Granted Granddad informed me privately that I still had to mind him since I was a minor. I gave him that one.

I tried to make Granddad proud as I listened to everything the Uncles proposed for dealing with the fey that had created this mess and I did agree with what they wanted to do. My only request was that Willow be dealt with too. Granddad was the only one that stepped up and sided with me and the others had no choice it turned out. When everything was said and done, I was happy with the results.

It was only another couple of days before we found

ourselves standing on the path leading to town. Laven had requested a chance to tell me he was sorry before he was banished to Alainn along with two of his sisters who had survived. Neither Aishal nor Rayni were heard from again. Both were on the fey version of *the most wanted list,* I had been told. I doubted they would ever be found.

It was hard, standing there as Laven was walked toward me between two fey I'd never seen before. When he came close, he looked at me with the largest, saddest eyes I had ever seen, and knelt with his head down.

"Why Laven?" I asked moving closer to him. "Why did you try to ruin everything?"

"Oh Ey-vey, I…we…were reckless and brash and so full of ourselves. We thought that it would be easy to take a Meadhan from a mortal and an Alltha." He spoke in his familiar silky sweet voice.

"It wasn't, was it? You brought demons into my forest, made my friends sick and screwed up big time," I said, none too kindly.

"No my lady," he replied and I actually snorted at his using that term. "I do mean it, Ey-vey, if not for you, we would have all died and if not for your friends, the Eilibear would have remained inside us. You saved us and we owe you our lives," he said bowing his head in what I hoped was shame. "I am sorry, we all are sorry. Please accept our apologies and forgive us."

"I don't think that is what you are sorry for. I think you are sorry you got caught in your own little web of deceit. Can you honestly tell me that if the Eilibear hadn't come, you wouldn't have just done the same thing, tried to take the forest and my friends from me?"

He was silent for a time; I think just trying to find words to make me believe him. Finally he was able to force some tears out and looked up at me, pleading. "No, we would have come to accept you and your ownership. Please, I beg you, forgive us."

I didn't believe him. Not now, maybe not ever. He looked good enough to eat, but was rotten on the inside. I wondered how he was going to fare in the normal world. He'd probably end up a male model.

"Not today, Laven. You need to prove yourself first. Play nice with the other Alltha and then we will see," I answered and nodded to the fey that I was done. Zack and Margo came up and stood with me as Uncle Geraint led the fey away. Yep, the mortal world didn't know what they were in for with that one.

When they were out of sight, we went to meet with Granddad and Uncle Eddie and a whole lot of fey I didn't know, but Granddad did. We stood in a small glade surrounding the hallowed willow tree. It was the first time I had seen Willow up close and I felt tears gathering. Here he had been stuck for hundreds of years and still when I asked for help, he gave me what he could. I had been worried about telling Granddad what I planned on doing. I shouldn't have been, as he readily agreed. It *was* time to finish the story.

Together we held the axe to his trunk and asked for him to be released. The tree shook, then shimmered before it transformed into a young fey. His face was instantly filled with terror, and he looked like he was going to bolt. I hurried up and hugged him. His body was stiff with fear.

"It's over Willow. It's okay now, you are safe. No one is going to hurt you." His little body relaxed, but I could still feel him shaking. I looked into his eyes, and he stared back at me baffled.

"I didn't mean to do it, I really didn't," he said in a voice that reminded me of Laven.

"I know." I glanced up at the others standing near us. "We all know. You can't go back to Firinn, but this nice fey is going to take you somewhere safe and you will be able to live a nice life." I motioned to Uncle Eddie. He looked up at the tall man and leaned into me fearfully.

"That's a Druid," he whispered to me.

"I know. He's really nice and he has agreed to protect you," I answered him, trying to sound as motherly as I could. I felt like I was babysitting again and one of the kids had woken from a nightmare. Which was a pretty good description of what was going on here.

"A Druid is going to protect me?" he asked, his eyes going wide. A mischievous little smile started to play around his lips as he looked up at Uncle Eddie. "Really?"

"Really," Uncle Eddie said and reached out his hand to the boy. Willow took it and allowed himself to be pulled up. "I'll be back in a short time. We have plans to be making," he said looking at his son.

Zack pulled me close and put his arm around my shoulder, rather protectively I might add. "I'm not leaving, Dad," he announced firmly.

"I'd be believing that," his dad replied with a chuckle, then put his hand on Willow's shoulder and blinked.

"Well, that's done, good use of our magic today kids," Granddad said, shouldering his axe. "I've got some chores to do. See you all tonight."

"Wait Granddad," I said and waited for him to turn around to face me. "Something's been bothering me. You and Marmaw and Skyler were all shifted by magic and now I know about the powers you and Skyler had, but what about Marmaw? What was her magic?"

He seemed shocked that I would ask the question, but recovered quickly.

"She didn't have one," he replied calmly, then briskly walked away.

It wasn't long before he started to sing one of his favorite songs and we watched him and his axe disappear into the forest. Zack still had his arm around me, holding me tight and it felt so good. Margo popped into Sprite form and landed on my shoulder. Life was good and Granddad still couldn't sing worth a lick.

"Do you believe him?" Zack asked.

"Nope...not at all,"

As Granddad's voice died away into the forest, we strolled back down the path to our home. It felt right, and for the first time I felt like dreams really did come true. Granddad and I never spoke a word about the Sumair stone. Granddad and Uncle Eddie had taken the old cabin as their room now, and the first time I went into it with Granddad alone, he had motioned with his eyes at the stove.

"Been doing some painting I see," he'd said quietly, and I had nodded, smiled a crooked smile and left him humming some unnamed tune. The day might come when we'd have to do something about it, but today was not that day.

ABOUT THE AUTHOR

C.R. Cummings starting penning her first stories in high school and completed her first novel soon after. She never published it, just had it waiting until the time was right. Her oldest sister's battle with ALS and her request that she would like to see her book published prompted C.R. to get to work.

Quest of the Evensongs was published in 2011 as an eBook and her sister was the first to receive a copy. Since that time she has published numerous works and currently is revising each for paperback. Her love of fantasy, the forest and 60's music led her to write The Ivy Chronicles.

A self-proclaimed Oregonian, she spends her free time reading, walking in the woods and hiding from the mountain of clothes that needs folding.